JUSTICE ...
IS JUST US

Dear Keith,
thank you for the kind
comment. I hope you
enjoy the character's
courage, which pales compared
to yours.
    your friend
    Harold Smiten
    9 March 2009

JUSTICE ...
IS JUST US

Harold B. Wooten

iUniverse, Inc.
New York   Bloomington

Justice ... Is Just Us

iUniverse books may be ordered through booksellers or by contacting:

iUniverse
1663 Liberty Drive
Bloomington, IN 47403
www.iuniverse.com
1-800-Authors (1-800-288-4677)

Because of the dynamic nature of the Internet, any Web addresses or links contained in this book may have changed since publication and may no longer be valid. The views expressed in this work are solely those of the author and do not necessarily reflect the views of the publisher, and the publisher hereby disclaims any responsibility for them.

ISBN: 978-0-595-49873-4 (pbk)
ISBN: 978-0-595-49563-4 (dj)
ISBN: 978-0-595-61287-1 (ebk)

Printed in the United States of America

iUniverse rev. date: 2/16/2009

DEDICATION

To the probation and parole officers who, day in and day out, give their hearts and souls to help offenders become the best they can be, while working tirelessly to keep their communities safe.

Contents

FOREWORD

As one who has spent fifty years in public service, many of them attempting to bring reason to the world of criminal justice, I congratulate Harold Wooten for bringing his considerable talents to this field by utilizing a "novel" approach as a means of getting the reading public to help create a societal shift in confronting crime. By bringing far more rationality to helping reduce runaway counterproductive incarceration, his approach will not only create a safer society, but one where the modification of the current culture will breed a "shot in the arm" to the pursuit of happiness. It will also produce major reductions in the current national expenditure of at least fifty billion dollars per year designed to reduce or control crime. The argument that greater incarceration creates greater public safety is simply not in accord with the facts and is often utilized by those who have a demagogic self-interest in promoting the prison expansion complex.

My two major mentors in this field were Congressman Brooks Hays of Little Rock, Arkansas, who was not only the hero of the Central High School desegregation crisis in 1957, but also was President of the Southern Baptist Convention, and Chief Justice Warren Earl Burger, who was determined to reduce the number of those incarcerated by promoting literacy training and meaningful job training for those already imprisoned so they would not recidivate. Both Hays and Burger shared the view of the great Russian novelist Fyodor Dostoyevsky, who said in his novel *Crime and Punishment*, "A civilization will be judged by how it treats its wrongdoers."

Back in February 1969, Brooks Hays wrote for the magazine *Christian Century* a review of the book written by the eminent psychiatrist Karl Menninger called the *Crime of Punishment*. In that review, Hays said, "Karl Menninger presents a thoroughgoing indictment of our system of justice in the United States and provides ample evidence of the distorted approach to the concept of justice on the part of lawyers, psychiatrists and other persons concerned with the maintenance of the instrumentalities of law enforcements.... Justice is rarely the goal of those who are involved in the law enforcement process.... Society should be giving far more attention to preventive effort."

Chief Justice Warren Burger made an historic speech to Lincoln, Nebraska's bar association in 1981, where he said that "factories with fences" should be created in prisons because "when society places a person behind walls and bars, it has an obligation--a moral obligation--to do whatever can reasonably be done to change that person before he or she goes back into the stream of society." He, too, identified with Menninger that "there are ways we can meet the crime and punishment challenges, that offenders can be treated and changed, and that love can conquer hate in the hearts of men if only we make the necessary commitment in our society."

Back to where we are today: since the late 1970s, this nation has embarked, unbridled, on a tough-on-crime agenda that has resulted in the federalization of many state crimes, guideline sentencing with long sentences, mandatory minimum sentences, and the abolishment of parole for the Federal system and many state systems. Harsh punishment is at the fore of almost every criminal justice decision. We have come to rely on prisons and jails as solutions. Today, the United States has less than 5 percent of the world's population, but almost a quarter of its prisoners. About 7.2 million people—one in every thirty-two adults—are either incarcerated, on parole or probation, or under some form of supervision.

My colleague and friend Harold Wooten, who is in the tradition of Hays and Burger, anticipates that a human revolution will come from the bottom up, led by the people who do the work, who will rise up and say, "Enough is enough." Let's hope he's right.

Warren I. Cikins
Senior Staff Member (Retired)
Brookings Institution

ACKNOWLEDGMENTS

Writing is a lonely affair. Clearly, I could not have written this book without the constant love, support, feedback, care, and humor of my wife, Nancy Smith Wooten. I am forever indebted to her.

I thank my mother, Glenny White, and my four daughters, Robin, Evey, Gabriele, and Emilee, for their interest, curiosity, and support. Each, in her own way, spurred me on when I felt like quitting.

I thank my writing coach, Barbara Esstman, the distinguished award-winning author of *Night Ride Home* and *The Other Anna*. Without her guidance, this effort would still be in manuscript form on a dusty shelf. I did extract a promise from Barbara. At the reading of my will, she has agreed to read to my children, verbatim, every single page she cut from my manuscript, before they get a nickel.

I thank Marina Koestler Ruben and Peggy McEwan, my line editors, for their stellar performance. Their insights and tightening of the bolts were outstanding.

Structure of the Maryland
State Criminal Justice Authority

Independent Agencies	Executive	Judicial
County Prosecutors	Governor	Judges
	Parole Commission	Probation Officers*
	Prisons	
	State Police	
	Public Defenders	
	Parole Officers*	

*These officers wear two hats. Probation *and* parole officers can supervise parolees and/or probationers in the community.

Parole - A person is convicted of a crime and sentenced by the courts to prison. The end of the prison term may be spent in the community on parole, during which time the offender would be under the supervision of a probation/parole officer. In the event of alleged rules violations or new crimes committed by a parolee while in the community, revocation hearings are held by the Parole Commission.

Probation - A person is convicted of a crime and sentenced by the courts to a period of probation supervision in the community. The probationer is under the supervision of a probation/parole officer. In the event of alleged rules violations or new crimes committed by a person on probation, revocation hearings are held by the courts.

1

MEETING THE NEW PAROLEE

Gee Brooks

Gee Brooks was one of the few Maryland probation officers who didn't think a new case was a new burden. She actually enjoyed meeting offenders, always looking for ways to connect with them. Today, she had a light green, cotton jacket slung over her right shoulder and assorted files in a brown leather case as she left the clerk of court's office in the Montgomery County Circuit Courthouse in Rockville, Maryland. Because she was traveling outside the district to the Maryland Correctional Institution - Hagerstown (MCIH) in Hagerstown, Maryland, she was required to use a county vehicle, so she allowed extra time to walk to the motor pool. Her plan was to attend a prison liaison meeting and then meet individually with parolee Thomas Smith, who would be released to her supervision in September, just three months away.

Alone in front of the courthouse elevator, the thirty-three-year-old officer, who was attractive enough to turn men's heads, managed to push the down button with her little finger. The elevator doors opened, revealing only one person on board, a gentleman in the right rear, probably in his fifties. She noticed that he had on wrinkled dress pants, a blue sport jacket, and a collared blue shirt, but no tie. The doors closed.

"How are things in the probation office?" the man asked.

"Oh, fine, fine ...," Gee said, staring at him.

"I'm sorry. I recognize you but don't know your name. I'm Jon Rhodes of the We Watch Together Society, or WWTS. I sat in on one of your probation revocation hearings," he said.

"Of course, sure, I know who you are. I love the WWTS newsletters. I'm Gee Brooks. I shouldn't say this out loud, but my buddies in the office pay more attention to your newsletter's take on local court issues than to the views of our bosses. But things are OK, I guess. I'm headed to MCIH to attend a meeting and meet an inmate who'll be released on parole soon," she said.

"If you don't mind me asking, who?" Jon said.

"Well, no, Thomas Smith," she said.

"They call him TJ," he said evenly.

The elevator doors opened and they exited together on the basement floor.

"You know him?" she asked.

"No. But I'll never forget his trial."

"Really? Do you have time to tell me about it?"

They meandered into the cafeteria line behind two women. Gee felt awkward, standing relatively close to Jon Rhodes with little, so far, to talk about except TJ Smith. She wondered what Her Highness Deputy Chief Probation Officer Dora Kingmaker would say if she saw her talking to the enemy—that is, someone who might advocate for offenders. Like everyone in the courthouse, Gee knew what initially brought Jon to the courthouse every day—the trial of the thug who murdered his wife; but she wasn't comfortable expressing sympathy for Jon's deceased wife.

They both ordered iced tea and found seats at a small table in the rear of the large room, alone.

"Tell me all about him, please. Why do you remember the trial? You must see so many," Gee said. She knew, as did everyone else at the courthouse, that Jon Rhodes sat in on trials as a vigil for his wife's death.

"Well, it's been four to five years, or so. I was relatively new at observing trials, but I remember clearly that TJ was caught up in a drug sweep in Lincoln Park by county police and ATF agents. I think he ended up getting five or six years. He was really caught in a no-win situation," he said.

"Right, he got six years for conspiracy to distribute drugs and interfering with a law enforcement officer. I just reread his file. What happened?" she asked.

Rhodes expressed his view that a lot of folks in Lincoln Park were involved in drug distribution on a small scale. For instance, he explained, to earn $50 they might agree to serve as lookouts for two hours and send signals if police were spotted. Gee knew this but listened politely anyway. Others, he added, carried out the sales negotiations, while still

2

others distributed the drugs to drop-off points. He didn't doubt that at some time TJ may have been on the periphery, maybe standing lookout in exchange for marijuana or selling small quantities of marijuana. But during the trial, before Judge Clarke, one of the defendants testified TJ had nothing to do with anything that day. The public defender representing TJ immediately motioned that all charges against TJ be dismissed, but Judge Clarke denied the motion.

"It was a very unusual trial. Here's what got him a conviction: about seven guys, it seems to me, were clearly either negotiating marijuana sales or bringing bags to the salesmen. They were selling drugs, plain and simple. Testimony from three witnesses, however, said that TJ was walking away from a corner grocery store with two paper bags full of groceries when all hell broke loose," Jon said.

"He'd have to have known these guys and what they were doing, or they'd have run him off," Gee said. Her comment was a subtle message to Jon that she understood the street culture.

"Absolutely. The cops, dressed in undercover clothes, starting swarming all over the scene. TJ was either lookout and intentionally tripped one of the undercover cops, as the prosecutor stated, or, as TJ said in his testimony, had a knee-jerk reaction when he saw guns and heard them shout 'police' and thought it was a rival crew robbing his friends, *pretending* to be cops, so he tripped the officer. Either way, the cop he tripped fell, knocked out four teeth, split his mouth open, and broke his wrist. So, what's the judge going to do? Drop charges against TJ because one defendant and two shaky witnesses said he had nothing to do with the drug sales? Or should the judge be persuaded by the police officer who, by the way, testified with his front teeth missing, as he described how TJ intentionally interfered with the arrests?" he said.

"Why did you believe TJ's testimony?"

"Gut instinct, that's all. When you meet him, several things will stick out. He's quiet—smart, I think. This part puzzled me: he seemed to expect to get hosed—or he was stuck in the middle. If he testified against the others, his life or the safety of his family could be in jeopardy. That's my guess. My sense is he's a follower. Here's the weird part: in a plea agreement, all the other guys got shorter prison terms. TJ refused to enter a plea or testify against them. He received the *longest* sentence.

I thought the court had the right verdict, the wrong villain, and way too much prison time for him," he said.

"Wow! And he didn't appear upset?" she asked.

"No. He sorta turned to someone, an attractive light-skinned black woman, who I took to be his wife, and looked, well ... embarrassed. I'll never forget it."

"Well, thank you, Mr. Rhodes. Wow!"

"Call me Jon, please."

"I go by Gee."

"I'm sure our paths will cross again."

"I'll let you know how he turns out."

"I'd appreciate that."

They shook hands and went their separate ways.

On the seventy-five-minute drive to the western Maryland prison, located in farm country, Gee felt increasingly disturbed by Jon Rhodes's story about TJ's trial. What if he had nothing to do with helping the crew sell marijuana and was really trying to protect his friends? Homeboys *do* stick together. She wondered if he'd be hostile to her. How do you spend nearly five years in prison without a chip on your shoulder?

Her mind raced back and forth between meeting TJ and the distance she felt from her husband, Ed, to whom she had been married for five years. She was constantly anxious lately, feeling like she was walking on eggshells with Ed—she wanted children now; he put the topic off the discussion agenda; she said nothing. She tried to please him, so he'd change his mind. It never worked. She felt she had waited long enough. She also felt helpless. She had withheld showing her anger and frustration with Ed's no-child-until-I-say-so policy for so long, living in his ordered world; she didn't know how to break her pattern of pulling her punches with him.

When her self-talk landed on the words "pulling punches," she thought of Deputy Chief Kingmaker, or The Kingmaker, as she referred to her, and how she'd like to punch the bitch. Gee flashed back to a sentencing hearing before Senior Judge Cox three days ago. She remembered with great precision Kingmaker's every comment, as

Kingmaker grilled her from behind her spacious desk with a picture of the governor over her shoulder. Gee could still hear her cold tone.

"Chip Faulknour, you remember him—your *supervisor*—tells me that you've recommended that this Wilson defendant, a burglar, receive a sentence of *no* prison time, only probation, correct? And that you refused his request to change your sentencing recommendation to the judge. Did I hear the story correctly from Faulknour?" Kingmaker had said.

Gee had wanted to be sarcastic but chose to try to explain that she had twenty-two letters written by local community leaders … all reporting what a wonderful person Wilson was and how much he cared for the children in the community. She had started to elaborate but was cut off.

"I don't care what they think, really, Ms. Brooks. I don't care if one of the letters is from Mother Teresa.… She doesn't work. Sentencing recommendations run through me. I do know and care about what Senior Judge Cox expects in our reports. He isn't called "Slamming Cox" for nothing," Kingmaker had said.

Gee had tried to needle Kingmaker by implying that Kingmaker was usurping Gee's responsibilities as an officer. "Dora, aren't you trying to get me to second-guess what the judge wants? Why do I even make recommendations based on my best judgment?"

"I'm changing that recommendation. I don't care what you call it.… I call it survival. Don't let this happen again, if you know what's good for you. The recommended sentence will be ten years in prison," Kingmaker had said.

Gee was grinding her teeth recalling the humiliation she felt—*belittled, really,* she thought. She glanced down and realized she was driving 80 mph. She slowed down to 65 mph. Other than Ed, she had told no one about The Kingmaker incident, not even her fellow officers Pepe, Huggie, and Hattie, her soul mates … or the Cuatro Amigos, as they jokingly called themselves. Now, she regretted telling Ed anything about how vulnerable and angry she felt at work.

She thought back to Jon Rhodes's comment that TJ appeared to feel embarrassed at his trial—*an odd reaction*, she thought—embarrassed.

Why am I pulling punches at work and with my husband? Oh, of course—I've memorized my life commandment, so I can be a good little girl … like Mom ordered.

Gee finished her quarterly Pre-Release Coordinating Committee meeting in the non-air-conditioned Hagerstown prison on this bright June day. The meeting with prison officials was cordial, and she gained what she came for: a list of parolees who would be released in the next ninety days to Montgomery County. Still, she always felt uncomfortable inside prisons and jails. The MCIH was over one hundred years old, made of brick and concrete. Razor wire and guard towers held the inmates in—inmates generally considered medium-security risks by state correctional experts. To her, most just seemed to be rough-edged, lower-class, and undereducated. A few looked like gang members—caricatures, really, in their exaggerated tough postures. The muscular appearance of many inmates reminded her of folks she saw in Rock Creek Park on the weekends, either on the soccer fields or the basketball courts. These inmates just had more defensive, guarded postures.

In keeping with policy, correctional guards escorted Gee when she walked around the prison. Although she never feared for her safety, the aura of human spirit rotting behind cell bars saddened her. Today, a chatty guard named Easter Hope Jones led Gee to the administration building, where TJ Smith worked. Gee marveled at how Jones, like so many other prison guards, had mastered the art of being friendly to visitors, while speaking condescendingly to every inmate she came in contact with during this short walk.

Gee made a habit of personally meeting parolees assigned to her months before their release. She believed these visits helped build rapport in a way that could never happen from behind her desk at the probation office in the formal courthouse. It was a strategy she had learned from her father, a retired federal probation officer.

She found TJ Smith, as expected, just outside the associate warden's glass-walled office at a gray metal desk typing on an old desktop computer. He appeared to know she was coming because, before she spoke, he asked her if she was looking for him. Information traveled faster than people walked inside prisons, even without cell phones. His polite, relaxed demeanor; his welcoming, large, brown eyes; and his small smile made her feel comfortable—less hurried. He turned off his computer and led her to a quiet corner in the large, open office area. He sat on a green, faux leather couch and she on a matching chair, both made by prison industries, and began what turned out to be a two-hour talk—the longest she had ever spoken to any offender in or out of prison. She was struck by TJ's handsome looks, mostly by his bright eyes and his long Tupac-like curly eyelashes. His hair was short and slightly wavy. To her, he looked like a graduate student at a university. She guessed this light-skinned African-American man was in his late twenties—she couldn't recall from reading his file. He was taller than she, maybe six feet. He was fit, but not overly muscular—certainly not skinny. He had a quiet voice—several times she found herself leaning in to hear him—particularly, she noticed, around subjects that were unpleasant for him to talk about. His infrequent laugh was spontaneous, reflecting his thoughtful responses to her quips. TJ, she thought, was relaxed, and surprisingly comfortable. She noticed when they walked to get bottled water from a small refrigerator that he had a habit of cupping his left hand over his right hand in front of him, almost a Mideastern style. She wondered where he picked up that pose. Most inmates appeared to have a tough veneer; TJ appeared to be someone in thought.

He seemed pleased to talk to her, which, in and of itself, was different than most parolees. Parolees also sought to downplay their role in past criminal conduct and exaggerate their optimism about the future. TJ did neither. Their conversation, an interaction, really, had a natural flow—not one just between an officer and a parolee, not one between two friends, but a conversation about him and his hopes for after his release from prison. *He seemed so … what?* she thought to herself on the long ride home that afternoon, *mature, and, well, not much like an inmate*. He would end up like so many of the "success stories" her father talked about. She would remember, too, that TJ commented to her that the two hours flew by. He quipped that it was fair to say he would have enjoyed talking to Goofy or anybody other than the same convicts he talked to day in and day out.

He told the story of his one friend, his cellmate for the past two years, Hardroc, who was halfway through a twelve-year sentence for running numbers out of his Baltimore barbershop—his second conviction for numbers. Hardroc, TJ said, was acquitted for the eighteen marijuana plants growing under black lights in the basement of his shop because of an illegal search and seizure; nonetheless, he was sentenced to significant time *as if* he had been convicted of the marijuana—a process that was known as backdoor justice.

It was obvious that TJ admired Hardroc, who was twenty years his senior. Based on the stories, Hardroc had taken TJ under his wing, and, according to TJ, helped him to cope with the daily stress of living in difficult circumstances with difficult people.

"He likes to say 'Boy, your constant need for approval would be refreshing in a puppy,' or 'What happens in the dark got to come to light some day.' They're part of my repertoire now," TJ said.

Repertoire? Wow, from a parolee, Gee thought. Most parolees talked about going home. Most, she presumed, although they didn't talk about it with her, were focused on a renewed sex life with their wives or girlfriends and spent little time talking about their cellmates.

TJ shared a few more Hardrocisms, and Gee marveled at Hardroc's sage pro-social advice, wrapped in succinct sound bites. If Hardroc had used these same observational skills to come up with pithy, mean-spirited slogans, she joked with TJ, he could have been a successful presidential campaign strategist. TJ said he had tried hard to embed into his actions the lessons Hardroc had taught him. Gee wondered what would have happened to TJ had he experienced a more anti-social cellmate.

She also heard from TJ, at length, of his now advanced computer skills. She already knew much of this story from an oral progress report she had received earlier from his institutional case worker. But she wanted to hear the story from him, *de novo*. He had received his GED within twelve months of his arrival at MCIH. After being assigned to the administration building, he received his AA in Computer Science from Hagerstown Community College, with all As. He was, she had heard, the poster child for the small community college's contract to teach inmates at the prison.

TJ had been given the task of helping a correctional administrator write a newsletter that circulated statewide throughout the prison system. When the administrator went on maternity leave, the newsletter and the prison Web site were his to manage. TJ showed Gee some past hard copies of the newsletter, and they appeared flawless. He walked her through the Web site, showing her the many features he'd added. He had been given expansive responsibilities, like conducting Internet searches and doing online research for staff. Proudly, he said, there was never a suggestion that he had misused his Internet privileges for personal reasons. If he did, he said, he would have had to answer to a higher authority than prison officials: his cellmate.

As was typical, TJ had secured no job back home, even though his release from prison was pending. She mentioned, out of the blue, really, that she knew a survey expert, Art Coleman, who lived in Tampa Bay, Florida. Art conducted surveys for various corporations, churches, and schools. Art was an old friend of her father's and, over dinner with her father recently, he had told her that he was looking for an IT virtual assistant. Art wondered if Gee had any friends who would want computer work for twenty to thirty hours per week. The work could be done from home on a PC. Art would supply the PC, and reports could be e-mailed. Gee had told Art she'd get back to him if she could find someone. *Today*, Gee thought, *I may have found someone.* She described the work to TJ.

"Would you be interested in this job?" she asked.

"Interested? Holy—uh, yeah … yeah! I can't believe this. You trust me?" he asked.

"Well, the prison trusts you. Why wouldn't I?" she said.

"I can't wait to tell Hardroc," TJ said.

Again, Gee thought it interesting that the person he most wanted to share the news with was his cellmate—not his wife.

TJ, upon her prompting, talked about his first family, or the fragments of his first family. He appeared to speak in a measured tone in an attempt to be factual, as if he had been coached to downplay seeking sympathy. *Maybe that was learned internal constriction*, she thought. Still, to her, TJ's sense of being abandoned by his parents was a sad story, a story about loneliness. He said he was raised by his maternal grandmother, of whom he spoke warmly. It didn't sound like she was able to keep much of a close eye on him, suffering from high blood pressure, diabetes, and chronic arthritis. Often, he said, it was his younger sister Dee and him taking care of their grandmother.

"I dropped out of the Mason Technical School in Rockville in the tenth grade. Mason generally had kids with behavioral problems. They were idiots," he said.

Gee recalled reading in his file that he had an IQ of around 130.

"I was never close to my mother. My sister, Dee, says that she left us when our father and she went different ways. I don't like to talk about her. I only see her if Dee bugs me—you know, on Mother's Day or on her birthday. She had an alcohol and drug jones for years. Then she found God. I never believed her act in church, anyway. Dee says she was sixteen when she had me. Maybe she wasn't ready to be grown-up," he said.

"We all have a different pace, don't we?" Gee said.

He didn't answer but raised his eyebrows and continued talking. "My father, Thomas, had his little flings with the law as a kid, Dee said. But it must not have been too serious, 'cause he went to Vietnam. My grandma took me to see him when I was about twelve. He said or did nothing that I can remember. Like he didn't want to know me. Dee said he lives in Sunshine, off Route 108, but I don't see him. He's got a live-in girlfriend. He's a carpenter ... I hear. You know, Ms. Brooks, it's easy to miss someone you don't know—but hard to fill that hole up. Missing him got worn out," he said.

"I know, TJ.... I know," she said. She felt a knot in her stomach thinking about her mother.

"You, too?" he asked.

"Well, me, too, TJ. Yes, me, too," she said. She changed the subject quickly. "Tell me, TJ, what do you expect ... with your wife and kids when you get home? What's her name?" she asked.

"Junie. Well, Mrs. Junie Edwards-Smith and I have been married seven years, legal and stuff. I have my hopes," he said, looking down at his sneakers.

After a long pause, he continued.

"We have two kids. Tommy is seven, and Natasha is five."

"Are you close to the kids?" Gee asked.

"Not as close as I want to be," he said.

He paused again.

"It's like I'm a stranger. Like ... I'm new. Five years is a long time for a man and woman to reconnect, or a seven- and five- year-old who never knew me 'cept on visiting day. I want them to understand I'm going to *be somebody*. Inmates say that shit all the time.... 'You watch,' 'this time,' and so forth. I'd keep on goin' down the road if I didn't believe that I'll be somebody. I used to try to be somebody by hustling, small-time stuff. I must say, I ain't used to being around regular people. That part's going to be different," he said.

"Well, you're going to make it, TJ. You've got what it takes—a brain, a good attitude, a good job, I hope, a good woman, and two kids who'll love having their father around. Be patient, don't be hard on yourself," she said.

"Does it send the wrong message for me to bring home gifts?" he asked.

"No, not at all.… It's a nice start," she said.

"What's good? I've got $300 saved up in my prison account. You know, 15¢ an hour 'mounts up," he laughed.

"Well, how about a baseball glove for your son and a doll for Natasha? You're on your own for Junie," she said.

"Would you do me one favor? Would you call Junie and tell her about the job? It'd be nice coming from you, and I'm not allowed to receive a call from her for three days," he said.

"Sure, give me her number," she said.

They said good-bye. *Hope is in the air*, she thought.

On the way out of the prison, Gee bumped into Assistant Warden Davis, whom she worked with on the Pre-Release Coordinating Committee. When she mentioned she had met with TJ, Davis asked her if TJ had told her about "the scene" four months ago, then told her this story:

An "old girlfriend" visited TJ and had the misfortune of selecting the same visiting day as his wife. According to two guards' reports, Ms. Taunja Suggar of Southeast D.C. left the prison visiting room in a semi-sprint. The two reports were in agreement that Junie warned Taunja with a finger-pointing in-your-face gesture not to come around her man again or select features of her anatomy would be in numerous pieces. Junie delivered this message at megaphone volume … in front of roughly seventy-five other visitors. Taunja Suggar was subsequently removed from the approved visitors list, for "safety reasons."

Gee thanked Davis for the information. When and how she would bring it up was dicey. Fidelity was a ticklish subject.

As soon as Gee got into her car, she called Huggie, her buddy and fellow probation officer.

"Huggie, I just left the MCIH, and I wonder if I've stepped in it," she said.

"What'd you do, girlfriend?" Huggie laughed.

Just hearing his voice comforted her. His deep tone, usually with a tinge of playfulness, gave her a sense of comfort, of being under his wing. His attentiveness on the phone today, as usual, was as if he was solely focused on her. He never drifted or multitasked on the phone, or in person, unlike her husband, Ed. Huggie's Barry White tone was so smooth; in her mind's eye she could see his massive, muscular, six-feet-five-inch frame, his shiny black shaved head, a la Michael Jordan. She loved the image of his cell phone in his massive, ham hock hands—it always looked like a child's toy. He frequently had to dial a number multiple times because he'd strike two numbers at the same time. An artist's caricature, she had joked with their buddies, would pass over his athletic appearance and focus on the large, black, horn-rimmed glasses that made him appear to be an intellectual.

"Well, I met a new parolee who's going to be on my caseload in September, Thomas Smith, Jr.," she said.

"I know TJ. His barely sober mother used to drag him into my father's church when we were kids," Huggie said.

"Really? We'll have to talk more. I like him.... He's doing great. Anyway, my dad's friend in Florida was looking for an IT specialist to work from home, and TJ doesn't have a job lined up, so I agreed to hook up the two of them. Then I remembered The Kingmaker's new policy that we can't refer parolees to friends or people we know. Shit, I can't take the offer back now. That's the only job possibility he has!" she said.

"You can avoid doing what you *need* to do.... But it *will* come back to haunt only you," he said.

"Oh, for God's sake, Huggie, where did you get that one from?"

"My mother," he said, laughing. "Listen, girl, you'd better schlep into your prissy-pants supervisor Faulknour's office or talk to The Kingmaker directly before they find out and make an example of you."

"I'll think about it."

"OK, I take that as a no, but … you listening? Two years ago, I had this old car advertised in the *Silver Spring Gazette* for $500. A parolee who landed a construction job needed a car to get to Northern Virginia every day. I thought, the car runs good—I'll sell it to him. I guess he must have mentioned it to another dude in the waiting room, or something, because Faulknour found out about it and dragged me into The Kingmaker's office. She reamed me out for the 'appearance of impropriety.' The Kingmaker decided that Faulknour should put a letter of reprimand in my personnel files. The letter's still there."

"I'll think about it," Gee said.

~

"Mrs. Smith, my name is Gee Brooks. I'm going to be your husband's assigned probation officer in Rockville when he's released in September," she said.

"How can I help?" Junie said.

Gee thought her tone was terse. "Well, I met him at MCIH today and I have some news he wanted me to share with you: I'm 90 percent sure I can get him a job working in IT from home with a reputable colleague. The pay is great and I'm pretty sure the job will be from twenty to thirty hours a week to start, maybe more," she said.

"Oh, Ms. Brooks," Junie said, "I'm overwhelmed. I didn't mean to sound—"

"Please, call me Gee."

"Call me Junie. Did he tell you Hardroc stories?"

"Some, but tell me more."

"Well, nothing produces more stress for an inmate than changing prison cells. It's like two dogs sniffing when they first meet. TJ had three previous cellmates who he hated but never had any problems with. In December of 2001, he was transferred to Hardroc's cell in Denton cellblock, the best and cleanest cellblock, I've heard. He quickly found out that Hardroc 'ran' the administration building and decided who roomed with whom. The way I hear it, Hardroc had access to everyone's files and he saw all of this potential in him. So he picked TJ as his cellmate. The administration building is the best place to work, TJ said.… It's cleaner and with smarter inmates."

"That's obvious when you walk around," Gee said.

"I remember how jiggy he was…. You know, one old cellmate was a child molester. But prisoners don't have choices; they're like Ping-Pong balls on mouse traps. He hated being pushed around by anyone—his father, his mother, the school system, the cops, and now the prison officials, who could and did move him around when they felt like it. At the time, he said that he felt like an item, a piece of meat. He was hurt, although no one ever expresses *that* feeling in a prison. He just wanted to do his time and come home. He said the next morning, his first eye-to-eye contact with Hardroc, when he kept asking TJ, 'Why you here?' I guess TJ kept giving him different answers…. You know, like 'the crime,' 'because Hagerstown prison had medium-security inmates,' and on and on. Finally, Hardroc said, 'No, here, on this earth. If you don't know, you'll be dead before you're thirty, boy.' TJ never forgot that. Now, my TJ is a smart-ass, so he asked Hardroc, 'Why *you* here?' TJ remembers the exact quote: 'Because I can't control my passions and I don't command the nights.'"

"Really…. Wow!"

"TJ said he started off toward the laundry facility, where he had been assigned for nearly two years. This fat, nasty guard, said, 'Boy, you ain't going that way no more. You're working now with Mr. Hard-Ass Rock in the administration building.'

"TJ said he turned to Hardroc and said, "I ain't *no* bitch for *nobody.'* Believe me, Gee, I can just hear him saying that…. Am I talking too much?" Junie asked.

"No, no, Junie, please go on. I don't hear much from the wife's perspective. Maybe families think I'm just going to try to catch their man doing something wrong. Please go on."

"I feel like I've known you all my life. Well, TJ said Hardroc smiled and said, 'Boy, if a cop gave you a $500 bill for nothing, would you take it or spit in his face?' TJ answered, 'Take it.' I'm told Hardroc said, 'Then shut *the fuck* up!'"

"Now that's funny."

"TJ said they didn't talk for a week. He went about his new job learning how to use the copiers and fax machines and how to fill out requisition order forms for parts and supplies. Those tasks, taught to him by Hardroc, were far better than those in the laundry facility with its backbreaking work of taking twenty to thirty wet sheets out of a large washer at a time. TJ used to say it felt like pulling against an angry mule. He said that no inmates on assignment to Hardroc called each other the N-word or started their sentences off with the MF-word either. He noticed Hardroc used a pleasant tone with all of the professional and clerical staff and even had a half-smile, although TJ said that, back then, he never looked at Hardroc directly. I remember, Gee, that around a week later, TJ told me that he asked CD, a fellow worker in administration, 'What's up with Hardroc?' CD said that Hardroc was a very smart dude, and he advised TJ not to mess with him. 'He told me, "You, brother, won't be here if he don't like you."' TJ tried to figure out why the prison officials liked Hardroc so much and gave him so much power. CD did say something like, 'You weren't listening, brother, and I can tell you one thing: Hardroc will fire your ass if you don't listen when he talks. Man's smart. He makes sense. He figure stuff out.... That's why they let him run things. God knows what cellmate you gonna end up with if you cross ole Hardroc. He run the joint, TJ. He run it.' TJ was petrified."

"Please go on. This is great information."

"Well, in letters to me, TJ wrote that he was curious about why Hardroc couldn't 'control his passions and command the nights.' He said finally Hardroc explained to him that his behavior *outside* the prison resulted from his inability to control his feelings—loneliness, anger, a pain inside his gut. Hardroc ended up looking for something to ease the pain, particularly at night. Honestly, Gee, it was the most complex sentence TJ had ever heard, and he told me he thought he understood it. Hardroc told him that his father was a drunk. He'd come home from the docks of Baltimore all liquored up, pissed off about this or that. You know, stuff like not enough work hours, feeling cheated by white supervisors, gambling losses, God knows what else. Then, his mother would provoke his father and they'd start name calling, cussing, and slugging. His brother would try to break them up. Cops would come, and the father would get arrested. He told TJ that cycle went on for a long time. Then his father left and never came back. He was found dead in D.C. when Hardroc was fifteen. Hardroc started drinking and using pot. He said he couldn't kill the pain. I swear, Gee, I feel like I know him through TJ's letters. He told TJ he hated the nights. Hardroc spent two years in the jungles of Vietnam and came back more screwed up. Hardroc said he wanted to get away from the nights, the memories. He said that he burned up a lot of good women along the way," Junie said.

"Wasn't TJ's father in Vietnam, too?" Gee asked.

"Yes. His father disowned TJ because of something that happened with TJ's mother.... Who knows?" Junie said. "I'm sorry I'm going on and on—I'll finish. Hardroc said something that hit TJ on the nose. He said, 'The stuff in your files, it don't say *nothing* bad about you. And, there ain't many dudes in here that you can say that about. It's a messed up world that would want to put a boy like you in here. But it's the world we live in. Same one brought my Daddy home, drunked up and beatin' on my Momma.' Then TJ said, 'I been thinkin' about your "Why you *here*?" question. I like fixing the copier and stuff.' I think Hardroc said, 'That's nothing.' TJ got all hurt and stood toe to toe with Hardroc, who said, 'That ain't nothing ... the copier. If you want, I'll teach you how to use a computer. That's where the money is! Do you want that, boy?' That was the start. TJ said he was so excited that he didn't sleep ten minutes that night."

"Thank you, Junie. What a great story. Will you please call me if I can help?"

"Of course, Ms. Brooks. I know TJ will make it. Thanks for listening. Honestly, I must say, I didn't think the system cared."

"Trust me, Junie, we do." Gee thought about bringing up the Taunja Suggar incident but decided to avoid the sensitive subject.

Close to the motor pool and seeing the front of the courthouse, Gee felt very angry at Kingmaker, her mother, and herself. *It's time to get things straight with Ed, too*, she thought, *about the icy distance between us and about having kids*. The anger quickly disappeared when a counter-thought emerged—*maybe I haven't tried hard enough to please Ed, like Mom did with Dad.*

2

DEAD LEAVES ALL AROUND

Gee Brooks

The day's run was an unusual struggle for Gee, who could comfortably run long distances even on hilly terrain such as today's path through the outskirts of Rock Creek Park. For most of last night, and all of last week, she could barely distinguish between ruminations about her caseload, disconnected angry feelings, and actual dreams. Typically, when under stress, Gee felt tightness or sometimes even mild pain in her lower back. This morning, her back hurt, and she had difficulty finding a running rhythm. When she was troubled, like today, she preferred running alone.

For Gee, running long distances was an exorcism of inner voices. She considered the voices her "running demons." Sometimes, a male's voice, a voice that almost sounded like her father's, would suggest in a kindly tone that maybe today she should just go a short distance, perhaps a mile or two; any longer would be too strenuous. Her mind would shoot back an angry, snarling response: "Stop it. I can do it." She said her responses aloud.

"What difference would it make?" a kindly, female voice might interject next. "Why not just walk a few blocks?" Or, "Why not go back to that comfortable bed and sleep?" "I'll show you," was Gee's typical response to the female. Then, nameless, faceless voices might pop in to talk to each other. The experience made Gee feel like she was in that twilight stage before surgery. Gee could hear them whispering, mocking her. "What's the point?" one would ask. "Why does she do this to herself?" asked another. Often a woman would ask in a serious tone, "What's she running away from?" That comment always made Gee furious. She suspected that the speaker was Deputy Chief Probation Officer Dora Kingmaker.

Today, she left Rock Creek Park and headed straight uphill toward East-West Highway. The assertive-sounding female voice raised the "running away from" question as Gee approached the top of the hill at Connecticut Avenue. Once over that long, steep hill, the voices stopped, as if she'd sent them scurrying. The voices always made her feel alone.

Five miles out, she began looping back toward the northern tip of Rock Creek Park and her Meadowbrook Lane home, with its azaleas in full bloom, battling with the forsythia for attention, all hovered over by old oak trees. She looked forward to sitting on the screened-in side porch that Ed had built. While cooling off, she liked to drink her morning coffee and peer across the street, watching the privileged arrive in SUVs to ride their boarded horses or drop their kids off at Rock Creek Park for riding lessons. Some riders rode in circles within a large soft dirt corral, observed closely by instructors. Others left the stables for one of numerous dirt trails that headed past the basketball courts and soccer fields where city boys played three-on-three and Latinos kicked soccer balls.

Gee usually experienced a sense of balance in this visual array—the wealthy on horseback, the African-Americans playing basketball, the mixed crowd of tennis players, and the predominantly Hispanic soccer players in their bright team uniforms. For Gee, this mixture of cultures, languages, and varied interests was the way things were supposed to be—and exactly why she always chose this running route in the spring and summer. It was why she loved the location of her Meadowbrook Lane home.

Today, Gee noticed a few unkempt backyards adjacent to Rock Creek Park. Her annoyance caught her off guard. Why should she care if some of these lawns were messy?

She found herself annoyed, too, with Ruppert, her black, curly-coated retriever. That, also, was unusual. Ruppert did what he typically did on runs—rambled along and slobbered all over himself. His joy at being with her made him a wonderful companion, except when a floating leaf, a racing squirrel, or another dog set him off, and it was all Gee could do to keep the ninety-pound, sweet brute on course.

She tracked her irritation to a nightmare she had had the previous night. Gee always paid careful attention to the possible implications of her dreams. Piece by piece, elements of the dream came back to her consciousness as she ran. She adjusted, or rearranged, the snippets in an effort to create a mosaic she could understand. She remembered being in the audience of a quiz show. Lighted signs prompted her and others in the audience to applaud or laugh, on cue. One sign had the silhouette of a cowboy with a horse and boots and said "Hoot and holler!" But in the dream, she subtly refused to follow the rules. She simply feigned compliance. The host of the game show was Kingmaker—someone Gee despised, as did her probation officer buddies Pepe, Hattie, and Huggie. The contestants were fellow probation officers whom she barely recognized. Kingmaker asked the officers questions about minute details of office policy that she, Kingmaker, had developed. Gee clearly remembered one question Kingmaker asked: "The old policy on the number of required face-to-face field contacts with offenders was changed by my superseding policy of what date?" The officers didn't know the answer, of course, and were obviously embarrassed. Each officer apologized, with head bowed. Gee noticed one of the officers was giving Kingmaker the finger, pretending to scratch his eyebrows, the way prisoners of war do when videotaped by their captors. At times, Kingmaker was herself and, at other times, she morphed into Nurse Ratched from *One Flew Over the Cuckoo's Nest*.

Off to the side of the stage were four offenders, handcuffed and in leg irons. All four were dressed in black-and-white-striped prison uniforms. Every time the officers gave a wrong answer—and every answer was the wrong answer—two muscular, sneering correctional officers dressed in army green prison guard uniforms with black trim—one guard on the left side of the four aligned offenders and the other at the right end—smacked hard, plastic, black batons against the offenders' hands, legs, backs, and faces, drawing blood from the facial whips. Gee remembered trying to scream, "They had nothing to do with the answer!" but no sound came out of her mouth. At times, the correctional guards would smack an offender for no obvious reason, except, perhaps, to remind the offender who wielded the power. This act infuriated Gee but not the audience.

As a consequence of the officers' wrong answers, eventually one by one the offenders were dropped through a trapdoor. Oddly, the offenders didn't seem surprised by the trapdoors. The audience screamed in delight. Gee remembered waking up in a sweat, furious with game show host Kingmaker's arrogance.

Running hard downhill, Gee was baffled about the context, the rules of the game. She sensed that, in the dream, Kingmaker intentionally made the officers appear foolish, but, oddly, there was no direct indication that Kingmaker targeted the offenders for cruelty—instead, that consequence appeared to be more like unintended collateral damage. The image of a military general at a press conference emerged, where the general chose to focus on the destruction of the enemy's infrastructure while dodging a question from the press about civilian casualties. She asked herself, aloud, "Where did you get the military press conference image?" Kingmaker's sarcastic remarks, of course, made herself look smart, the officers stupid, and the offenders helpless. That Gee was a part of an audience that laughed at others' misery enraged her ... even though she tried to remind herself that it was only a dream.

The dream left Gee feeling anxious. She wondered just how much she had been in denial about the angst she felt about the culture of the office—which was, essentially, it's OK to be condescending toward offenders. Stereotypes had become shortcuts.

She wondered if the dead leaves all around her were symbolic of her spirit dying at work. Surely, without her friends Pepe, Hattie, and Huggie, being in "the system" would be unbearable. Who could she talk with about this growing discomfort? Her father, a former federal probation officer? *Absolutely not.* Ed? *He'd never sit still long enough to listen.* Maybe her best friend, Ali? *Maybe,* she thought. No wonder.... No wonder she had coffee every Saturday with Pepe, Hattie, and Huggie. *No wonder,* she thought. *My God, they're my hold on sanity.*

Then, almost as that thought emerged, another source of her anxiety came to her in a burst of clarity: last week's distance from Ed was *less* about his five-day business trip to Los Angeles and being apart and *more* about the distance and annoyance in his tone and his obvious disinterest in talking to her. She had called him six times; he returned two of the calls. Even then, the conversations were awkward and stiff. She tried to pinpoint the last time she had felt emotionally close to Ed ... really close ... but came up with a blank, and that frightened her. She simply couldn't remember when they had last held hands or snuggled in bed when they weren't having sex, or even watched a movie together on the couch.

She decided that she was going to reach out to him and reconnect. Since he had arrived home from L.A. after midnight, perhaps he would still be in bed, and she could wake him up with rousing sex and close the distance she now felt so terribly uncomfortable with. She missed the simple things: laughing, holding hands, talking, and actually listening to each other. She felt … isolated.

She got Ruppert, who was still breathing hard, freshly drawn water in his bowl, with the mandatory four pieces of ice, and put it next to the small island range in the kitchen. He ignored the water until she gave him a congratulatory cookie. Then, after lapping up half of the water, he headed for the screened-in porch, where he liked to collapse on the cool, red-painted cement floor and pant until he fell asleep.

The home, purchased five years ago, right before they were married, was decorated throughout with her efforts at creating a warm home—one like her grandparents' but not like the home where she was raised by her father and mother. At her urging, Ed had added oak rail and crown molding throughout every room. They used a bold dark green for the living room walls, adorned with smartly framed photographs of outings and action shots in a mixture of color, black and white, and sepia. There were pictures of Ed and Gee everywhere— on camping trips, whitewater rafting adventures, Ed playing softball, Gee riding a bike in a one-hundred-mile MS bike tour, Ruppert as a very small puppy, and numerous friends and a few family members. In the center of the family room, dominated by a large, dark brown, overstuffed leather couch, stood a huge plasma TV and a surrounding entertainment center made of heavy oak. On the right corner of the entertainment center was a small picture of Gee playing catch with her mother. It was the room where Ed liked to be, where he liked to receive his constant business-related cell phone calls. A machine-quilted throw made by Gee lay over the couch. Numerous quilted wall-hangings and comforters she made were found throughout the house. Live plants, each of which Gee talked to, were scattered about the living room and family room. But clearly the simple screened-in porch, built by Ed, her father, and their friend Huggie, was their favorite place to relax. In the spring and summer they enjoyed the two dark-brown, Acadia gliding chairs with matching table centered between them to rest newspapers, drinks, and books. Two years ago they had added a copper, wood-burning fireplace to complement late-night, after-dinner drinks when they entertained friends.

After a cup and a half of coffee, and, more importantly, cooling off, Gee headed up the steps and past the master bedroom, where she peeked in on Ed and found him still tossing about in bed. She headed for the hall shower, which she used as her private bathroom. After drying her hair, she covered herself in Magnolia Blossom body cream and slipped into a short, emerald green, silky nightgown, which, of course, was a message in and of itself. The nightgown placed on display her long blond hair, shapely breasts, and long, tanned legs. Gee never just walked.... She bounced as if her feet were spring-loaded. It was her signature. She put a simple, small blue ribbon in her hair that matched her light blue eyes.

She slid under the light covers, snuggling up to Ed from behind, and pressed her breasts into his back. He let out a slight moan. Like a chef orchestrating a presentation in front of delighted patrons, she moved her middle finger deftly around his ear, neck, and down his back. Then she reached around his body to gain his full attention. She began to kiss him gently. He was nonresponsive. Instantly, the hypersensitive Gee felt his lack of interest. She wanted him to want to connect with her. *Maybe*, she thought, *he's just jet-lagged. Stop it, Gee*, she said to herself. *Stop it! He's just tired.* She rubbed his chest and kissed him on the neck. Still, he showed little interest in taking charge of any sexual foreplay.

"Are you OK, Ed?" she asked. "Is my baby jet-lagged?" she asked, massaging him.

"No, I've just got a lot on my mind."

"Already? So early in the morning? Well ... there's a time and place for everything, booby," she said, kissing his neck.

She tried to roll him over and mount him, which he always liked. He resisted. It was apparent that this morning he didn't want her to be in charge. *Maybe that's not all bad*, she thought. He climbed on her and climaxed quickly, in less than two minutes. He bolted out of bed, without a word. *Wham, bam, thank you, ma'am*, she thought to herself. Neither spoke directly of this brief interaction, this awkward interplay. She fought against her instincts to make meaning of this encounter.

She heard Ed start the shower and followed him, after putting on jeans and a sweatshirt.

"I'm going to meet Pepe, Huggie, and Hattie at Starbucks. You love Huggie—you'll like Pepe and Hattie, too. Join me, please. They're important to me.... They help me survive. After coffee, maybe the two of us could go to the Farm Women's Market, or just browse around Bethesda, like we used to. I miss doing that with you," she said.

Ed came out of the shower and wrapped a towel around himself. "I've got a lot of work to catch up on. The West Coast trip was very successful. I'm not real interested in hearing about your cases today," he said, without eye contact.

"Oh, stop it," she said, smiling. "Let's have some fun. I feel like all you do is work."

"Well, you know, the quarter is ending in three weeks. I've got to close some deals if I'm going to lead the office in quarterly sales. That's a $10,000 bonus, as you well know, not counting the commissions. You can't have it both ways," he said.

"I can't have what both ways? What does that mean? I don't care if you're salesman of the quarter.... I care about you!" she said.

"Oh, that's rich. Have you been reading too many beach books?" he asked.

"OK, OK. Let's stop this. You must be under pressure," she said, touching his shoulder. He recoiled. She tried, unsuccessfully, to ignore the gesture. "How about we split the difference? Let's go play this afternoon *before* we go out to dinner.... Whatever you'd like to do. Let's have fun together.... Remember when we had fun together, Poopy? I miss fun with you!"

"No thanks."

Gee looked down at the floor and sighed. "Let me know if you change your mind," she said. *My God*, she thought, *things are worse than I thought. Wake up, Gee!*

"Do you need your hearing checked?" he shot back.

"No. No, I don't. I hear you—I just don't understand," she said, and left the room. She gathered her keys and wallet downstairs in a flailing motion, as Ruppert followed her to the door.

"Stay, Ruppert. Stay here ... with the jerk," she said, closing the front door hard.

At coffee with her buddies, they talked about the ever-present reality of too many offenders, too little time, and the accompanying feeling of being overwhelmed and disorganized. Of the four, Gee seemed most equipped to handle the overload. She had to-do lists referencing other lists. Hattie joked that if there was such a thing as a National Association of Organizers, Gee would be selected to organize it.

That afternoon she asked Ed to join her raking leaves left over from the winter, which was no small task, given the four oak trees in their yard, each of which towered over one hundred feet. He refused to help, which was a first for their jointly managed yard work. Raking leaves, she peered at the back door every few minutes, expecting Ed to emerge and join in the spring ritual. The work, she fantasized, would create a segue to small talk, which, in turn, would open the door for a breakthrough moment. Two hours later, after thirteen lawn bags were filled with oak leaves, she tried to start the twenty-two inch, push lawnmower. It wouldn't start.

"I can't start the lawnmower. Do you know where the lawnmower manual is? It's not where I left it," she said, hoping he would move his PC off his lap and join in solving the lawnmower problem.

"It's in the garage, in a canister on the workbench," he said.

She waited a second for him to move away from his notes and laptop. He didn't. "Jerk," she mumbled to herself, audibly, as she headed for the garage.

Fifteen minutes later, with the owner's manual at her side, she yanked the cord, and the lawnmower started. While she cut the grass, she kept glancing at the back door, anticipating his appearance. She finished the yard work and headed for the shower.

Around six o'clock, with the awkward silence between them in full force, Gee hollered up the steps from the kitchen, asking Ed to come downstairs. As he landed on the bottom stair, she greeted him with a forced smile, handed him a cold Heineken, held one for herself. She walked back into the kitchen, turned at the marble-topped bar, and said, "Let's talk."

"I'm more comfortable in the living room," he said. Once there, he settled in an oversized green-and-white-striped chair. Having followed him, Gee chose the couch. The small formal living room was usually the location of their serious talks ... talks labeled by Ed as the "OR Talks," or "Our Relationship Talks."

"What's up?" she asked.

"What do you mean?"

"I'm concerned. I feel like we've become distant housemates in college. We interact, talk, but about logistics, not sharing who we are and what we feel. I feel alone. I'm not blaming you.... It's just what I'm experiencing. Have I done something to anger you?"

"What do you mean?"

"What do I mean? Well, we used to be ... what ... action-oriented. We rode bikes together, ran together, shopped together, did nothing together. Now, you work and I seem to manage the house and support your schedule. That's OK, but I want more from you. I miss you ... *us.*"

"Oh, here we go again. 'You don't do this. You don't do that....' What do you want from me? To be everything you ever needed ... whenever you need it?"

Gee's sigh reflected the instant pain in her gut.

"Is that what you think? I make too many demands on you and your precious time? You mean like asking for conversations? 'How's your day?' 'Nice dress?' 'What's up with work?' 'How do you feel?' 'How was your run?' 'What do you think?' 'Let's have some fun together.' Stuff like that?" she said, placing the beer down and gesturing more actively with her arms with each sentence.

"I always thought it would be enough for you if I busted my butt at work.... You know, got ahead and made lots of money for a bright future!"

"And I always thought if would be nice to take care of you.... Share your life and experiences. Am I asking too much by asking to be let in? How is *that* asking too much? Stop this babble, Ed. What's wrong?" she said. After a silent moment, upon reflection, his comment about "be everything you ever needed" didn't seem extemporaneous to her.

"It's clear to me that the distance you feel, Gee, is because we've lost that sizzle, the ... the spark that we used to have. All you really do anymore is ruminate about—" Ed started.

"You mean *you've* lost that sizzle? And how do you know what I think about, or *ruminate* about, as you put it? You've got your nose in a PC."

"OK, I've lost something. This ... this is a nightmare. It's dawned on me lately that I've become my father, a thoughtless, coldhearted deal maker. I don't like that. You've become ... what ... like my mother—a shallow Sister Mercy, going on and on about the flowers on the altar of the church. Except you've mastered the art of musing about the petty-assed problems of offenders—or, worse, about mean ole Kingmaker did this ... The Kingmaker did that. God, I can't imagine having snot-nosed kids whining at my heels, adding to this mess!" he shouted.

"Oh, so your nonsense about saving enough money.... *Je-sus*.... So *not* having kids is about me? About me? Is that how you feel?"

"I can't be all you need. I feel you're *at me* ... *after me*! I feel strangled!" he yelled.

"*At you? Je-sus!*" she shouted. "I never thought I'd *ever* hear me described like that ... *ever!*" she screamed.

She got up and paced around the room.

"I feel trapped in a spiderweb!" he shouted to her back, as she continued to circle the room.

Gee paused, turned to him, folded her arms and glared. Ruppert came to her side. She kneed him away.

"I'm bored," said Ed. "When we first married we had fun together. That fun turned into work. You in your world of cases, people you want to save or whatever. I'm surrounded by competitors from other companies and *within* my own damned office. I live in 'I can beat his deal, your deal, their deal.' I'm trained not to show emotions, to be cool and collected. You want to talk about saving souls. Now, what's the connection between us?"

"Why can't we separate our two worlds of work?"

"You're not paying attention. It doesn't work that way. You live what you do.... I live what I do. And I like the power of being number one. I never thought I'd like to slay colleagues and competitors over deals. But part of me does. There's just no room ..."

"For me? For us?"

"I don't get the point of marriage anymore, really. I can take my clothes to the cleaners. I can find food. I know we do little together anymore. That's fine with me. It's not with you. We're on different courses and it's been coming for quite a while, really."

They were quiet for several minutes.

"Where have I been?" Gee asked. "You live on an emotional island, Ed. When we go out with other people it's like you get in one of those rubberized boats and jettison out to their yacht. You laugh, you smile, you wine, you dine—you're just a wonderful guest ... but a visitor. Then, you go back in your little boat to go back to your island, so you don't have to talk about yourself or what you feel."

"And you're different? How are you different? You're always *at* people. You're very comfortable with *their* problems, *their* issues. You want to delve into others' problems, solve *their* problems. Margaret-Fucking-Mead wants to save the world. You think anybody knows what goes on inside of you?"

She thought to herself that, like it or not, that there was some truth to that. She was more comfortable talking about other people's problems. Even her best friend Ali had said that.

"Do you care about what goes on inside me?" she said.

She would have welcomed a "yes" but got only a long silence.

"And I don't get your emotional island stuff. What are you talking about? I work, I focus, and I go out with friends with you. How's that different from anyone else? Not enough 'OR' sessions? Why don't you tape Dr. Phil or watch Springer—he's closer to the people you want to save," he said.

"That's nasty and elitist ... at best. I need some time to collect my thoughts.... I'm going to the grocery store," she said.

~

She almost threw the groceries in the car.... *Je-sus*, she said to herself.

~

She put the six plastic bags on the kitchen counter and, without putting the grocery items away, walked into the family room, where Ed didn't look up from his PC.

"You want some more information, some actual examples? Really?" she said. "What about last week when you were pissed off with your father's comment about how much money your brother made last year? What an insult. You make twice as much as your brother. For four days I asked you what was going on...."

"Voila! That's my damned point," he said. "For four days you asked *me* what was going on...."

"That's *my* point," she said. "And on day five, Mr. Invisible, again at my prompting, mumbles something like, 'Well, I was just annoyed.' 'No big deal,' you said. I know you were hurt. But you made sure to wait until the moment was gone, the emotions were gone," she said.

"I'm way past tired of your telling me about my emotions, my anger, my shortcomings! Live your own damned life. When I want to say something to my father, I will—not when you want me to! Why don't you deal with your own anger?" he said.

"What anger?" she said.

"Go read the letter from your mother in your top dresser drawer and see if that doesn't get you in touch with your big swollen secret—rather than everybody else's problems!" he screamed.

"How dare you bring my dead mother into your need to retreat from life! Have you no shame?" she said, crying.

Suddenly, she felt like vomiting. She quickly headed for the downstairs hall bathroom, fearful of throwing up. She slammed the door behind her, burped several times, and splashed cold water on her face, slowly resettling her wavering stomach. *At him,* she said over and over to herself ... *at him!* My mother's letter.... You'll regret that.

She heard him walk out of the house.

She sat on the side porch, exhausted from a week of restless sleep, today's run, the yard work, and the pain from those words—'*at me,*' '*strangled,*' '*trapped,*' '*swollen secret*'—which she repeated over and over again. Fueled by Heinekens, her mind raced, with scattered thoughts that were barely connected. Somewhere around 9:30 PM, she threw up.

Back in the kitchen, leaning against the wall, she remembered reading an article several months ago in a women's magazine—"10 Clues Your Marriage is on the Rocks"—while waiting to get her hair trimmed. She had most of the "symptoms." Back then, she thought her score on the quiz was a joke. She felt then that her life was entwined in Ed's. She never considered being single again or starting a new relationship. How could this be happening? She was embarrassed by the idea of a potential separation. The word "separation" felt like a dagger in her heart. How did this happen so quickly? How long had he been wishing he wasn't married? She thought about their sex life—it used to be so exciting. In this moment, it came to her that they used to have sex four or five times a week. Now, it was more like once a week. She thought they had just settled into a different pace. Maybe that was a clue she had ignored. But why was this happening? She thought the obvious thing to do was to get couple's therapy. She hoped that therapy would help them get back to where they used to be: two people in love who enjoyed each other. Money wasn't an issue.... They had over $400,000 dollars in investment plans. Then how could they get back on track?

She heard him return sometime after midnight and settle, she guessed, on the couch. Her mind raced with questions. There were no answers that made sense.

One week later, the anxiety of the silence between Ed and Gee was building in Gee. She thought back to last Saturday's coffee at the Bethesda Starbucks with her work buddies. She could still hear Hattie's joking words ringing in her ears, "Gee's not going to show anyone her feelings." The image of a bright red cell wall sprang to mind, drawn by herself in eighth-grade biology class. "The cell wall keeps everything inside," the teacher had said. *How am I any different than anybody else? I guess maybe I really don't share my feelings with Ed ... or my friends ... or my father ... but there's my best friend, Ali.... I share who I am with Ali.* This thought comforted her, but not for long. *God, maybe I just push back and forth with events, thoughts, reactions ... but maybe not my actual feelings.... Oh my. Why do I feel like a stone, skimming over a pond?* The picture of a still pond, right out of a scene from *On Golden Pond* jumped into her consciousness. *Am I a stone skimming over a pond?*

She dug deeper for answers. *Ed makes few emotional demands on me. All of the unpleasant emotions he expresses around me are work-related, the intrigue of the deals, the backstabbing, the double-talk he experiences. He talks about those things over dinners, but not about his feelings with me. Those just come out in sound bites with tonal shifts, like "I thought you were going to do that!" It's true; I press to hear his feelings. He backs up. I press lots of people about their feelings. But what am I doing with him? I can't remember talking about a feeling other than frustrations at work or worrying about this or that offender. What was it like when we were first married? We did fun stuff. We were outdoors together. Then his career and my career overtook us. Or did they, really? The contrast seems so stark: then and now. What is now?*

She slid into a dramatic question-answer mode, as if she were answering someone else's questions. *Well, let's see, now, you ask? Now I spend more time by myself, away from the very busy, oh, and preoccupied Ed. Now, I no longer recreate. Now I exercise to exhaustion, pushing the limits. An example, you ask? Well, I used to exercise with Ed three or four times a week … road bikes, hiking, running, mountain bikes, rowing— stuff like that. Now I exercise every day, mostly running and riding … every day, for longer and longer distances. How often with Ed, you ask? Maybe once a week, maybe none. Why am I pushing myself harder and becoming more compulsive? I'm not compulsive, I'm … what … finding my emotional equilibrium … my emotional gyro.*

Her answers were becoming more sarcastic in tone. She laughed at her haughtiness. She abandoned the stone-skimming metaphor with this thought: *if I'm the rock, who's throwing me?*

⁓

Two days later she dug into their relationship *before* they were married. *What was it like when we dated?* She thought back to the West Virginia trip five weeks before they were married—the whitewater rafting down the very dangerous, Class V Upper Gauley River. She remembered waking up around dawn on a chilly October morning in a small, rented cabin with the light ricocheting off the mixture of orange, red, brown, and partially green leaves and screaming to her, "I'm here! Get up! Come see me!" She remembered Ed shuffling around in the kitchen. She could smell coffee brewing. She recalled rolling over in a grand gesture, grabbing Ed's fluffy pillow and squeezed it between her legs, realizing that within an hour they'd be blasting through chaos in a three-person, thick, rubber raft with a guide. New to a sport that Ed had mastered, she both wanted to ask Ed questions and she didn't. She wanted to leave her safety in his hands.

She could still remember the smell of burning oak in the cast-iron wood-burning stove in the adjacent living room. She deftly slipped off Ed's T-shirt she had slept in while he was in the kitchen. She was naked under the warm covers. There was something about Ed's worn T-shirts … the smell … his smell … that both comforted and aroused her. When Ed came into the near-barren, simple bedroom, standing near the waist-high bed, she recalled how the sunlight behind him illuminated his six-feet-one-inch frame. It reminded her of the light in the strained-glass picture above the altar surrounding Jesus' head in the Episcopal church of her childhood. She tried to wordlessly entice Ed with sex, and he smiled, placed the two cups of coffee in white, thick glass cups—probably, she thought, stolen from a nearby Cracker Barrel—on top of magazines that advertised local restaurants and activities. She remembered that he gently, deftly, climbed into bed, placed his hand on her back, and leaned her forward. His legs straddled her from behind as if they were children playing choo-choo train. He grabbed one of the coffee cups and handed it to her. From the side of his shorts, he pulled out a hairbrush that he had slipped into his waistband. He said nothing. He softly brushed her long, blond hair. Several times he leaned forward slightly, kissing her on the neck or on her back and shoulders.

What is now? Now, *he says I'm a busybody like his shallow mother.* She flashed to the rock skimming across the pond. *Am I swallowing my feelings with him? Who else? Well, that's easy … Her Highness … The Kingmaker. What am I afraid of?*

⁓

Fourteen days later, having exchanged only essential information with Ed, like who was going to feed the dog, Gee decided to break the silence. *I can't take this*, she thought. *For the past two weeks, I've been cornered by his passive-aggressive trap. If I go to him, he'll say I'm at him. If I keep the pain inside, I lose. I hurt all over. I'm angry, really angry … and frustrated. Why can't he give me a sign to show me how to reach him? This is cruel.*

At seven o'clock at night and now fully in "couples' silent mode," she slammed her book down, went downstairs, walked into the family room, and said, "Join me in the living room," which interrupted his laptop work and caused a frown.

"Two weeks of silence, Ed. What's the message? How can I reach you? What do you want? What do you want to happen?" Gee asked in a factual tone.

"Nothing," he said.

"So you just want to get out of the spiderweb, huh?"

He didn't answer.

"Is there another woman?" she said.

"No," he said, looking at her squarely.

She remained silent. She got up off the couch and walked into the kitchen to let his response settle in. Her instincts led her to believe him. After putting water on her face and drying it with a paper towel, she returned to the living room.

"Then, it's just me.... It's *me* you want to get away from, correct?" she asked.

"I'm sorry...."

"'I'm sorry' doesn't work. I love you. I'd like to get professional help with you to save this marriage. I recognize we've been ... drifting apart. This isn't *all* your fault. I want to know what I've done. I want our marriage to work."

He paused before answering. "I don't want to try to save something that isn't working for me," he said.

"Why can't we find some middle ground while we get help?" Gee asked.

"Middle ground would put us somewhere lost at sea, wouldn't it?"

It came to her in that moment with that one message that the one theme she kept hearing over and over again was *no*; just like his present posture, arms folded across his chest, his message was that he was closed to her and her ideas. She pushed out, he pulled back.

"So there's nothing I can do to reach you?" she asked.

He said nothing and did not move.

"Have it your way.... Have it your way," she said.

Tears fell from her eyes, but she made no crying sounds. Her mind raced. What did she feel—what? Anguish, anger, frustration ... and mostly emptiness. She allowed new feelings to surface.... She felt hollow … empty … invisible. But she returned to being angry and hurt. She felt as if she were experiencing a bad dream, where an evil force was slowly, painstakingly torturing her with pinpoint accuracy.

In the silence, she also felt sudden flashes of desperation, and her natural response was belligerence. "I see," she said, breaking the silence. "Too much work, huh? I'm not a person who can stand coldness, particularly intentional coldness and the idea that I'm not fun to be around."

He did not respond.

"OK, so you don't know what you want, but you do know what you don't want: me. Do you want a separation?" she asked.

He said nothing but nodded.

"That's it, nothing but a head shake?"

He said nothing.

"You can't even say the words? Nothing?"

Ed got up, which ratcheted up her anxiety level. He walked over to the living room window, looked out at the riders at the stable across the street and said, "It's just like them. They go round and round all day. Oh, they look good, but they're really getting nowhere," he said. He turned and looked at her. "The more things stay the same, the more they seem to change."

"So, you're bored with me, is that it?"

"Stuck," said Ed.

"And I can't help, right? Except to leave you alone?"

He nodded.

"I can't stand torture. I guess all that stuff about waiting until we have plenty of money saved before we have kids was just bull," she said.

"Kids are the last thing I want to talk about," he said.

"I bet," she said.

She walked into the kitchen to get a Heineken. This time when she returned, she didn't bring him one.

"Do you want a divorce?" she asked.

He made a palms-up gesture with raised eyebrows, which she interpreted to mean, "I guess so."

"That's it. I'll give you your wish. You like to make deals, so here's one for you—you find an attorney to draw up the *fucking* voluntary separation papers. If you find a nasty one, I'll do the same. I want the VW—oh, and fully paid off. I'll find a condo and I expect you to pay for it—*in full*. I'll pay the taxes and condo fees. You pay in full for all of my outstanding educational loans *outright*. You pay all of my *future* therapy bills—when I get a therapist. You can have my share of this house. I need some of the furniture, and I'll need new stuff, too. *Jesus*…. I can't believe I'm having this non-conversation. I didn't see this coming. In the meantime, please stay downstairs. I can't believe we're actually separating. This marriage is important to me. You're important to me. But you've got me in a box. *At you!* How do I come to you now, without being *at you*? Nice job, you stupid jerk," she said and headed toward the stairs.

"Why don't we just call it a voluntary separation?" he asked, before she made it out of the room.

"Why don't you voluntarily kiss my ass!" she screamed at him, turned, and headed for what was to become her temporary quarters—their bedroom, upstairs.

Still, as she reached the top step, she paused, hoping that he would call to her, stop her, bring her back downstairs, and talk her out of this twisted nightmare.

He said nothing.

⁓

Several weeks later, on a Saturday when Gee returned home from her run with Ruppert, the legal papers were on the kitchen table in a large envelope with a yellow sticky attached, with this handwritten note:

Here is the agreement. The attorney suggested that you consult with an attorney.

⁓

She read the document carefully. It gave her everything she asked for plus $50,000 of their joint savings. The document required her to agree not to seek any additional money from him through alimony or retirement funds. She signed the papers and put the original back in the envelope, keeping a copy for herself. She expected to get a great deal of flak from Ali about not consulting an attorney and perhaps from her father, too, even though he liked Ed.

~

That afternoon she drove to Ali's house. "What'd I do wrong?" was the ruminating theme as Gee drove into Ali's large driveway and up to her cedar-shingled, three-car garage with a massive children's game room above it. Before she got out of her car, she settled on the only explanation she knew for the separation: "I don't know."

She sat on the veranda of Ali's six-bedroom brick home in Olney while Ali made iced tea. Seated in a padded patio chair at a wrought iron table with a red umbrella, Gee felt embarrassed. Even though they had already talked about the recent turmoil, she still expected Ali to ask her how Ed could drift away emotionally without her sensing it. Gee had practiced an answer—she'd try to explain that the relationship had seemed to unravel, rather than tear apart. *But how could that actually happen?* she kept asking herself while waiting for Ali. The answers Gee came up with didn't meet the expected question head-on.

In some ways, Ali was like an older sister. No subject was out of bounds between the two of them. Like Gee, Ali was in her mid-thirties, but she had also finished medical school, married, and had two children before she reached thirty-four. The size and elegance of Ali and Michael's home looked more like the home of a pediatrician, Ali's profession, than that of a professor, Michael's profession. With the aid of maids, the house was spotless, and the yard was well-attended by a lawn service. Formal pictures of the two children and snapshots of them at play were everywhere.

On the stone veranda, overlooking the figure eight-shaped pool, the two friends drank tea and picked at the small plate of veggies and fruit. Michael had taken the kids to the zoo. As usual, the tall, black-haired Ali, dressed in very short, white shorts and a light blue T-shirt with a green and blue scarf in her hair, looked like she belonged on the cover of *Vanity Fair*. Ali was energetic, very bright, warm, a great listener, funny, and simply charming. She had a magnetic laugh that burst from every muscle in her face. Ali, at ease and comfortable with herself, was never reluctant to provide direct feedback to Gee, even when the message might disturb her.

"Somehow, seeing 'Virginia Brooks, Defendant,' in black-and-white feels so final ... like we're strangers. God, that hurts," Gee said.

"Are you going to take his advice—or his attorney's advice—and retain an attorney?" asked Ali.

"No, I don't want to jinx him. He's agreed to what I want. His instincts are to drift. I don't want martyrdom to be his companion, too. I've signed the papers," she said. "I've picked out this one-bedroom condo with an underground parking garage at the Willoughby in Chevy Chase, near the District line. He's agreed to give me a check for $227,000 the day before closing on Friday the twenty-first. I move in three weeks from today, on Saturday. It's a nice place. Will you go see it with me?" she asked.

"This is moving fast, isn't it?" Ali asked.

Gee looked down at the ground and nodded once.

"Of course, I'll go with you to look at it. Let's go now, sweetie. For gosh sakes, you know you can count on me being there to help you move in. I have lots of questions, but they can wait. Actually, one can't.... Is there another woman?" she asked, leaning forward.

"I don't think so. He says no," Gee said.

"OK. Just realize this isn't the end of the world. You'll figure it out. Just stick to your guns. But really, things are moving very, very fast. Is there any way to talk through this? Any other options? Have you considered therapy?" Ali asked.

"He refused therapy. *Je-sus*, this is awkward," she said.

"We'll get through it, girl," said Ali, moving across the table to give her a big hug and kiss on the cheek. "We'll get through this," she repeated.

~

Tommy Joe's was a lively restaurant, mostly thought of as a bar, perfectly positioned in the heart of revitalized Bethesda. Its mauve walls gave customers a sense of a being in a bar in Key West. Huggie was seated in a booth near the back when Ed arrived with his two-day-old beard growth. He waved to give the searching Ed his bearings. It would be impossible to miss the presence of Huggie.

As Ed approached the booth, Huggie stood up and hollered out,

"How's my man?" There was nothing subtle about Huggie's social ease.

They shook hands in the fashionable clasp handshake, plus raised elbows, plus the one–arm-over-the-shoulder-semi-embrace sequence made popular by black athletes.

"Oh, all screwed up," Ed said.

"Because …?" Huggie asked.

The waitress delivered two large amber drafts in twenty-ounce, chilled glasses, which Huggie had ordered before Ed arrived.

"Before you get into some long-winded epistle from Paul, I'm your friend. Dump the broads … but don't dump me!" Huggie roared with laughter.

Ed looked down at the table.

"That's a joke," Huggie said.

"It's just … I don't know what the fuck I'm doing … I … I …"

"I don't think you need to know what you're doing to drink a beer. Haven't NASCAR fans done proved that?" Huggie asked.

"I don't know what's wrong. Is it Gee or me? Is it, whatever *it* is, my job, or what? I keep having this fantasy that I want to buy a Harley and head for Alaska," Ed said, taking another large swig of beer.

"Isn't this time to get some professional help, my brother?" Huggie asked.

"I don't know," Ed said.

"Well, I guess I want to deliver one message tonight, and that's this: you're my friend and I love you like a brother. I don't intend to lose you. And I have a pact with that nasty bitch you're still married to. I have a pact with ole sugar britches, who, by the way, is going to be my second wife. She and I won't talk about you, the issues, the problems— none of that. Gee and I are great friends, but you are my buddy, and I cannot—*cannot*—be torn down the middle. I ain't no movie ticket. I'll be separate friends to each of you, and both of you will have to accept that," Huggie said. "She ain't the enemy.… You ain't the enemy. Deal?" Huggie asked.

"Deal, Huggie," Ed said.

Huggie held up a big hand—as in *stop*—as the waitress approached the table. She did a 180 degree turn that befitted an Olympic ice skater.

"I'll just sit back and hope you two assholes get your shit together," Huggie concluded.

They sat in silence for about two minutes, which is a long time for men to be in silence. Then, they did what other rational men do.... They talked about college adventures and baseball for a couple hours before leaving the bar for their quite different home bases.

3

BOTTOMING OUT

Gee Brooks

For days after receiving the separation agreement, Gee confined herself to the bedroom while Ed slept downstairs. She was miserable. Three hours earlier on this Monday morning, Ed had left town on an eight-day business trip. He left only his hotel location and phone number on the kitchen counter, without discussion. It made Gee edgy and miserable to purposely *not* talk to him while living in the same house, not even to say, "Have a safe trip." *What the heck*, she thought, *I would have said that to a stranger*. Countless times she started to pick up the phone and call him on his cell phone. Each time she was jolted, as if anew, by an inner voice reminding her of the impending separation … to which she would say to herself, "Oh, that's right.…" Coldness was abject pain for her. It wasn't in her family experience.

She began to think ten days ahead—to the moving day. *What did she feel?* she incessantly asked herself. *Confused* was the answer that came back. At this moment, and only for this moment, her feelings bounced around like a young child on a trampoline—they were … in suspension. She was certainly not comfortable in her own home yet not emotionally prepared to move into her new condo. She was stuck. But the clock was ticking. The clock was ticking, she kept thinking. She laughed when she remembered the ticking clock in *High Noon*. But the smile didn't hang on her face for long. For the first time since her teens, Gee felt not just alone but lonely and out of touch.

In her office on this dreary, rainy, Monday morning, she focused on catching up on her written reports and assignments. Busy work helped hold off the thoughts about her crumbling marriage and the empty home on Meadowbrook Lane. After a quiet lunch alone in the cafeteria, she unexpectedly hit a wall. She crashed into herself and felt panic. The idea of going home alone that night to all the memories, the dashed hopes, the carefully framed pictures of happier times, the home seemingly tailored and decorated to their personae and the idea of being cornered by a needy dog was more than she could tolerate. She rushed to her office and closed the door behind her, a sign to staff that she was not available.

Her small office had a rather large wooden desk and two chairs, one to each side. Her diploma and three pictures of her with Ed hung on the wall behind her desk. She stared at the pictures. At 5:45 PM on this terribly gloomy Monday, with the probation office now empty, she crawled under her desk sitting in a near-fetal position, her arms wrapped around her knees and her pleated, checkered skirt. Gee Brooks began to cry. Bawl, really. The pain rolled over her in waves, constricting her chest. Her first instinct was to call Ali, but she chose not to. The pain was too intense, too overpowering to talk about or analyze. She wanted to go to Ali's home, but, with the children present, it was no place to unravel.

She joined her hands together, fingers intertwined, to literally hold onto herself.

She considered calling her father, but she didn't want to upset him.

She was in a panic.

She fantasized about Ed calling her to say it was all a big mistake, really, and, oh, would she please take him back? She would be harsh with him, she thought, but, over time, she'd forgive him.... But he must somehow find a way to erase the words *at me ... you're always at me.*

Screw him, she snapped back at her pleading, helpless fantasy.... *No, fuck him—for wasting my time. No man, no man, has ever said I was at him. To hell with men—I'll find a lesbian lover!* The thought made her both laugh and cry harder.

How did I get myself so wrapped around one man's self-centered needs? She rubbed her temples. The back and sides of her head ached. Her back was taut. Her shoulders and neck felt like they had needles in them. Her stomach cramped. She hadn't really slept in three days. The sides of her desk made a natural cage, one she welcomed.

She asked herself in a whisper, "How in God's name did I get here? Ali has kids, Huggie has kids, where are mine? Am I not good enough to be a mother? Ed, it was your stupid idea to make money first.... 'You know, Gee, like doctors do,' you said. 'Then, *then* we can enjoy life and kids. We'll fix up the house and sell it for a whopping profit, maybe buy a cottage in Colorado, or Utah, and live an outdoors lifestyle.' Except, Ed, you got lost on the way, didn't you … lost in a world of finance and competition. Ed's number one—yahoo! And me, what happened to me? I'm in a profession that hates people."

Eyes closed, she saw herself in a pulpit with a lavender robe flowing as if large electrical fans were aimed at her. She imagined herself bellowing to the worshippers, "Welcome to the world of justice, where we seek to punish the weak and meek!"

"That's good, Gee, the weak and meek," she said aloud, mocking herself. She felt the presence of a black deacon standing behind her, clapping his hands together.

He said, "That's good, Pastor Brooks. Amen, Pastor. Now let's hear from Pastor Brooks's mother, Anne. Come on up, Anne."

"Oh," said Pastor Brooks, "Deacon, we can't…. She's dead. You're pretty dead, aren't you, Mom?" She glanced down in this racing fantasy at a brown, wooden coffin, draped in roses, resting on wheels, below the pulpit … Mom's coffin. She sobbed, trying desperately to muffle the sound.

She urgently wanted to go to her car in the parking lot and drive away. But Officer Brooks was afraid someone in the probation office or courthouse would see her acting distraught and out of control. "Not in *this* courthouse," they'd say. "My God, *not* in the marbled halls of justice," the collective *they* would say privately to each other … but not directly to her.

She crawled out from under her desk and sat in her chair. The door had been shut for over six hours, an emotional lifetime. Wads of Kleenex were strewn under the desk, around the desk, on the floor, and on the desk.

Maybe I need to be in a hospital, she thought. She picked up the phone and started to call 911. She slammed the phone down. She tucked her feet underneath her and folded her arms around her chest and closed her eyes again. *Stop it, you helpless baby, stop it!*

"Come, everyone come," the attending physician, a psychiatrist, said while waiting in the hospital lobby until the entire group of observers arrived, like interns on their rounds. "Come on up to the seventh floor to see the helpless baby in the hospital."

"I'm fine," Gee said to the rows of visitors at her bedside. Those in the back row were eating popcorn. "I'll be OK, just fine. I have my juice and apple right here. We have group therapy tomorrow and TV time in the afternoon. I like *Search for Tomorrow.* I'm just, well, nutso!"

The visitors all looked down at the floor, hands clasped, and said nothing. She heard one of them whisper, "You were so full of life back then, honey!"

I need help. God, I need help! Her jaw quivered uncontrollably.

She pulled out the yellow pages from her bottom desk drawer and thumbed through until she landed on a reasonable sounding name: "Dr. Steven Weinman, Psychiatrist, 5900 Connecticut Avenue NW, Washington, DC." *That's near Chevy Chase*, she thought. She dialed his number.

A recorded message instructed the caller to leave a message, and Dr. Weinman would return the call.

Gee was only able to say, "Ah, ah, I need help," before she started to sob.

"This is Dr. Weinman; I was just screening my calls on the way out the door. What's your name?" he said.

"Ah ... ah ... Gee ... I'm sorry ... Gee Brooks...."

"You sound in a great deal of pain. Are you safe?" he asked.

"Safe, but I feel like I'm coming apart."

"Are you nearby?"

"I'm in the courthouse in Rockville. I work here."

"Well, Gee, you have some options. You can call 911 and they'll take you to a hospital for observation. You'll be safe there, until you can make up your mind what you want to do to feel better. Is that best for you now?"

"No, I can't do that. My supervisor wouldn't appreciate such a show of emotion."

"And what office is that?"

"The probation office."

"Damn, I better stop jaywalking then."

She almost smiled.

"If you can pull yourself together, I can see you in two days.… Let's see.… At six o'clock on.…" he said.

"No, that won't work. I'll call someone else."

"Can you get a ride here now, or a cab?"

"I'll drive myself."

"Well, let's see, you can't wait to be seen in two days, you feel like you're coming apart, but you're OK to drive? Listen and focus, Ms. Brooks. I'll wait here for one hour for you to arrive. Either you have a friend drive you here or you get a cab or you call 911. That's my advice, and so far it's free. You decide." He gave her his office address and suite number. She wrote it on a scrap of paper.

She headed out of the courthouse, furious at his demand that she not drive. She was unsure if she was headed for her car or was going to hail a cab. She just wanted to be outside of the courthouse.

Out on the corner, she raised her hand to try to hail the one cab that drove by in the first five minutes. The cabbie ignored her. Catching a cab from curbside in Rockville in the early evening was unlikely; this wasn't downtown D.C. Suddenly, a BMW screeched on the brakes and pulled over to the curb, startling her. She saw it was Pepe, her friend. Cars honked at him to move on. He ignored them.

He shouted out of the rolled-down window, "Gee, what are you doing?"

"Oh, God, Pepe, help me.… Help me, please," she said.

"Get in the car. Of course, get in the car before we both get killed."

That might not be a bad idea, she thought. She was unable to talk. She grabbed his arm, bawling, and buried her head on his right shoulder.

"It's OK. I'm here. Your friend Pepe's here. It's going to be all right. What can I do to help?"

She handed him the scribbled address and phone number, with the name Dr. Steven Weinman, Psychiatrist.

Pepe picked up his cell phone and rang the number.

"This is Dr. Weinman."

"My name is Pepe Gomez. I'm a friend of Gee Brooks. I know nothing about what's going on, but I'm guessing that I should drive her to your office now."

"Yes. I'll be waiting. I'm in Suite 520. Park across the street."

"I'll be there directly."

Pepe and Gee arrived in the now-empty waiting area outside Suite 520. Four offices were in Suite 520, two on each side. The waiting area had a small foyer with no receptionist. Patients sat in one of four chairs with the option of using the bathroom, drinking water from a water dispenser, watching psychiatrists walk from their offices to a kitchenette without making eye contact, or reading magazines, including the *New Yorker*. Or they could stare at one of several Picasso prints. Pepe chose a *New Yorker*. Gee stared at her lap.

Soon a door opened from one of the two offices on the left. A kind-looking man, about five feet, eight inches, perhaps in his mid-sixties, slim, with short, black, curly hair, and slumped forward slightly at the shoulders, said, "I'm Steven Weinman. Come in, please." He smiled and nodded at Pepe as Gee entered his office.

"I'm Gee," she said, crying. She noticed the couch, which looked more like artistic deference to Sigmund Freud than a working couch. Like her own home, the walls were hung with tapestry and eclectic art. He signaled with his left hand for her to sit in the green leather chair, while he sat in a black reclining chair, facing her. Another chair matching hers was adjacent to her. It was empty. She looked at the chair and wished Ed had chosen to accept her invitation for couples therapy. Dr. Weinman seamlessly handed her a box of Kleenex.

"What brings you here?"

"I feel like the world is collapsing around me."

She told him of her separation from Ed, of her plan to move into a condo soon, and of feeling more disconnected and alone than she had ever felt in her life. She added in a very soft tone, while staring into her lap, "I miss my mother." She started to cry, gently. It was the first time that she had ever verbalized missing her mother to anyone.

"Where is your mother?" he asked.

"She has been dead for over twenty years," Gee said.

"Oh, I see. Do you feel suicidal?"

"No. Unsafe, but not suicidal," Gee said.

"Have you ever been in treatment before?"

"No."

"The reason I ask, Ms. Brooks, is that I don't do suicides. It's not my shtick. Personal reasons, really. I'm kind of picky about who I treat. I have my quirks. My style may not match your requirements. For instance, I'm really not too cool on anti-depressants, but they could be necessary for you. Sometimes I cuss. I wish I was more temperate. You and I might need to meet several times and, if necessary, I can help you find a therapist that meets your needs, or your preferences," he said.

"What do you mean?" she asked.

"Well, some women like to be treated by other women. Some patients like therapists closer to their own age. Some prefer to be on anti-depressants. Others want to be in a group setting. Some expect only comfort and reassurance from a therapist. They want therapists who do *feedback-lite.* I don't do 'lite.' So, I guess what I'm saying is that all of this treatment business is really hit-or-miss. The way I see it, you and I working together well really depends on how well we connect and on how curious you are—how tired you are of the status quo. My assumption is that whatever is going on with you isn't working well. Do you understand what I'm saying?" he asked.

"Yes, I do. Listen, I have no intention of taking anti-depressants. I don't give a rat's ass about the sex or age of a therapist. I want to stop feeling out of control, unsafe," she said.

"OK. So, you're angry?"

"Very, but I don't know with who, or why," she said.

"Granted. That's where we start. Describe your recent sleeping patterns, please," he said.

"I'm sleeping in our bedroom, and Ed's downstairs. I've been drinking three or four beers every night. Then I sleep until about four o'clock. Then I'm up until the day starts," Gee said.

"Are you safe in the home? Is there physical or psychological abuse?"

"Oh, no, Ed's a wonderful—"

"A wonderful guy who's merely breaking your heart? May I call you 'Gee'?"

She nodded.

"Gee, you're depressed. I suspect it's a situational depression, which is good news. That's a small joke. Well, it's better than clinical depression, but not too good news for you, is it?" he said.

She almost smiled, didn't, but thought, *that's actually funny ... good news for me.* The quick diagnosis made her feel she wasn't crazy.

"My point is, as you got into this pickle, you'll get out of it. As strange as this might sound to you right now, feeling out of control might well be a sign that you're quite rational—even right now. My guess is that you've been trying to juggle, balance, control, and maybe conceal. Now, your mind and body are saying 'enough' ... 'That's enough.' Do you follow me?" he asked.

"Yes, I think so," she said. A sense of relief came to her in the midst of the pain. The fear of checking into a hospital evaporated instantly. *I'm going home,* she thought.

"But watch the drinking. I suggest your limit is now one or two glasses of beer a night. That's fine, no more. So, no suicide, homicide, boozing.... Deal?"

"Deal, but I like that homicide idea," she said.

"You're joking?" he said.

"Yes," she said.

"There's a difference between feelings and actions," he laughed. "Now, I suggest we see each other tomorrow, and we'll take it from there. Do you want something to help you sleep?"

"No, knowing I have help—I have you...." she paused, crying again, "It helps."

"Here are my ground rules: again, suicide, homicide, boozing are all no-no's. I suggest we meet weekly for three months—more frequently, if you feel the need. But let's meet tomorrow and then set a weekly time. My fee is $115 per fifty-minute session. I like to get paid on time. I start sessions on time and end on time. Call and cancel if you can't make an appointment. Now, I'm no picnic. I don't have a cozy, meandering style of treatment. I will be direct with you. We'll break a few eggs in your recovery and transition. Oh, and I want you to write an autobiography for me. Tell me everything. At my prices, it speeds up the process. Starting tonight, keep a journal of your thoughts and feelings and particularly your dreams. Write it all down. This is fertile ground for us. Do you have any hunches as to why this marriage is on the rocks?" he asked.

"I don't think I have been sensitive enough to Ed's needs."

"Interesting. I'd bet my money elsewhere. See you tomorrow at 11:00 AM. Hang in there," he said.

"Thank you," she said, crying hard.

"I'm on your side," he said.

The thought made her cry harder. *My God, I have someone I can talk to about everything*, she thought.

As she rose, he added, "At these prices, it's the least I can do."

This time she could not hold back a small laugh, and that brought on more tears—but tears of mild relief in this mighty emotional storm.

After a few seconds, when the crying at least slowed down a little, she left his office. Pepe met her and walked by her side without saying a word.

~

At 5:30 the next morning, Gee's phone rang on the table beside her bed. Ed's been hurt, she thought.

"Gee, it's Pepe. I'm outside, waiting for my running partner," he said.

Moments later, she came outside and tried to talk but welled up. She managed to eke out, "Thank you."

"My pleasure. After I kick your butt up and down the hills of Chevy Chase, I'll wait for you to change and take you to work. I work for coffee," Pepe said.

"I'm not going to work today, but I'll make you coffee, and I'd appreciate a ride to my car at the courthouse," she said.

She stayed home that Tuesday and away from work for two more business days. During that time she wrote her nineteen-page autobiography and began journaling feverishly.

For days, Pepe called every night at ten o'clock. He pretended he needed to check on some issue. Gee never spoke to Pepe about the details of her visits to Dr. Weinman, but she did have a running partner outside her house every morning. Around the eighth day of Pepe's oversight, Ed, now back in town from a business trip, was leaving the house very early, primarily to avoid seeing Gee. On the way to his car in the driveway, he noticed Pepe in his black running shorts, white

Nikes with red stripes, a red University of Maryland T-shirt, and a blue, tattered New York Yankee hat, leaning against his black BMW in front of the house.

"Can I help you?" said Ed.

"Nope."

"What are you doing in front of my house?" asked Ed.

"I'm Pepe, a friend of Gee's. We're going for a run," Pepe said.

"Oh, Pepe, from work. I'm sorry, I ... I ..." Ed said, making a palm-up gesture with his right hand. He didn't finish his thought. Instead, he turned, got into his car, and drove off.

Several days before moving into her new condo, Gee fired Pepe from his morning escort duties and was actually able to thank him without crying. She baked him an apple pie and delivered it to him at Starbucks, where they had coffee.

Pepe told her that during the past weeks he had been a stalker.

"What on earth are you talking about?" she said.

"Over the past few weeks, I've driven by your house, gone around the block several times, and called you from my cell phone. I'd drink a beer or two and wait until the lights went out and I was sure you were safe," he said.

"I didn't even know you were calling from your cell phone. I've been out of it, haven't I? Thank you, Pepe, you're a wonderful stalker and friend.... I'm lucky to have you," she said.

She cried softly, fiddling with her fingers.

"I've been there, Gee. The worst thing is being alone and feeling cut off ... and lonely," Pepe said. "I didn't want that to happen to you. You're ... you're my friend."

4

MOVING DAY

Gee Brooks

Gee talked about moving day for hours with Ali, Pepe, Hattie, Huggie, and Dr. Weinman. Her journal had sixty-two pages dedicated to the issue. Moving out of a home she had personalized, cared for, and loved for nearly six years would be a difficult experience, no matter how well-organized she was. Emotionally, she was barely prepared. Moving day, a late June day in 2003, was one day away. She tossed and turned all night. Her memories spun like a lazy Susan in the hands of a five-year-old boy: the first Christmas, the day they brought Ruppert home, the spring she planted the two Japanese maples and the azaleas, and, of course, the time Ed built the screened-in side porch. Together, they had completely redecorated the interior, adding a black range island, marble counters, and new cherry cabinets and refurbishing the hardwood floors previously buried under rugs. They added area rugs from a Persian rug dealer on nearby Wisconsin Avenue, with whom, of course, they haggled over the price. Ed painted the exterior brick white, against her father's advice, and the shutters and wooden front door black. She knew every inch of this home. It was an extension of her spirit and sense of well-being.

It's my home, she thought—*well, was*, she corrected herself.

She suggested to Ed three weeks ago in a clipped conversation that it might be better for both of them if she ordered new furniture, silverware, plates, cups, and glasses, rather than disturb "his" house. She proposed to take with her two dressers and an antique table that had been her grandfather's. She'd need a new bed, lamps, dining room table, and chairs. He interrupted her and simply agreed that she take what she wanted and buy what she needed. He handed her his Visa, which she accepted.

Gee and Ali shopped for three straight days until they found what

Gee wanted. The merchants had to meet one condition: all goods would be delivered before noon on moving day.

On Wednesday and Thursday nights, Gee and Ali packed clothes and personal items in boxes. Ali labeled them carefully while Gee created a Goodwill pile. Ed was conveniently absent each night.

Gee had insisted to Ali that she'd be fine alone on Friday night, the day before moving day. In fact, she was asking for privacy. Ali got the message. Gee was surprised, then, to hear her doorbell ring at 6:30 PM.

"Hello! I'm selling encyclopedias, *and* I just happen to have free pizza!" Pepe said. He muttered something about being in the neighborhood. He had brought with him not only a large pizza from Tortellini's Greek Pizza House, loaded, he said, with goat and other cheeses, which she had told him before was her favorite kind of pizza, but also a blue-and-white cooler with lots of Heineken iced down. She drank a beer with him and nibbled at pizza. She found it hard to talk. Emotions welled up in her throat in volleys, like waves rolling in on an ocean shoreline at high tide.

"What can I do?" he asked.

At her direction, without mentioning the events of tomorrow, Pepe helped her transport boxes and her heavy sewing machine to her car. She walked out of whatever room he was in, every now and then, without saying a word. He said nothing but returned to the kitchen to wait, gobble pizza, and drink cold beer.

At eight o'clock, seated at her counter, after having been repeatedly assured by Gee that she needed no further help, he said, "So, you're all right tonight?"

"Yes, dear, I'm OK. I've been preparing myself. I'm not like you found me on the corner, outside the courthouse, light-years ago," she said, propped against the island range.

Pepe looked down. "I'll leave on one condition—two, actually," he said. "You call me on my cell phone at any time tonight if you need me—for any reason. Couches and I get along. I'm fifteen minutes away. Second, I'm the Hertz truck driver tomorrow, not Huggie—and, for God's sake, not Hattie. Deal?"

"So, the pizza was so you could drive the truck?" she asked.

He smiled, kissed her on the cheek, and left without responding.

Around midnight, Gee heard Ed open the front door. She could hear his keys drop to the floor. After several minutes, he called up the steps, "Do you need anything from me tomorrow?"

"No," she said.

"I'm leaving about six o'clock tomorrow morning. I'll have my cell phone on if ... Gee ... I ..."

"Oh, please.... I'm tired," she said.

She awoke from a light sleep at 4:30 AM. At six o'clock she heard Ed walking out the front door. She got out of bed, walked to her bedroom window, and saw Ali getting out of her car at the curb. Ali walked to Ed, stood close to him, and talked briefly. She could have stayed in her car until he backed out of the driveway and just waved, she thought. She couldn't hear what Ali was saying to him, but it was Ali who was doing the talking while Ed looked at the ground. Ali reached up and touched his shoulder. The intimacy made Gee furious. Then Ed got in his car and backed out of the driveway, while Ali opened the front door.

After brushing her teeth, quickly combing her hair, and placing her pony tail in an orange baseball cap, Gee put on shorts, a tank top, and sneakers and bounded downstairs.

"And what did he have to say?" Gee asked.

"And, hello to you, too!" Ali said.

"And just what did he have to say?"

"Honestly, Gee, I don't think he said a word," Ali said.

"Now that's classic. Once again, Ed doesn't say a word and yet he's the center of attention. *Je-sus*!" Gee said.

Ali approached Gee, put her arms around her, and said, "You're right, honey. I've offended you. I'm sorry. I'm here for you ... not him. Forgive me, please."

"It's just ..."

Ali held her as she cried.

"Leave the Kleenex box out today," Gee said.

Ali reached into her black Bermuda shorts, pulled out a small pack of tissues, and said, "I'm armed and ready." Ali's red T-shirt said "Life is Good."

They laughed and poured coffee. Ali noticed the Tortellini's Greek Pizza box. "Oh, I love their pizza. Next best thing to Ledo's."

"Pepe brought it over last night," Gee said.

"Well, that's one thing I am looking forward to—meeting your friends. All this time, for whatever reason, you kept your work separate from the rest of you ... even though you talked on and on about Pepe, Huggie, and Hattie," Ali said.

"I know—stupid, really. At least something good will come from today."

"OK, that's your last negative crack. You're moving into a wonderful new condo with beautiful new things and great friends surrounding you. Today is today ... not yesterday ... not tomorrow."

At seven o'clock sharp Hattie arrived.

"Hey, hey, hey, everybody. What's up?" Hattie said, letting herself in.

Gee introduced her to Ali. Hattie had on a blue-and-white Howard University T-shirt, her alma mater, from which she received a MSW, and cutoff jeans, maroon high-top sneakers without socks, and a black bandana. The five feet, two inches, thirty-two-year-old African-American woman with big, brown eyes, looked like a refugee from an Emo concert. Gee felt that Hattie wore a look on her face that said on-duty.

"I've heard so much about you, Hattie," Ali said.

"It's *my* ... well, maybe *your* job, too, to keep this girl on the straight and narrow ... no small feat," Hattie said.

"It's a career—not a job," said Ali.

"The real job is keeping Huggie and Pepe in line," Gee said.

"I can't wait to meet them. What're they like?" asked Ali.

"Trouble," said Hattie. "Let me tell you a Huggie story before he gets here. Gee, go piddle, or whatever organizers do," Hattie said.

"Oh, the 'I' story?" Gee asked as she left the room, heading upstairs.

"Yep. Realize that Huggie Winston is a tall, handsome, African-

American brother with chiseled, you know, muscular features. He's a hunk. He's well-read, somewhat reserved … until he gets to know you. He was my first friend on the staff. We spent many a day in a car together as field investigation partners. Huggie's about a foot taller than his soft-spoken wife, Rosa, who's an elementary school teacher. I think she's coming today, too. Trust me, Ali, Rosa isn't small in influence. I love her. She and Huggie have three little boys. I love to watch this— Huggie might holler at them, but barely a whisper from her will stop those three hyperactive boys in their tracks … and their not-so-small father," Hattie said.

Hattie added that Huggie's father was the pastor of a mega-church in Rockville.

"I've heard about his father and his civil rights connection with Dr. Martin Luther King," Ali said.

Hattie said she had learned from Huggie's stories that from the time he was a young child until he went away to Mississippi State, his father demanded that he sit in the front row of church every week and pay attention. "Rosa told me once that Huggie always focused on his father and was … well … in constant fear of his disapproval. So much so, Rosa said, that as a toddler, Huggie would ask her to hug him when he felt he might have done something that could disappoint his father. His three older brothers and four sisters cast on him the name 'Huggie' because he would whisper to them, 'Please huggie,' … and it stuck. People are easily drawn to Huggie as a confidante, particularly young black men on supervision. They seek him out when they're in a jam, no matter who's their assigned officer. A psychodrama expert would call that 'positive tele.' People are just drawn to Huggie. But I swear, Ali, he does have some hilarious quirks. We have monthly staff meetings, which are always occasions for managers to announce new policies and procedures and go over things officers are doing wrong—"

"You mean they never speak to what's going well?" interrupted Ali.

Gee hollered from upstairs, "No.… Never!"

"Well?" Hattie said, with raised eyebrows and a gesture with her hands that Ali interpreted as "What is, is." "It's always a tell-listen format. Anyway, Gee and I started to notice that Huggie usually had a smile on his face—almost a grin—while everyone else was miserable, staring at the floor, or feigning interest. You know, with looks on their faces like, 'Oh, that's interesting.' Our inner voices are screaming, 'Please share with me more examples of how I screwed up this month!' So, safe in his car after one particular marathon management whipping, Gee asked him point-blank, 'What's up with you, fool?' Five minutes later, Gee told me, after a solo belly-laughing uproar, Huggie said, 'I won't tell you. Just sit next to me at the next staff meeting.' So, at the next meeting, Gee sat right beside him, her leg, she said, touching his," Hattie said.

"You don't need to make it sound so lewd, Hattie!" Gee hollered.

"You were the one touching his leg, girlfriend!" Hattie said, as she and Ali laughed.

"As I was saying, this is what happened. Out of the blue, Huggie started to mumble to himself, "I, state your name," as if he were at a swearing-in ceremony. Then, barely audible, he mumbled the response of a second person, a flaming idiot.... "I state your name." "No, state *your* name!" said the first voice. "No, state *your* name," responded the idiot. I believe *girlfriend* upstairs peed her pants, right on the spot," Hattie said.

"I *almost* did," Gee said from the upstairs hallway.

"You guys must be very bored in meetings," Ali said.

Gee realized that she had never considered the context of this story, with the misbehavior in management meetings as a symbol of systemic problems.

"He told Gee after that meeting that he used to practice this ritual in church. It helped make it look like he was following the presentation," Hattie said. "After that, when she heard him mumble even the slightest sound in a staff meeting—an 'I' or 'state'—she would tremble, trying not to laugh. The more she tried not to laugh, the more acute the pain in her ribs. Then, over beers at Tommy Joe's one snowy Friday night, she blabbed Huggie's ritual to the rest of us. After that night, our officer buddies were very excited to be in staff meetings, on the edge of their seats. Funny, the officers' body language made management think everyone likes their stupid meetings," Hattie added.

"Oh, God, yes.... A minister's son, no less," Ali said, as the door opened, and Huggie peeked his large face around the corner.

Ali and Hattie screamed with laughter.

"What the ..." Huggie said, swinging the door open fully.

"I'm sorry ... I ... I ..." Ali said.

"Oh, oh, big mouth, Ms. MSW, is telling stories on people," Huggie said, looking at Hattie.

"It's not her fault," said Gee, bounding down onto the bottom step.

"Never is, according to her, but trouble is never far away from her, is it?" Huggie asked, squeezing Hattie gently around the head with one mammoth arm. "Hi, I'm Huggie Winston," he said, reaching out his hand to Ali.

"I know...." said Ali, bursting into laughter again. "I'm sorry.... I'm Ali...." grasping his mammoth hand.

"Hey, who left the door open? I guess you don't pay the electricity anymore!" Pepe said, walking in behind Huggie. He noticed the uproar and said, "Well, I'm glad we've decided to dispense with the funeral parlor tone. Hi, I'm Pepe.... You're so gorgeous, you can only be Ali, right?" he said, extending his hand to Ali.

"Well ..." Ali started to say, shaking his hand. "You didn't tell me this tall, handsome fellow had such beautiful eyes, Gee. Shame on you!"

"Oh crap, get the shovel out of the garage—it's getting deep in here," Hattie said.

"Hello, lover," Pepe said, kissing Hattie on both cheeks as she held his face gently.

"And where's the party girl?" he asked, swirling around to find Gee for a hug.

"Some party," she said, returning his hug.

"Oh, I got your rental truck outside. Tell him ... you know," Pepe said, looking at Huggie.

"What? Oh, Rosa can't make it. She says she'll help you get settled next week," Huggie said.

"That's fine. We have enough help. A lot of new stuff is being delivered anyway. I'm glad I rented a small truck. Oh, Pepe bought me pizza from Tortellini's, so I told him he could be the driver," Gee said.

"Oh, a pizza slut! OK, since you've told a Huggie story ..."

Hattie, Gee, and Ali burst into laughter.

"How about the Pepe-Judge Brayer story? That's always good for a laugh!" Huggie said.

"Hey, it's only fair," said Ali, smiling at Pepe.

"OK, but I'm still the driver, Huggie," Pepe said.

Hattie said, "Well, first, let me say this about lover boy here. One white female administrator in the office said that if Pepe and Antonio Banderas were on the cover of *GQ*, back-to-back, 90 percent of negative attitudes toward Hispanics would disappear. Like with my African brother here, it's impossible to miss hearing Pepe coming down a hallway. He could charm the pants off Ursula the Sea Monster."

"Ahh," cooed Ali.

"This is what I love about him. It is impossible to tell where the boundary is between his work with folks on supervision and his community-centered activities. I don't think he sleeps," Hattie said, while Gee disappeared upstairs again.

"Hey, can I join you up there?" Pepe said.

"No!" hollered Gee.

"There's not one person on probation or parole in the region that doesn't know him as Mr. Pepe. And our man here is the bane of management."

Then Hattie added, "There's not one manager that doesn't want to tie and quarter Senor Pepe because Pepe's sentencing recommendations always speak in glowing terms about the defendants. One time when Pepe was ordered by supervisors to correct formal reports to the court that typically include numerous grammatical errors, his corrected reports came back—corrections made, but with numerous new errors, making the process a correct-the-corrections nightmare."

"We think he's baiting them, saying, 'This is the way Hispanics talk and write.... Get used to it!'" Gee hollered down.

Pepe just held his hands up like, *who knows?*

"Pepe has a unique history with Chief Judge Brayer. In his courtroom, Brayer is this stern, egocentric man. That's how we know him. Lucky for us, he stays out of the affairs of our office. The judge tends to see others' faults more clearly than his own. Now, on this one occasion, Brayer methodically skewered the office managers because of the grammatical errors in Pepe's report, and he chewed out Pepe directly, in open court, with an intentional glance toward the press," Hattie said.

"Tell them what happened next, Huggie—you were there," Hattie said.

"I ain't playing on the girls' side. You women stick together enough as it is!" Huggie said, giving Pepe a high-five.

So, Hattie went on to describe how, at first, Judge Brayer summoned Pepe's supervisor, the effervescent Chip Faulknour, who was also Hattie's supervisor. When Faulknour arrived, Judge Brayer took five minutes from the elevated heights of the bench to criticize Pepe's report that had somehow managed to circumvent the elaborate supervisory editorial police process. Judge Brayer implied that he'd put the entire management of the probation office under a contempt order if he ever received "another schizophrenic bilingual cacophony of lard." "Did I say that right, Huggie?" Hattie asked.

"Who knows?" he said.

"Folklore has it that while receiving this tirade in front of the bench, Pepe never stopped smiling—as if he were receiving the court's annual award for the most outstanding probation officer," Hattie said.

"Over whose dead body, Hattie?" Gee hollered down.

She went on to add that, after the grilling, Faulknour ran somewhere, probably to get back to the Deputy Chief Kingmaker's office to make sure that all of the blame landed on Pepe and none on himself.

"But the press piece backfired on Judge Brayer—the theme of the article in the Metro section was judicial bullying in Montgomery County. Finally, managers gave up and took him off all report-writing for the court," Hattie said.

Pepe rubbed Ruppert's head.

"How come they haven't succeeded in firing you?" Ali asked.

Pepe only gestured *who knows* with his hands and smiled.

"My guess is that managers can never quite find the exact moment to do the nasty deed. Would you do it after he orchestrated his annual fall clothes drive for the needy? Or, would you fire him before the annual Thanksgiving food drive, as featured on local TV? Or, would it be late on a Friday afternoon when the staff have left and Pepe is just getting started with a new parole release who has no place to live? Or maybe they could try in the summer when much of the staff is in and out on vacation—except that he coaches two softball teams for underprivileged children in the toughest parts of town. So, you could say the timing of the thing seems to be problematic," Huggie said.

"Let's get to work, or, as they say back home, let's get the hogs off the truck. Where do you want us to start?" Pepe asked Gee, who was standing at the top of the steps.

"Well, how about the women come up here, and you guys load the boxes and the furniture that's in the garage?" Gee said.

And the moving out party began in earnest.

As the last box was placed in the eighteen-foot truck, Pepe pulled down the sliding door. He jumped into the truck, and Huggie and Hattie went to their cars. All three waited for Ali and Gee.

Up in the bedroom, the two had concluded they had corralled everything Gee planned to take. Gee sat quietly on the bed. Ali sat nearby in a rocking chair. After several minutes, Gee said, "I'm ready."

"I know you are, honey.... I know you are," Ali said.

~

When the entourage arrived at the Willoughby's freight elevator at 11:15 AM, chaos erupted. The driver of the Hecht Company's truck, delivering Gee's new bed and mattress, dining room table and chairs, couch, and living room chair, and the delivery man from Carpetland, unrelated to Gee's move, began arguing over use of the freight elevator. Pepe tried unsuccessfully to find the building manager to settle the matter.

Gee went up to the Hecht Company driver to get the full story but was nearly accosted by the disheveled driver from Carpetland, who shouted at her, "Listen, lady, I'm delivering this truckload now, whether you like it or not!"

"I have this freight elevator reserved until noon, and I intend to use it now," Gee said.

"Bitch, I don't give ..."

In a flash, Huggie's face was six inches from the face of the irate Carpetland driver.

"Now, now, brother, I wouldn't say another word to my friend here. You've got it all wrong. This is her elevator until noon. Now I suggest that you call your dispatcher and check the time you were *supposed* to deliver whatever it is you're delivering. Now!" said Huggie, peering down at the top of the driver's head.

With a snort, the driver turned and pulled out his two-way phone. Huggie heard the dispatcher say, "I said, as soon as you can!"

"Well, they're telling me as soon as I can is after noon. What do you want me to do?" said the driver.

"Do the Silver Spring delivery and then come back. Make that delivery first," said the dispatcher.

"No problem, man," the driver said to Huggie.

"I didn't think there would be, brother. Be cool," Huggie said.

"You, too, brother. Be cool. Sorry, ma'am. I just got this job, and, you know—"

"Forget it," Gee said.

The Hecht Company driver and his aide delivered all the furniture to Gee's condo. Huggie began the assembly work while Pepe carried the remaining boxes up from the rental truck on a hand cart. Ali and Hattie carried up the lighter things. Then the women turned their attention to unloading boxes while Pepe and Huggie finished the assembly work, hung pictures, and took out trash. Pepe and Ali went to a nearby bagel shop for carry-out lunches.

Around four o'clock, all of the work that the helpers could do was finished. Without fanfare, the moving entourage began to prepare to leave, except Ali.

"What can I say...." Gee said, before tears welled up.

"We didn't break anything!" Pepe said.

"No, you didn't break anything, Pepe," she said.

The doorbell rang.

Gee could hear Hattie say, "Oh, my God."

Hattie took the large array of tulips and assorted flowers from the deliveryman and held them for Gee to admire.

Gee stared at them in Hattie's arms and reached for the card:
To Gee, my friend. May your new start be as fresh as these flowers!
Love, your friend
Pepe

5

A CAREER LADDER EMERGES

Dora Kingmaker

Probation officers, like police officers, communicate in tightly drawn circles. Each use code words, inside jokes, and unique gestures. Probation officers and police attend each other's public ceremonies and the funerals of key officials. They share files and information and publicly try to appear as comrades in arms. Still, age-old stereotypes work in both directions—probation officers believe that police are only interested in making arrests, not solving problems, and police hold the viewpoint that they arrest the criminals and then probation officers mollycoddle them. Today, Thursday, February 5, 2003, was a ceremonial occasion calling for the appearance of unity—the Montgomery County Corrections Department and the entire statewide criminal justice community took great pride in the opening of the 1,100-bed, state-of-the-art prison, known as the Montgomery County Corrections Facility, or MCCF. Its pod-like construction was being heralded as the future of prison layouts. The facility's goal was to reduce statewide prison overcrowding by housing local prisoners for up to eighteen months. Private guided tours of the two-story facility for the media directly preceded the keynote address by Maryland governor Harry Ward. On other occasions, the auditorium of the MCCF would be used for training, special events, and basketball. But today the stage was decorated with bunting for the governor. There was an impressive showing of state officials, including the governor's newly selected chairman of the state parole commission, J. Trenton Axelrod, the head of the state police, the county executive, the county police chief, several Department of Corrections officials, and, of course, Robert Kasten, the county's chief probation officer.

Dora Kingmaker, the forty-year-old deputy chief probation officer, dressed impressively, as usual, in a dark green suit with a short, tight skirt, watched the elbow-rubbing of the powerful on stage. Her red hair shone. She fantasized about one day being introduced to a large group as *the* honored guest. One colleague put it aptly: Dora Kingmaker suffered from hero-hunger. Even she realized that she had no sense of moderation when it came to power and authority: she had to have it all. She felt no compelling reason to adjust that drive.

Just moments before the ceremony was to begin, a buzz erupted with the appearance of four heavily armed state police officers with automatic, lightweight assault rifles escorting the tall, handsome, handshaking governor. Before 9/11, police didn't carry assault weapons, but no one questioned their use now. Dora had long been an admirer of the governor. She was enthralled with the ease and grace with which he handled the print press and the TV media. He was born for the camera. Today, in his dark blue suit, white shirt, and red tie, she noticed that he sliced through admirers and well-wishers like a speedboat on a calm, flat lake. She wondered whether it was just she who felt enthralled with him—who noticed the virile sexuality in his every movement. To Dora, he seemed to be flirting publicly with women, something nearly every politician avoided like the plague. *Maybe*, she thought as she watched him, *it was just the way he hugged women, chest-to-chest, and how they always came away laughing, as he appeared to be whispering secrets to them.* His raw exuberance for life made her smile. He was like a beloved gladiator, now freed, telling admirers robust stories of survival against the greatest of odds.

About fifteen years older than she, the governor inspired Dora to create a fantasy world around him. Governor Harry Ward: lover and father figure. She longed to be recognized by him, but not just as another admirer in the crowd. They were foolish, she said to herself, these silly feelings, foolish. Still, she raced to the first row of seats and crossed and uncrossed her legs repeatedly. She felt awkward, having allowed teenage-like fantasies to overcome her usually measured, in-charge behavior. In her office and the courthouse, she acted with precision, in role, under control, as if a camera were always on her. At that moment, in the first row at the MCCF, she might as well have been a teenager at a concert, yearning for eye contact with Justin Timberlake.

After a few, brief, blah-blah-blah speeches, the governor surged to the podium and praised everyone present for their roles in furthering the ends of justice by building this new prison. Defining this moment as a victory—building a prison to house inmates—was later described by a writer from the local *Gazette* newspaper as praising the development of a new cemetery to bury the dead. That irony escaped the correctional officials. Governor Ward said that the audience was now safer than they were yesterday. No precise definition as to what that actually meant was provided. His message on this day was that overcrowded prisons in Montgomery County were now a thing of the past and that community safety and justice remained everyone's obligation. He declared it was a new day in Maryland. Dora was annoyed to hear an old-timer next to her whisper to his wife, "Remember in 1965, when the governor—what was his name?—announced at the opening of the 495 Beltway that overcrowded roads in Montgomery County were over as we know them? Remember that?" His wife elbowed him to hush. Dora frowned at him.

From the first row, Dora couldn't help but smile at the larger-than-life governor, who, in spite of all of his hubris, couldn't help but notice her. She winked at him as he delivered a witty line. Thereafter, on three separate times, he looked at her, squarely in her eyes, and, each time, she returned his smile with one of her own. He seemed to be speaking to her.

As the crowd roared with approval, Ward concluded his presentation, which also concluded the formal events, shook hands with the dignitaries on stage, and started out of the facility, shaking hands and patting backs, with his state police escorts surrounding him. As she watched him leave, Dora turned to find her boss, Chief Kasten, to get a ride back to the office. He was talking jovially with Parole Chairman Axelrod, who, she saw, had one arm locked around Kasten. Dora decided to wait for Kasten at the white county car they had driven over, so she meandered slowly past the chatting guests toward the parking lot.

Wrapping herself in her favorite alpaca scarf, she was startled by a tap on her back.

"Ma'am," said a muscular state trooper with his stiff-brimmed hat tilted toward his nose.

"Yes ...?"

"I'm Corporal Casey. The governor would like you to have this," he said, placing a business-size card in her hand.

Before she could respond, he was gone.

One side of the card was blank; on the other, these words were written in cursive:

> *Thanks for the smile.*
> *Call me, Harry.*
> *410-349-0798.*

She waited until she got back to the office, where she shut her door and placed the call from her own personal cell phone.

"Corporal Casey," answered in a voice she now recognized.

"Hi! This is the woman—"

Before she could finish the sentence, the governor, who had taken the phone from Corporal Casey, said, "Hey! This is Harry. Thanks for coming today! What's your name?"

"Dora Kingmaker, Governor," she said.

"What brought you to the ceremony today? Not the thirty-degree weather!"

"Well, I'm the deputy chief probation officer in Montgomery County, and—"

"Well, Doah," he said, creating for her a pet name, "I need criminal justice expertise and count on folks like yourself at the grassroots level to help me with my public safety initiatives."

"Well—"

"I hope we can talk about your justice ideas some time," he said, starting a pattern where, as he did with so many others, she could hardly finish a complete sentence without him talking over her lines.

"I'd like that—"

"Well, Doah, my time is so limited. Can my main man, Corporal Casey, exchange some possibilities with you for us to get together to talk? Does that sound doable?" he asked.

"Sure, sure it does, Governor," she said.

"Call me Harry, Doah. Corporal Casey will call you back on this cell phone," he said.

"OK," she started to say, as the phone went dead.

She wondered what started this— her smiling at him? *My God, can he read minds?* She laughed to herself. *Where might this lead?* The unknown, usually a source of irritation, excited her. The governor was, of course, married with two children. *Well,* she thought to herself, *what do I have to lose?* She thought back to her lengthy affair with the former Montgomery County state's attorney, now a federal prosecutor. The affair ended amicably when he ascended to his new position in Greenbelt. But, before he left, he helped her get the promotion to deputy chief probation officer with his recommendation, full of high praise, to the selection panel. With his key endorsement, she beat out three qualified internal candidates and twenty-seven outside applicants, many of whom were more highly qualified for the prized position. Dora had been virtually handed the reins by Chief Kasten and was barely able to bide her time until his expected retirement.

Three days later, on a Sunday afternoon, Dora's cell vibrated and rang in its holder on her waist as she entered her townhouse. Dora kept it on all of the time now.

"Hello?"

"Ms. Kingmaker, this is Corporal Casey. I'm—"

"I know who you are, Corporal."

"The governor will be attending a fundraiser in Damascus next Friday night, the thirteenth. You could be invited.... You don't have to donate," he said.

"Sure, sure. Friday the thirteenth. What do I have to lose?"

After the call, she fantasized about being on the governor's cabinet as a high-ranking, trusted official. She could see herself in a Christian Dior suit with a white silk blouse, using a Mont Blanc pen to take notes in a leather-trimmed binder at a long, dark mahogany table. She knew the governor was interested in politics beyond the borders of Maryland. *Maybe he'll want me to represent his interest in the Department of Justice,* she mused. *Now, wouldn't that shut the ole man up,* she thought to herself. Dora's father had always been openly partial to her two older brothers. After she turned thirteen, he stopped trying to hide his disinterest. The oldest brother, Jeff, was the vice president for marketing at a grocery chain, and the middle child, Phil, coached baseball at Elon University, after a brief stint in the minor leagues. She was painfully used to being treated as third fiddle ... third fiddle with a large chip on her shoulder. *Never quite good enough,* she sneered to herself now in memory of the painful neglect. *Fuck him,* she thought.

"Yes, sir, Governor, I'll have that white paper in your hands in three days," she said aloud to herself in her foyer mirror as she left for the grocery store.

~

At dusk on Friday the thirteenth, when Dora pulled up to the expansive two-story Damascus farm house with six white columns, she noticed the house had a main section with four appendages—as if one had been built after each bumper crop, she thought. There were foot-high harvested corn stalks as far as she could see, two large silos connected to a massive barn, and off to the north side of the house a very large swimming pool area, tennis court, and a small guest house. She could smell cattle and saw six horse trailers on this Bethesda Church Road farm. This was not the lifestyle she dreamed of. As she drove into the yard, she was instructed to stop her red Mazda convertible so an attendant could park her car in a field. Just inside the front door, she was greeted by several folks who seemed to accept her immediately, as if she was as an insider. They placed a nametag on her chest.

"Oh, Ms. Kingmaker. How nice to meet you," said Edward Strock upon introduction by a youthful volunteer. The handoff made Dora swell with importance.

"Nice to meet you, Councilman Strock," she responded.

"Please, Eddie," he said. "And you are with whom?"

"I'm by myself."

"I'm sorry. I meant who's your firm? I assumed, for some reason, you're an attorney," he added.

"Oh, no. I'm the deputy chief probation officer in the county."

"Oh, you work for Bob Kasten! He's a great guy."

She quickly folded her arms and said, "Yes he is ... a nice guy," she said, looking down, thinking to herself, *nice but through.*

"Well, keep up the good work, and give my regards to Bob, will ya?" he said and turned away, not waiting for an answer.

Within seconds of his whirlwind exit and quicker than water fills a hole in the sand at the beach, his vacated space was filled by a sixty-something woman, who had what didn't seem like her first glass of wine in her hand.

The woman introduced herself. All Dora heard was Lydia something-or-other.

The woman talked incessantly about God knows what. The only thing she seemed to require of Dora was for her to nod her head every now and then and make an appropriate facial expression or sound—mostly "uh-huh" and "ooh!" *Who is this idiot?* Dora wondered, *and how do I get rid of her?*

Then, something Lydia said brought Dora's wandering eyes and attention squarely back to her.

"My husband and I give at least $100,000 every year to the party. Harry owes us plenty of attention," Lydia bragged.

Dora guessed that the heavy-tongued Ms. Lydia was the hostess.

"Well, Lydia, dear, I hope I can get a word in with the governor tonight," Dora said.

"Oh, honey, what's your name again?" asked Ms. Lydia.

"Dora, Dora Kingmaker."

"Well, I'll make sure Harry says hello."

Ms. Lydia continued to talk, taking time out only to grab wine from a roaming server's silver tray. That is, until the buzz in the room suggested that the governor had arrived. Then, Lydia excused herself, found her husband, a red-faced, potbellied man, and went to the veranda to greet her buddy.

Within fifteen minutes, as everyone pretended to be engaged in conversation but was really casting an eye to catch *his* presence, Lydia began escorting the governor deftly from donor to donor. As Dora watched him carefully, she thought to herself, *my, the governor is good at this*. Everyone he spoke to would burst into a smile, laughing the instant he shook their hands. He gave every attractive woman an embrace. Dora felt competitive, even aroused, when he hugged several good-looking women, who in turned gushed at him openly.

Finally, they approached, and Ms. Lydia started to introduce her as she had done so flawlessly with the thirtysome folks that preceded Dora. She placed one hand on Dora and one hand on the governor's arm, which was the setup.

"Governor, this is—"

"Hello, Doah. How are you?" he said, not waiting for completion of the introduction, as he placed his arm around her back squarely on her bra fastener and quickly pulled her breasts against his chest. The embrace was lighting-quick, short in duration, and almost intimate to her.

"I'm great, Governor...."

"Doah is the deputy chief probation officer in the county, and we all have our eyes on her career," he said.

"Well, Governor, thank you. It's nice to know we have a governor who believes in the safety of our citizens as much as I do," she said. She had practiced this line at home before the mirror and in the car on the way over.

"I wish everyone understood as you do, Doah, that we must stop the violent predators," he said, sounding a campaign standard.

"Oh, yes, we must," said Lydia, who grabbed his arm, demonstrating that it was time to move the governor on to the next guest. He understood the cue.

"Nice to see you, sir," Dora said, shaking his hand.

"See you later, Doah," he said.

Forty-five minutes and three Sea Breezes later, Dora headed for her car. In the parking lot, yards from her car, she was approached by Corporal Casey, this time with no brimmed hat. A large light, mounted tonight on a nearby shed for security reasons, revealed his short, brown crew cut and the skin on the top of his head. Why men thought this was attractive was beyond Dora. Over his shoulder she could see a cluster of police officers chatting and laughing. Dora avoided eye contact with the officers. She hated it when groups of men stared at her, particularly buzz cut jocks and cops.

Corporal Casey wasted no time with small talk.

"The governor would like to, ah, meet you after this event is over," he said.

"Sure. Where?"

"Well, it'd have to be your place.... He's fairly easy to recognize.... You know, the press."

"Well, OK. What time?" she asked.

"I'd guess in about an hour or two," he said.

"OK," she said. She noticed that he didn't move.

"I need the address again," he said, handing her a blank card and a pen.

She scribbled her address and phone number again, and handed him the card back.

"Thanks," he said and turned and walked away.

⁓

At 11:30 PM her doorbell rang. Dora had changed into a newly purchased fuzzy jogging suit and matching T-shirt. She opened the door to find the governor.

"Governor, come in, come in," she said.

Two steps inside the foyer, after the door closed behind him, he held out his arms and she walked toward him and kissed him politely on the cheek.

"How about something to drink?" she asked.

"I'd love that. A beer?" he said.

She walked toward the kitchen and gestured for him to follow her. She opened two Miller Lites and handed him one.

He took a long gulp and smiled.

"What'd you think of the fundraiser?" he asked.

"Interesting, really," she said.

"Bob and Lydia are simple people but dedicated to my career. I could ask them for anything. All they want in return is fair tax protection for farmers. You'd be surprised what the most powerful people in Maryland want in return for their donations. Just attention and protection, that's all."

"That's a fair exchange. I've been a supporter of yours for a long time ... from a distance ... but, I must confess, not a donor," she said.

"There's more than one way to contribute. Your thoughts and views are like gold pieces for me. You know, you're the prettiest redhead I've ever laid eyes on."

"Well, thank you, Governor."

"Harry, please. Doah, it's awful comforting to have a few private friends I can count on. I like to keep a group of tight friends around me who can help me stay on target. You know, insiders who I can count on, and also, frankly, unwind with. Is that something you'd like, too?" he asked.

"The idea of unwinding with such an interesting person as yourself is very appealing, Harry," she said.

"I'd like to think I could get your views on criminal justice policies, too."

"You can, Harry. I'd be pleased to help in any way I could be useful."

"From time to time I have commissions, special investigations, fact-finding reports, focus groups, things like that," he added.

"Honestly, it's all very stimulating, Harry."

"Good, then I can count on you to be on my team?"

"Yes, and you can be on my team, too!" she said, smiling.

"You know, you should keep a close eye on guys who come over late at night to talk politics and to enjoy your beauty," the governor said.

"Oh, really? What should I be on the alert for?"

He stood up and walked behind her chair and began to rub her shoulders.

"Well, you know … making advances.…" he said, as he began to kiss her neck and earlobe.

"Well, it's hard to resist that which is *so* exciting," she whispered.

With that, she stood up and faced the very tall governor. They embraced and kissed with slightly opened lips.

He grabbed her breast as they kissed. She cupped his butt.

They exchanged mouth positions and direction for several moments.

"Whew! Why don't we give politics some time off?" she said.

She grabbed his hand and led him up the stairs to her bedroom, where they undressed each other.

They had noisy, urgent sex. The intimacy left her without a clue as to what to say next. It helped that when he was relieved of his tension he left the bed and used the bathroom in the hallway while she put on her jogging outfit in the privacy of her bathroom. She stayed an extra minute to think of what to say next.

Downstairs in her kitchen, he smiled at her as they sat on chairs turned backwards, facing each other. "Do you travel a lot?" he asked.

"Good guess, Harry. I like to go to the Caribbean at least once a year," she said.

"Maybe we can meet there sometime," he said.

She made an approving facial gesture.

He declined a glass of wine, although she poured one for herself.

"Wow, Doah.... You *are* something!" he said.

"So are you, Harry," she said.

"I must return to Annapolis. You'll hear from someone, but I'd prefer you not bring up this conversation.... You know—"

"Oh, sure, sure, I understand," she jumped in to save him from finishing his sentence.

"Good, good. Well, I've enjoyed myself. I can call you again, Doah?"

"I expect you to, Harry."

She reached over and kissed him, flush on the lips.

They rose, holding hands, and walked to the door. He turned and kissed her again.

"Goodnight, Doah!" he said, opening the door and leaving swiftly.

God, she thought, *I hope I didn't make a fool of myself. Commissioner Kingmaker*, she thought to herself in bed, unable to sleep. She felt empowered by her new secret.

Five weeks later she had had no further contact from the governor. Dora felt angry that she had been used for a one-nighter. That is, until she received a call from Tara Cower, executive secretary to the commissioner of juvenile justice in Maryland.

"Ms. Kingmaker, the commissioner would like to invite you to participate on a statewide ad hoc commission investigating the treatment of juveniles in state institutions, particularly prisons. Does this sound like something you'd be interested in?" she asked.

"Absolutely," Dora said.

"Let me give you the format. The commission will meet three times, for two days each session, and consider data, reports, and expert testimony, as well as review citizens' comments from public meetings held across the state," she said.

The big time! Dora thought to herself.

"What would my role be? You know, I work with adults in the

criminal justice system and have no experience with juveniles," Dora said, waiting for the title "Commissioner," which would, of course, springboard her career onto a statewide platform.

"The chairman of the ad hoc commission would like you to be an adjunct adviser. There's no pay, but our office will, of course, pay all expenses and work out the details with your court," she concluded.

The air was almost out of Dora's lungs, but she managed to contain her excitement sufficiently to ask, "What will I be asked to do before the commission meets?"

"Well, I don't think anything, really," Ms. Cower added. "We'll send the letter of invitation to the chief judge with a copy to the chief probation officer and you, and we look forward to your participation."

At the first commission hearing on April 12, Dora expected to see the governor, at least for the opening remarks. It would give her a chance to at least send a nonverbal message, since she had not seen or heard from him since their tryst. She chastised herself for not appreciating that the governor had many duties that required his attention. *But clearly*, she thought, *he had kept his word by this assignment.*

The chairman welcomed everyone and said the governor sent his regards but that, because of the press of duties, he could not be with them. He looked forward to the commission's report. The chairman laid out the context of the commission's task. Then he asked everyone to introduce themselves. There were ten commissioners: four assigned staff members from Juvenile Justice, including a staff attorney; two recording secretaries; one IT fellow; two graduate students; and Dora Kingmaker. The commissioners and staff members from Juvenile Justice knew each other and talked freely among themselves. Dora felt they were all very unfriendly to the IT expert, the graduate students, and herself. She was pissed.

As the introductions were made, she said, "I'm Dora Kingmaker, the deputy chief probation officer in Montgomery County. Although I have no experience working with juveniles ..." She waited for everyone to laugh. Only one graduate student responded to her throwaway line. "... I hope my considerable experience will be of value to this important inquiry."

Whether it was true or not, she felt like an outsider. Most of these folks moaned that poor juveniles were being mistreated in mental institutions, group homes, and juvenile prisons. It was a theme that turned her off. She would have rather talked about boot camps and more punishment-oriented approaches, but she could never find the opening. After the commission completed its second day of balderdash, as privately as possible, she approached the chairman.

"Is there anything I can do to help this important mission, Mr. Chairman?" she asked with great dignity, as if she were talking to Senator Sam Ervin at the Watergate hearings.

"Keep your head down, and listen to the BBC," he said with a laugh while scanning the room. "I'll let you know if anything develops where we could use your expertise."

What was that about? she wondered. Dora began to conduct her own background inquiries both online and through select individuals in the know. There was a consensus that the governor had been forced to look into this issue—juvenile treatment in state institutions—by a coalition of statewide liberals and the *Baltimore Sun* newspaper. The ad hoc commission's report was going nowhere intentionally, and its report would be buried before the ink had dried. *Aha! That was it.* Now she understood the BBC message: keep your head down. *Harry was just building her resume*, she thought. It was the last time she would say anything during the balance of her commission experience.

This is just the start of my new career, she thought to herself.

In the first week of May on a Friday night at 11:48 PM Dora's cell phone began to rattle on the end table next to her bed. She tried hard to sound awake and alert—as if she were working on some noble cause.

"Ms. Kingmaker, *he* would like to know if this is a good time for a visit," said the corporal.

"When, precisely?" she asked.

"In twenty minutes," he responded. She could hear *him* talking on the phone in the background but couldn't make out the conversation. *Maybe he's creating an alibi for his wife*, she thought.

"Fine, Corporal. The front door will be ajar. Just have him let himself in," she instructed.

She splashed cold water on her face, combed her hair, brushed her teeth, changed from flannel pajamas to a mid-calf navy blue, floral, lace nightgown and matching robe, also newly purchased. She raced downstairs, poured two glasses of red wine, and put on soft background music.

"How are you, Harry?" she said from the kitchen, handing him a glass of wine after a quick kiss on the lips. He appeared to Dora hornier than a sailor touching the docks after months of sea duty.

"Fine, Doah," he said, receiving the wine. He removed his jacket and tie.

"Oh, I've missed seeing you," she said.

"Doah, my life is very public. I'm always in front of a camera or a reporter trying to destroy me," he said.

She rubbed her fingers through his hair with her right hand, as if he was a ten-year-old little brother who had been beaten up by bullies, while deftly placing her left hand above his knee. "You're safe here, Harry. There are no cameras here," she said.

"God knows who will use what private information about me to sink *our* ambitions. Can I talk freely?"

Noting his emphasis on the word "our," she said, "I wish you would, baby."

"I stay married because my wife is, well, very good for my career. But there's no real warmth left between us. I noticed you right away and was struck with how beautiful you are … how … what … in control and … ah … how firm you look. I hope we can have a *special* relationship … where I can help you get what you want in your career … you can make me look like I know what I'm talking about … but, on a private side, help me relax and feel good. Maybe we can be good for each other. That's what I hope for, Doah," he said.

She liked the contract. "Well," she said, leaning into him and biting his ear, intentionally inflicting pain as an experiment, "if I get your drift, you like things—how should I put it?—I don't want to make a fool of myself…." she said.

"You won't, Doah," he said.

"You like someone to be in control—to be a little forceful, Harry?"

"Very," he said.

"I don't do costumes, Harry," she said, sitting back in her chair but feeling very much in control. She got up and walked behind him, putting her hands on his shoulders. She was flushed with excitement, having a very powerful man who could open many career doors apparently under her thumb and at her whim. Now, if she could only find the right pattern, tone, and combination of stimuli to meet his urgency.

"Talk to me," he said.

"Harry, have you been a bad boy?" she said, standing behind him, her breast against the back of his head.

He moved his head from side to side.

"Oh ... yes ... *very*."

She knew she had him.

"Well, maybe *Mommy* is going to have to take you upstairs and slowly, slowly ... well, we'll see what Mommy will do!" Suddenly, the governor was wiggly, like a six-year-old child after drinking a twelve-ounce Coke. He nearly ran up to her bedroom. Once in bed, she repeated the question, "Have you been a bad boy?" She allowed him to grovel and grope until she was on top of him, engulfing him. When he was near satisfaction, she stopped. He begged and wiggled. She increased her movement, then stopped again. Mommy was now fully into her new role ... and in control. The script was nothing less than a fantasy come true for her ... and one she had hungered for, longed for, really, but had never acted upon before. She never thought that she would find a man she could trust enough to let go of some natural instincts. And so, their sexual interaction had a basic format.... She smacked his fanny ... let him feel her ... kiss her ... touch her ... until he begged her and whined. She let him reenter her, but made him withdraw and then reenter her while choking his neck lightly. Finally, he roared with relief. He put his head in her lap and she stroked his hair.

It was a role she had yearned for, yet one she was simply too narcissistic to explore the root feelings of—the powerful feelings that literally made her dizzy. It was, then, a *folie à deux*.

Moments later, he thanked her and excused himself for having to make a phone call—but made it from the corner of her bed. She felt this was done intentionally, so she could enjoy the thrill of his power. He demanded "deep background" and went on to lambaste a

Washington Post reporter, whose name, if she'd ever heard it before, she didn't recognize now. In between sips of wine, she rubbed his back and repeatedly slid her breast against his back to divide his attention.

When he completed the call, she began tying a knot in the ole cherry stem, as he put it, and then she began riding the pony, uttering non-stop, "Mommy wants you to please her, that's it, good boy." He yelped again, spent. She, too, had simultaneously enjoyed a release, which was unusual for her with a man. She enjoyed arousing him and that, in turn, excited her. She enjoyed the way he whined, the way he smelled, his excitement, his crying out his pet name for her, "Doah … Doah … oh … Doah."

Having exposed herself to the possibility of being entirely off-track and making a fool of herself with this sexual play-acting, and sure he wouldn't want word of this encounter to be repeated, she was determined not to let him escape without making her grander needs known, with specificity.

"Was that good for my boy?" she said.

"Oh, very, very good," he said.

"Good. *Mommy* liked it, too."

She went into the bathroom to break the role. Putting her robe on, as he dressed, she said, "Harry, thank you for getting me on the Juvenile Justice Commission."

"You're welcome."

"Can I look forward to more time with you and more opportunities to help …" she said, smiling, "politically, too?"

"Of course. Say, do you have any brandy?" he asked.

"Sure, let's go downstairs," she said.

Downstairs, while she poured brandy in the family room, he made another call.

He finished his call just as she entered the room, making a Loretta Young-style entrance.

"Harry, I have a favor to ask," she said.

"Sure, kitten. Fire away," he said.

"I expect Chief Kasten to retire soon. I *think* I'll be the next chief. Can I ask you, nonetheless, to make a well-timed call when the selection time comes?" she asked, rubbing her fingers through his hair.

"Let me say this about that…. The decision is really the chief judge's. Brayer and I know each other, but I don't feel comfortable calling him. These things can find their way into the press, and you'd be sorry I called. But here's what's more likely.... I play cards with Senior Judge Cox. Now, if he asked me what I thought, or even gave me an opening, I'd recommend you in a minute, darlin'. Cox could carry my view back to Brayer, and it might be in Brayer's interest to please me for some future chit he might have," he said.

She thought his answer certainly sounded plausible.

"I've got a Part Two also, for us, sugar," he added.

"I'm all ears," she said, again with her hand in his hair.

"When you're selected chief—and *if* I'm re-elected for a second term—all things being equal, your experience as chief would fit nicely for a correctional cabinet position in my administration. How's that sound?" he asked.

"Like a deal," she said. "God, you make me hot!" she said in a lusty voice, driving her tongue deep into his mouth.

"Hell," he said, interrupting the kiss, "we might end up in Washington some day. Wouldn't that be a trip?"

~

They met about once every two weeks for the next three months. Then, the calls stopped. Still, she was patient. She felt she could afford to be.

~

For her part, Dora took great liberties to exaggerate her role on the commission to her boss Robert Kasten and every judge she spoke to, particularly when the commission's interim report was released publicly that September. She manipulated her way into giving a comprehensive review of the report to the court family the next week. Although attendance was voluntary, twenty-two people showed up in the ceremonial courtroom of the old courthouse. Afterward, she felt anxious that she appeared shallow in response to some questions, particularly those addressed to the nuances of the commission's recommendations. Still, she had stood in front of a large number of interested courthouse employees, some of whom might be on the next selection committee for Chief Kasten's replacement, including two magistrates, and that, in and of itself, was valuable. Since the doomed message of the ad hoc commission was to use community interventions for youthful offenders rather than institutions and prisons, it was ironic that Dora Kingmaker used this occasion to emphasize her new mantra—we must protect the public from the enemy: juvenile predators. Surely, Dora reasoned, the governor would be pleased with her.

6

WHY A PROBATION OFFICER

Gee Brooks

Changes in Gee's life were both subtle and bold. Today, she pushed hard on her road bike as she headed up the last hill, heading east toward Wisconsin Avenue, near the District line. Gee thought how odd it was that just days ago she jogged the nearby area with Ruppert. Now, during the week, Ruppert was with Ed. As she entered her *No Pets Allowed* condo, her light, red bike on her right shoulder, she gave out her usual mission-accomplished grunt.

Her anger toward Ed was always expressed with an "I'm home, dear!" as she entered her condo, which was surprisingly comfortable, even quaint. All of her personal photos and significant pictures graced her bedroom and living room. It was really the first time she'd been alone as an adult since the years between college and her marriage to Ed. At fleeting moments, she felt free from the burden of taking care of someone else. The bedroom had a large four-foot by five-foot window, facing south, which facilitated afternoon naps in the sunlight. Her father, Thomas Burns, had already come to dinner twice and helped install oak shelves on several walls. Ali, her husband Michael, and their children had enjoyed a Sunday brunch.

The condo was just one block from the Chevy Chase Athletic Club. She worked out regularly—morning abs class, lifting weights, and evening boxing aerobics—in addition to running and riding one of her two bikes. She had her favorite bagel shop at the District line, just two blocks away, and the Bethesda Starbucks where she regularly met Hattie, Huggie, and Pepe was just an easy jog or bike ride away.

She was developing new routines to go with her new surroundings. For brief moments, they made her feel alive. But, seconds later, she sometimes suddenly felt pensive, unsure. The feeling was like she was in the desert, unable to figure which way was out, which way was home, which way would lead to death by dehydration of the spirit. *But*, she thought, looking around her living room, *I have my things … and my friends.*

She had weekly therapy sessions with Dr. Weinman, which made her feel increasingly in charge of her emotions and responsible for them. Journaling brought an odd sense of both discomfort and awareness, bundled together. She was learning to live with paradox and ambiguity. She no longer felt the sense of panic that she felt two months ago. Her life still felt turned upside down, but the nights of crying herself to sleep had stopped. She wasn't here or there—she was *in-between*—a place barren at times, fruitful at others. Dr. Weinman coached her to be curious about, rather than retreat from, her feelings. She was at the intersection of her past and the present. The future was for another day. She was beginning, awkwardly she thought, the process of facing her ending with Ed. But that ending set off a cluster of other endings she had avoided.

She turned the coffee maker on and headed for the shower. It was a Monday in July and she wanted to get to work before the traffic got too heavy—no small accomplishment in Montgomery County. In a field heavily influenced by women officers, Gee Brooks was in her sixth year on the job. Most of her free time was focused on learning why a marriage to a pretty nice guy didn't work and how to manage the complex and vexing behavior of the offenders in her caseload. A small part of Gee hadn't stopped wishing she could reach Ed. But he remained emotionally unavailable—he was there, but he wasn't there. He pretended to have an interest in connecting with her, but he was never completely in the present. *Why hadn't she faced that reality before?* She was obsessed with that question. She wondered what else was she blind to and why.

She tried to reassess Ed from a distance. In her internal monologue, Gee concluded that he wasn't very different than many of their peers. He was an advanced multitasker. There was his career in mortgage banking, the associated travel, the ever-present wireless Internet, the buzzing or ringing Blackberry, the cell phones, the instant messaging, anything that allowed him to multitask and to be here, there, and everywhere at the same moment, but not totally present—even when he was in the same room. He commanded a comprehensive understanding of complex financial data for leveraging the next, better deal. He was a top producer, one of the best in his business. His annual bonuses alone over the past two years averaged $40,000 to $50,000.

Considering her voluntary separation toward divorce was based on not "connecting," she had feelings similar to those of family members after the suicide of a loved one—irrational guilt, anger, constant second-guessing, and nagging feelings of failure. Then, there was the unending self-flagellating question: *what is wrong with me that I can't reach him?*

After making herself a large salad for dinner in the comfort of her condo's small kitchen, she sat in her favorite green-and-white-striped padded chair. She thought about her admiration for her father, Thomas Burns, and his take on the field of probation. Now retired, he too had been a probation officer—one of those "rehabilitation" relics. During his career, he had found his niche working with offenders. He told stories about women he helped get off welfare and about young men he helped find work, young men who had gone on to become responsible community members. Thomas Burns would gladly tell a variety of uplifting success stories to anyone who asked.

Thomas Burns knew the exact number of folks—twenty-five—he helped send back to prison. He told Gee that he met with each one of the twenty-five in a personal meeting before they left the county jail for designation to a federal prison and told each one why he had recommended prison. He also told each one he'd be waiting to help them, if they wanted help from him when they got out. Then he asked—and it was not his responsibility to do so—what he could do for their families while they were in prison. He tried hard to attend to their wishes. He had no enemies ... anywhere.

He also had no answers for what to do with young anti-social gangbangers. When asked about "our society going to hell in a handbasket because of gangs and crack," he'd just smile and change the subject. He'd talk about what he did do well—listen to the stories of those under his supervision and try to help them re-author their given scripts—scripts that made them permanent outcasts. While Thomas Burns had a niche, Gee was uncomfortable with her own county probation office.

She concluded, after biting a carrot from her salad, that weekly logistical conversations with Ed remained a disappointment. Trial and error confirmed that, no more than twenty seconds into the phone conversation, she would hear his computer keys clicking. But increasingly the discomfort she felt, the constant unease, was less about Ed and her separation from him and more about her own demons. Who was she? Why did she feel constantly edgy? Why was she so happy the moment she had a motivated offender and yet so miserable in staff meetings? She sensed now that the separation from Ed was about his self-centeredness and, maybe, about her trying to be a nice girl and pulling her emotional punches. She asked herself, *If I'm not Mrs. Brooks, who am I? How did everything become so awkward? And how will I get out of it?* She thought about dating but felt uninspired. She knew that she'd never had a hard time attracting the attention of men. For the present, she wanted to focus on herself and not someone else's needs. Men could wait.

At times—mostly weekends—she had custody of Ruppert, which meant she had to sneak the ninety-pound dog up the garage elevator. Unfortunately, the elevator often stopped right outside the front desk on the lobby floor. If someone in authority looked into the elevator or a frowning tenant got on the elevator, she carried on this Mommy-to-doggie conversation, "OK, baby, we're going to get Mommy's hat, and off we go on an adventure!" Stupid ploy, she thought, but it effectively staved off complaints from neighbors. During rational moments she realized that holding onto Ruppert, with his slobbering kisses and wagging tail, was really holding on to the dream of herself, Ed, Ruppert and three, maybe four, children. It pissed her off that Ruppert was closer to Ed than she was. *Jerk got an A+ with his dog*, she thought. Still, while angry and hurt, she never hated Ed. Instead, she felt the emptiness of not reaching him and of her own unfulfilled dreams of life with him. Sometimes, when he was busy with their former friends and she was with Ruppert, Gee would burst into tears with no apparent prompt. Ruppert needed her, touching a very vulnerable spot deep within her—one that she did not understand in its urgency.

Their mutual friends continued to invite either Gee or Ed, but not both, to parties, cookouts, ballgames, bike rides, whitewater rafting—all the things they used to do together. She yielded to him for most events. Truth was, she probably did more distancing from friends than they did with her. It was hard for her to tell. Gee heard through back channels, particularly gossip shared by one mutual friend, that Ed said at a pool party that he had not stopped caring about Gee but that he no longer had a sense of connection with her. He looks lost, the confidante said.

Part of Gee's new activities, besides daily workouts and weekly therapy, included reading voraciously—mostly self-help books. And, at Dr. Weinman's encouragement, she continued to write down her feelings—exploring who she was, how she got there, and where she might be headed. Even she recognized a surprising theme emerging: much of her energy was spent on trying to please others, which often required her, she realized, to bury her own needs. She considered Dr. Weinman a brilliant, ever-probing agitation, and, like Ali, an emotional bedrock.

As she had done for eleven years, she talked every day with Ali, who had been her roommate for three years at the University of Maryland, before Ali went on to medical school at UNC. Ali had been Gee's maid of honor and vice versa. Gee loved Ali as only a woman can love a best friend, and she treasured the time they had together. Every other Friday night, with Michael's blessing, Gee and Ali would have dinner at one house or the other, over a select bottle of wine or two, while Michael acted or was learning lines for a new play. Their two children stayed at grandma's.

Gee complained about her supervisor Chip Faulknour, who insisted that offenders who can't obey the rules should receive rapid and significant punishment. Gee balked at Faulknour's favorite saying: "If you *can* punish, you should."

"Friedrich Nietzsche would've been proud. All Faulknour needs is a pair of pince-nez glasses for a look to match the attitude," Gee said.

While Faulknour was really the only one in the probation office to use the "if you can punish, you should" expression directly, more so than not it represented the unspoken practice of most managers. This viewpoint was evident in sentencing matters where officers were coached to add factors to increase the proposed prison term when writing their sentencing recommendations.

"I just got chewed out by The Kingmaker for breaking that cardinal rule," Gee said.

On this Friday night, after her first sip of 2000 Columbia Crest Merlot, Gee revisited Ali's thorny question of two weeks ago: "Do you do probation stuff because you're trying to please your father?"

"With regard to the probation profession and the pleasing-my-father question, the answer is *no*, I don't feel the need to work for his approval. My father's love of his work has always been a source of pride to me," she said.

Gee thought that now was not the time for her to tell Ali about the endless alternative career fantasies she had had over the past few months, like becoming a school counselor, or getting a MSW from the University of Maryland. The idea of having her own patients appealed to her, particularly away from the confines of the courts. But the fantasies had little momentum.

"Why then, *Leibchen*, do you have so many stories about a career with idiotic policies, nasty and condescending attitudes by managers, and a way of thinking about the people you supervise that you'd never condone outside of work? *Never*," Ali emphasized.

"But that's what everyone expects for offenders," Gee said.

"If everyone else put their head ..." Ali mocked. "I bet it's not that simple. No one has stereotypical, condescending attitudes toward just one group. It always bleeds over to others. Those punishing attitudes can't be reserved just for the offenders!" Ali said, rolling into an interrogation without a pause.

"Just give me a 'yes' or 'no': is your office culture fairly *unfriendly* to defense attorneys?"

Gee mumbled, "Yes."

"Fairly *disinterested* in the families of offensive offenders?" Ali asked.

"Stop it," Gee said.

"Oh, sorry. Fairly *disinterested* in the families of persons on supervision. Did I say it right?"

Gee said, "You said it right, smartass; and, yes, disinterested unless someone is hurt."

"Fairly *removed* and *distant* from the local communities and the families that live in them?" Ali asked.

Gee said, "Yes."

"Somewhat *rude* to the offenders—oops, the persons *on* ... or is it *under*? ... supervision?" Ali questioned.

Gee said, "Yes. Accurate."

Slowly, like a not-so-bright runner-up in the Georgia Peachtree Beauty Pageant, Ali said, "But you, Gee Brooks, share none of those beliefs ... values ... and attitudes.... Now, do you?"

Gee reared up, like a horse rising on its hind legs.

"Look, there are all sorts of health insurance policies, defensive medical practices, threats of malpractice lawsuits rippling though every pediatric practice—not to mention the difficulties of getting and holding onto good staff—stuff you hate! How are our fields any different?" Gee asked.

"I'm on your side. Sorry if I was being a jerk. I agree with your view of the potholes in my profession. But, at the end of the day, I feel good about my service to my patients. I feel happy when I know I've done the best I can to make my sick little patients feel better and to reinforce healthy lifestyles. When I run into suspected child abuse, I've never backed away from the truth, as I see it. That said, I've almost quit because of 'managed mis-care' pressures. Also, I'd like about half the hours and twice the money. But, my Leibchen, as they say, at the end of the day, I feel good about what I do. Do you feel good about your work—really good?" Ali asked.

"*Je-sus* you piss me off. I hate your stupid questions. I hate thinking about it, but I do think about it to myself all the time ... and whine to friends. Is it the system that's crazy, or is it me? It's not very often I leave the office feeling good about myself. Can I really do anything that helps one person make it? But, when I really get further into your question, and I've asked myself that 'end-of-the-day' question a thousand times, I start developing categories," Gee said.

"I know, you always subdivide, layer, and create a matrix—I just wanted a simple answer and another glass of this great wine," Ali said. Her dark hair flipped from side to side, secured by a tight scrunchie, as Ali skated on her socks into the kitchen, still listening. Friends at college used to say that Ali seemed to skate, while Gee bounced. Both were pure energy and grace.

"The simple answer is no, no, and yes," Gee said.

Ali laughed.

"*No*, I seldom leave the office feeling good about my organization. Every day I'm doing something that's stupid, 'because it's policy.'"

Gee continued without taking much of a breath, "And *no*, I don't feel good at the end of the day with the meanness in my office. It embarrasses me—the 'us' versus 'them' tone. It's a similar feeling you get in some stores—you know, that feeling that customers are an interference with the employees' business.

"But *yes*, I love working with people, listening to them, giving back to them what I hear them saying to me. Sometimes they're startled by the profound things they've just said to me. I love trying new things out. Two weeks ago I went to a funeral of one of my charge's grandmothers. He introduced me to his family as his 'friend'—he didn't want to say probation officer. He cried openly at the loss of his grandmother. The experience changed our relationship into one of community teammates. Now he helps me find resources in his neighborhood and takes the time to introduce me to behind-the-scenes leaders, like the barber who's really the block 'gatekeeper.' But here's the crazy part. Officers are a very diverse group: some aren't brain surgeons. But, I swear to you, almost all are caring folks. You know, the ones you'd call for help with a flat tire at two o'clock in the morning. Most are people-persons. It's not the officers: it's the officers in stupid roles, *in context*. Imagine, Ali, an atmosphere where mostly warmhearted people are doing mean-spirited things every day to offenders—actions they'd never normally do to strangers," she said.

"Customers? Did you just imply that offenders are customers? Seems to me you have some decisions to make about your no-no-yes career. Cheers," said Ali, as they clicked their wine glasses.

"Nuevos Principios, Ali."

"Nuevos Principios, Gee."

Gee remembered when Ali first came up with the term "Nuevos Principios" in college during a two-bottle wine night. The expression was loosely translated to mean "new way," or sometimes it meant, "Don't take the B.S." Over time, it came to mean, "Find the truth as you know it." From that college night on, they called themselves the Nuevos Principios Sisters. The salute always cracked them up. It also loosely translated to "I love you and cherish you—don't ever stop being my friend."

"Do you see any similarities between what you let into your consciousness about your work and what you let in about Ed?" Ali asked.

"Oh, crap. More homework," Gee said.

~

The next morning, on her Saturday long run, Gee thought sadly about Willie Parker, a parolee on her caseload who had a revocation hearing on Monday. He had two recent positive urinalysis results for cocaine and a possession-of-marijuana conviction. She could not reach Willie, and she accepted that. He kept his distance from her. Still, he was his own worst enemy. She knew there was nothing she could do that would prevent his return to prison. *Too bad*, she thought, *that he had stopped going to drug treatment.* Now, treatment wasn't going to be an option—only prison was next. He was looking at two years.

She thought about Ali's career probe. Gee knew this about herself: she was a kind person, and she tried to treat everyone she met kindly. Still, she was far from a pushover. She also knew that, like it or not, she was part of the *punishment übëralles* army—where management reinforced punishment for offenders over all else—because she was painted by the same brush that they were: by judges, prosecutors, defense attorneys, public defenders, court personnel, persons on supervision and their families, the community, and the general public. She liked to believe that her unseen acts of kindness toward her offenders mattered. Gee railed against stupid policies and procedures along with Huggie, Hattie, and Pepe. Still, people under her charge were in prison because of the "rules."

Somewhere deep inside, her spirit was becoming increasingly unsettled, but she wasn't yet ready to own the pain of being a kind, caring person in a punishing profession. Her kindness was being lost in a morass of punishment … and in the context of her chosen career, she was painting over chipped paint. It wasn't the only pain she had buried. She had given Dr. Weinman a clue as to the primary source of pain in her life—the person who could rightfully take a seat in a second empty chair in his office.

Nearly five miles into the run today, she could almost see her old house as she passed an out-of-season outdoor ice rink in Rock Creek Park. She imagined herself as a lone skater. Only she had the ability to watch herself. She wondered how long she could skate on one leg.

7

THE OFFICE POWER DEBATE

Gee Brooks

Gee's head was spinning from her conversation with Ali about the culture of the probation office. She thought it might be helpful to explore her feelings with Hattie, Huggie, and Pepe. The foursome loved to debate the real and imagined power of key players in their organization, as well as focus on their quirks. Today, Saturday, in mid-July, instead of selecting their usual table at Starbucks near the side door facing Woodmont Avenue, the four friends sat outside. The iron chairs weren't comfortable, but that didn't bother them—at least, no one complained. Gee wanted to talk about how she despised the tough-guy cop culture of many, if not most, of their fellow officers and supervisors and how she tended to think of the culture in the office as a boys-will-be-boys power trip … and quite stupid.

"So, Hattie, how's your fiancé?" Gee asked, annoyed with Pepe's lack of juicy information.

"Breighton's fine. We've decided that I'm going to leave the probation office in about a year to focus on children's advocacy issues…. Don't know where yet," she said.

"You sure spend a lot of time mothering the cleaning staff. I see someone in your office sometimes at seven o'clock in the morning and even after work," Gee said.

"I tell them what I believe—that everybody can change their behavior. *Everybody*," Hattie said.

"I know in the last year alone you've made hospital visits, gone to funerals, and made at least three 'loan' payments on soon-to-be disconnected power bills for your *informal* caseload," Gee said.

"Hush, girl," Hattie said.

"I know this: you scare the crap out of the managers because of your family connections with Judges Johnson and Clarke," Gee said, naming the court's two black judges. "And officers say your family is friends with Maye Lee Williams, too," Gee said, adding the name of the sole black Maryland Parole Commission member.

"I'm black, if you haven't noticed, Gee.... Where're you going with all this?" Hattie said.

"My friend Ali asked me if we're at war with the management of the office. I didn't know what to say. Do you feel at war? Is part of the war racism, stereotypical thinking, anti-Hispanic, a class struggle? Are you armed to defend yourself? Am I in denial?" she asked.

"To answer your questions, no, I'm not at war. I don't hate management. I find most managers annoying. The supervisors we like best—who, unfortunately we don't work for—talk about their own frustrations with the condescending culture of the office. I do feel like I can relate to the black judges and the parole commissioner, and I like the idea that they could have my back if I needed support, but I'm not going to be here forever because of the way the power system is built. I don't fit in," Hattie said.

"Tell us how the power system works. Let's see if you have it right," said Huggie.

"OK, first the power starts with the governor, who masters the press and public opinion. Then it moves down to politicians, followed by the judges at the local level. Really, the Parole Commission affects our people directly, as do the prosecutors. Daily, though, our probation Chief Kasten has power, but The Kingmaker runs our office; then come the supervisors. Then, there's us and the clerks. Some community advocates have influence, maybe not direct power. Then come the defense attorneys and public defenders, who we have little connection with—they're like adversaries, not allies. Next—now we're really dipping down to those on the bottom of the totem pole, those who have little or no power—the offenders and their family members. Now, how exactly did those on the bottom of the totem pole land there? That's what's screwed up," Hattie said.

"The system doesn't set out to destroy people.... Individuals with a personal agenda do. And that would be The Kingmaker, not Chief Kasten. You know, like reprimands in personnel files," said Huggie.

"Chief Kasten really doesn't want to interact with anyone that's not the governor, a politician, a state official, a judge, or the chairman of the Parole Commission. He avoids public speaking and chooses to stay in the background. He claims he's 'developing' the leadership skills of The Kingmaker. That's B.S. He'll retire soon. At least, that's what his administrative assistant told me. Kasten is a minor factor in policy, and no factor in the daily operation of the office," Hattie said.

Huggie added, "But, don't forget, Kasten is quite effective at blocking officers' complaints from reaching Chief Judge Brayer and the other judges. Mostly, though, his style is one of benign neglect."

"Now that ... *that's* pure bullshit. And dangerously naive bullshit!" Pepe said, nearly coming out of his chair. "There's no such thing as "benign" when neglect affects people's lives. You care.... You're there, you act.... Or you don't care because it doesn't affect you directly. Benign is cowardly and selective blindness.... Trust me. The useless pabulum we feed ourselves! Benign neglect! Hah! Like 'government intelligence'—who made that crap up? Mark my words, folks, I don't give a rat's ass about office politics, but neglect's the door to harm!" Pepe said.

"Whoa! Well, what I meant to say is that, as far as I know, he's never done anything to harm me," Huggie said.

Pepe started to smile. "Sorry, Huggie. I had a flashback."

"Acid?" Hattie asked.

"No. I remember going to a counselor in the first week of my freshman year at the University of Texas. I told this woman, a student affairs counselor, who I waited for hours to see, that I felt homesick and neglected. I don't know why I used the word 'neglected,' it just came out of my mouth. Actually, I felt more like a foreigner. She had the balls to say that what I was experiencing was really benign neglect or a 'neutral reaction' by others, not intended to harm me. I told her to buzz off with her benign listening skills and walked out. She was, as it turned out, actually pretty helpful. I figured out I had two choices: go home, or stop feeling sorry for myself," he said.

"I can't imagine you feeling sorry for yourself. Well then, gang, where's all of this discomfort I feel coming from at the office? Where does the mindless, stupid decision-making come from—the stuff that makes me so damned miserable?" Gee asked. "Help me figure this out."

"The real force in the office, puddin', is The Kingmaker. She's an evil witch. Something in her must tap into a spot in you that suggests you guys need her approval," declared Hattie.

"Well, well, tell us more," Pepe said.

"You might use some interesting skills to deflect her nastiness, Pepe, but if you guys paid attention, there's nothing that comes out of her mouth that isn't crafted and measured ... measured better than a Betty Crocker recipe. The agenda is always her power and her control. Think about it! Kasten should be involved with all of the judges around the sentencing process and *all* of the personnel issues—instead, *she* tells us what to do and walls us off from Kasten and the judges," Hattie said.

"I just went through that," Gee said.

"She gets a special kick out of targeting folks that she feels are against her will. You look at her—every day, I swear, she wears a different business suit ... every day ... as if she were a prosecutor in a major white-collar trial. Rumor has it The Kingmaker has a 'special' relationship with the Governor," Hattie said.

"Where have I been? Oh, I know: above this drivel. Who cares who she goes to bed with?" Pepe said.

Gee said, "Hattie's right. Who knows, the rumors seem to have a life of their own. I figured they're either right on the mark, somewhat accurate but taken entirely out of context, or simply the product of her enemies. But the rumors are her subtitle," Gee said.

"Her what?" asked Huggie.

"Her subtitle, as in *Death in Hyde Park: One Girl's Love of Knives*, the story of one girl's—"

"Got it, Ms. Borders Books Information Help Desk," said Huggie.

Gee punched Huggie on the arm.

"I know The Kingmaker overrides other supervisors' recommendations on personnel issues. One of them told me they just try to guess what she wants and avoid the hassle. Every one of us should fear her. For officers who've had the poor judgment to appeal to Chief Kasten, I'm told that Kasten gave them an explanation that sounded like, 'Well, that's just the way Mom is!'" Hattie said.

"Mom knows best! And you call that benign?" Pepe said.

"Everyone knows her Achilles' heel is her burning desire to be the next chief—at all costs. She's 'form over substance.' I hate the woman,"

Hattie said. "Oh, you'd better keep her in front of you, Miss Gee. No wicked witch wants to share the throne with another woman."

"I worry about our boy, Chip Faulknour, the Citadel grad, who somehow never made it in the military like Daddy wanted. Like the lady-in-waiting, he dresses like an attorney, too.... I'm sure he does that to identify himself with prosecutors and distance himself from us, the lowly probation officers. I bet he spends all of his waking moments thinking about positioning himself to be the next deputy chief—once The Kingmaker is promoted," Huggie said.

"Why couldn't Ed be more like him—you know, manageable?" Gee joked. "Here Ed.... Good boy!"

"How long would that last?" Huggie shot back.

"I wasn't serious. Back to Ed—I mean Chip. He's a shameless brownnoser. He has that super-annoying habit of laughing at the slightest opportunity at any semi-witty remark made by high officials. Have you noticed that he varies the decibel level of his laughs based entirely on the speaker's status? A comment by a judge about the rising barometric pressure would send him into a guffaw that could be heard fifty yards away," Gee said.

"So, we're not at war with this setup ... these characters?" asked Pepe.

"Not yet. But the time will come—trust me, the time will come when we'll have to get off our plump asses," said Huggie.

"Speak for your own supersized buttocks, Huggie," said Hattie, punching him in the arm.

8

HIRING ON

Carrie Springer

There was only one thing missing in Carrie Springer's life: meaning. After a few glasses of wine at a neighborhood cocktail party, Carrie had shared with her friend Dick Felton that she was searching for something she could get her heart into. She wanted to do something with passion. Her bitter divorce had drained much of her creativity and energy. Her ex, Carl, had thanked Carrie's devotion to his career and caring for their two boys by having countless affairs with younger women. Since the separation and divorce, Carrie had plenty to do to keep her busy— plenty of friends, a variety of board meetings, and tons of money. She was once a very good golfer, and she pined to get back to the game. She loved her two sons, both doing well at Ivy League colleges. She had given up her career as a newspaper writer to be a mother, but that was far, far in the past—almost another lifetime.

In a few minutes, Carrie was meeting Jon Rhodes in the cafeteria of the Circuit Court in Maryland's Rockville Courthouse complex. Dick had referred Carrie to Jon, suggesting to Jon that Carrie had skills that he needed in the We Watch Together Society, or WWTS. While WWTS was getting plenty of public attention lately, Dick, a savvy PR consultant, felt its image was too lackluster and could use improvement.

WWTS had concentrated its attention on the justice process in the Circuit Court, focusing on the propriety of guilty or not guilty verdicts, plea bargains that seemed to benefit the wealthy, evaluations of Circuit Court judges, and the overarching sense that the court paid too much attention to sound bites for the six o'clock news rather than to the reality that many county residents were being sent to prison for minor offenses. WWTS had gone from a society of lightweight court observers to a nuisance for the judges and prosecutors, who would have preferred to conduct their duties away from public scrutiny.

Carrie told Jon Rhodes in a brief phone conversation that she would be wearing a green sweater on this balmy Thursday in late March. She really had nothing to lose today; she was just exploring options. As she breezed into the cafeteria, she reminded herself that she was here to listen; still, the courthouse evoked many unpleasant memories of her domestic court experiences. Pretending to be writing an above-the-fold article for the *Washington Post*'s Metro section, she whispered to herself, "Can a middle-aged woman turn the court system upside down?" *I'll have to work on the headline*, she thought.

Jon Rhodes was seated at a table at the rear of the cafeteria, his back to the windows, where he could see and reach out to courthouse players—judges, prosecutors, public defenders, marshals, court security officers, and probation officers—as they came for carry-out coffee, and, today, where he could spot Carrie Springer's arrival.

Dick Felton had told Carrie a great deal about Jon Rhodes. She knew that he was in his mid-fifties, was slightly overweight, and had short brown hair with highlights of gray. He had been a CEO of his own commercial real estate company. Felton described Jon Rhodes as a civic activist and an avid amateur golfer; he had millions in the bank, and every successful businessman in Montgomery County knew him. Carrie had done her own research in the county library and learned that Rhodes had walked away from his business on February 3, 1997, exactly one week after his wife Lucy was murdered in a botched robbery attempt. The killer, a twenty-eight-year-old black D.C. parolee, was high on crack. According to newspaper articles, Rhodes told friends that he never once entertained the notion of going back to work after her death. Dick said that he told confidants that he managed his overwhelming grief by obsessively attending every court filing, motion, and hearing related to the thug that killed his wife. He said that this was his vigil and the only place he could stop shaking. He told intimate friends that sleep abandoned him. Until the conviction and sentencing, he told his sister, who shared the story with Dick, he felt nearly insane; only the vigil, an overt expression of anguish, pulled him from the abyss.

It was common knowledge that Jon Rhodes watched court proceedings and scribbled notes incessantly. Both casual observers and court employees, who saw him every weekday, treated him with great empathy and kindness, but they kept an awkward distance from him.

"My God," a cafeteria food server would say to anyone who broached the topic of Jon, "there but for the grace of God go I."

"Jon?" asked Carrie from about ten strides, dressed in a green sweater that covered an above-the-knee floral print dress. Her dirty blond hair was cut just above the shoulders. Her hazel eyes smiled. Carrie was astonishingly attractive. At five feet, eight inches tall, she was about three inches shorter than Jon. Unlike him, she was slender and fit. Her friends remarked that she seemed to glide with the elegance of a dancer. It was as if a breeze flowed around her. Carrie was, quite simply, radiant and fresh.

He stood, smiling, and said, "You must be Carrie Springer."

Up close, he looked so serious, so worn out, and so without energy that, in a blink, Carrie asked herself, "What have I gotten myself into?"

"That I am," she said. "Dick Felton said that two years is enough time for me to mope about divorce and that I might enjoy exploring working with you."

She noticed Jon smile. *Maybe there is someone alive inside that ash-colored face*, she thought. Still, she felt put off by his seriousness.

"Good," he said.

She considered, but decided not to say, that Dick had stood by her in very tough times during the long contested separation and divorce process. Although Dick and his wife were friends with Carrie and Carl at the Chevy Chase Club, Dick was disgusted by Carl's womanizing, which shifted from rumor to common knowledge, like ... her, *too* ... he didn't with *her, too*, and so on. After the legal separation, Carl left the family home and turned unashamedly to women fifteen to twenty years his junior. That was the last straw for most of the club blue bloods, except for his golfing buddies.

"I have no financial concerns," Carrie continued. "But there are only so many yoga and pilates classes one can get lost in. Or half-marathons or boards to serve on. So, I told Dick that I want to do something important. Something exciting and, well, *useful*. My girlfriends and I have our favorite charities, but Dick suggested that I explore your WWTS. I trust his judgment, and that leads me to you."

Carrie thought these words appeared to light a small spark in him. *My God*, she thought, *am I connecting with this dour man?*

Jon began the story of WWTS, a recitation he had given a hundred times. Carrie awkwardly expressed sorrow over his wife's death. *How*, she wondered, *does someone survive the pain of a brutal murder?* She told Jon that she understood loss all to well. Her empathy appeared to touch him, she thought, and she reprimanded herself for losing patience with his quasi-monotone.

He continued his presentation, describing how he began attending court hearings, trials, jury selections, anything that seemed important in court, while he waited for the trial of his wife's murderer. She knew all of that already.

"One day I was pausing in the hallway to collect my thoughts when I was approached by three senior citizens … cute folks, really. I'd seen them numerous times in the courthouse halls. I once heard a security officer at the Magnetometer refer to them as the 'geezer court patrol.' I wanted to smack the shit out of him," he said.

"Geezers…. That's so cruel," she said.

"The triad invited me to join them for breakfast in this cafeteria on the days they were here. We always sat at this very table. It was like court employees reserved it for us," he said.

"They showed me how to read the daily court dockets to follow trials and court hearings. Over time, they discussed how they informally rated the performance of judges, prosecutors, defense attorneys, public defenders, and probation managers and officers in court. They had their favorites and their villains. For them, this was sport—their own reality show. It probably gave them something to do, something away from the Asbury Nursing Home, something that beat going to the doctor or watching TV. The three old characters said they were the stars at dinner in the nursing home, regaling their peers with the day's top crime stories like a live newscast. They only attended the most sensational trials. Rarely did they stay for more than two or three hours. For them, the experience was recreation—for me, it's a compulsion. But I'm less intense now," he said.

Damn, Carrie thought to herself, *he hasn't changed his facial expression once…. He was more intense than this?*

"Slowly, the experience of being in the courthouse became more of a passion—a public advocacy mission—for what I call 'the pursuit of simple justice,'" he said.

"What does 'simple justice' mean?" Carrie asked.

"Well, back then I came to appreciate that if I could experience through direct observation in the courtrooms that a rational sense of simple justice existed—that it existed in *this* courthouse *every day*—then I could control the ruminating and find a smattering of internal peace. I felt it was as sane as I was going to get," he stated.

"So you think your internal well-being can only be controlled if you observe simple justice?" she asked.

"Sounds crazy when you put it like that. Let me say that another way. I've discovered, removed from my wife's murder, that the idea of simple justice has carried me into uncharted waters. It's become a journey that's inseparable from me.... The journey and the traveler has become one and the same," he concluded.

He looked her squarely in the eye. "Does that make any sense to you?" he asked.

"It only has to make sense to you."

He cut to the story of the trial of Lucy's murderer. There was a noticeable change in his tone—anger filled his voice. His body stiffened.

"The bastard got life imprisonment without parole, meaning he'll die in prison. The sentence didn't make me happy—or disappoint me. I wanted two things: to ask the slime 'why my Lucy?' —and to strangle him. But it's what happened *after* the sentencing that caught me off guard. For three months, nearly every night, I had the same dream," he said. "I'd break into his cell or sometimes just float in, or even walk in, and start smashing his head to bits ... sometimes with a bat or crow bar, or my bare hands. But each time I'd be stopped by Lucy's soft but firm voice: 'No more, Jon.... I'll wait for you.' The dream—or nightmare, really—finally morphed into me approaching his cell and hearing Lucy's same message *without* me smashing his head to bits. After that, something changed in me. That was about two years ago," Jon said.

"Changed how?" Carrie asked.

"What I began to see in the courthouse appalled me. I observed serious criminals, who I thought were guilty as hell, get their charges dropped for questionable legal procedural reasons. I saw cases where young black men and a growing number of Hispanics, including women, were caught up in small-time drug distribution cases and sent to prison for five years under mandatory sentencing laws … three, four times a day. The offenses seemed so minor to me. The young men looked so hard, so lost. If you closed your eyes, one case sounded just like every other case. By contrast, I saw short sentences or just probation for crimes like tax evasion or fraud. Hell, all that time I sweated over business taxes for nothing!" he laughed. "I saw or, I should say, *see*, the wealthy with gifted attorneys—as I would have had—from well-known law firms, achieve favorable outcomes. All the while, the poor are represented by well-intended but swamped public defenders," he said.

"Go on," she said.

"And I've witnessed jury verdicts that troubled me—both guilty and not guilty findings," he concluded.

He paused to drink from his coffee cup.

"Then it came to me…. Why not do what that triad of senior citizens did, but in a more formal and data-driven way: why not rate the performance of the court as a whole? So the centerpiece of WWTS became the annual rating of the court's operation. What has resulted is a very public sense of justice in the Circuit Court. Over the past few years, I have become increasingly concerned that the court players seem to operate with various agendas that co-exist for reasons that are unrelated to justice or fairness. It feels to me that this court is more focused on careers than justice. You would only be able to pick that up by watching them every day. Then, you pick up their patterns in repeated comments like 'we're sending a message that we will not tolerate this in Montgomery County.' The real message is, 'I'm tough,'" he said.

"Give me an example of these questionable agendas," she said.

Jon explained that usually players in the courtroom drama kept one eye focused on pleasing their constituent base—whether that constituent group was the political hierarchy, the public, the press, or their supervisors. "That's true," he said, "for everyone except the public defenders. Most of them seem to mount well-intended if convoluted tales about what adverse circumstances combined to propel their unfortunate and naive defendants into criminal behavior. Then the public defenders say that the defendant is at 'the crossroads' and that, therefore, the court should be motivated to save him from prison by being lenient. It's bad theater played to the court's deaf ear. Having heard this overused metaphor hundreds of times, I began to wonder if the court was located at a very significant crossroads of helplessness and hope—like Routes 270 and the 495 Beltway. Mostly, this strategy doesn't work," he concluded.

"How, in God's name, did you come up with that pitiful name— the We Watch Together Society?" she asked with a smile on her face.

"I did get carried away with the name. Thankfully, people just call it WWTS," he said.

"All right, I think I have enough background. So tell me where you want to take WWTS," Carrie said, moving closer to avoid a noisy conversation behind them. "What do you want to focus on, and how do you envision me helping? You don't need me to observe trials," Carrie concluded.

"You don't beat around the bush, do you?" Jon said.

"My husband beat around numerous bushes, if you know what I mean. He wasted a lot of my time—and charm," she said.

They both laughed.

"This might sound strange coming from a man whose wife was murdered by a crack-smoking young man.... Maybe it's part of healing, but I'm concerned about the number of young black and Hispanic men returning to prison after an unsuccessful period of supervision in the community. Back they go for more prison time. I guarantee you that if this was happening to white kids the press would be all over it like they'd follow a sitting president having an affair. But no one, *no one*, seems to notice! It used to be a rather infrequent experience to have a revocation hearing on the court's daily calendar. Now there are five to ten every week," he said.

"What is a revocation hearing?" Carrie asked.

He explained that a revocation hearing was like a trial before the judge who originally sentenced the person before he or she went to prison. It determined if the person had lived by the conditions of supervision since being back in the community.

"A revocation hearing pits the probation officer and the prosecutor against the person on supervision and the public defenders," Jon stated.

"Who wins?" she asked.

Jon said, "The prosecutors."

A chill went down her back—like she suddenly realized she was with a person with whom she had fundamental, deal-breaking differences. She shifted to a sarcastic tone. "So, these young people are committing new crimes and being sent back to prison. What part of that scenario bothers you, Jon? Is it the new crimes or the drug use?"

She didn't wait for an answer. "Let me be clear," she said. "I'm not prepared to get into some bleeding-heart drama about the poor drug users who are making crack babies. It ain't me." She prepared to stand.

"I'm not being clear. Please hear me out," he said. "I may be pigeonholed by some as a wacko, but I'm not stupid, and I have no goddamned sympathy for those who willingly want to be criminals. I'm not talking about thugs! I swear to God, from what I can tell from the data—which, by the way, has been a study in obfuscation—and from what I've observed, a significant number of people in this county are going back to prison for violating rules—*not* for committing new crimes. This is *petty* shit. My hunch is that it's not unique to this county or to Maryland. There's a massive cover-up going on, like with the Vietnam War or the search for WMDs in Iraq. The prison-industrial complex is the only winner. I'd bet my life on it. Meet this issue head-on, here and now, and who knows the ripple effect. Now, that's not chicken-shit liberal mush! I might be wounded, but I'm not delusional," he said.

"OK, Jon," she said, abandoning her standing motions. "Still, that doesn't make sense. Why would the court send people to prison for violating rules? What rules? And who benefits by having them in prison for rules violations?" she asked.

"Good questions," he said.

He explained that the original sentencing hearings are frequently covered by the press. The courts sentence offenders to prison with five or more special conditions, or rules of conduct. Certainly, these conditions make judges *seem* tough on crime in front of the press. It's a public shell game, Jon felt. After all, judges are elected officials. He gave examples of special conditions imposed at sentencing: no drug use, no alcohol use, pay a hefty court fine, pay restitution, pay court costs, do hundreds of hours of community service, like cleaning up parks. These conditions *seem* to make sense and send a message to deter crime. But, he explained, if you walk in the shoes of the person who returns from prison three to five years after the sentencing and find the rules still waiting, they are hefty demands for young adults twenty to thirty years old, especially those who aren't that well organized in the first place. Add into the mix the idea that probation officers seem to be instructed to try to catch them doing something wrong. "It's a sad, sick game. Nothing more, nothing less," he said.

His viewpoints resonated with her. She liked taking on bullies. She didn't know if she could tolerate his sullen demeanor, but she did like the glimpse at his anger.

"With no money, no job, no skills, living in the projects—with *your* back to the wall, what would the rules mean to you?" Jon asked.

"Not much, I imagine," she said.

"Sit in on a revocation hearing, and you'll see," he said.

"How big a problem is this?" she asked.

"My preliminary data shows this to be a sleeping giant on a national scale. For instance, I got a hold of a Blue Ribbon Commission Report in California—a commission that was formed to try to do something about the problem of prison overcrowding. The Commission determined that 47 percent of new entrants in prison, more than 34,000 people, were for rules violations—*not* new crimes. They call it technical violations. Now, a few years later, *after* the commission's report, the number of inmates in prison for technical violations in California is over 65 percent. I'm convinced we have a similar problem in Maryland," he added.

"What are the consequences if you're right?" she asked.

"Well, let's see," he said, using his fingers to count off the ways. "Hearings crowd judges' calendars and require personnel from various factions of the court family. One would hope, instead, judges would attend to backed-up criminal and civil suits that take sometimes five years to be heard in this county. Maybe each hearing costs $2,000 to $5,000. Think of the infrastructure—warrants and arrests for the defendants executed by police officers and sheriff's deputies take days, which, in turn, takes them away from their job of protecting the community. These revocation hearings lead to time in local jails waiting for the hearing. This is like the costs of an expensive hotel for about two to six weeks. And the loss of the offender from his family's and community's perspective—what price do we put on that? Have you ever imagined what imprint it might make on a young child to see his or her father chased down by the sheriff's deputies like a stray dog, thrown to the ground, handcuffed, and led off to prison? Then, of course, we could throw in the cost of state prison for one year, somewhere between $25,000 and $35,000," he said.

His eyes looked ablaze with engagement to Carrie.

He went on. "Have you noticed the new 1,200-bed correctional facility on Route 270 built to house the swelling number of new inmates, the MCCF? It just opened in February. Why would we need that new prison facility if we didn't have these rule violators locked up for a year? They are the base population. They keep beds filled. You wait. In the next few years you'll hear a cry for the construction of yet another new jail and more new prisons throughout the state. If you liked the military-industrial complex, you'll love the prison-industrial complex. You know, 'If you build it, they will come.' Where does it stop? When does it stop?" he asked.

"Well, to answer your question, yes, I've seen the facility. What will happen to the person when they get to prison for their rules violations? Will they be in some sort of program?" Carrie asked.

"There are usually no programs. They'll mop floors or work in the kitchen," he added.

"Then what?"

"Then they start all over again in the community with the same conditions or even more conditions."

"Who in the hell dreamed up this stupid idea?"

"Now, there's the rub. Apparently no one. It just emerged ... as practice. What do you think? Do you want to spend time on this issue? And, if yes, how would you approach the problem?"

"Yes, I'm interested for several reasons. To put if succinctly, I always bristle when people say, 'There's nothing we can do.'"

She told him that she'd like to find out what held this stupid idea together and where the cracks were. How could such an obviously flawed idea stand the test of time? Was the data correct? How could such a smoldering problem exist under the noses of public officials? And how do they sleep at night?

"I'd take the tack—in what ways can I help tell this story? Rather than prison, what can be done locally, more effectively, and safely? Who can *I*—or should I say *we* —link with and offer support? How do we manage the politics? How do we influence the players behind closed doors, without public ridicule? Ridicule would only make those responsible bury the truth, causing otherwise helpful folks to run for cover. How do *we* get the teeter-totter spinning? And, I'm interested in who in the community *should* be upset about this ... and how I can help organize them," she added. "Now, there are some interpersonal connections you should be aware of that I'd use carefully. I'm friends with Chief Judge Brayer. Bill and his wife Mildred are old friends from the Chevy Chase Club. We've dined and played tennis, golf, and cards together, although the social interaction stopped after Carl and I separated. But I still consider Bill my friend. I would want him to be a friendly ally, although we'd need clear boundaries," she said.

"I've tried to have an open and direct relationship with Judge Brayer. Some judges, particularly senior judges, hate me and what I stand for. Brayer does not. I always go over my annual findings with him, before we go to press. Actually, he offers sound, balanced advice. More than once, I've pulled stuff out based on his counsel," Jon said.

"Sounds like Bill. I also know Judge Harry Johnson. He and I played golf alone when one of our playing partners became ill. Harry's tighter than a bull's ass in fly time."

"Oh my God! Tighter than a—" Jon laughed.

"Harry's wife is wacko. But I think he'd be open to me, maybe behind the scenes. You know, I thought I'd go back to writing or reporting. But this sounds like investigative reporting, problem solving, and community activism, all rolled into one, which I love. Now, Jon, I must break a few eggs with you, if I'm to work with you. Do I have your permission?" she asked.

"Yes, please be frank," he said.

"We'll see if you like my frankness," she laughed. "You need to treat yourself better. I'm sure that selecting this cafeteria was, in part, intended to give me a sense of the environment—"

He interrupted her, "Well, I'm sorry if—"

"Hear me out. This cafeteria is very public. The work you asked me to help you with is rather dicey. You should've treated both of us better by getting out of this place so that we'd be able to talk more openly."

"Point taken."

"Secondly, there's an aura around you that seems to blend ever-vigilant and on guard. We—you and I—can get to the truth better without unnecessary drama. I'm not saying lose the passion.... But lose the off-putting. Use the passion for the truth."

"I think you're right, actually."

"Which brings me to me. Did I mention that right out of college I was a beat reporter for the *Cleveland Plain Dealer*? I love putting the missing pieces of the puzzle together. But, at my age, I want to be more of a player. I'll gather information objectively, but I'm going to want to get involved in doing something with it—what I think is right. I don't give a rat's ass what people think of me. You're still comfortable with keeping a vigil. I don't mean this unkindly, but I don't share that with you ... thank God."

"Do you think that's twisted?"

"That's for you to decide. For my two cents, if I were you, I'd heed Lucy's words in your dream: 'No more.... Move on.' Let's *solve* the problems, not just point them out. Let's crank this baby into another gear."

"Message received. I trust you'll be patient with me."

"No, I won't."

"Maybe I need to be pushed by someone with your energy into more passion and less vigil."

"Just get back to the executive skills you have, and I'll get my skills going. I have a nose for what's important. I need to get to know some players and find people I can trust inside the system. I'll need to see some revocation hearings for myself. We'll need to talk with folks in the state's attorney's office and public defender's office together; plus, I need some probation officer insiders. I'll figure that out. I'll need you on some of these departmental visits. I want to be part of something important—and not act like a bunch of angry, blind squirrels banging around in the dark for some nuts," she said, smiling.

"Was that a double entendré?"

She merely held her arms out with palms up.

"I accept your terms. Welcome to the WWTS. Would you like a title?" he asked.

"Yes. Boss!"

"Will you help me write a heralding piece on you?"

"Of course."

"Seriously, what title do you want, Carrie?" Jon asked.

"First, in the next newsletter, I want you to drop the 'Founder' title behind your name and declare in the lead paragraph that WWTS is reorganizing. Your title is now 'Executive Director.' I will be the 'Assistant Director' in charge of community outreach. How's that?"

"Fine by me. You got it!" he replied. "Anything else?"

"Yes, a handshake and a great dinner with good wine to celebrate our partnership. Thank you, Jon. Let's see what we can do together."

As she stood to leave the table, for a second Carrie thought Jon Rhodes's posture appeared to be similar to that of a sixteen-year-old boy watching his car come out of the car wash. She, too, left the cafeteria with added lightness in her step. There was a sense of mystery, with bullies and injustice and sinister motives—things that really turned on her creative juices. *But damn,* she thought, *Jon Rhodes is so serious.*

Three weeks later, Chief Judge William Brayer, sitting in his chambers, read the bi-weekly WWTS newsletter announcing the reorganization and the new Assistant Director, Carrie Springer.

"Well," he said to Gabby White, who walked through his open chamber door, "there goes the neighborhood."

"Excuse me?" Gabby White said.

"Expect a call from a Ms. Carrie Springer from WWTS. If she wants to meet with me, set up a meeting for lunch. If she doesn't call, well, forget I said this," he said.

An hour later, Gabby said that she had Ms. Springer on the phone. "She wants a meeting. Where should I tell her?" she asked.

"Noon Tuesday at Il Pizzico on Rockville Pike," he instructed.

"There goes the neighborhood!" he repeated to himself.

~

Sharply at noon, Carrie entered Il Pizzico and, without having to introduce herself, was guided by the owner to a table in the rear of the large dining area.

There, in the corner, was the handsome, slightly graying, six feet, six inches tall Chief Judge Brayer in a navy blue, pin-striped suit. He stood and kissed her on each cheek. "Hello, Madame Assistant Director," he said.

"Hello, Judge Brayer," she said.

Leaning close to her, he said, "Carrie, in public, it's best not to use my title … for security reasons."

"Sorry," she whispered.

"How are you?" he asked, adding, "I miss you, you rascal. The dinners, the cards, the dancing, the golf."

"Speaking of golf, how's Harry Johnson?"

"He still talks about you nearly beating him in front of his friends at the club, by the way. He's fine. You know Harry."

"You know, I forgot about almost beating him. And that miserable woman he's married to?" she asked.

"What can I say? Miserable, I guess. Come see us…. Catch up with Mildred. She'll give you the gossip. Are you still on the inactive rolls at the club?" he asked.

"Yes. Maybe that'll change before too long. Who knows?"

The waiter arrived. He said, "Sir, Madame. What can I get for you today?"

Judge Brayer turned to Carrie and asked, "May I?"

Carrie nodded.

He ordered lunch in impeccable Italian.

"*Grazie,*" said the waiter, enjoying the native dialogue. He whirled around with added flair.

"*Grazie,*" said Judge Brayer.

"You never cease to amaze. What did you order, and where did you learn Italian?" she asked.

"A surprise…. You'll be pleased. After law school, I enlisted in the Army. I was considering a political career at the time. But I learned in the Army that I'd rather stick with the law than learn the art of spinning, non-sequiturs, double talk.... You know, the skills of politicians. Of course, our president has since shown us that part-time reserve duty works just as well as an actual military tour of duty. At any rate, they chose to station me in Italy for two years. When in Rome ..."

"I'm impressed," she said.

"Don't be. I only speak Italian when ordering food and wine.... What's on your mind, Carrie? You didn't call me just for lunch. You could've done that a long time ago," he said.

"Well, sir, you're right. I met with Jon Rhodes—"

"Poor bastard—" he interrupted.

"Well, yes, but—"

"Some of the judges are spooked by him. His ... his ..."

"Vigil. I know," she said.

"Yes, vigil. I don't blame him for being enraged. Maybe I'm numbed by what I see and hear in my courtroom all the time—man's inhumanity—but he can put some on the defensive. To his credit, he's always informed me fully before he did his annual evaluation thing. And he's allowed me to clear up misperceptions," he added.

"What kinds of misperceptions?" she asked.

"Well, the purpose for sealed indictments, plea agreements, the need for settlements reached under agreement with nondisclosure, ongoing police investigations, things that might make the public suspicious," he said.

"Bill, I want to ratchet up the investigative reporting aspect. Jon's going to continue in his role as a court observer. He's really a brilliant man!" she said.

"Oh, I remember him well—*before*, as they say. But how can I be of service to you, my dear?" he asked.

"Well, I don't know right now. Maybe we can be of service, as you say, to each other—while maintaining the necessary distance, given my role as a seeker of the truth and yours as someone clearing his calendar as quickly as possible so he can get out on the links!" she said.

"Funny."

"I'm a little concerned about one thing. I'm too old to play nice. I like digging into areas where political ambition overrides the right thing to do," she said, sipping her water.

"And …?"

"And, if the court's family—judges, prosecutors, sheriffs, probation officials—are part of what I conclude is unjust …" she paused.

"I know you well enough to know you're not asking for permission. This notice is more like a driver on Route 270 who puts her blinker on at the same time she swerves in front of you. She's not asking for permission. She's just informing you a slight second before she acts, right?"

"Right," she said.

"Well, I'm so warned. I trust your judgment," he said.

The food arrived. He made but one more comment about their new roles, and it, for her, made the lunch a business success and not just a nice way to reconnect with an old friend.

"We'll find a way to collaborate. It's good to have you on the train. It's a complicated world, this criminal justice stuff. In this adversarial drama, I welcome different views … I think," he said.

"We'll see what we see," she said, smiling.

"Gee, I wish the timing was better, given all of the changes going on in your life … but …"

"Oh, no. What, Ali?"

"Well, my wonderful husband has received a prestigious scholarship to study at Oxford," Ali said.

"And you don't mean Oxford, Mississippi, do you?" Gee said.

"No, honey, I don't."

"And what about my best friend, Ali? Will she drag the kids across the pond?"

"Yes … yes, honey, I will. I'm going to work in a clinic that works with underprivileged children … I've always wanted to do that anyway. I suspect we'll be there for several years and then see what comes next," Ali said.

"I'm so happy for you," Gee said.

"Are you sure …?"

"Of course. They do have phones, Ali," Gee said.

Gee could hear Ali crying, uncharacteristically unable to talk.

Gee paused a second and said, "Listen, dear, we've talked on the phone every day since college. We'll use e-mail, cell phones, whatever. You come over once a year. I'll come over there ... What the heck, we'll manage."

The words of encouragement only made the usually composed and in-charge Ali cry harder.

"Can you come over tonight for dinner?" Ali asked.

"Of course ... Nuevos Principios, Ali."

"Nuevos Principios, Gee. I love you."

Five weeks later, Gee said a tearful goodbye to Ali and her family at Dulles International Airport.

9

DID I BLINK?

Gee Brooks

Early on a Saturday morning in August, Gee peddled hard on her road bike toward Starbucks. She and Hattie would be alone today—Pepe and Huggie were crabbing. Whizzing down a near-deserted Wisconsin Avenue, Gee ruminated about how quickly her relationship with Ed had come crashing down. *When did he begin to feel differently about me? What did I do? Why didn't I see it coming?* She arrived at Starbucks, hopped off her bike, removed her cleats, placed them, her gloves, and her helmet on the bike seat and leaned it against the side of the building, and walked with socked feet to the counter, where she ordered her regular coffee, a *grande*. She quickly grabbed the sole unoccupied outdoor table.

Within seconds, the effervescent Hattie arrived in her jet-black car. Hattie stood out in her orange high-top Keds. She had on red shorts and an orange sweatshirt over a barely visible, white T-shirt. She wore her usual broad smile.

"So, we finally drove the two knuckleheads away and instantly raised the average IQ a hundred points!" Hattie said, hugging Gee.

"Woman power, baby," said Gee. "That's funny … driving folks away…. I've been obsessing on that issue."

"As in, how did I drive *poor* Ed away?"

"Something like that," Gee said.

"Why didn't you warn me? I'd have brought some vodka to kill the pain. The question is a fruitless question, hon. From my experience, a postmortem analysis is, at best, a guess. It's not like we can reconstruct who caused the accident by looking at the bent fenders. Even if we had lover boy here to question him, and even if he tried to be totally honest, I doubt he knows. So how are we going to know the unknowable?"

"How do I stop my mind from racing around these questions?"

"A physical object can only be at one place at one time. And the mind can only think about one thing at a time. Move on and enjoy life. It's impossible to be miserable when you're enjoying life. But what can you learn from the experience? Now that's a different question. Pay attention to the little actions, the dialogue, the tone, and the body language from everybody as if your sanity and happiness depended on it. Turns out it does. Want to hear a story of the White Prince Charming who took his flies and flew?" Hattie asked.

"I'm all ears," Gee said.

Hattie told of living off-campus during her sophomore year at Howard University in a large, old, wood-framed group house with five other students: one other girl and four boys. Within two weeks, she found herself head-over-heels somewhere between love and lust with "the very white" Donnie Krebbs, surfer boy, replete with curly blond hair, blue eyes, and strong, lean body.

"Donnie Krebbs was the first boy I ever made love to. He swallowed me up," she said.

"Damn."

Hattie described how she loved to listen to him talk, this southern boy from Gulfport, Mississippi. He seemed to paint pictures with his words. She noticed other kids in the house and on campus didn't seem to take this shy young white man too seriously, which seemed perfectly fine with him. When she asked him why he attended a predominantly black school, he just said, "Why not?" She liked that.

He had no clear sense of his future, and it really didn't seem to bother him. It did, however, bother her mother greatly—that and his skin color, which actually made him more attractive to Hattie.

"We dated, well, virtually lived together for two years. I thought things were going great. I was in love. One day was never like the next with Donnie. He always had some new thought, some tweak on how he saw the world, some new idea that seemed to sway him. I can only say that the word 'bored' never entered my thinking. He was a joy to be with—and, oh, was he good in bed!" Hattie said.

"Damn. What happened?"

"One day, about a week from the end of the school year, our second year of virtually living together, I came back to our room and noticed his bags were packed, a large duffle bag and a backpack. Because he had high grades—he majored in environmental sciences—he had no exams, just a paper to finish within a week. I asked him why he was packed already. I had expected that we would travel together over the summer, like we'd talked about. He said that he was heading for Chile and then Australia. He wanted to get into fly-fishing. He said he'd finish his final year of college some other time. I asked him, 'What about us?' What did he want? He just said something like he wanted nothing, really. He said that he was crazy about me but that whatever was inside of him that was pushing him toward fly-fishing—whatever it was—called him, and he had to answer the call. I said something like, 'And that's it for us?'" Hattie said.

"Oh my," Gee said.

"He said, 'Yes, I suppose, and I'm grateful for our two wonderful years together.' I think he said grateful," she said.

"Grateful?"

"Grateful. He kissed me on the forehead, turned, grabbed his bags, and left. I was devastated for months. By the end of the summer I realized that people change. He was the same Donnie—but he wasn't. Donnie had changed in subtle ways. I'd just chosen not to talk to him about the ways he was morphing into a new iteration of Donnie. I was infatuated with the old Donnie. But drip by drip, a little at a time, I realized that what he really loved and cared about, the environment, was becoming a new passion within him. I just hadn't paid attention. I was still hooked on the old Donnie. So he moved on. I moved on. For months, I couldn't get him out of my mind. So, I compartmentalized him: he became part of a fantasy ritual, if you get my drift. I still miss him, but that was then," she said.

"Wow," Gee said. "I think I was really on cruise control with Ed, too."

"Heraclitus said change happens so rapidly that we never step in the same river twice."

"I get philosophy *and* a dollop of wisdom today? Did you ever hear from him again?" Gee said.

"Hear, no. I did get one postcard from Brazil. It said nothing personal, except 'take care' or something. And, I did see him referenced in a fishing magazine at my father's house—something about his being a public relations fishing guide with Patagonia. Things just change. None of us is really the same person for very long. Same body—just altered values. And those altered values seep into our attitudes. That's why I keep such a sharp eye on the cleaning ladies at work.... I look for little changes that change everything ... like unpaid electric bills that lead to disconnected lights that lead to evictions and so on. Nothing stays the same," Hattie said.

Gee nodded slowly. She thanked Hattie, hugged her, and left the table in deep thought. It was an aha moment. She realized that her obsession with reconstructing what happened with Ed through an endless cycle of questions produced no real answers; rather, her answers were simply a series of second-guesses that neither appeased her, comforted her, nor brought peace.

Hattie's words "nothing stays the same" jolted her, as if a rubber dart had landed squarely on her forehead. Starting then, on her way home from Starbucks, Gee Brooks became interested in the unglamorous hard work of living in the moment. She was determined to let her feelings—as she was experiencing them, in the moment—lead the way to the future. If the past became clearer, that would be good, too. No more guessing, she thought. "What the hell," she said aloud to herself, "By the time I understand what happened with Ed, I'll be a different person anyway."

She hopped on her road bike as if she were mounting a horse. Reaching a steadying speed, she lifted her head toward the blue sky and screamed, "I'm alive! I'm alive!" causing several heads to turn in her direction.

As she rode down Wisconsin Avenue toward her condo, she couldn't help but ask herself one more useless question, *how did I get into this mess? Well, so much for living in the moment,* she laughed to herself. This time, though, she didn't fiddle with an answer.

10

MIDTERMS ARE IN

Gee Brooks

The start of a therapy session is so weird, Gee thought, as she rushed into the waiting area, seconds before Dr. Weinman opened his office door and summoned her in with a smile. *What will we talk about today?* Sometimes that decision was easy—a crisis was at hand. Other times, topics just seemed to emerge, unplanned, unscripted. She grabbed a quick cup of cold water, trying to cool down from the run to his office from her home, a distance of about four miles.

"Whew! I thought I was late. I think my watch stopped," she said.

She brought him up to speed on her recent move into her condo. In previous sessions, they had spent time reviewing her autobiography. That review was now completed. Today, she reported that she no longer cried out of the blue.

"The symptoms of the depression reaction are dissipating, aren't they?" said Dr. Weinman toward the end of the day's session. "Well, then, I have an interim report card for you. You know, like midterms," he laughed.

"Have I've failed?" she said, only half kidding.

"Interesting. Why would you assume that?" he asked.

"Well, I just ..."

A long silence followed.

"When did time stop?" he asked.

"When did time stop?" she repeated.

Silence.

"When Ed said on a camping trip in the Blue Ridge Mountains after we had been married for about a year—at sunrise, for God's sake—that he thought it was best that we saved up money, a large nest-egg, like his parents and older brother had done. Then, we could *consider* having kids. He was just buying time. I went along with that plan. Good ole Gee. Time stopped then for me. Something began to die very slowly

in me—the idea of nurturing my own little girl, combing her hair ..."
She paused, looking down at her lap.

"I've been on probation," she said. "You know, a dutiful wife, making the house a warm place, being there for him. I've swallowed my pride at times at work, taking shit from jerks, so his master plan would work. I've sort of tiptoed around his plans, his needs. In the meantime, he disappeared into cell phones, e-mail, deals, accounts, business dinners, and travel. Whatever he needed, I was there, saluting his plans."

"You might think about when else time has stopped for you," Dr. Weinman said.

"And my report card?"

"I thought you'd never ask. In our first few sessions you had a high response rate for despair, depression, and hopelessness. Since then, anger and curiosity have been your companions. I'd say you're on the way to understanding the changes you're in the midst of. Do you feel in accord with my view?" he asked.

"I do."

"I'd be curious, then, why your initial reaction was that you're failing. Our time's up," he concluded.

⁓

A week later, Gee dawdled with small talk.

"And, boys and girls, the pregnant question left in the air?" asked Dr. Weinman.

"I wish I was pregnant ...? Oh, the question about why I thought I was failing my midterms, as you called it. I think sometimes that I've disappointed my mother. That's a large mouse in the snake that I've been unable to talk about," she said.

"Have I got it right—you've disappointed your *dead mother*?"

"Yes."

"Unable or unwilling to talk about your mother, Madame Snake?"
He got no response to the question.

"What kind of snake are you?" he asked.

"A green garden snake."

"Harmless and cute, right?"

She smiled, clasped her hands together, and looked down at her lap.

"'Unable or unwilling?' the good doctor repeated," he said.

"Unwilling. It's been too painful."

"If it's been too painful to talk about, then you've done something else with the pain. Perhaps you've developed methods to cope physically, emotionally, spiritually. Let's get to work, Gee. Time and happiness are being pissed away," he said.

She was silent for a moment.

"Oh well, here goes. Mom—Anne—was a gifted woman. She was a well-known artist—she painted exclusively in water colors. She and Dad, I'm told, were married right out of college—like Ed and I were. They are … were … a warm, loving couple. I remember her always holding his hand, kissing and stuff. Oh, and sending flowers to each other. She laughed a lot. She had this big laugh. It was as if they were having a contest to see who could be the funniest," she said.

Gee said she always felt her mom loved her and enjoyed caring for her. She was eleven years old when she was cut trying out for a boy's baseball team, because, the male coach told her mother, her legs weren't strong enough, which, of course, she reported to Dr. Weinman in a cocky tone, was a crock.

"The rejection broke my heart. I was embarrassed. I remember crying in Mom's arms, leaving the ball field in disgrace. Some of the boys were laughing at me. The two of us just sat there in the parked car, staring at the field, and my mother came up with a plan. She said that the two of us would run every day until I could run three miles without stopping. That distance would be much farther than the boys on the team were expected to run. Within three weeks, I was up to three miles a day, without stopping once and without major discomfort," she said.

"Stage Two of the plan was a confrontation between Mom and the coach. This part embarrassed me, but Mom insisted. The team was to play at two o'clock on a Saturday. The coach required players to show up thirty minutes before the game to warm up. At exactly 1:25 PM, Mom, with me partially hiding behind her, confronted the coach."

"Her tone was like ice—'I'm Anne Burns. This is my daughter, Gee. You remember us. You cut her from the team three weeks ago because you *said* her legs weren't strong enough. Now you and I know that's crap, don't we?'"

"Sounds like Mom knew how to be pretty direct," Dr. Weinman said.

Gee continued her story. She remembered shaking all over. Before the coach said anything, her mom held up the palm of her hand—as in, "talk to the hand."

"'Now you watch this,' Mom said. She turned to me and said, 'Go, honey.' On cue, I ran around the field for thirty minutes, about three miles. We walked back to the coach, and the one-way conversation continued. 'Now you either have your boys go farther than Gee after the game to make your point that her legs are too weak, or you and I will be in the office of the league commissioner Monday morning,' Mom said, with her arms folded. I remember him motioning for her to join him, away from the boys and from me. She told me later that he said something like, 'Maybe I was wrong. I did it because I thought the boys would be cruel to her and I didn't want to deal with all that. How would it help for her to be miserable on a team that didn't want her?' She responded, 'That's her problem. She's a big girl.' I actually heard Mom say that. He went to the dugout and said something I couldn't hear. I remember several boys turning toward me and frowning. I didn't care. The issue was resolved, and we left," Gee said.

Gee went silent again for several moments.

"So, you played with the enemy, the boys, right?" he asked.

"I wish," she said.

She spoke about the ride home, when her mother first experienced a piercing pain in her head. Once home, the pain intensified. Gee's father rushed her mother to the hospital. He told her he thought it was allergies or a migraine. After days of tests, a conclusive diagnosis was made: she had secondary brain cancer.

"Our family life, as I knew it, collapsed. Doctors, chemotherapy technicians, pharmacists, pills, home nursing aids, visiting friends, were our lives now—the world of illness. I didn't know what was going on. I felt angry, hurt, and alone."

She started to cry.

"My parents tried to act like nothing was wrong—like this crazy event would go away, and we'd go back to normal. But it was getting harder to remember what normal was. We were into this thing for about a year—this pattern of treatment, hospital stays, the end of treatment, and hope again. And then, another episode, another cell group popped up. I remember hiding in my room after the news of the new cells," she said.

"It came to me right then: my job was to just help her. I begged for God to heal her. I could sense that they weren't telling me everything. But I focused on how I could help her. Shit, to see her smile made my day. I slept with her blue nightgown wrapped around me. I called it Bluey. Then she entered a hospice care center. At age twelve, I thought the word hospice meant 'small hospital,'" she said.

"It didn't, did it?" he said.

The pace of the story was slowing. Her words were labored. She took deep breaths. Tears flowed down her face.

"Keep in mind, the rest of the story I only remember images, some vivid, some fuzzy, like her gray hospital room and the white square tiles in the ceiling with little snake-like imprints in them. But most of the memories are more like tones in my head and looks on her face or feelings," she said. "Dad told me to go into her room. He sat quietly in the corner. I was to pretend, he said, that he wasn't there. He wrote down the words she said to me. I don't remember them from her," she said

"Why would your dad feel the need to memorialize such painful words?" asked Dr. Weinman.

"Oh, he made a copy of everything she said that day for me. I have it at home. I've memorized every word. I used to say them over and over, before I could go to sleep," she said.

"Interesting, isn't it, Gee, memorialized words from a dying woman to a child? For what purpose?" he asked. "Please, go on. Now what did your father do?"

"He stayed in the room. I guess he was afraid she'd die in front of me. When I walked in the room, she looked asleep. She seemed so pale, so old. I couldn't help but look at all of the tubes and machines she was hooked up to. I almost threw up, but bit my lip. I started to cry.... I couldn't help it. She woke up and smiled at me and started humming a tune I remember from when I was a little girl—you know, the kind

117

mothers make up for their babies. Dad wrote that she said, 'My little darling.'"

Tears rolled down Gee's face like out of an open spigot.

"According to Dad's notes, Mom said, 'You make me happy, sunshine. From the moment I saw your fuzzy blond hair and held you in my arms for the first time, I've been happy and always, always very proud of you. Proud you were *my* daughter. My little darling, my time is up. I know you'll be OK, won't you? I'm going to be waiting for you and Dad on the other side. I'll be there for you again. I'll see my little darling again, but not just anymore now. I want you to promise to use your life to take care of yourself, your father, and other people. Promise me that, my little darling.' I remember hugging her and crying. After a few minutes, Mom fell asleep," she said.

"You *did* memorize the words...." he said.

She described how her father took her home and a few days later, he came home from the hospice, sat her in his lap on the couch, and said Mom had died in her sleep.

"We cried together for a long, long time. I've always wanted to please my mom. Sounds stupid, please someone who's not here," she said.

"No wonder you work for the courts!" he said.

"What?" she said.

"What do you think I mean?" he asked.

"Like she or, rather, the recorded words were a sentence, like judges sentence defendants to prison?" she said.

Dr. Weinman made an exaggerated, sweeping, two-armed, palms-up gesture, which she interpreted to mean, *who knows?*

"Our time's up," he said.

Gee made an extra appointment, the first available, which was the next day at noon.

Without saying hello, she sat in the chair and began talking.

"I've always thought my mother was judging me," she said.

"I'm sorry, that darned road construction noise outside. Did you say *was* judging you?" Dr. Weinman asked.

She started to respond but paused. "OK, *is* judging me," she said.

She noticed he looked nonplussed, which pissed her off.

He leaned forward and said, "How did you get from loving, nurturing parents, to an unfortunate, painful, untimely death, to a sentence of perpetual judgment that resulted in a failing performance on your part? Mother lives, loves daughter. Mother dies, tries to say good-bye and I love you. Daughter trapped in judgment. How does that happen?"

"By those words Dad wrote down," she blurted out in agony. "By those *fucking* words on those two pages of yellow paper.... 'To Gee' ..."

There was silence—maybe two minutes—as Gee stared into her lap, wringing her hands.

Then Gee fell into a deep, agonizing, painful sob, her head in her lap, her hands intermittently covering her eyes, then balled up, banging against her legs, stomping her feet. She thought of the hundreds of hours of agony stored up within her, the countless dreams and daydreams, the visions of her mother coming back from the dead, or the hope that Mom would send some clear signal that Gee was doing well and that she was pleased. But instead nothing for the child, or this young woman, *nothing*, ever came back from her dead mother that suggested she was a good girl or that she was doing fine or that she was OK. Nothing. And, at this moment, that realization burned into her, lodging in a spot so deep in her gut that she realized why she had been unwilling to talk about, or release it, until now in the safety of his office.

"What are you experiencing?" Dr. Weinman asked.

"I've learned to shut up with conflict, to run from it, avoid it, act like it's not affecting me, be a good girl, don't show your anger, take care of other people, forget what I need ... just be good, Gee. I'm fed up with that!" she screamed.

"The words have been a sentence, haven't they, Gee?" he asked.

After a very long time sobbing with rage, where only disconnected curse words jumped out of her, Gee, armed with a Kleenex box gently nudged toward her by Dr. Weinman, looked up at him knowing, instinctively, it was time to quit the session. A quick glance at the clock confirmed her guess. She was furious. She didn't want to leave.

To her surprise, he ignored the time and spoke.

"I don't know why we parents do what we do, why we do stupid things. It's part of the mystery of parenting and life. One day you may also be a parent and ask yourself a thousand times why you did this, why you said that, why you blamed your kids for your own inadequacies. I would suppose that the last thing Anne Burns would have wanted was to place some collar around your neck, some choker, a choker-collar that even slightly suggested that you were doing anything wrong by being who you are, by feeling what you feel. Anne Burns would never do that, would she, Gee?" he asked.

Gee could not talk but shook her head side-to-side in agreement.

"Give some thought to why your father chose to write down every detail and what the results have been. I'll see you next time," he said, standing.

She grabbed two more tissues from the box.

"Two for the road, bartender," she said, smiling through tears.

She started to leave but turned and stood in front of him.

"Thank you," she said and hugged him. He received the hug and held her.

"Anne," he said, looking skyward, "What's not to love?"

"Thank you," she said.

Gee turned and walked out the door.

~

Gee started the next session by saying, "You look upset. Are you OK?"

"Do you always focus on other people's feelings?" Dr. Weinman asked.

"No," she said, "I was just wondering—"

"You pay me to think, I'll do that. You focus on your feelings," he said.

"OK. I don't know why my father wrote down every word. I'll ask him. It was a year until he even removed her clothes from the closet or emptied her dresser. Even then, it was my aunt, his sister, who did that nasty deed while he was playing golf. When he came home and saw what had been done, he was furious, beside himself. He was screaming and yelling. After my aunt left town that day, I came home from doing something and it was the first and only time I've ever seen him drunk. It scared me. I left the house and went to a friend's house for two days."

She told the story of returning home that Sunday evening and hearing him hammering in the living room. She looked around the foyer, kitchen, and hallways. Everything had changed. There were now thirty, forty, fifty pictures of Anne and the family, some hung poorly, some framed sloppily, some beautiful and touching. The couple had made a habit of always having an expensive camera available, and these were the offspring of their desire to capture the little moments of their love … Anne and Thomas … and Gee.

"The place is an art museum," she said.

"What was the effect of this act, of creating a museum of photographs?" Dr. Weinman asked.

"Well, when I was a teenager, I stayed in my room a lot or went over to friends' houses. As an adult, I've avoided going over there. I prefer his coming to my house—my condo now," she said.

"Avoid the conflict? How does he spend his time?"

"He plays golf, we go to dinner about once every week or so, he watches football and sports on TV, reads, plays poker with men friends, and, oh yeah, every Tuesday night he plays couples bridge with a woman who was a friend of my mother's—they used to play as a foursome before Mom died. Then, some time after Mom died, her friend's husband died, and the two paired up. I think they go to the movies, too, every Saturday night. And I hear about sightseeing every now and then. I just don't ask him about that part of his life," she said.

"I'm confused. I thought you're close to your father," he said.

"I am," she said.

"Are they intimate?" he said.

"What?"

"Oh, there's a young child here today who doesn't understand the adult world. Does the woman play with your father's Twinkie?" he said.

She felt like calling him a smart-ass. "I'm sure that—"

"Sure? Have you asked the obvious question? Or have you avoided that, too?"

"No, I haven't asked," she said.

"Because …?" he asked.

"Well, good question. My first impulse is to act like a little child and say, 'because that would be cheating on Mom.' Now, isn't that stupid!" she said.

"So, who knows what's going on? Does the woman have a name, or is her name Mom's Friend?" he asked.

"Linda."

"Well, if they're *just* friends, how come Thomas, Linda, and Gee are in solitary confinement, in separate prison cells, unable to talk to each other? Sorry for the prison metaphor," he said, smiling.

"Good question," she said.

"And one you've been unable to ask, because you're a good little daughter, right, Gee?" he said.

"Hey, fuck you!"

"You're the one who's been screwed out of an appreciation of yourself."

"Message received. Sorry for the nasty—"

"No offense taken. What nips your curiosity?"

She started to answer.

"Sorry, Gee, that was a rhetorical question intended to suggest a topic worthy of exploration on your part. Our time's up," he said.

She stood and started to leave, but turned to him and gave him a hug.

"God, you irritate me. I love you. Bill me overtime for the hug," she said.

11

THE WOMEN'S GROUP

Gee Brooks

Offenders are required to meet with their probation officers at least once a month, typically in the officer's courthouse office or sometimes in the community, at the offender's home, or at their workplace. Gee noticed that some of the female offenders seemed to like to talk to other women offenders in the office waiting room. They stopped talking when she appeared.

"Hattie, have you ever considered working with those women in a group setting?" Gee asked in Hattie's office.

"No, but it's an interesting idea. Just be sure you don't lend them money or get caught up enabling their anti-social behavior. Some of these women are very streetwise hustlers," she said.

Gee laughed, "Why thank you, Mom."

Realizing that all new initiatives required the prior approval of Deputy Chief Kingmaker, Gee wrote Kingmaker a memo seeking approval to hold weekly women's groups for the purpose of helping women find common interests and bonds, to find child-rearing support and counsel, to move from welfare to work, and to gain support for family problems and challenges.

One week later, Kingmaker responded, by memo, that Gee could not hold group sessions, because the term "group" implied therapy, and Gee didn't have an advanced counseling degree, or an MSW.

Gee responded, with a copy to Chief Probation Officer Kasten, that in view of the agency's mission statement—"to find all suitable means to bring about the rehabilitation of persons on supervision"—it was her intent to begin two-hour Women in Dialogue discussion sessions every Thursday night at the Rockville Civic Center. Staff were invited to attend, if space was available. Gee knew that this little caution, "if space was available," meant that not one officer would attend.

After a unit meeting, supervisor Chip Faulknour took Gee aside in a small conference room and told her that Kingmaker was on the warpath.

"Gee, she told me that she has her eye on you. Please realize that I have no choice but to follow her orders," he said.

"Since when did helping women offenders make it out there constitute poor probation work?" she asked.

"I'm just saying," he threw up his hands, turned, and left the room.

Gee knew Kingmaker disliked her, which made her more determined to do what she felt was right. Gee was beginning to lose the desire to be a nice little girl. That approach, she accepted, neither worked with Ed nor with her dead mother.

The first night of the discussion session was to begin at seven o'clock, in a small meeting room at the civic center. There were no rugs, only a grayish tile floor. One window with blinds looked out onto a wooded area. The walls were white with pictures of men who looked like civic center founding fathers. Gee set up ten metal folding chairs in a relatively tight circle. Then she sat and waited. She stared at the clock: 7:05 ... 7:09 ... 7:13 ... 7:22 ... 7:29. She fiddled, waiting for someone to show up. Two women offenders arrived together at 7:35. They apologized for being late; they apparently had childcare issues. The three women, counting Gee, talked about children, crime in the streets, broken school systems, and unfair school administrators until nine o'clock. They agreed to meet again the next Thursday night.

Gee and the two women met for three more weeks. The discussions went deeper, into relationships with men and hip-hop's influence. By the fifth week, a total of eight women offenders showed up, including the original two. Five of the women were black, two Hispanic, and one white. The group included one former armed bank robber, now a very stable women in her late fifties; three women who were convicted of drug use; one transporter of drugs; a black three-time-convicted shoplifter; one woman convicted of bank fraud; and a foxy, white prostitute. They spoke primarily of how society's rules are stacked against women.

At the next meeting, this same core group showed up, but a new person arrived—an obvious transvestite, dressed in a skintight dress with high stacked heels and a bright red wig, as if he was going to a disco. Gee wondered how to handle the situation; she said nothing at first, waiting for the group's reaction, but there was none. The person introduced himself as Tyronia and said that he was referred to the sessions by Ms. Kingbuster after his sentencing to probation for prostitution.

"Kingbuster? Do you mean Kingmaker?" Gee asked.

"Whatever floats your boat," Tyronia said.

After a particularly exaggerated and awkward, "*Oh, my God!*" from Tyronia, which made it clear that Tyronia was more interested in pretending to be a woman than engaging in dialogue, Viv Watson, the shoplifter, who had emerged as a woman who talked freely about how difficult it was to raise two children by herself and was clearly a positive influence on the others, walked outside with the new guest during a break. Tyronia did not return.

A conversation started, but Gee interrupted.

"What happened to Tyronia?" she asked.

"I told him I was going to dump his makeup in the toilet if he didn't find his own group," Viv said.

"What'd he say?" asked the bank robber.

"He called me a hussy and left," Viv said. Gee thought to herself, *The Kingmaker's referral of Tyronia to disrupt the group had failed.*

After the laughter died down, Gee felt the need to develop ground rules: everyone was entitled to finish their thoughts; no one person should dominate the group; Viv would get two teenage girls, neighbors of hers, to babysit any little children in a play area in the Civic Center while the women met—everyone who used them had to share the bill; carpools, if possible, were desirable; everyone would only use their first names; and what was said in the group was confidential.

"I won't come back if two ladies present tonight continue to be high at our sessions," the bank robber said.

"I didn't think we needed to be high to be comfortable here," Gee said.

She got no response.

The sessions now had a core group, with varying degrees of regular attendance and participation. A few other women seemed to come and go.

It was a fascinating experience for Gee. She felt in league with these women of character and spirit, whose vision of the future always had a tinge of defeatism. No one, they reasoned, ever really made it out of the trap of poverty and misery, unless they hit the lottery, and none of them knew anyone who had hit the lottery for big money. As best they could, they were strong. Their families and relatives depended on them to deliver the impossible, though they never measured up.

There was never a session where Gee didn't learn something new about herself. She shared with the ladies that she, too, had believed that somehow conflict and anger would go away if she was good enough to others. In the midst of the challenges these women faced every day, Gee's old standard, the magic of avoidance, became, well, laughable to her now. The ladies made a pact to lean into conflict as best they could and have faith that they'd make it through. Baby steps, they coached each other, baby steps.

While she might have guessed offenders were angry at the system, she never imagined how rational and reasonable their complaints were. She was beginning to feel that the more she remained quiet, the more she owned the outrageous pain inflicted on these women and their children. The more she heard their stories, the angrier Gee became toward the probation and parole system.

~

The group no longer focused on what was going on *out there*, with the schools, courts, or the police. Now, more comfortable with each other, the women's favorite topic was family relationships. Gee understood the pain and loneliness shared in their stories. Viv Watson, now a group centerpiece, particularly told stories that touched her. She was Gee's favorite. Some less confident women were energized by Viv; she helped them dream, Gee thought. Her role shifted to more of a facilitator then a group leader.

Tonight, Viv spoke of trying to care for her own two young sons, ages five and six, plus for her two nephews, who were thirteen and fourteen. She cried as she spoke of the conflict between loving their mother, her sister, who was on crack and out of sight, and trying to care for the boys, who, she was certain, were entering the drug scene. She wanted to care for them, guide them, but they wouldn't allow it. Her sister could be dead, for all Viv knew. She said she was tired—

physically and emotionally. The group cried with her, including Gee, who understood the feeling of being overwhelmed.

Viv said she had just started her second job; she already worked in a school cafeteria from 7:00 AM to 3:00 PM, and now she had started cleaning offices from 7:00 PM to 10:00 PM. She had requested a night off to attend these sessions. She said she was grateful to have people to talk to. The ladies offered her suggestions and sources of help in finding her sister, without getting her arrested, and ideas on ways to get the school counselors to help her nephews before it was too late.

"Be strong, baby, be strong," said the bank robber.

The Monday morning following Viv's story, Supervisor Faulknour stood in the doorway of Gee's office at nine o'clock and informed her that Viv Watson had been arrested on Saturday for aiding and abetting minors in the act of a felony crime and shoplifting—her fourth arrest for shoplifting.

Gee said, "I know this woman, and this makes no sense. Trust me, Chip, trust me on this one."

"You know, I'm going to have to report this to Ms. Kingmaker, since she warned you not to hold these groups," he said.

"You do whatever you need to do, Chip," she said.

In view of the arrest, Gee was required to write a revocation report within twenty-four hours and give it to Faulknour, listing the arrest, any other conduct issues, compliance or non-compliance with general and special conditions of the court, and a recommendation for action. The supervisor then, by policy, reviewed the report and checked off on a form whether they agreed with the officer's recommendation, or, instead, recommended another course of action. If there was a difference in the two recommendations, then, again by policy, the arbitrator was Deputy Chief Kingmaker, who had written this policy.

At their next Thursday session, Viv, now out on bail, was animated. It was a riveting, passionate session. It was new emotional territory for the women, now more trusting of each other and in full crisis mode. Viv told her women supporters, to whom she was closer than her own family, that she took her nephews to Target to get them some clothes. She noticed the nephews disappeared, and she became anxious and scared. She waited in the checkout line with her two wiggly boys, hurried the clerk up, and rushed toward the exit. There were two internal security officers wrestling with the older boy, while another security officer had the younger boy in a choke hold on the ground. Viv said she screamed and lashed out at the second officer so he would release her younger nephew. The Montgomery County Police arrived during the fray and confirmed that each boy had hidden electronic gadgets and video games in his clothes. Plus, the older boy was found to have a joint on him. The boys were arrested and sent to a juvenile detention facility for processing. Viv was arrested as the mastermind, the one who orchestrated the action. A female officer took her crying boys to a neighbor's house. She spent the night in the Montgomery County Detention Center and was released Sunday morning in a bail reduction hearing. Olivia Lopez was her assigned public defender.

Gee's mandatory report to the court through supervisor Faulknour referenced the arrest. She added a lengthy explanation offered by Viv Watson. She also stated that Viv had not paid a $50 fine and had not reported to the office on two occasions—but that both missed appointments were very early in the supervision process, almost a year ago. Gee recommended that no revocation hearing be held, because it was her view that the charges would be dropped or Viv would not be found guilty. If she were found guilty, Gee argued, the issue could be revisited.

Without informing Gee, Deputy Kingmaker ordered Supervisor Faulknour to override Gee's recommendation. Kingmaker stood over Faulknour's shoulder and watched him check off a box that indicated the supervisor did not agree with the officer's recommendation.

Typically, a summons letter would be used to get Viv into court for a revocation hearing, because she was not a violent person and had no history of failing to show up for court hearings. However, Kingmaker ordered Faulknour to check a box that indicated an arrest warrant was necessary for the safety of law enforcement officers and the community, and the only way Viv Watson would appear in court.

The court agreed with Management's assessment, rather than Gee's, and an arrest warrant was issued and a revocation hearing ordered, upon her arrest and detention. The sheriff's office was advised directly by a secret Kingmaker phone call that Viv Watson would be at the Rockville Civic Center on Thursday evening at 7:30. They could arrest her there.

"Now let's see if I get her attention. And you, sir, will keep *your* mouth shut about the warrant," Kingmaker said to Chip.

Gee was anxious about how Kingmaker had handled her recommendation for Viv. It felt odd that she'd received no direct response. *Maybe*, Gee thought, *Kingmaker took her time notifying the officers when she agreed with them* not *to hold a revocation hearing.* Gee felt very unsettled that she couldn't give Viv, or the ladies, a straight answer as to what to expect.

The women's session started on time, as it had for the past two months. Viv arrived with her two boys, who stayed with the teenage babysitter, as did four other kids. The women's bond was undeniable—they were invested in the process and in each other. Gee noticed that their dress and appearance seemed to be sharper each week. Viv reported to the others that she had a trial set for one month from today, which Gee already knew. They spoke tonight about men who had dominated them, yet who had abandoned them when they were in pain. It was a riveting discussion. But the discussion also left an elephant in the room.

"Gee, with regard to Viv, what will the judges do about her probation?" asked the criminal justice veteran, the armed bank robber.

"I hope they'll wait to see what happens in the shoplifting and aiding and abetting trial," Gee said.

The bank robber bore in, "What will you do, Gee, if they don't?"

"I'll tell the truth, as I know it!" Gee said.

The group cheered.

At nine o'clock, the session ended, and everyone gave Viv a hug. Individuals expressed encouragement for her to be strong. One woman warned her not to take the nephews back when they were released from detention.

"But they're my blood!" she said, crying.

"Be careful, Viv, be careful, whatever you do," Gee said, having the last word.

As the ladies left together, Gee stayed behind to put the folding chairs back on a rack. When she left the room she heard a scuffling sound in the parking lot.

Three sheriff's cars, lights blinking, had formed a semi-circle. Viv was on the ground with a heavy female sheriff's deputy's knee on her back, her hands locked in handcuffs behind her back. Her face was in gravel and dirt. Small spots of blood were below her right eye, near her mouth, and in her hair.

Viv's two sons cried aloud, nearby. The older boy screamed, "Momma, Momma! Leave my Momma alone!"

"What are you doing?" shouted Gee.

"Lady, unless you want to be next, you'd better shut your pie hole," warned a male, Hispanic deputy, standing Gee down.

Gee looked at the departing ladies in disbelief. They had gathered up Viv's two sons.

"We know you had nothing to do with this. It's the system!" shouted the prostitute. They moved away quickly.

Gee got in her car, grasped the steering wheel, and, realizing who was responsible for this, shouted, "You bitch!"

~

Two days later, Gee received a call from her Civic Center liaison. "I'm sorry, Ms. Brooks, but we'd prefer that you hold your meetings elsewhere," the lady said.

"I'm sorry. I knew nothing about this," Gee said, hanging up the phone.

~

"Are you surprised by the affront, Gee? Did you really think this woman, Kingmaker, who you describe as a control freak, would accept your citing the mission statement to her boss kindly?" asked Dr. Weinman.

"I didn't think she'd target an offender to get back at me," she said.

"I'm confused. For months you've talked about how you and your friends—hold on, I have their names written down here in my notes—Huggie, Hattie, and Pepe, have talked about the injustice of your system at Starbucks, case after case. You felt you're surrounded

130

by colleagues who try to catch people doing things wrong, so they can send them to prison to enhance their careers. Wasn't it you who said the judges are blind to all this? Help me understand. How does this act surprise you?" Dr. Weinman asked.

"Because it's personal," she said.

"Did you see *The Godfather*? Remember when Salvatore Tessio said to Michael's henchmen, when he knew he was going to be whacked, 'Tell Michael it was business—it wasn't personal'? This is the business of your deputy chief's career. Salvatore was wrong.... It's very personal to her. *Very* personal. Be careful." he said.

In a preliminary discovery hearing before Viv Watson's trial, where the prosecutor was required to reveal the nature of the evidence to the defense, the prosecutor said that the security officers' report stated they had no direct knowledge or evidence from their video cameras that Viv orchestrated the conduct of her nephews. Since the two teenagers also said they acted alone, as did Viv Watson, all charges were dropped by the state. Viv was a free woman again.

However, at Kingmaker's insistence, the revocation hearing was scheduled on technical grounds. The basis of the charges—with which Gee was required to proceed—were:

1. An arrest for Aiding and Abetting Minors in the Act of a Crime and Shoplifting.
2. Failure to pay a court ordered fine of $50.
3. Failure to report as instructed on two occasions to the probation officer.

Gee was now in the position of walking a thin line between supporting her values and defending her revocation report, albeit technically overridden on court papers by Chip.

The courtroom appeared far too spacious for the small gathering. There was a court stenographer and a courtroom clerk below the judge's level, two deputy sheriffs hanging around for security, and the bailiff whose tasks seemed limited to holding a Bible for witnesses to swear on and pointing them in and out of the witness box. The jury box was empty. The judge would hand down the final ruling on this revocation matter, since they were *his* terms of probation that Viv Watson was accused of violating. Down below, even below the courtroom clerk and stenographer, at the floor level, sat the assistant state's attorney, and, at another table, Assistant Public Defender Olivia Lopez and Viv.

The oak-paneled walls and giant American and Maryland state flags gave the room a sense of formality. The only people who stood to have their lives directly altered by this hearing were Viv Watson, her two children, and her two nephews, whom she fed and housed—*they* would pay the ultimate fare. The taxpayers, albeit indirectly, had a financial stake. The hearing was also a point of no return for Gee— stuck squarely between the Women in Dialogue and Kingmaker—and, to a lesser degree, Chip Faulknour.

"Good morning. All right, Mr. Prosecutor, state the reason for this hearing, and then call your witnesses," said Judge Clarke.

The demeanor of the assigned prosecutor, an assistant who the state's attorney did not know well, was, Gee thought, one of impatience and indifference—almost as if he had more important things to do with his time.

He argued that although all criminal charges related to the Target arrest had been dropped, he had spoken directly with Target's security officer Robert Haynes, and Haynes was satisfied that Ms. Watson, who had three previous convictions for shoplifting, orchestrated the acts of the young boys.

"Moreover, Ms. Watson had willfully ignored the court's order to pay a fine of $50 and had missed scheduled appointments with her assigned probation officer. It appears obvious that because Ms. Watson, no stranger to this court, is employed full-time, there is no excuse for her not paying the fine," he said. "In short, Your Honor, even a casual observer would conclude that she's been given her chance—chances, I should say," he concluded.

"I presume you're calling on security officer Haynes to testify as to what he observed?" asked the judge.

"Actually, he is unable to come today due to a family conflict," said the prosecutor.

"Remain seated, Ms. Lopez. I understand," Judge Clarke said, waving her hand toward Ms. Lopez. "Well, then, Mr. Prosecutor, we can ignore the hearsay you just provided us."

"That's my objection, Your Honor," said Assistant Public Defender Lopez.

"Who would you like to have testify, Mr. Prosecutor?"

"The prosecution calls probation officer Gee Brooks to the stand."

As Gee approached the bench, out of the corner of her eye she noticed four of the women's group members and, right behind them, Kingmaker and Faulknour. Her stomach tightened. Her Thursday night colleagues believed they knew the truth about Viv. These women, Gee thought, were very hard to fool and unlikely to take time to come to court to support a liar. As she neared the witness box, her mind locked on the simple idea that she should be herself … and let the chips fall where they may.

"State your name for the record," said the prosecutor.

"Virginia Brooks."

"Are you the assigned probation officer?"

"Yes, I am." she said.

"And for how long?"

"About thirteen months," she said.

"And are you the author of the revocation report?" he asked.

She looked at Viv and the four group members over Viv's shoulder and said, "I'm required to file a revocation report. However—"

"Just answer my questions, Ms. Brooks. So, you determined that this woman should be revoked and sent to prison," he said. Gee noticed he glanced at The Kingmaker, who winked at him.

Olivia Lopez stood, "Objection, Your Honor. She said she was *required* to file a revocation report. Required by policy. We haven't had a question as to what she actually recommended."

"Objection sustained," said Judge Clarke.

"Did you recommend that Ms. Watson have a revocation hearing? Let's start there," said the prosecutor.

"No."

"Well then, why are we here?" he said.

"Good question, Your Honor," said Ms. Lopez, standing.

"Be seated, Ms. Lopez. What's your point, Mr. Prosecutor?" Judge Clarke asked.

"I have in my hand—for the record, this is Exhibit Number One—a revocation report," he said, handing the report to the clerk for a numbered label and a brief visual review by the judge, and then handing it to Ms. Lopez.

"Ms. Brooks, read where it shows your revocation recommended," he said, handing her her own report.

"You're reading the supervisor's approval and comment line. Above that is where I checked 'No revocation requested at this time.' I attached a memo stating my reasons," Gee said.

"Well, then why is the 'No revocation requested' box xed out with a 'Revocation requested' box checked and the initials 'RF'?" he asked, seeming confused.

"I suppose my supervisor disagreed with my recommendation and placed an X over my recommendation," Gee said.

He grabbed the paper back, studied it, and said, "Well, I guess it says 'No revocation requested,' then 'requested.' Excuse me, Your Honor. Whose initials are these?" the prosecutor asked.

"Your Honor, I can explain," said Chip Faulknour, standing with Deputy Chief Kingmaker at his side.

"And you are?" asked Judge Clarke.

"I'm Ms. Brooks's supervisor, Richard Faulknour," said Chip.

"Objection, Your Honor, are we going to have shout-outs from the audience?" said Ms. Lopez.

"Ms. Lopez, please restrain your sarcasm. I understand the protocol. If we need your testimony, Mr. Faulknour, we'll call for it. Mr. Prosecutor, can you move this along?" said Judge Clarke.

"Ms. Brooks, why would your supervisor disagree with you? Do you know this offender, or don't you?" he said.

"I know her. She has two jobs. She cares for her sister's children, the two teenage boys. Her sister has disappeared...."

"Into drugs?" asked the prosecutor.

"Objection, Your Honor. That's speculation," said Ms. Lopez.

"Sustained. Mr. Prosecutor, Ms. Watson is the subject of interest, not her sister. Proceed," said Judge Clarke.

"She impresses me as a good woman, a good person. She told me her version of the story. The boys acted alone. She feared they were being hurt, and she reacted to the security officers out of a knee-jerk sense of protection," Gee said.

"Did there come a time when she didn't report to the office as required by the rules, the conditions?" the prosecutor asked.

"Twice. But, over the thirteen months, she has reported nineteen times, when you add her attendance at weekly discussion groups," Gee said.

"Well, then, what about the unpaid fine?" he asked.

"I asked her to have it paid as soon as possible last month. She said she would. I know she has two jobs and has borne a lot of the expenses for her nephews. I trust she will pay it soon," she said.

"You trust? So, paying a fine ordered by this judge, the presiding judge today, is *not* a priority for you, Ms. Brooks?"

"Living, surviving is a priority. I trust that—"

"*Trust?* Did you *trust* that she wouldn't assault a security guard? Did you *trust* she wouldn't be arrested for a fourth shoplifting offense? With all of this *trust*, why did you ask for a warrant for her arrest, rather than summon this *trustworthy* person in here today?"

Dora Kingmaker covered her eyes with her right hand.

"I didn't request a warrant; I didn't request this hearing. Check up the form a little higher for that answer. I have faith in Viv Watson. I believe she's on her way to being a wonderful citizen," Gee said.

"Mr. Prosecutor, are there any more holes you'd like to dig?" asked the judge.

"No, Your Honor," he said, trying to find a piece of paper to shuffle around to appear organized.

"Ms. Lopez."

"Thank you, Your Honor. I'll be brief. Ms. Brooks, how many cases do you have—that is, offenders on supervision?" she asked.

"Probably seventy-five."

"Do you know them as well as you know Ms. Watson?" Ms. Lopez asked.

"No. I know Ms. Watson better, because she's been in weekly discussion sessions for the past few months, as have some other ladies here in the courtroom, and she speaks up quite openly," Gee said.

"Do you suspect that she uses illicit drugs?"

"No, I don't," Gee said.

"When she was arrested for this last creative exercise in law enforcement folly—"

"Reword that, Ms. Lopez," said the judge.

"When she was arrested for this last incident, did she test positive or negative for drugs upon her detention?"

"Negative for drugs," Gee said.

"Is she an alcohol abuser?"

"Not to my knowledge," Gee said.

"Hustler?"

"No."

"If you had to put a label on her, what would that label be?" asked Ms. Lopez.

"Objection, Your Honor, she already has a label: a three–time, convicted shoplifter," said the prosecutor.

"Objection overruled," said Judge Clarke, glaring at the prosecutor.

"She's a hardworking single mother of two, who has recently taken on a second job and has tried to care for her two nephews, who seem to have minds of their own, while their mother roams the streets. She's an honest woman," Gee said, noticing Viv staring at her hands.

"And you do this work for a living, day in, day out, correct?" asked Ms. Lopez.

"Yes, I do."

"How were you rated last year on your annual performance appraisal?" Olivia asked.

"Excellent in all categories," Gee said.

"Not again," mumbled Kingmaker to Chip. "Not anymore, Ms. Brooks."

"Your Honor, I have but one more question. Then I'll call Ms. Watson, if the court believes there is something left to discuss. Ms. Brooks, what do you recommend as an outcome today?" asked Olivia.

"I'd expect the court to give Ms. Watson an additional fine, maybe $25 more, and require that the entire amount be paid within thirty days. Then wish her continued success with a caution that she cannot save her nephews if they have chosen crime as a lifestyle—she can only love them. But she must protect herself and her own two children from further conflicts with the law," Gee said.

Judge Clarke did not miss the "yes" uttered by some of the women seated tightly together.

"Thank you, Ms. Brooks," said Ms. Lopez.

"You may step down," said the judge.

Gee walked to the front bench, rather than taking a seat at the prosecutor's table, the person who by law defends her *against* the defendant and the defense counsel. The symbolic act of not sitting beside the prosecutor was not missed by Kingmaker.

"Your Honor, I request that this hearing be concluded, and I think that Ms. Brooks has found an excellent remedy," said Ms. Lopez.

"Mr. Prosecutor?" said the judge.

"One closing comment, Your Honor. We're a nation of laws. One day Ms. Watson will understand that. We stand by our request for a revocation and seek six months in prison," he said.

"Ms. Watson is continued on probation—"

"Yahoo!" screamed the bank robber.

"Quiet in the courtroom," said the bailiff.

"—with the following revised special conditions: I order that an additional fine of $50 be imposed forthwith and that the entire fine of $100 be paid in thirty days. If not paid in full and on time, Ms. Watson, the prosecutor's recommendation will become very attractive. Let me say I'm disappointed that county funds were spent on an arrest warrant rather than a summons in this case. I'd ask Mr. Faulknour, who appeared so eager to correct the record today, to get his own shop in order. This hearing is concluded."

"All rise. This court is now adjourned," pronounced the bailiff.

Gee felt a hand tapping on her shoulder. She turned to see a stern-faced Kingmaker.

"If you can tear yourself away from the victory party, I'll see you in my office—immediately, Ms. Brooks," Kingmaker said.

To Kingmaker's left, Faulknour had an ashen appearance. He disappeared through the wooden doors into the hallway, two steps behind Kingmaker.

Viv Watson gave Olivia Lopez and then Gee a big, tearful hug. The four group members, understanding the dynamics of what they just observed, were wise enough not to approach Gee; they just gave her subtle smiles, and one gave a thumbs-up sign. Judge Clarke watched the scene, in its entirety, from her partially opened exit door.

12

COFFEE'S BREWING

Gee Brooks

With the courtroom emptying, Gee smiled at Olivia Lopez. Knowing the Public Defender was new to the job, Gee was amazed how at ease and unfazed she was with the courtroom protocols in this hearing. She seemed to know when to mock the prosecutor and get him into an exaggerated posture and when to appear serious.

Olivia grabbed Gee's arm and squeezed it. "That took a lot of courage," she said.

"Maybe. It's what's next that will take courage, or maybe not. I think I'll just be me and let it go at that," Gee said.

"You go, girl," Olivia said.

Gee turned to take the long walk to Kingmaker's office. Then, she decided to treat herself well, so, instead of rushing up to Kingmaker's office, she headed for a cup of coffee in the cafeteria on the basement floor.

Standing in the cafeteria line, she saw Jon Rhodes at a corner table, by himself, scribbling on a yellow pad. He didn't see her. She thought to herself, *Jon Rhodes* is *courage. Viv Watson* is *courage. The four ladies in court* are *courage. Dora Kingmaker is a nasty woman.* No mas, *Dora,* No mas, she said to herself.

Gee, coffee in hand, headed for the elevator and the long walk down the tiled fifth floor to Kingmaker's office.

"Please tell Dora I'm here," Gee said to the frowning secretary, who promptly got up, opened Kingmaker's door, and leaned into the office, mumbling something.

"Go on in," said the secretary, avoiding eye contact.

Kingmaker sat behind her desk. Three maroon leather chairs with brass buttons made a small semi-circle around it, with Chip Faulknour seated at one end already. Gee noted the three pictures on the wall: in the center, a state-released picture of the governor standing in front of the American and Maryland flags; over Kingmaker's left shoulder, her diploma for an M.S. in Government and Politics from George Washington University; and, on the right, a picture of Kingmaker standing alone on the Great Wall of China.

"Sit down, Ms. Brooks," ordered Kingmaker.

Gee sat as far away from Chip as possible. She made a point of taking a sip from her coffee cup. She was nervous and pissed off, but she wanted to appear unrattled.

"I've asked your supervisor to be here for a moment, and then you and I will have a little talk, privately," she said.

"Fine, although let the record reflect I've requested a neutral party in this room to observe this, what, meeting?" Gee said.

"It ain't going to happen. Mr. Faulknour, if I ever have another performance appraisal from you with excellent on it, it better be for an officer that understands who she works for! Do you understand me?" Kingmaker asked.

"Absolutely," said Chip.

"Please leave," she said.

Chip scurried out of the room without making eye contact with Gee.

"Who do you think you are?" asked Kingmaker.

"Who do you think you are, Dora?" responded Gee.

"What did you say?"

"Who do you think you are, deciding how I should do my job? I'm paid by the state, hired by this court to do the job of rehabilitating offenders—at least, that's what our mission statement says," Gee said.

"Don't give me that mission statement crap!" said Kingmaker.

"Our mission statement is just crap? Really? It doesn't mean anything? I don't think I got that memo. So, the part about 'find all suitable means'—"

"You listen to me, and you listen to me good! I'll have your job. Maybe not today, maybe not tomorrow, but make no mistake: I'll have your job. Your future here is over. You'd be smart to leave now. I run this office. I stay here late at night. I get us resources from the state, from a central office that seems to care only about what Baltimore needs. I keep the judges off our backs. I sit in meetings with the court leaders and tell them how safe we make the community. I do that. *I do that!* Your little show today undermines me and this office. I won't tolerate that," Kingmaker said.

"Oh, Dora, you were at the wrong show then. The real show was in the parking lot of the Rockville Civic Center when a fat cop had Viv's face in the gravel. You know, with blood and dirt all over her face as she was screaming and crying in terror, as were her two young boys. *That* was the *real* show. Have you no conscience?" Gee shouted.

"Next time, you'll listen to me! What difference do the Vivs make in this world? Do you think for a moment that all of her whining and moaning in your sessions is going to change the outcome for her? How long before she decides to smoke a little dope, or steal this or that in a store, or spread her legs for money? How long? Who made you the savior, Gee? Are you delusional?" Kingmaker asked.

"Now that's the first intelligent statement you've made today, Dora. I may well be delusional, but what the heck, so was my father. So was my mother. So are my women. So are my buddies. We have this crazy delusion that we can help people change. And I think I can, in spite of the insanity around us," Gee said.

"Did you just call me insane? Did you dare call me insane?"

"Nope, sorry, Dora. I said in spite of the insanity *around us.* You know, it's a complex world!"

"Your days are over, Gee. Be careful. I'm watching you," Kingmaker said, standing.

Gee got up and started for the door but stopped short. She turned to Kingmaker, who was staring down at her desk, "Why don't you just get a job in Annapolis, you know, in politics, where the stakes are just careers among willing sharks—you know, instead of trampling the little people?" Gee turned to leave.

"I'm very disappointed in you," Kingmaker said.

Gee stopped again. "Dora Kingmaker, you're not my mother," she said.

As Gee opened the door, Chief Kasten looked up from talking to the secretary.

"You'd better learn who runs this place," bellowed Kingmaker.

Hearing the shouted comment, Chief Kasten said to Gee, who had stopped in her tracks, "Oh, maybe I better learn, too."

Gee guessed he was there to read her the riot act. "Did you want to see me?"

"No, go on about your business," he said, appearing agitated. Gee took his advice and moved on quickly.

As she left, Chief Kasten walked toward Kingmaker's open doorway, and Gee heard him say, "That's good advice, Dora—remember who runs this place."

The next Friday, Dora Kingmaker called a whole staff meeting in the ceremonial courtroom of the old courthouse.

"Why'd you set this thing for Friday? I told you some time ago, in your office, that I'd be in Baltimore next Friday. You even wrote it on your calendar!" Chief Kasten said.

"My mistake. I couldn't read my own handwriting. Do you want me to cancel it?" she asked.

"No, just let me know how it goes," Chief Kasten said.

For the professional staff, attendance was mandatory unless excused by their supervisor. Today, no one was excused from this meeting.

Promptly at 8:00 AM, Deputy Chief Kingmaker stood before all of the officers. She had no notes. At her instruction, officers were herded toward seats at the front of the courtroom, thus avoiding the typical text messaging and other playful, teenage-like antics that tended to occur in the rear of the room. Supervisors were seated in the front row.

"Thank you for being on time. I'm sorry the chief couldn't be with us today. He's headed to administrative meetings in Baltimore. He and I called this meeting, because we have been disturbed lately by a trend that seems to be rearing its ugly head more frequently. It's time to get back to a basic understanding," she said.

With a long pause to try to make stern eye contact with each officer—a difficult task, because nearly all of the officers were staring at their shoes except Gee and Hattie, who were staring at Kingmaker directly—she continued.

"Why do we do what we do? Our work—serving the court and the

Parole Commission and protecting the public—is being treated by a few officers as if it's a back-burner issue. I intend to put a stop to it. So, I wanted to share with all of you what the views of this office are, what we are about, so there'll be no misunderstandings," she said.

She went on to point out that over the past three years the number of convictions for violent acts by gang members in the county had risen 75 percent, the number of violent offenses by young women had increased 22 percent, the number of positive drug urinalysis tests taken by officers was up 17 percent, the number of inmates statewide was up 41 percent, and the number of revocations based on technical reasons, without new convictions, was up 78 percent.

"Do you suppose those figures are connected? Of course they are! I have reported over the past three years that we need stronger and more effective tools to really know what's going on in offenders' lives. Do you really think that offenders are telling us the truth?" Most officers laughed. Gee, Hattie, Huggie, and Pepe did not.

"Why do you think we have such a large budget for electronic monitoring equipment? Why do you think you have more breathalyzers than other offices? Why have I argued for five years that you need firearms for your safety—and we're getting very close to getting approval on that, by the way. I've done that for you. Why have I encouraged you to recommend special conditions at sentencing so that offenders actually feel the punishments they deserve? Why have I pressed your supervisors to send all noncompliant behavior by offenders to the court, even if they don't commit new crimes? It's real simple, folks: special conditions *control* offenders' behavior. When they don't abide by them, we're notifying the court and the Parole Commission *each* and *every* time. Is there anyone in this room who thinks that just because they haven't been caught, they aren't committing crimes?" Kingmaker asked.

Again, most officers laughed.

"The judges expect us to protect the community. The judges do *not* want to see their names in the paper or on the six o'clock news for letting offenders run wild. The Parole Commission carries out the criminal justice policies of the governor. As best I can tell, he's very passionate about crime and victims. Since the people of this state elected him, I have to assume he speaks for the values of the people of Maryland—and Montgomery County," she said.

"That's our job. Those of you who can't do this job the way we want it done, we'll help you find the door!" she said. "Now, are there any questions or comments from the peanut gallery?"

Looking out over the room, she saw Gee with a raised hand.

"Ah, Ms. Brooks has a comment," she said.

"Yes, Dora, I do have a comment. I understand the theme of stopping violent behavior. I'm all for it. According to recent national data, 10 percent of folks on supervision can't make it—you know, they're so anti-social that prisons are a good place for them. Now, Dora, data also shows that about another 30 percent, mostly drug users and those with some form of mental illness, have a split review. Some make it in the community without committing new crimes; others don't. Effective treatment is the huge variable. If my math is accurate, that leaves about 60 percent who are *not* a risk to commit new crimes or otherwise harm the community. Do you suppose that it's possible to crack down *too hard* on people and cause them to fail?" Gee asked.

"No, I don't. We could debate our philosophical views—and your suspect data—for a long time. I care not to. The point is, Ms. Brooks, officers work at the pleasure of the court and at the direction of the governor, through the Parole Commission. In this county, I have just laid out our policy and views toward offenders. It *ain't* up for debate, but thanks for the comment," she said.

Again, the officers laughed.

"OK, since we're all on the same page, this meeting is over. Have a nice day, and be safe out there!" she said.

~

In spite of Kingmaker's threats, the group of eight offenders and Gee met in a room in Huggie's father's church every Thursday night for four more months, until, finally, personal circumstances changed. The group had fulfilled its purpose.

At their final meeting, they went around the room, recounting what they had been through together as a group. At Gee's suggestion, they made simple statements of appreciation for those in the group who had helped them. They cried and laughed together.

Gee thought the session was over, so she stood to give each one a hug.

"Well, I want to tell you—" she started.

"Hold on, Ms. Brooks, we're going to have the last word," said the bank robber. "And that would be Viv's job."

Everyone laughed nervously.

"Whew! Well, for a loudmouth, this is harder than I thought," said Viv. "We got you this magnolia-smelling powder, because you always smell so good," Viv said.

Gee blushed.

"I came to count on that smell, week after week. I came to count on your pretty little smile, on your kindness, on all the ladies. When things were darkest, I knew if I just held on till Thursday, I'd be OK. This group and you, Ms. Brooks, were my rock. I can only thank you by always trying not to let you down. I asked myself time and time again: if I gave up, what would the ladies think? I've even gone back to church. Well, from all of us … I can do this.…" she paused to try to compose herself. "God bless you, and we all thank you for helping us when we needed someone to believe in us," Viv said, handing Gee the store-wrapped box tied with a red ribbon.

Gee found it hard to talk at first. "Well, don't be so sure you haven't helped me more than I've helped you. I've cherished our time together. It went by so fast, but it's been so valuable to me. I count you as my sisters. I know the greatness in each of you.… You trusted me.… You let me in.… And I'm proud that you're proud of yourselves. Don't let anybody turn you around. You know where to find me," she said.

They started singing the civil rights gospel song with the "turn you around" theme. One by one, they hugged each other and laughed and cried.

On the ride home, Gee thought that there was one common thread: the women believed that the group's active, vocal presence in their lives was critical to their success. She instantly applied that lesson to her marriage: just because you have people around doesn't mean you aren't lonely.

In the month ahead, Viv's supervision ended without further issue. When Gee last had contact with Viv, she was working full-time managing the kitchen staff of a family-style restaurant, earning a relatively good salary. Her two boys were doing well in school, while her two nephews sold crack and marijuana. The bank robber was also off parole supervision, working every day and living with a partner. One of the former drug users was back in federal prison; the second drug user had married and moved to Las Vegas, with the court's permission; the third drug user had died of a heart attack; the drug transporter worked in a Hispanic congressman's office on Capitol Hill; the bank fraud woman worked in real estate; and the prostitute married her dentist, who had six children. Gee kiddingly said to Hattie that the former prostitute, with six children, had the longest, toughest sentence to serve.

13

THE ROOKIE OUTSIDER

Carrie Springer

Carrie heard about the new assistant public defender, Olivia Lopez, who had first appeared in the courthouse on a Monday in June, from an assistant prosecutor. It was clear the buzz was started in part because Ms. Lopez came directly from the law firm of Arnold & Porter, a career shift some would presume to be backward. Why would a person trade high-paying, front-page clients for those unable to pay for their defense?

Undeniably adding to the excitement, she was flat-out gorgeous. Had she been plump and disheveled, few would have cared about one more public defender. Ms. Lopez, in her early thirties, had jet-black, shoulder-length hair, complemented by blue eyes the size of nickels. While just five feet, three inches tall, she was chiseled with classical lines. It was odd, then, that given her rare beauty, one of the first things Carrie noticed about her was her body language. She defined the word "wiggle," like a three-year-old girl at a family event who knew that her father and grandfather were watching her every move with delight. She seemed to know in every cell of her body that a constant spotlight announced her presence, front and center. Matching this panache, when she spoke her sharp wit and exceptional listening skills became apparent. She played off what was said to her, putting her in complete sync with the speaker. And her reputation preceded her. Colleagues in the legal community and at her former law firm of Arnold & Porter in Washington called her "an intelligent, charming woman." Still, there was a quality, a characteristic she possessed, that warded off envy: she cared deeply about others, particularly the powerless—those who might be easily taken advantage of. It was her driving value to care for others. In this domain, she was well beyond assertive—she was Top Gun—and she came across as authentic and engaging.

Carrie thought this might be just the connection she needed—a strong-willed woman who was as new to her task as she Carrie was to her own. So, after the Il Pizzico lunch meeting with Chief Judge Brayer, Carrie asked Jon Rhodes—ordered him, really—to set up a meeting with Hubert Brown, the chief public defender in Montgomery County. On this occasion, Carrie would seek a separate audience with Ms. Lopez. *I'll call her first*, she thought.

"Jon, I want you to run interference. Introduce me to Brown, and then you two go talk about stuff—you know, renew old acquaintances. I want to get Olivia Lopez alone and see if I can build rapport with her," she said.

Carrie called Olivia Lopez.

"Ms. Lopez, I'm Carrie Springer, Assistant Director of the—"

"WWTS. I know. I read an article about your new appointment. Interesting, really. The old WWTS articles helped me appreciate some courthouse hot buttons," she said.

"You hit the ground running, don't you!" Carrie said, thinking to herself, *I like this lady!*

"Well, now, that stone would hit both of us, wouldn't it? What can I do for you?" she asked.

She gets to the point, Carrie thought. *I like that.*

"Well, I'm coming over to your office tomorrow afternoon with Jon Rhodes. I thought while I'm there…. There's something I'd like to talk to you about privately," she said.

"Sure, so we shouldn't include Chief Brown or Jon Rhodes, right?" Olivia asked.

Bingo, Carrie thought, *She gets it.* "No, that won't be necessary."

As Carrie and Jon Rhodes waited in front of the receptionist's desk in the Public Defender's Office, Olivia appeared from one wing of the interior hallway at the same time Chief Hubert Brown arrived from the opposite wing.

"Hello, you must be Carrie Springer, and you must be Jon Rhodes. I'm Olivia Lopez. Oh, and Hubert, you know Jon. This is his new assistant director, Carrie Springer," said Olivia, as if *she* were hosting the meeting.

"How nice to see you, Jon, and a pleasure to meet you, Ms. Springer," said Chief Brown.

"Please, call me Carrie. Actually, I have a brief meeting with *your* new assistant here," Carrie said, nodding toward Olivia.

"Good, good, then, Jon, let's go catch up. Please know, Ms. Springer, you are always welcome to stop by without an appointment … like Jon has always done," he added.

Carrie didn't know if that was a sign of Jon's informality or a thinly veiled reference to Jon's reputation for everything being "urgent."

"Well, with my ever-present cell phone, Mr. Brown, I'll call first … as a matter of courtesy," she said. She intentionally did not look at Jon, but her cell phone remark was a message directed to him, meaning *slow down, Jon.*

"Well, Carrie, shall we?" Olivia asked, pointing to her office.

"Wow!" said Carrie upon entering the office and noticing a large arrangement of flowers. "Those flowers are lovely!" She was, of course, nosing around to find out who sent them.

"Yes, they are. I'll take that subject up with Mr. Hector Gomez. Do you know him?" she asked.

"No, I can't say as I do," Carrie said.

"He stopped by on my second day on the job to welcome me—Tuesday, I think it was. He left the flowers with a cordial note. He's a probation officer. I called to chastise him for spending his money on a stranger, but I don't think he heard a word I said," she added. "How can I help you, Carrie? By the way, I love that suit. Where'd you get it?"

"Bergdorf Goodman," Carrie said.

"Oh, I shop there, too!" Olivia said.

"I love their New York store."

"Me, too!"

"Would you like to join me on my next extravaganza?"

"Well, let me know when you're going up to the Big Apple. I go all the time to get away."

"I can do better than that. Let me check my calendar," Carrie said, pulling out her pocket calendar. "I usually take the train, but because of a commitment I'm headed up by plane on Saturday, July 12. I always stay at the Plaza. We could meet for lunch Saturday, shop, and then get into whatever mischief we find! I'm flying back Monday morning."

"I don't even have to check my calendar. See you in New York on July 12. Shall we share a suite, or should I get my own room?" Olivia asked.

"I'm going alone, so let's share a suite. They're big enough."

"Great. I'll probably head up on Friday and come back on Monday morning. I use Amtrak. Should I explore theater or opera tickets?"

"That would be wonderful!" said Carrie. "A friend of mine has an art exhibit, if you're interested."

"Sounds like fun. Now, how can I make *your* day?"

"Have you picked up—in your brief time here—any talk in this office about the revocation hearing practices in this court?" Carrie asked.

"I had one case, but that was over before it started. So, as they say, I have a sample of one. Gee Brooks was the probation officer. Keep your eyes on her—she's special. I came out of Arnold & Porter because— well, that's a long story. Chief Brown is giving me few assignments. He believes I need time to observe court proceedings, meet folks, set up the office.... But in my—how shall I put this—*marginally necessary* quasi-observation period, I've had a few very simple cases."

"I won't load you up with any of my biases, Olivia. Let's do this: will you call me after you've experienced a few revocation hearings?" asked Carrie.

"Sure, of course. Realize that I won't be on the record," Olivia said.

"Of course. I'm really fact-finding, but I think it's in the interest of the clients you serve to look into this issue," Carrie said.

With that, the ladies chatted at length about fashion and New York.

Two weeks later, Olivia called Carrie. "I've got some information on theater tickets, and I also want to talk about that *thing* you brought up," Olivia said.

"What is this, *The Sopranos*? Did you take care of 'that thing'? I presume you mean the revocation process?" Carrie said.

They both laughed.

"Yes, that's it! That 'thing' troubles me. Let's meet outside the courthouse for lunch," Olivia suggested.

"I've got a better idea. How about dinner at Ruth's Chris in Bethesda?"

"Next Tuesday works," Olivia said.

—

Sharply at seven o'clock, Olivia entered Ruth's Chris Steakhouse and greeted Carrie with a handshake. They were seated immediately. For several days after Olivia's "thing" reference, Carrie had been full of curiosity. What do we have on our hands? Could Jon be right? Why did Olivia insist on meeting outside her office?

After chatting and getting to know each other better, they jumped into the revocation process. Carrie was impressed with Olivia's extraordinary ability to get to what was important.

"Well, I've held one probation revocation hearing and observed three others since we spoke. What a mess! My colleagues just roll their eyes when I asked them about the process … the end game. This is an exercise of shooting fish in a barrel!" she said.

"My God, Jon's onto something," Carrie said.

"By the way, most people in my office are put off by Jon Rhodes. He touches a place, emotions, where they don't want to go," Olivia said.

"I know. I'm working on that. He'll find the ground. In his defense, the insane pain of a murdered wife can't be placed neatly on a shelf. I understand how uncomfortable he can make people, but he *is* a wonderful man," she said.

"OK. I just wanted you to know that folks in my office keep him at a distance," Olivia said.

"Thanks," said Carrie.

"Here's my take on the revocation hearing process: I went back six months—that's as far back as I could go without drawing unwanted attention to myself. I found five revocation hearings for new crimes while in the community, all of which resulted in new, lengthy prison terms. I have no issue with that. The system is working. Then, get this, I found forty-seven revocation hearings during this time that were based solely on technical violations, Carrie, meaning there were no *new* crimes," Olivia said.

"I know—rules violations," Carrie said.

"You got it! Two of those forty-seven were continued on supervision without any consequence. I guess you could say our office won those two," Olivia said.

They laughed as the waiter poured red wine and took their order.

Carrie offered a toast: "May friendship find us."

"Oh, that's so sweet. Cheers," Olivia said.

They paused to let the moment resonate.

"Now, six other cases were continued on supervision, but with *new* special conditions. That leaves the balance—thirty-nine, Carrie, *thirty-nine* were sent to prison for technical violations for periods ranging from six months. Actually, there were only two that got off that easily. Eleven months was the average, up to eighteen months. Now, I repeat: none of the thirty-nine had new arrests," she said, pausing to take a sip of wine.

"What are the rules violations? What do they feel like? Serious stuff or chicken poop?" asked Carrie.

"I'll get to that. First, you should know that all of those I read had the fourteen standard conditions and *at least* four special conditions!" Olivia said.

Olivia explained that there are no surprises with standard conditions—no drug use, no gun possession, no leaving the state without permission, be employed full-time, and file income tax returns. But the special conditions were more difficult—be in your home by 9:00 PM every night; wear an electronic anklet 24/7; every day write down five places you looked for a job and hand it to your probation officer by 8:30 the next morning; go to A.A. meetings; go to treatment three times a week; come into the probation office twice a week and submit to a urinalysis; and on and on. The highest number of special conditions she found any one person having was eight. She said that it was as if the sentencing judge was trying to control behavior with rules.

"Guess what—the rules come back to nail these guys, time after time!" she said.

"Trip wires. Jon calls then trip wires. Can you give me some examples of what behavior actually sent offenders back to prison?" asked Carrie.

"Yes. One positive UA for pot. Two missed appointments with the probation officer. No job. Missing a curfew. Late payments on fines. A speeding ticket. Stuff like that. There were two cases that ended back in prison that I thought had solid grounds without new offenses; oddly, both were supervised by my flower-giver, Hector Gomez. In both cases the probationer was either psychologically abusing his wife or children or physically threatening them. But these two were the exception, not the norm. The system has gone off its tracks," she said.

"My God," said Carrie. "What can be done about it? What can we do? What should I focus on to change things?"

"Let me think about it. Let's talk more in New York," said Olivia.

"Deal."

One week after this conversation, Carrie and Jon had an appointment with the state's attorney for Montgomery County, Wayne Elkin.

"Come on in, Jon—and you must be Carly!" bellowed the pudgy Mr. Elkin from his doorway.

"Actually, it's Carrie, Carrie Springer, and it's nice to meet you," she said. Instantly, she disliked Elkin.

"Oh, sorry. My bad!" Elkin said.

"*My bad*"? thought Carrie. *How old are you?*

"Nice to see you, Jon. I hope all is well.... You know...." Elkin said.

"Oh, please," Carrie mumbled under her breath.

"I'm well. Thank you, Wayne. I thought we could take a few moments and talk about an issue that has come up," Jon said.

"You know, I'd love to, Jonny, but I have an unexpected and contentious pretrial hearing and must take my leave. I'm sorry. Perhaps another day, or, better still, let me get Bradford, my deputy—"

"Of course, I know Bradford. That'll work," Jon said, rising to leave, followed by Carrie, who felt like she was being pushed out the door by Elkin.

It was an unfriendly environment, this state's attorney's office, she thought. Assistant prosecutors and support staff alike looked at her as if she was an un-indicted co-conspirator, ready to be led to a conference room to provide damning testimony by ratting out her buddies. As they were waiting outside the office of Bradford Shuster, he waved through the open door, indicating he'd be with them as soon as he ended his phone call.

Elkin hustled away, with a ta-ta sort of wave over his shoulder.

"My God, what a shallow jerk!" Carrie whispered to Jon, watching Elkin nearly skip away.

"Oh, there's more to come," whispered Jon.

"Holy cow! No wonder you're obsessed with watching these birds!" Carrie said, abandoning the whisper.

Now off the phone, Bradford waved them in.

"Hello! Hello, Jon! How *are* we?" said Bradford.

"Fine. Thanks, Bradford," Jon said.

It dawned on Carrie that at one time in the early stages of his vigil, Jon must have needed this pathetic pandering. Maybe, just maybe, Jon would get his fill.

"Bradford, this is my new assistant director, Carrie Springer," Jon said, pointing an open palm toward Carrie.

"How nice to meet you! Listen, I'm *so* sorry, I have a conference call in ten minutes, but is there something we can address briefly, other than meeting your lovely new assistant?" asked Bradford, who was the deputy state's attorney for Montgomery County.

"Well, yes, there is—" started Jon.

However, before he could finish, Carrie jumped in, disliking Shuster's flippant demeanor and having lost all patience. "Mr. Shuster, I have been able to determine that in the last six months about forty persons on probation were revoked and sent to prison for technical violations. You know, *without* a new criminal offense," she said.

"Well, that number sounds high, but let's assume you're accurate, for argument's sake," Bradford said.

"Why aren't these folks handled in local community facilities—you know, like halfway houses, alcohol and drug treatment centers, work release centers, places like that?" she asked.

"Well, I couldn't tell you, really. That's the call of the judge or the probation office. Ms. Springs—"

"Springer," Carrie said.

"Sorry! You people ought to hand out cards!" Shuster said. "Ms. Springer. To be perfectly frank, that's not what we do here. Our office's job is to act as the attorney for the probation office in these hearings. We seek revocations. We don't make recommendations as to *where* to handle the punishment—other than prison. We do have many issues with the arguments made by the Public Defender's office, but that's just the way the game is played," he said.

"Oh, and what a game it is!" Carrie said.

With that, Jon jumped out of his chair. "Well, Bradford, thank you so much for your time. You've been most helpful!"

"More than you know, Mr. Slusher," Carrie said.

"Actually, it's Shuster," he corrected.

"My bad," she said.

Bradford didn't appear to be offended, but she knew based on the tart look on Jon's face that he had caught her intentional slight.

"Well, have a blessed day!" Bradford added.

After leaving Shuster's office, Jon turned to Carrie and said, "Carrie, is that your best restraint mode?"

"You're right, Jon. I just couldn't stand that slimeball."

"Prosecutors have one of two goals."

"And they are?" she asked, her arm entwined in his as they walked through the courthouse halls.

"To be elected to higher office or to become partners in law firms, plain and simple," Jon said.

"God help us!" she said.

"Indeed, Carrie.... *Now* you get it," he said.

14

FUN? WHAT'S THAT?

Carrie Springer

Carrie, in a relatively short time—a matter of months, really—cherished the WWTS investigative work. She felt full of herself, like she was back at the *Plain Dealer*. She sensed that Jon had become almost perky. To say he had a bounce in his step would be an exaggeration, but something was different, she thought. At her insistence, WWTS moved into newly leased office space one block from the courthouse. She decorated the office with pastels and floral framed pictures. There were times when Jon would burst into the office with excitement, starting his sentences with, "You're not going to believe this!" She noticed that he began to touch people on the arm while talking to them. Even his use of dour facial expressions, which he had mastered, was far less frequent. Also, she knew that he enjoyed being around her. She began to feel connected to him. They had a rhythm to their conversations. Although quite different, she felt they complemented each other. They were capturing powerful data, turning the rock over, as she liked to say. They joked that they were the next Woodward and Bernstein.

On this particular April day, Carrie and Jon left their offices to retrieve the previous year's tax returns from their mutual accountant. They drove toward the Rockville post office in Carrie's new Lexus.

"What do you do for fun, Jon?" she asked.

"Fun? What's that?" Jon replied.

"That's what I thought. Bill Brayer said you were quite the golfer," Carrie said.

"I was, before—"

"So was I before *my* before—before Carl's extracurricular extravaganzas surfaced. I was too embarrassed to show up at the club, or in shock. So, during the separation, I put my membership on inactive status."

"Columbia Country Club?" he asked.

"No, Chevy Chase. And I just stopped playing. That was over three years ago. Two weeks ago I reactivated my membership," she added.

"Good for you!" he said.

"Wait, I'm not finished. I have this great swing coach, Marcus Schmidt, who's really helped my game. I'm seeing him Saturday. Pull out your clubs and join me. I can take you as a guest and we'll get back-to-back coaching," she said.

"I really can't—"

"I really can't? Horse poop. Stop it, Jon. Right now, stop it! You and I both know that in the spring and summer court calendars slow down, because attorneys and judges are playing golf. We can slow down, too," she said.

"I just feel I can't leave the courthouse," he said.

She said nothing, and there was a long silence.

"Now, isn't that stupid? I can't leave the courthouse. I can't leave the courthouse!" he was getting louder and louder. Suddenly, he rolled down his window, stuck his head out, and screamed, "Help! Help! I can't leave the *damned* courthouse—my pants are on fire!"

With an abrupt swerve, Carrie pulled the car over to the service lane. They laughed hilariously for quite a while, as Jon kept repeating "my pants are on fire" every time they were catching their breaths.

"Whew! Oh God, where were we? Oh, yes, Carrie, I'd love to join you!" he said, and they went into another laughing spasm.

"I haven't laughed that hard in years," she said.

"Any more questions?" he asked.

"Oh, no, no, no more questions, I swear! Not while I'm driving," she said.

"What time?" he asked.

"I'll call you for Saturday's time. Hell, on second thought, let's go to the driving range at the club late tomorrow afternoon," she said, touching his arm.

"Deal!" he said.

At the CCC driving range, Carrie noticed, without trying to be obvious, that Jon had a sweet swing. He seemed to struggle with his first few shots. Then it was like something clicked for him. Whack,

whack, whack.... Shot after shot went within a twenty-yard width, right down the middle.

"Wow!" she heard him say to himself.

Carrie introduced Jon to the assistant pro, Marcus, who watched Jon on one knee, made an adjustment to his left hand, and moved the setup in his stance back exactly one inch. Then she overheard Marcus go into an extensive discourse on why Jon should replace every iron and every wood in his bag with the latest and the greatest must-have stuff, including rescue woods. Marcus said only Jon's sixty-degree Cleveland pitching wedge was a keeper. They agreed to meet on Tuesday for Jon to be measured and order clubs. Of course, he'd need new shoes, bag, and on and on. And, so, the long-in-coming relaxation prescription began its healing ways.

"God, this is fun!" Jon said to Carrie as Marcus headed for another golfer. "How can I thank you, Carrie?" he asked, placing his hand on her left shoulder.

"Have fun, and play with me," she said with a smile. As her words reverberated in her head, she turned bright red.

"Well, Carrie, this is my day!" Jon said.

"Actually, I meant you should play *golf* with me," she laughed.

"I'd love to," he said.

"I don't want to pin you down. You might get bored with me, although I'm fast—oh, shit—*play* fast," she said.

They laughed again, but this time Jon made no funny looks.

"I used to play to a fourteen/fifteen handicap, but I've got a lot of work to do to reach that. And you?" she asked.

"Well, I had a seven, but that was *then*," he said.

"Well, let's have some fun," she said.

Four weeks later, Carrie and Jon were playing every Thursday and Saturday afternoon at 1:30. Dinners seemed to flow naturally after Saturday's round. Over drinks at the clubhouse on the fourth Saturday, Jon said, "Carrie, I'm going to apply for membership here."

"That's wonderful!" she said. She reached over and squeezed his hand.

"Thank you. I'll need the sponsorship of three members. May I use you?" he asked.

"You know the answer to that. You can expect the two judges from the court to support you: Bill Brayer and Harry Johnson."

"Are you sure?" he asked.

"I'm sure. I'll test the waters, and, if I get a *yes*, then you can call them directly. I know their answer now. They're old buddies. I'm so pleased. Dinner and drinks on me! Woo-hoo!" she screamed.

15

FLOWERS AREN'T A GIRL'S BEST FRIEND

Hector "Pepe" Gomez

Pepe always observed people around him in great detail, particularly beautiful women. He took one look at Olivia Lopez in the courthouse cafeteria on just her second day on the job, and he felt most of the air being sucked out of his lungs.

"Huggie, who in God's name is *that*?" he asked.

"The new assistant public defender. I don't know her name. Not bad," Huggie said.

"That … that'll be my girlfriend," replied Pepe. He felt drawn to her like a child to candy and snooped around with his courthouse buddies to learn her name. He had his answer before noon. He immediately ordered flowers. Huggie had never heard Pepe use the term "girlfriend." Huggie knew that single guys in the office liked to go out to bars with Pepe. It was said that guys used him like fishermen go after their prey, loading the waters with chum. The dirty deed—chumming in bars—would usually take about thirty to forty minutes. By then, Pepe would have what the boys described as a "school" of attractive women "nailing the hooks." Pepe gladly entertained them. Then the boys tried to pick off his discards; "follow his wake" was their exact nautical term. The chumster always delivered.

~

Three hours after ordering flowers for Olivia, Pepe sat in his office, daydreaming.

"Gomez," said Pepe, answering the phone.

"Good morning, Hector, this is Olivia Lopez," she said.

"How are you, Ms. Lopez, on this beautiful June day?" Pepe asked, as if butter wouldn't melt in his mouth. He hadn't been called Hector since he was scolded by his mother twenty years ago. Olivia pronounced

Pepe's given name with a tone a teacher would use with one of her misbehaving boys. Actually, her chiding tone made him smile.

"Do you have a moment for a cup of coffee?" she asked.

"Now? Uh, sure. Where?" he asked.

"Oh, the cafeteria's fine," she said. "See you in five minutes," Olivia said.

"Ten-four!" Pepe responded.

~

Entering the cafeteria, Pepe noticed half a dozen men were craning their necks, in unison, to catch a glimpse of the short-skirted woman's adorable presentation in the cafeteria line. It wasn't the pastry they were looking at—he knew Olivia was already there. He joined her in the line, several people apart, made eye contact, smiled, and gave a little wave of the hand. He noticed her stern face and almost giggled. *My, what a feisty one*, he thought.

He followed Olivia to a table in the southeastern corner of the cafeteria, where the sun seemed to rest above her head, as if, he thought, it had been placed there by the director of a movie. *Where's the music?* he laughed to himself.

"Good morning, Hector," Olivia said, removing the lid from her coffee.

"Hello, Olivia. To what do I owe this moment of joy?" asked Pepe.

"Well, Hector, this is a follow-up conversation to the flowers you sent me," she said.

"I hope you enjoyed them," he said.

"Is it your custom to send flowers to every new employee in this courthouse?" she asked.

Sensing an interrogation, an on guard Pepe responded, "Uh, no—"

"Oh. Oh, then you send flowers only to new employees in the Public Defender's Office, correct?" she asked.

"Well, actually, no...." Pepe eked out.

"The day I started, another new defender, Allen Northington, joined the office. He didn't get flowers from you," she said.

"Actually, no, he didn't, but please convey my best wishes to Allen," he said, trying not to smile.

"Well, then, you must give flowers to only new *women* employees in the Public Defender's Office?" she said, sounding puzzled.

"No, actually," he said, trying not to smile.

"Oh, then the flower-giving is just for me. Correct?" the attorney asked.

"Just for you, Ms. Lopez," Pepe said.

"You've embarrassed me. Everyone thinks they're from a boyfriend. You don't even know me, and you send a fellow courthouse employee flowers? We work in the same building. Have you ever heard of creating unwanted gossip, Hector? I have an impeccable professional reputation, Hector," she added.

Before he could answer, she continued, "Do I look that easy? That stupid? Oh, *my God*, flowers for me? Oh, how can I ever thank him? No more lonely nights! I know you have a high school ring I can put some wax in or a varsity sweater I can wear! Daddy, get Momma on the phone—quick! Hello! 9-1-1, you'd better send a fire truck, because I'm on fire!" she mocked, using various voices and tones.

"Point taken, Ms. Lopez. I apologize," he said. *Oops*, he thought, *time for Plan B*. "Actually, aside from your charm and beauty, I really wanted to get your help, pro bono, of course, to draw up some legal liability papers so some of my kids in the community can get rides to baseball games and homework clubs from faith-based organizations and other community groups," he said.

Olivia had a puzzled look on her face, which he had counted on.

Pepe whipped out some folded papers from the left interior pocket of his sport jacket. "I got these off the Internet. They're sample forms. Until I get them in an acceptable format, I've got seven organizations willing but not able to give boys and girls a ride. Without rides, those kids are going to hang out on the corners. You know how that ends up," he said.

She grabbed the papers from his hand and looked at them. Sure enough, he had handwritten notes in the margin. She noticed with a quick glance that his handwritten notes signaled that he had overly complicated some simple liability issues, while underestimating the significance of others.

"All right, Hector, I'll bite. Give me a week and I'll mail you a version that your organizations can use safely, or they can use them to draft their own documents," she said.

"Well, Ms. Lopez, it's the least I can do to show my appreciation for your dedication to children to take you to dinner. Do we have a contract?" he asked.

"Oh, God.... Did I step into this one?" she said, shaking her head and looking at the floor. "I guess—for the children," she said. She tucked the papers under her arm and, without another word, marched out of the cafeteria.

Five days later, Pepe received an inter-office, legal-sized manila envelope. Inside, he found his original notes and a cleanly prepared three-page legal document with signature and date lines. There were ten copies.

A yellow sticky was attached with this note:
Hector … for the kids.
OML

"Olivia, this is Pepe. Thank you so much for the documents. How kind of you! You can't imagine how much this helps. By the way, there're plenty of young girls and boys who will be affected by your *future* kindness, too! I've got a story to tell you about how the legal papers already helped. Would you like to join in some opportunities to work with kids who need our help?" he asked.

"Hector, of course I'd love to help little children, but do I have the time with my new job? That's another question," she said.

"What're they going to do, fire you?" he asked.

"I'll get back to you, Hector, when I have the time," she said.

"Wait, wait. No need to get back to me, Ms. Lopez. We can talk about it over dinner.... You recall our contract: pro bono legal work for dinner. Friday night work for you?" he asked.

"My, my, Hector. Smooth as a baby's behind, aren't you!" she said.

"I have no idea what you are talking about. What time shall I pick you up?" Pepe asked in an even tone, as if he were dealing with a twelve-year-old girl's temper tantrum at summer camp.

"No, no, Hector, I'll meet you.... Where?"

Well, at least we're off the snide, he thought.

"How about seven o'clock at Brasserie Monte Carlo in Bethesda on ..."

"I know where it is. Good-bye," she said.

Good-bye, fair Princess, he said to himself with a gigantic laugh. *Shall we dance?* There was still one deal breaker, one hurdle with this lawyer. Pepe had a deeply rooted fear that she'd act better than he would, because she was a lawyer. He wouldn't tolerate that feeling in any setting, under any circumstance—the feeling of not being good enough. Kidding from Gee, Hattie, and Huggie about his writing skills was one thing—not being recognized for his intellectual prowess was another.

Pepe was so excited that he was singing to himself all the way to the restaurant. He tried to slow down his every movement. *Be cool, Pepe, be cool*, he said to himself.

Olivia arrived at Brasserie Monte Carlo, took off her jacket and yellow scarf, and revealed a black cotton sweater and a black skirt that stopped four inches above her knees. Black stockings and pumps completed the outfit. Pepe had on a black linen sports coat, a blue collarless shirt, and black slacks. It was as if they had coordinated their ensembles.

"Olivia, thanks for your help with the liability thing. Already, three organizations have used the document to create their own liability agreements. Worry-free transporters have arrived—like the cavalry," Pepe said.

"You're welcome. They're welcome," she added. Now that they were seated at their booth, for the first time the edge to Olivia's voice was lessened, though not completely gone.

With Olivia's approval, Pepe ordered a bottle of BV Coastal Estates 2004 Cabernet Sauvignon. For dinner, Olivia ordered grilled rainbow trout in lemon caper sauce, and Pepe chose beef in herb de Provence cream sauce.

"Well, aren't we saucy?" he said.

She gave him a quick smirk.

"May I share the story I alluded to on the phone?" Pepe asked.

"Of course. What happened?" she said.

"You may have saved a little girl from harm. By accident, several days ago when I was riding by in my car, I came across this six year-old Hispanic girl, Lupé, who I now know lives in an apartment with her mother, brothers, and sisters near the Lakeforest Mall in Gaithersburg. She was sitting underneath a covered bus stop, about three blocks from her home. She appeared to be crying—you know, with her hands covering her eyes," he said.

"Wait, wait. I'm confused. What does she have to do with your caseload—your work?" she asked.

"Nothing," he said, and without hesitation continued his story. "Two teenage boys were sitting on their bikes, one at each end of the bus cover. The scene looked suspicious, so I circled the block and parked my car. I walked up to her and said, 'Are you—' and then I pretended I forgot her name. 'Little Lupé,' said one of the boys. 'She's hiding from her mom's boyfriend!' they laughed. I motioned to the boys to beat it, and they did. As one rode by me, he spit on the sidewalk near my foot," he said, pausing for a drink of wine.

"What happened?" asked Olivia.

"Where was I …? Oh, I told her I was a friend of Father Dominic of the Catholic Church around the corner—"

"Are you?" Olivia asked.

"Well, I had met him several times…. Friend was a stretch," he added.

"Clearly, Lupé knew Father Dominic. I said, 'Where do you live?' She pointed. I go, 'I'll walk you home.' We walked about three blocks in silence. Finally I said, 'Lupé, I know you don't know me, and it's not a good idea to trust people you don't know, but you can help me a lot if you would answer one question. Is *he* going to hurt you tonight? If he is, let's go see Father Dominic *now* … together…. I'll go with you.' Her little voice said, 'He's asleep.' When we approached her apartment, I reached out for her hand. She started to go in, but I held her hand firmly and knocked on the door. Her mother came to the door. She looked at me and Lupé and said, 'Lupé, get in this house.' 'I said, one second, please.' Lupé moved into her mother's arms. 'I'm a friend of Father Dominic's.' Olivia, I swear, I was waiting for lighting to strike me for my second lie, but it never came," he said, pausing to drink more wine.

"God should have taken his opportunity then. What happened?" Olivia said.

"The mother then looked and sounded slightly less defensive, but not much. I told her that I came across boys teasing Lupé at the bus stop about her being afraid to go home. The mother turned her head toward a room inside the apartment. 'Now,' I go, 'I must be certain that she'll be safe tonight.... I must tell Father Dominic she'll be safe tonight. Please be truthful.' Tears came to her eyes. She said, 'I'll speak to the Father tomorrow. Lupé is safe. I promise you, sir, Lupé is safe.' I go, 'Then I don't need to call ...' implying the police. 'She's safe. Father Dominic will help me figure out what to do,' she said.

"I left the apartment and headed for the parish. I interrupted Father Dominic's dinner. I told him the story. He went over to the phone and picked up the church directory and called Lupé's mother. His call must have touched off emotions for Lupé's mother, because he spent a lot of time trying to comfort her. I heard him arrange a time to for them to meet the next morning before she went to work. Now, here's where you came in," he said, finishing the last ounce of wine in his glass.

"Me?" Olivia asked.

"I took your legal papers to a small Hispanic outreach group in the neighborhood two days ago, and they signed it on the spot. The next day—the *very next* afternoon after this event, with her mother's blessing, that group transported Lupé to an afterschool program for girls her age, a place where she'll be surrounded by warmth until her mother gets home at night. I spoke with Father Dominic this morning, and he's optimistic Lupé's mother will do what's right for her daughter—we hope. So, there you have it, Ms. Lopez. We're successful in our first team effort," he said, tipping his glass toward her, which she complied with, reluctantly.

"Thanks for that story," she said.

"You and I—we're drawn to helping children in pain, aren't we?" he asked.

He didn't need words from her. He saw the answer in her face. *B-7.... Bingo!*

"My hunch is that we share some similar feelings from childhood. I'd like to share some of the pieces of me with you some day," he said.

She didn't make a sound.

"I bet that no matter where each of us is on the planet, we'll be connected by our concern for children! How's that for a prediction?" he asked.

"Will you excuse me?" she said as she rose and headed to the bathroom without making eye contact with him.

For a rare moment, Pepe was too caught up in his own emotions to catch Olivia's facial expression. He was mesmerized by Olivia— her sharp-tongued wit, her apparent sensitivity—which led him, instinctively, to believe that underneath that competent surface, he'd find a person who understood pain and loneliness. He wanted to learn more about her. But at this moment, he was in touch with painful memories of feeling like an outsider as a kid—like a foreigner, alone, like Lupé, in a hostile world. Before she returned to the table, he regrouped; tonight wasn't the night to expose *that much* about himself. As a matter of fact, he had never exposed *that much* about himself to anyone.

⁓

Inside the ladies room, Olivia doused cold water on her face.

⁓

Back at the table, Olivia said, "Well, sir, your contractual obligation has been completed, and I've enjoyed myself and the dinner. Thank you."

"Now, now, Ms. Lopez. I am a very good listener. I appreciate the dilemma, the complexities of courting a woman who works in the same network—"

"Courting? My God...."

Pepe noticed she smiled but quickly replaced it with a stern look. He wanted to laugh but didn't. By design, he moved into overdrive.

"Courting, yes *courting*! I know, people shouldn't eat where they poop. So, here's an idea. In the courthouse, we're friendly, cordial. We never talk about work or cases—ever. If we end up with a case together, like a revocation hearing—which would be rare, since I don't have many—you do what you do and I'll do what I do. We're big boys and girls, OK?" he said.

"Hector, tonight, *this* is a stretch for me," she said, gesturing with her hands to the restaurant walls.

"OK. I understand. Most folks don't get too far in relationships anyway. So, what are the odds against us? Significant, right? How about if we just enjoyed each other *outside of* Montgomery County for a while? What's the harm?" he asked.

"I'm sort of in a lull in the relationship-building enterprise. I've got a new career and am feeling my way along," she said, staring at him.

He didn't fire off one facial muscle.

"I guess you're just not going to just ride away into the sunset, are you?" she asked.

He didn't respond. The ball was still in her court.

"I'm going to New York City in two weeks to have fun with Carrie Springer. Do you know her?" she asked.

"I don't, but I've heard her name recently," he added.

"I'm meeting her on Saturday around one o'clock or so. She's flying in. Carrie and I will stay at the Plaza Hotel. We could hang out in New York, you know, doing nothing really. But understand—I'm not talking about a date thing. You and I could take the first train up, very early Friday morning and just hang out in the city. Here are my ground rules: one, you pay your fare, I'll pay mine; two, I'll get a suite at the RIHGA Royal Hotel on West 54th Street for Friday only; three, I'm returning Monday morning on the train—you return on your own," she said.

"Great, but one suggested amendment to your lovely proposal," he said. He knew instinctively from her tone that she wanted more time with him.

"Go ahead," she said, seemingly annoyed.

"Can we split the suite at the RIHGA? I'm couch-able. You know, like college friends. I have a cousin in the Bronx. I'll go visit him on Saturday and Sunday and get the train back with you on Monday. If we can't stand each other by then, I'll sit somewhere else on the train. Deal?" he asked.

"Deal, Hector," she said, with only a very slight smile.

"May I follow you home—for safety, of course?" he asked.

"No, you stalker, that won't be necessary," she responded.

Outside the restaurant he gently touched the outsides of her arms and kissed her softly on her left cheek.

"Good night, Olivia, I enjoyed the evening," he said.

"Hector, Hector …" she said, as in … what am I going to do with you? She turned toward her car, a green British racing convertible, which was parked on the street nearby.

He watched her drive off. He blew a kiss.

She smiled, then snapped her head forward, away from his gaze.

On any given night he could easily land any attractive woman in bed; but never had the ole chumster fallen—like a rock off a cliff. She brought out a playful kid in him, and he was especially attracted to the fact that she was a Hispanic woman. She had a way of listening to him, embracing his thoughts. He felt alive with Olivia. He felt sparks.

The "All Aboard" call for the 6:08 AM Express came moments before the little café stand opened at New Carrollton. So close to having their first cup of coffee, but still so far away, he thought.

Moments after they'd boarded and found their seats, the train started, the sojourners had their tickets punched by the conductor, and the announcement came that the club car was now open. They raced to get in line. As they drank their coffee, they talked about politics, music, and friends and what they liked to do. They spoke with ease, Pepe thought.

Pepe asked, "When you were a kid, did you brush your teeth every night, Olivia?"

"Of course!" she said.

"Who made you, your mom or dad?"

"I'm sure it was my mother," she said.

He noticed a shift in her tone with the word "mother." "Tell me about your family," he said.

"No, you first," she insisted.

"OK, me first," he said.

Pepe felt anxious. *Just how much detail do I care to share?* "My father jumped over the fence at Brownsville and said, 'Run, Isabella! Run your fat ass off!'" he said in a very loud voice.

Olivia lost it. "Stop it," she begged, bent over laughing.

He took a deep breath.

"My father, Joaquin, was an influential and powerful figure in his town. He raised and trained quarter horses at our family ranch. Most of the horses were sold in the U.S. He and my mother lived about one hundred miles outside of Mexico City. *Something* happened. My grandmother, Tia, told me bits and pieces, but she never gave too many details."

"Which grandmother?" she asked.

"The one who also chose to call me Hector—my mother's mother," he said.

"OK, maternal," she concluded.

"Yes. Apparently my father was accused of trying to fix a race. My grandmother, who's a hoot, said my father never did a dishonest thing in his life; the accusation was 'baloney' but came from dangerous men. At any rate, before I was born, she said, he sold most of his horses but brought two of his champion horses and my mother to the U.S. My parents ended up in San Antonio and bought a twenty-five acre farm, with me on the way," he said. "All of my father's family stayed behind."

"Hmmm...." she said.

"My mother's mother and two sisters followed her several years later and settled in San Antonio. I have eight cousins there, too. They all became naturalized citizens, as, I'm told, my parents did."

"And your parents, are they still in San Antonio?" she asked.

Pepe was upon the moment of truth. He considered whether he'd dare tell her the truth. He'd never shared this one particular aspect of his family's story with anyone. "My mother is. My father committed suicide, and my mother leased the farm and moved in with my aunt Aura when I went off to the University of Texas in Austin," he said.

"Oh, I'm *so* sorry," she said.

"I wish I could say that I'm over it, but I think there are certain events that we don't *really* get over. We just look at them differently," he said.

"Why?" she asked.

"'Why?' is too large a question. It was the first question I asked and then repeated to myself a thousand times. Sort of like, why would someone commit a robbery? Who the hell really knows why anyone does something? I was pulled out of class by the principal. It was the start of my sophomore year in high school. The principal wouldn't answer my question: why was I being pulled out of class—and by him? He just said something happened, and I needed to go home. He led me to the front of the school where the sheriff's deputy was waiting. The deputy motioned for me to get in the car. I asked him, 'What's up?' I thought I was busted for having sex with the mayor's daughter—free-floating guilt," he said.

"Go on," she said.

"The deputy said something like, 'Son, I'm taking you home.... There's a problem.' My first thought was that my father had been in an accident. When we drove up to the barn, I saw an EMS truck with lights blinking. Then I saw my mother holding my father's limp body in her arms, in the dirt, in front of the barn. A noose was lying at his side, cut off his neck by someone. I remember seeing a purple ring around his neck. It looked like a chicken's neck when it's rung. I hugged her, I screamed, I hugged him. He was gone," Pepe said, unable to hold back silent tears.

He paused.

"Sorry," he said.

"Please, don't be," she said, holding his arm. "Do you mind my asking again.... Why? Why?"

"No, if you don't mind me saying I really don't know. This is what I've pieced together. To this day all my mother can say is 'it was God's will.' With help from my grandmother, I learned this: his heritage, his pride, his reputation was who he was. Sixteen years after being in the U.S., he was not one of 'them.' He was just ... a gaucho. He knew I was not accepted as an equal at school. The Texan culture was the whites and 'us.' I never complained to my father or mother, but just about every day from the fourth to the ninth grade, I came home with signs of that day's fight. I didn't take too well to being called a wetback."

He was quiet for a moment, his mind racing. He'd never been so transparent. He wondered, in his silence, if this stain, this tragedy, would run her off.

"My father was proud of me. I know he loved me. He always hugged me and rubbed my hair," he said, eyes glistening again. "But maybe, I don't know, he wanted things different for me. He talked about me going to college. But we never saved any money for college," he added.

He told her his mother worked at a dry cleaner's for years. Then, new corporate owners bought out the family-owned business. Some corporate runt accused her shift of coming up short on the cash register.

"My mother ... stealing! What a joke. I remember my mother crying hysterically in my father's arms. She doesn't know how to lie, much less steal. I remember after that—at least, I think it was after that—my father stopped talking ... almost literally. Months later, he hanged himself. My grandmother said it was after his biggest customer, a man for whom my father had raised hundreds of horses, suddenly, without warning, gave all of his business to a younger man on another farm. The quarter horse business was over. I remember him crying, drunk one night on our back porch. I sort of approached him slowly and asked him what was wrong. He said something like 'What do I do now? Shovel shit in stalls? A *Gomez* shoveling shit?'" Pepe said.

"God, I'm sorry," she said.

"After his suicide, my mother bumped along as best she could. My grandmother moved in with my aunt and us and held all of us together. Every night for years my mother just sat on the back porch talking to herself. We gave her space. I turned to cross-country running.... You know, a Forrest Gump-like thing—run away from the pain. It didn't work too well. I'd have this anger. I didn't know what to do with it. I dreamed of my father coming back. I dreamed of building a monument to him.... Sounds silly now...."

"Not really," she interrupted. "Not practical, but not silly. We want to hold on to those we love. Your father sounds like a wonderful man," she said.

"I sort of went into no-man's-land for about a year. God, I don't remember much about the tenth grade, really. But then, by my junior year, I guess some sense of direction came to me. I realized that I was the last *Gomez* male. I didn't ever want to be in a position where some young jerk would be able to take my job. So, I figured I needed an education. I applied for and, surprisingly, got a full scholarship to UT. I think they felt sorry for Hispanics at that time. I remember in my senior year opening the envelope from UT and telling my mother that I got a scholarship and I'd be leaving for Austin in late August. The look on her face was one of shock. I went out on the back porch and stared at the barn. I felt like I was being ripped in parts. Stay, go, nothing made me comfortable. If it wasn't for my grandmother Tia's egging, I wouldn't have gone. Halfway through my four years at UT, it came to me: I wanted to be *useful* in the community—so that no child would ever have to go through the pain I did alone. My father stuck with me as long as he could," he said.

He was silent again.

"Thank you for sharing that," she said.

They sat in silence for a good while.

~

After a snack in the club car somewhere north of Philadelphia, Olivia said, "I have no family. I was raised in an orphanage in China and brought here at age twenty, when I entered college," she concluded.

"Uh huh. What does the M in your middle name stand for, Ming?" he asked.

"Maria, jerk," she said.

"Oh, so China isn't—"

"She was the only child born to the union of Dr. Raul Lopez and Dr. Maria Lopez," Olivia said, as if were a voice-over. Then, she returned to her normal tone.

"My father, Raul, his great-grandparents emigrated from Spain in the early 1900s; her parents emigrated from Cuba in the late 1940s. My father, a cardiologist, has headed up the Cancer Institute at NIH for many years, since I was in my early teens. He's a kind man who's still active in his laboratory at work. I love him dearly. He works from sunup until late into the night, every day," she said.

"A dedicated man," Pepe said.

"My mother, Maria, is a pediatrician in private practice. She's also on the faculty at the University of Maryland School of Medicine in Baltimore. Unlike my father, Maria's an extrovert who *must* be the center of things. That's quite an art form in her practice. But there came a time when her presence, always on center stage, became overbearing to me and no longer amusing. I suppose she is who she is.... We all are," she said.

"Who do you look like?" he asked.

"My mother. Exactly like my mother," she said. "I've always had a difficult relationship with her. Maybe, as I look back on it, we're very much alike and probably fighting for my father's attention. We both lost out to science," she added.

"I'd take you over a test tube any day," he said, nudging her gently.

"My gosh, Hector, those are the kindest words I've ever heard," she said.

"Scarlett—"

"Rhett—"

"Now shut up. It's my miserable turn," she said. "You were open with me; I suppose I should reciprocate—just kidding. I want to share who I am, although, I must say, I've never told this story to any man."

"Oh," said Pepe.

"In my early teens, I found my mother ... impossible. There was nothing I could do that was ever quite right. Seven As on a report card and one B would lead to a discussion about how careless I was in that one subject area. Had I planned well enough and executed with dedication and purpose, I'd have had all As, she would say. So, I retaliated. I'd tease her with something she held important for me and quit at the pivotal moment. A nasty little brat, really," she said.

"Like what?" he asked.

"I dropped out of classical piano lessons after my music teacher told my mother I had a great future. When I was elected the captain of the debate team in fourth grade at Madeira, I quit. But things really changed on a July day when I was fourteen," she said. "Let's see if I can get this out...."

"I'm not going anywhere," he said.

His arm pressed against hers.

"I had a fight with my girlfriend. I was supposed to be at her house for two days. I called my mother's office, but they said she wasn't there. I actually stomped home, about three miles. My mother's car and another car were in the driveway. I thought that odd. I went inside and called for her, but she didn't answer. I thought I heard a noise in the pool, opened the sliding glass door, and walked out onto the patio. I heard a muffled scream from my mother. She tried to get me to go inside, but something didn't feel right. I noticed from a distance that I couldn't see her bathing suit straps. Then, as I approached her, her tennis instructor from the club surfaced from under the water. It was clear they were naked. I screamed at her and ran inside," she said.

Pepe remained silent and looked straight ahead, not at her.

"I had a decision to make and she knew it. She came into my room and begged me not to tell my father. I said to her, 'Then you will.'

"Two days later, I came home and my mother was at the door, surrounded by suitcases. She said she was going to a conference, and she'd be back. My father was in the study and never rose from his chair to say good-bye. I knew she had told him. When she returned several weeks later, she moved her things out of their bedroom and into a spare bedroom at the other end of the house. As exiled as she was to him, I was to her, and he was to me. The family, as I knew it, collapsed. Some civil connection lived on between them, but they became replicas of my former parents. I chose a college as far away as I could: Stanford, in California. I think I came home each year for about two weeks. I went directly from Palo Alto to law school at Michigan without a stopover at home. After law school, I stayed in Ann Arbor, was engaged to be married for a year, but fortunately came to my senses and broke it off. One month later, I took a job with Arnold & Porter in D.C. and stayed there for two years," she said.

"My father's suicide has, I don't know, made me stronger, more alert to pain. How did this family turmoil change you?" he asked.

"Well, I guess the sense of helplessness was crushing, or so it seemed at the time. I said to myself, I'll find a way to survive. But it left me with very bitter and angry feelings about being powerless. Want to or not, I was repulsed by that feeling—being helpless, at the mercy of others. I know this: no one, and particularly no child, should feel that loneliness, the feeling that two people you loved were tearing your heart apart, the feeling that somehow ... I was to blame. No child should bear that alone," she said.

"Why didn't they get professional help for you, or for themselves?" he asked.

"They did for me. But it felt to me that the hired gun's goal was to get me to accept my mother's domineering behavior. I always felt that in some sneaky way my mother was telling the therapist, 'make her less angry.' When my mother asked me for an update on therapy, her tone was like, 'Aren't you over it yet?' I was never really angry with my father. I just wished he could have fixed things between them," she said.

"Does any part of this experience guide you today?" Pepe asked.

"Guide me? Well, maybe I'm constantly on guard for nuances in what people are saying to me. My antennae flap: is this the truth, or—"

"I can see that."

"I find that a useful skill. Are you being sarcastic?"

"No, not at all. I didn't mean that. I think it's a gift."

"OK. On the flip side, I have a hard time trusting men," she added.

"But it was your mom—"

"The tennis instructor had a penis, Hector," she said, as if a '*duh*' should follow.

"Oh, so all of us with a penis are going to get it?"

"Nope, just tennis instructors. I guess trust is everything in a relationship, and trust takes time. So that's my family story."

"You impress me as having a passion for honesty and that you're a caring person. There's an authenticity about you that the family tragedy hasn't dimmed. Maybe you're the best of both of your parents," he said.

"You're being serious?" she asked.

"I'm quite serious."

"That's a kind thing to say. Thank you," she said, her voice cracking ever so slightly.

"I've been so busy gnarling, stuck in some ways, that I've never seen that," she said, folding her arms over her curled-up knees.

They checked in at the RIHGA Royal Hotel around 11:00 AM. After a quick tour of the suite, Olivia announced that it was up to her expectations. Pepe set up his suitcase on a crossed-legged luggage stand in the living room area and unzipped his bag.

Olivia called from the bedroom, "Let's go eat. There's a great bagel shop. I think it's on 53rd Street, the, ah, Bagel & Bean, I think it's called. Sound good?" she asked.

After eating, Olivia stopped in a small Korean-owned convenience store for two bottles of water, while Pepe darted in a souvenir shop, jammed with New York City items. He quickly selected a lapel pin with an NYY configuration, which, of course, stood for the New York Yankees.

Out on the street, rejoining Olivia, he said, "Olivia, I'd like to give you something now as a memento of this day in New York City," and handed her the Yankees pin.

"Why, Hector, how cute. Why did you give it to me now, instead of afterward?" she asked.

"I may be riding back on a different train car!" he said.

They were walking toward Central Park down West 57th Street when Olivia spotted Nobu New York, a new restaurant.

"Wow! I didn't know this had opened," she said.

"What is it?" Pepe asked.

"Chef Nobu is a sort of pioneer in Japanese cuisine, and Robert DeNiro is a partner of his. We've got to try to eat there tonight!" she said, yanking him toward the restaurant.

"Olivia, we'll never get reservations on the spot," he said.

"Can't hurt to try," she said.

As they entered the restaurant, a handsome, distinguished-looking Japanese man in a black sport jacket and a white collarless shirt approached. His hair was white only on the borders around his forehead. "How can I help the hikers—directions to Central Park?" he asked.

"I know," she looked down at her casual outfit. "I've heard so much about Nobu. We only have one night in the city and I'd die to get a table tonight," she said.

"Which is it? If you die, then a table wouldn't be necessary!" he smiled at his own response, as did Olivia.

"Let me see," he said, grabbing the massive reservation book.

A young, attractive woman, *perhaps a hostess*, thought Pepe, appeared and gently nudged the gentleman on the elbow with her hand, "You don't have to do every job, sir," she said.

"You're not—" Olivia started to say.

"I am," Nobu said, still at the side of the hostess. "Find them something," he ordered.

"I have a cancellation for two at seven. But I was told to hold the table in case we heard from—"

"Release it," he instructed. "For …?"

"Olivia Lopez," she said.

"The charming Olivia Lopez and …?" he looked at Pepe.

"Pepe Gomez," he said.

"And Mr. Gomez is unfortunately a Yankees fan," Nobu said, looking at Pepe's frayed hat.

"I'll be working tonight on a very large private affair for Mr. DeNiro. Otherwise, I'd invite you to join me in the kitchen for some fun. But if you enjoy this evening, come back, and it'll be a pleasure to complete my wishes. But make a reservation. Alyssa, give me a menu," demanded Nobu.

She complied quickly.

He wrote a personal note on the dark brown leather menu: "To Olivia and Pepe—Enjoy!" Below, he signed his name.

"This will be here for you tonight. You don't want to lug it around all day. How pleasant to meet you two," he said and bowed slightly.

"You're a dream!" she said. She reached up and gave him a kiss on the cheek. He smiled, seemingly surprised. He shook Pepe's hand as Olivia and Pepe bowed slightly, actually in unison, and then moved away.

They raced out onto 57th Street.

"Wow!" she screamed. "Was that neat or what? I feel like getting dressed now," she added.

"The day is young," he replied. "Are you always this charmed?" he asked.

"Apparently only with you, Hector!" she said.

A few minutes later, Olivia, in the midst of babbling about meeting Nobu, getting a table, and the future promise of a guided interaction in the kitchen, almost stepped in front of a cab that had sped through a yellow light. Pepe grabbed her arm and pulled her back, the cab just barely missing her.

"Whoa! That was close," she said, eyes wide open. "Thank you," she added, her breath taken away.

"My pleasure. I better hold on to you—for your safety," and he slid his arm in hers. They remained arm in arm for a good while.

They entered Central Park, in no particular hurry, some time after one o'clock. He had no sense of time. The temperature on this cloudless day was eighty-eight degrees. As he held her hand, they sat by a giant oak tree. Pepe placed his back flush against the tree with Olivia at a ninety-degree angle, the back of her head resting across his legs. He fiddled with her soft black hair while they talked. Her hair felt to him like strands of silk. Their hands touched and released with ease. His back ached, but he didn't budge.

"I appreciate that we're not talking about our jobs. But let me ask one question. May I?" she probed, really in preparation for seeing Carrie tomorrow.

"Fire away," Pepe said.

"What's the culture of your office with regard to persons on supervision—on probation and parole?" Olivia asked.

"The best way I know how to describe it is … well, it's a white man's macho party. The managers somehow believe that being tough on offenders is helping the community be safe—or at least that's their cover. Really though, I think the process is just a by-product of stereotypical thinking. We label and put a stigma on a group of a people until we have a polarized end game. 'They' are the enemy. Then you can justify anything," he said.

"That's the most articulate explanation of the criminal justice system I've ever heard in my life," she said, looking squarely up at his eyes.

"I ain't stupid, Olivia. But The Kingmaker, the deputy, is another matter," he said.

After a marvelous experience at Nobu New York, they purposely walked past Carnegie Hall, because Pepe was curious to see what it looked like.

"Look, we missed Ray Romano live tonight!" she said.

"Olivia, we didn't miss *anything* today!" he said.

They walked slowly, the RIHGA Hotel sign visible just two blocks ahead. He wondered how to determine the appropriate distance-closeness ratio once they entered Suite 727. He was quite content to call it a day without pushing premature intimacy. But he realized that he already felt intimate with her in a profound way—a way that he had never experienced before.

Once inside she asked, "Are you going to stay up and watch TV?"

"Well, maybe there's a good movie on," he said, having no clear signal as to what she wanted to happen next.

"After I get my pajamas on, I'll join you. Just send me to my bed when I fall asleep. OK?" Olivia asked.

"Do your pajamas have little feetsies?" he asked.

"Of course," she said.

He changed into lounging pants with a red jalapeño print and a black University of Maryland sweatshirt.

He was standing over the TV, with the remote in his hand, when Olivia entered wearing two-piece white pajamas, ankle-length, with little red hearts. She approached him, opened her arms, and kissed him.

"Thank you for a wonderful day!" she said. "It was magical."

"Olivia, better than I could've ever imagined," he added.

He sat on the couch, and she lay across his lap, as she had done under the oak tree earlier in the day. It now felt like a safe, familiar position for her. Pepe found some movie that interested him.

Within fifteen minutes she was asleep. He nudged her into an upright position and walked her to the bedroom. He tucked her under a pile of covers in the cool, air-conditioned room.

"Good night, Olivia," he said, kissing her on the forehead.

"Good night, Hector," she said.

Some twenty minutes later, Olivia called out to Pepe.

"Hector, there is a strange noise in my room. Could you come in here and check?" she said, seemingly scared.

He rushed in. "What noise?" he said from the doorway.

"Over there, near the window," she said, sounding panicky.

He walked over to the window and opened the curtains. A fully lighted building was right next door, just yards away.

"Olivia, I don't hear anything," he said, looking around for some clue.

Then he felt two arms wrap around him in a tight hug, from behind, her breasts touching his back.

"Maybe it was just my heart—pounding!" she said.

He turned around and held her. Their lips found each other. Their kisses, alternating between firmness and movement, sent a sensation throughout his body. He glided her backwards, as if dancing, onto the bed. They touched each other, exploring each other's bodies, gaining a feeling of physical comfort and arousal. He encouraged her to enjoy him, and she responded; she in turn led him to places on her body. They laughed, held each other, and made love most of the night—playing, teasing, giggling, before finally falling asleep in each other's arms some time around five o'clock the next morning.

"I'm starving—and you?" she asked, coming out of the bathroom around ten in the morning.

"Me, too. Our favorite bagel shop?" he asked.

"Absolutely," she replied.

Arm in arm, they headed for Bagel & Bean.

An effeminate male waiter took their order efficiently. He smiled at Pepe—stared, really—before disappearing.

"What an unusual day," Olivia said.

"Wasn't a bad *night* either!"

"No, it was a very good night—the best.… Hector, I don't know how to say this—"

"I know, 'I'm not ready for a boyfriend,'" he said, with an edge of sarcasm.

"That's not *exactly* what I was going to say. It sounds, well, silly, when I hear you say those words," she smiled.

He shot back, "Well, actually, I'm not ready for a boyfriend either!"

Just as Pepe delivered that line, perhaps louder than he thought, their waiter passed by, and, overhearing him, frowned and twisted his head sharply to the side.

Pepe and Olivia caught his reaction and snickered quietly.

"Go on, Olivia. You were right in the middle of the 'while I'm in a reconnecting phase of my life, now that I've met you, I'm realizing that the timing really doesn't fit my I-can-go-it-alone mindset' speech," he said.

"I hope—I just wasn't looking for a boyfriend in my life now. I've got too much going on," she said.

"Listen, Olivia, I'm not a puppy. I'm a big boy. Be frank with me. Is this about the fact that you're a lawyer and I'm a probation officer?" he said, with anger.

"I resent that, Hector!" Olivia said.

"I don't do 'Pepe's not good enough' for anybody—you included!"

"Where did you get that from? This has nothing to do with professional status. Frankly, the probation office puts too many restraints on you. You're a brilliant person with great vision and a feel for people and their pain. Maybe that's what you sense in me when you talk about your probation work," she said.

"Maybe I just projected—" he said.

"Look, I'm getting settled ... in a job, back around my family. I don't rush through changes fast. I tend to process things slowly when they're important to me. Last night—last night was an exception. I don't let someone—*men*—in this quickly. My head's spinning. Exactly, how long have I known you, Hector? How long?"

"Months," he said.

"Baloney! Forget the flower-giving ceremony," she said.

"You didn't like the flowers?" he pretended to protest.

"Given the unfolding circumstances, it was the exact opposite of what you should've done!" she said.

"If I wanted to keep a secret. Is it because we work together, or is it something else?" "We've covered that ground."

"I understand the workplace rules. But is *that* the issue?" he asked, trying to read her eyes for a clue.

"Yes, and the fact that I have very warm feelings for you," she said, tightly entwining her fingers together, almost as if she was waiting for physical pain to stop. "It's not supposed to happen to me like this, Hector! I don't like being swept off my feet. I feel … vulnerable … in the open!" she said, her eyes racing around the walls of the restaurant.

"Good! Olivia, I've never enjoyed anyone more in my life. I feel like I'm with a friend. Well, a *special* friend after last night," he smiled. "Look, I feel happy … at ease, with you. I asked myself over and over yesterday, 'How can this be so natural, so much fun without trying?' I look at you and see such beauty. I'm crazy about you," he said.

The waiter delivered the food, glanced at the tears in her eyes, and smiled again.

"Lord, the waiter is gawking at me again," Pepe said, smiling. "One step at a time, Olivia…. That's all anyone can do. Can you handle that?"

"Yes, but let the dust settle. Let me feel what *Hector* might mean in my life."

"Then we go slow, right?" he asked.

"Right."

Olivia read her book in the lobby of the Plaza Hotel on a very comfortable couch, surrounded by large vases of freshly cut flowers. She rubbed her NYY pin in her hands and thought about his innocent face as they said goodbye outside the RIHGA.

"Olivia!" said Carrie. They hugged and kissed each other on the cheek.

Carrie was excited to see Olivia. Already they seemed to appreciate a certain common style—an attention to detail, courtesy, and a deft understanding of when they were having their chains yanked. Carrie was certain she had found a courthouse ally, which was critical to the effectiveness of WWTS, and, she hoped, a new friend, too. They checked into their room which had, as they had requested, two double beds. The suite's floral prints and elegant trim were breathtaking, even for Carrie, who was accustomed to the finer things in life. Olivia agreed with Carrie's assessment. They ate lunch in the hotel. Carrie surprised Olivia with reservations for a massage, which she had billed to her account. During this special pampering, Olivia, resting on a warm, fluffy, gray towel, fell asleep.

After their time in the spa, both agreed they were invigorated; so, they headed for Bergdorf Goodman. Once there, they were joined by a fashion consultant who stayed with them for a shopping extravaganza. Over a dozen boxes were shipped back to their respective Maryland addresses.

On the way to the Museum of Modern Art on this hot day, Carrie asked, "What did you do yesterday?"

"I met an old boy friend. He and I walked through Central Park— you know, just catching up," she said.

"An old boy *friend*, or an old boyfriend?" Carrie asked, picking up the obvious vagueness from Olivia. Particularly after Carl's dalliances came to the surface, Carrie missed very little in the congruence, or lack thereof, between words, body language, and tone.

"Well, uh, old boyfriend," Olivia said, trying to clarify yet conceal.

"I see…." Carrie said, avoiding eye contact with Olivia.

"You are *not* going to believe this, Carrie!"

"What?"

"We met Nobu!" Olivia managed to distract Carrie with the story, still without naming the "old boyfriend."

That night, over a quick salad, before they headed for the Majestic to see *The Phantom of the Opera*, Carrie asked, "Have you had a chance to think about the revocation process?"

"I have. There's a serious organizational culture problem. The probation officers—with some, like Gee Brooks, being exceptions— act like bullies, like they're *glad* to be in court. They're right off a *CSI: Miami* set. I talked to … one probation officer who said it's nothing more than stereotypical thinking against offenders. My office, like the prosecutor's, really doesn't have a lot to go on in revocation hearings. Assistants meet with the offender, maybe for an hour before the hearing, and go over the charges spelled out by the probation officer in a revocation report. The reports are mostly a summary of what the offender did or didn't do. Frankly, what we hear from offenders is usually excuses or descriptions of being helpless. Still, I swear, my instincts tell me there's a lot of fabrication going on by the probation officers on the stand," said Olivia.

"That's what Jon says. What kind of fabrication?"

"Stuff you can't pin down, like 'I told him to call me by next Tuesday,' or 'I left a card on his door with instructions to see me by Monday afternoon, but he never called,' or 'I warned him.' Stuff you can't defend against. Their testimony is crucial because it goes to the matter of intentional neglect, as opposed to offenders just being disorganized or unable to comply—like when they're unable to get a job. The defendants appear agitated, pissed off at the officers' testimony, like the officers have made it up to cover their own butts."

"Can't the court see that?"

"Carrie, as you know, the court is a family, for better or worse. They work with each other day in and day out. Defendants come and go. The prosecutor simply argues that the offender has had one bite of the apple at sentencing. It's an adversarial process—the judge is almost always going to accept the statements of probation officers in a 'he said, she said' debate, for the integrity of the process," Olivia said.

"And the beat goes on. If it's penny-ante stuff, why doesn't the court just slap the offender on the wrist?" Carrie asked.

"Now, there's the rub. I asked my new colleagues that question and they just sort of scratched their heads. No one seemed to know. My guess was that somewhere along the line, the court asked the probation office—maybe numerous judges asked at different times—what *other* community options were available to solve the presenting problems, and the probation office responded that there were none. The easy remedy, the new norm, became incarceration in state prisons. My guess is the court probably didn't ask to what degree an independent assessment of community-based resources was conducted or if the probation leaders ever really sought to develop new resources. The probation office's culture is to win revocation hearings. Same for prosecutors—you know, win the big game! They're not motivated to help solve the problems," Olivia said.

"Macho...."

"So, now we have a recurring process that probably *no one* is watching."

"Wow, Jon's right," said Carrie. "Is there a way to solve the problem, Olivia?"

"My public defender peers have to change their approach. I'm not sure if they're inclined to do that. They come across meekly in these hearings. True, they probe the probation officers, but they seem to back off of getting into dicey areas—like the truth. Instead, they rush to a 'please give this poor boy one more chance' argument."

"What would you do differently?" asked Carrie.

"In one case, Probation Officer Gee Brooks was all I needed. She shot it straight. I bet she got in trouble for her honesty. But I'd grill the probation officer on how and why, exactly, all those special conditions came about. The officer in front of me probably didn't make the recommendation for the special conditions, so I'd summon the officer who did recommend them and get their testimony. This, of course, is a presentation targeted to judges, who actually order the special conditions—or nooses. But I'd stay away from grilling the officer as to whether he is telling the truth; there's nothing to gain by doing that. Then, I'd grill the presenting probation officer on why his office doesn't use local community resources to resolve the problems he presented in his revocation report. He won't know, so I'd call the chief probation officer to the stand. Now, that ought to get things going. So, two things are of interest to me: hammering away at the role of multiple special conditions and finding local resources to handle the problems, rather than prisons."

"How would your peers react to this tactic?" Carrie asked, looking skeptical.

Olivia paused, "We'll see. I doubt a crown awaits me."

~

Early the next morning as Carrie was headed out the door, she noticed the NYY lapel pin near Olivia's bed.

Lord, another Yankees fan, she said to herself.

Carrie walked over to Olivia's bed and whispered, "See you back at the mill. Thanks for your thoughts." She was pleased that—besides gaining a new friend—she now had an ally inside the Defenders' Office that she could count on for reliable information.

"Have a safe trip," Olivia lifted her head to say, before flopping back into the pillow.

New York changed everything, Pepe thought on the train ride back with Olivia, presently napping with her head on his shoulder. *My God*, he thought, hearing her breath beside him, *I'm in love.*

16

NO EXIT

TJ Smith

Today, September 3, was TJ's last day in prison. On the day of their release from MCIH, inmates had to be removed from prison at 4:00 AM. The prison was located in the western part of the state in a rural area, hours from where most black and Hispanic inmates lived, and avoiding rush hour traffic was a priority for the sheriff's deputies who transported them. The deputies also liked to leave pre-dawn for the associated overtime. Plus, if another inmate had a score to settle, prison officials reasoned, the offended party wouldn't have the opportunity to do the nasty deed if the target walked through the facility so early in the morning.

At 4:05 AM, two Montgomery County sheriff's deputies, who had the responsibility to transport parolee's back to their district of supervision, backed up by two prison guards, clanged on TJ's cell. Because two sheriff's deputies once transported the wrong inmate in 1971, an elaborate I.D. quiz was required.

"Thomas J. Smith, Jr., what is your middle name?" asked the lead deputy.

"Joshua," TJ whispered, so the other inmates couldn't hear him.

"What?" asked the deputy.

"Joshua," said TJ, louder.

"What is your Social Security number?"

"O-U-8-12!" shouted out Cleon from two cells down.

Chuckles and snickers emerged from other cells, the inmates now rousing with voyeur interest. All of the inmates knew the identification drill used by sheriff's deputies. It was like a quiz for dummies.

"Quiet down!" said one of the guards standing behind the two sheriff's deputies.

"318-02-9889," said TJ.

"There goes another identity theft opportunity! Tsk, Tsk!" shouted Cue Ball from directly opposite Cleon's cell.

"Shut up!" repeated the same beefy guard.

"What's your father's middle initial?" continued the deputy, looking at a fact sheet.

"J. I'm Jr.," said TJ.

"What event should occur today?" asked the deputy.

This question started a Denton cellblock shout-out, a free-flowing my-turn-at-the-microphone babble, like a karaoke party gone mad.

"Queen for a Day!" shouted one effeminate inmate. "Don't leave your buddies behind!"

"Breakfast with the governor!" said another.

"A free fucking Jiffy Lube oil change!"

"A date with Cal Ripken's wife!"

"My release," said TJ.

"Hey, Mr. Stump-the-Stars, could we get this over with?" asked the smaller guard to the deputy questioner.

As they were opening the cell, TJ turned to the now-standing Hardroc. Oddly, neither man had discussed TJ's release directly, although TJ felt many of Hardroc's remarks over the last few weeks had started with the word "remember." TJ hated this moment more than he hated his first day in prison. Hardroc had become part of his identity.

"TJ, my brother-from-another-mother, you're in my soul. Be strong. Keep it real, brother," Hardroc said, exchanging an elaborate ritualized handshake and hug.

"I love you, man...." TJ said quietly.

The deputies handcuffed TJ's hands behind his back and guided him out of the cell and down the dimly lighted cellblock with its double-decked cells.

One inmate called, "Be cool, brother!" Another buddy in a nearby cell said, "Get some sloppy for yo' hang-down tonight, TJ." Other inmates observed TJ being escorted down their cellblock but remained silent.

Because the overhead lights on the cellblock were not illuminated fully, none of the inmates could see the tears running down TJ's face— *surely a first for an inmate*, he thought, *crying seconds away from walking out of a prison.*

At this moment, TJ felt profoundly torn between leaving the only father figure and, at times, big brother he had ever known and rejoining his wife and two children. Hardroc had set him up as an IT expert in the administration building. He had declared TJ had a career in computers. But TJ wondered if a free society would buy it.

On the way back to Montgomery County, from the back of the deputy sheriff's car, TJ thought about how Hardroc had said, "you're in my soul," to him, when TJ knew, in fact, that Hardroc was embedded into *his* heart and soul. TJ felt honored to have been under Hardroc's tutelage. He realized at this moment, more than ever before in his life, that he had plenty to lose. He feared failure in his gut. This time, failure would be on *him*, not the fault of the system, not his parents, because he had everything anyone would need to succeed: a promising job, a home, a loyal wife, and two loving children. *What the heck*, he thought to himself, *I even like Ms. Brooks, my probation officer.*

TJ's younger sister, Dee Smith, picked him up at the Montgomery County Detention Center, a sprawling building that had taken on multiple temporary building appendages in an effort to keep up with the escalating number of detainees awaiting trial. TJ wore a change of clothes Junie had brought him last week. He carried his toiletries and the $250 saved from his meager prison salary over the past four and two-thirds years. Outside the main entrance, Dee hugged him, like, he remembered, she used to do when they were kids. He flashed back to a memory of the two of them fighting, as brother and sister fight, yet trying to create their own sense of security in a parentless home. Together, they used to snuggle on the old worn-out couch trying to ward off fear of the night and the uncertainty of tomorrow. Until she was twelve, Dee used to fall asleep near him, then wake up and go into her own bed. Her breathing helped him fall asleep. In prison, he slept with his thumb close to his mouth. He wondered if Hardroc noticed that. If he did, he didn't mention it to TJ.

As a child, Dee's views on life had always influenced TJ as a big sister's would have, not a sister three years younger than him. She was just short of a mother figure to him. She was the one constant in his childhood and, along with his grandmother, the only source of female affection he had known, at least until he was fifteen.

"How are you, big brother?" Dee asked.

"Like a deer in the headlights. Jumpy, really," he said.

"You seem so … *grown-up*," she said. "Well, it's time for a new start."

He said nothing but kept looking out of her car window. She handed him new sunglasses. *What the heck are these buildings?* he thought to himself. Five years ago he had rarely ventured out of Lincoln Park. Everything felt new, he thought to himself, like he went to sleep in D.C. and woke up in downtown Chicago. It was an unsettling feeling—like being an arriving foreigner.

"I know for a fact your wife hopes troubles are behind you two," said Dee. *She should know*, he thought. Junie was Dee's best friend, and she told her everything.

"Good," he said, but instead of joy, he felt sad and awkward, out of place and on-guard. He could find no words to describe his feelings to Dee. He marveled in silence at the speed of the cars on Route 270 and how close they came to each other.

"Why, my big, handsome, *married*, African brother, did you let that skanky-assed Taunja on your visiting list? Are you *stupid*? I hope you got that bitch out of your system. She always had you under her thumb, but Junie ain't gonna be stupid for you now. And I ain't covering for you," she said.

"How long you been waiting to say that, Dee? Enough. I was stupid. Enough," he said. Yet he began to fantasize about Taunja's muscled body, her large, firm breasts, and her unsurpassed bubble butt. *Taunja could tear a man up*, he daydreamed, smiling slightly.

"I ain't kidding," she said.

"How are the kids—you know, 'bout me coming home?"

"The truth?" she asked, diverting her eyes from the road long to glance at TJ directly. "Yes."

"Scared. They hardly remember you. Well, Natasha doesn't. They didn't like coming up to that Hagerstown prison. Junie hasn't raised them like that. Junie hasn't told you everything, because she didn't want to act like she was *all that*, but girl's been on a roll," she said.

"Oh, tell me more!" he said.

"Listen to you! Who in the hell is sitting next me? Old TJ would never say, 'tell me more,' and you been up in Hagerstown with all them thugs. Most of *them* start their sentences with the *M-F* word!" she said.

TJ jerked his head back but said nothing.

"Well, brother, you know about the job at the doctor's office as a receptionist. They liked her so much, they sent her to school—paid for everything—to get a nursing degree. Then, of course, Montgomery College gave her a scholarship. You know that. But guess what happened this week—the doctor's office is giving her, as in *paying* her, although she's not there, for twenty hours a week to take classes. She only had to sign a contract to work with them six months for every semester of school she attends. She's starting on her B.S. at the University of Maryland next week. She wants you to be proud of her, so heads up," she said.

"Who watches the kids?" he asked.

"I do, at nights, when she studies or has classes. And several teenage girls in the neighborhood—responsible girls," she added.

"I don't like other people watching my kids."

Dee said nothing for a few moments.

"She's got this group of supporters—the Bethesda Women's Club—who mentor her. People believe in Junie, TJ. And, every Sunday, she takes Grandmomma to church and then cooks the Sunday meal," she said.

"How's Grandmomma?" he said.

"Not today, baby. We'll talk about that tomorrow. Better, let's just go over there Sunday," she said.

"Well, with Junie's new status, I take it the "Welcome Home, Con" party has been cancelled," he said.

Dee just gave him a scowl and tried unsuccessfully not to laugh.

Then, after a few moments of silence, they caught up on various cousins and her work as a pre-K teacher in Germantown.

"Junie asked me to take the kids out to a movie after getting, you know…."

"Reacquainted with their absent father, huh, Dee?" he said, peering over his sunglasses at her.

"Whatever. Is that OK with you? Is that what you want, Brother?" she asked.

"I'm cool with that. Reacquainted.... Shit.... How do you do that? Hi, I'm TJ. By the way, I'm your husband, so get me my newspaper...." He trailed off. "Dee, I've thought of you so many times.... How you held me together when things got tough, when Grandmomma was ill ... when that mother of ours dragged *my ass* into church so *she* would feel good about herself with church-cover. I remember eating all those mayonnaise sandwiches waiting for Grandmomma's checks. And our devoted father ... too good for us. Me hanging out in the street, trying to be something.... It was you who tried to help me...."

He paused, his voice choking.

Tears fell down Dee's face.

"God knows I love you and thank you," he said. "I can't tell you why I feel so violated and angry right now, but it ain't you I'm mad at," he said.

"Take your time, TJ. Take your time. It'll all work out," she said.

TJ had been in Junie's three-bedroom townhouse in Germantown for about half an hour, and he still felt awkward, like he was visiting a distant relative. He was pissed off that Junie was not there to meet him and make him feel welcomed, but he said nothing to Dee, who was making coffee in the kitchen. He sat in the small living room, just off to the left of the tiny foyer. It was the room closest to the front door; he stayed there for a good while because he didn't feel he could invade the other rooms, particularly upstairs. He walked around and felt two large comfortable chairs and a solid green corduroy couch with three neatly arranged pillows.

This room's bigger than the cells I've lived in for the past fifty-six months, he thought. The room was spotless. He guessed the children weren't allowed to play in it. Four pictures on one wall were hung in a square. Two of the pictures were of African women and two were of his children at play. He remembered his grandmother's apartment on the outskirts of Lincoln Park. There, only one old table had family pictures. He remembered studying those pictures, wondering why he never actually saw any of those people. It dawned on him now that his grandmother's pictures were of people from the past—Junie's pictures were about pride and the future.

On another wall, he noticed two pictures of himself holding his children: one with Tommy and the other with baby Natasha, in the prison visiting room. Two pictures of the past, he thought, but also a signal for the future.

"Dee, is there a bathroom on this floor?"

"Right here, baby, right here," she said, showing him a door in the short hall, steps from the kitchen.

He noticed how clean everything was in the bathroom. A map of the Metro system was framed above the toilet. He stared at the stops in D.C. near Georgetown.... He wanted to walk around, maybe go to the Kennedy Center to hear a concert with Junie.

TJ heard the voices of Junie and the children. He walked quickly back into the living room, where their gifts were wrapped in boxes—a baseball glove, doll, and nightgown—all selected by Dee. He had handed Dee $125 when he saw the wrapped gifts in her car.

"Hello, TJ," Junie said, giving him a hug and a kiss on the cheek in the foyer.

"Hello, Daddy," said Tommy and Natasha, simultaneously.

"Well, come here, you two, I'm not gonna bite—not yet, anyway," TJ said. Natasha looked to him like the spitting image of Junie, with her caramel skin. But she had his long eyelashes. TJ was surprised how tall Tommy was—almost up to his nose. He actually looked like a cross between TJ and Dee. Both children had soft, sweet demeanors.

They approached him together, slowly, and he hugged them at the same time, one under each arm. Both turned their heads away from him.

"I got you these small gifts.... I hope you like them," TJ said, pointing them to the gifts on the coffee table.

Dee stood quietly behind a chair, in the background.

Tommy was the first to get the wrapping off. "Oh, wow! But I don't play baseball," he said.

"I'll teach you, Lil'T. I'll teach you," he said.

"Oh, Daddy, I love the doll. She's *so* pretty," Natasha said.

"Like you, baby, like you!" he said, receiving her hug.

Junie took one look at her gift, the nightgown, shut the box, and said, "I'll look at this later."

"What is it, Mommy, what—"Natasha started to protest.

Junie gave her *the look*, and the discussion was over.

At Junie's prompting, the children talked about school, their friends, what they liked and didn't like—almost the kind of discussion families have when a member has been away on a long trip, it seemed to TJ.

Junie and Dee started frying chicken, TJ's favorite, with mashed potatoes, gravy, biscuits, and collard greens, while TJ unpacked and put his meager possessions away in Junie's closet and bedroom. Junie had emptied a side of the closet for him and had his old clothes ironed and hung up. After trying them on, TJ found that he still wore the same size, although he was heavier now. He pulled out some T-shirts that had subtle logos or messages associated with the street life, like his old favorite of a rapper, and threw them on the floor to give away. Given the few things hanging up, clearly Dee or Junie had preceded him in this effort. He would shop for casual clothes when he got a paycheck, he thought. He remembered Hardroc used to say, "Clothes trick a man into believing he's somebody."

"TJ, come check out your computer room. A box arrived from Art Coleman with the computer, printer, all that stuff—right there!" Junie said. "I set it up, but if you don't like it, move it around."

"Oh, wow! Thank you," TJ said.

"So, TJ, you have a meeting with Art tomorrow at the church. He called and said that he has a contract for you to sign, and he wants to go over the process with you. They'll have a small office the two of you can use," Junie said. "Are you excited?"

"Yeah. I'll be on my way to be a regular IT guy," he said.

Natasha and Tommy entered the small room, now with half-emptied computer boxes."What does IT guy mean, Daddy?" asked Natasha.

"Well, it means I'll be working with computers," he said.

"Oh, I know that, Mom told us. I work on computers at school, too, Daddy," she said, running off to get something.

She returned and handed him a computerized mock-up of a man in a suit working at a computer. The caption said, "My Daddy."

"Thank you, Baby. Let me tell you about my computer classes at college," he said, and he began a long discussion about computers and the importance of an education.

After dinner, Dee told the kids that it was time to head to the movies and give Mom and Dad a chance to catch up.

As TJ closed the door behind Dee and the two kids, Junie sat quietly on the couch, her hands folded between her long, brightly patterned green and blue skirt.

"How does it feel—to be home?" she asked.

"I don't know.... Odd ... like I don't understand time and place. *Your* townhouse is now *my* home."

"But *us*, TJ.... Where do we start? How do we start again?"

"What do you mean, 'again?'"

"*Again*, again. After all this time? After your little girlfriend was up at Hagerstown slipping and sliding around. I don't have it in me to play wet-nurse to a man who wants to treat me like a commodity! I *am* someone! My children are going to be somebody! And please, don't call Tommy 'Lil'T.' That's street talk. Call him that, and he'll be that!"

"What do you want from me? I just walked in the door. I haven't had a beer or dope since I've been in the joint. I haven't been with a woman in years. What do you want from me?"

"When you closed your eyes on that prison cot, TJ, did you fantasize about her, or me?"

"And who's comforted you, Junie?"

"Other than me, nobody."

"Why're we doing this, Junie? What do you want?"

"For the pain and loneliness to go away," she said. He noticed the tears in her eyes.

"So do I, Junie. So do I!" he said.

"TJ, I don't have it in me to just, on demand, open my heart.... I'll try.... Maybe time will help. You must understand. Parts of me have had to shut down, not just to you—to every man," she said. "I'm sorry, I'm not good at this, I'm sorry. I feel like I'm on pins and needles, waiting for something to happen. Listen, I'm not what I was back then. I'm different. I have people who believe in me. *I* believe in me. Please don't take us—"

"Junie, I'm going to work with computers. I'm in the IT field. You'll see. I ain't no con, no small-time drug user—you'll see. I'm never going back to prison. I want to be a good father, Junie, and a good husband. I'm not taking you on a bad trip anywhere."

"It's me, TJ, I'm sorry. Something—maybe trust—has died in me. I can't get it back, and I can't seem to move forward. But I'll try hard," she said.

The silence that followed was ended by Junie saying, "Let's go upstairs."

Without saying a word, they went to their bedroom. Beside the bed, she kept her back to him as she removed her earrings and necklace, gingerly kicking his soon-to-be discarded old clothes out of the way. He pressed his chest to her back and put his arms around her.

"I know.… I know, TJ," she said.

He went over to the bed, undressed, and lay on the covers. She removed her sweater, bra, skirt, slip, and panties, still keeping with her back to him. She glanced in the mirror and saw his obvious arousal. With arms folded over her breasts, she slid beside him, choosing not to put on the new nightgown he had bought for the occasion.

"Be gentle, please.… It's been a long time," she said.

He kissed her gently and mounted her. After a few uneven motions, they found a rhythm. Her eyes rolled back as she let out a moan, part-pain, part-pleasure.

"TJ.… TJ."

After just a few minutes, he was spent. He knew he would want another encounter, but Junie left the bedroom so quickly that he was sure it wouldn't be tonight … and it pissed him off.

What about me? he wanted to scream. In spite of Hardroc's teachings and admonitions, he felt sorry for himself—and *entitled.*

The Labor Day weekend was a very busy time for Gee, who reluctantly spent her break doing some early planning for the National Probation Association's bi-annual meeting, which would be held at the Baltimore Civic Center in January. The Montgomery County probation office was the official host. Like all staff, Gee had been assigned multiple tasks, including serving as a room monitor for a training presentation on interstate compact cooperation, a stupid topic, she thought; working at the registration desk; and serving as a member of the office social committee. This last task was to make sure the dinner-dance ran smoothly. Therein lay numerous little headaches. It was the last thing on earth she wanted to do.

Gee pulled out TJ's file to make sure she had not overlooked some remote special condition. She was excited about his future and happy to be able to help him find the IT job—as long as Kingmaker didn't find out about it.

17

THANKSGIVING DELIVERY TEAM

Gee Brooks

Because Pepe was on his way to San Antonio to have Thanksgiving with his ailing mother, Gee, Huggie, and Hattie were called on to take over his annual Thanksgiving dinner delivery for the needy. Pepe was prepared this year in a way that startled Gee. There were lists, Mapquest routes, even quotes they were supposed to say to certain families. It almost looked as if Pepe had been secretly getting help from someone more organized than he was.

At the rear of the A.M.E New Hope Gospel Church in Rockville, Judge Glenny Clarke spoke to the media about the court's great interest in this annual effort, traditionally spearheaded by probation officers.

The vans were loaded by community activists and then blessed by a covey of ministers, who competed for airtime. Huggie, Hattie, and Gee sat behind the driver's seats of the three yellow Hertz vans. The others each had two assistants, but Gee had three: TJ, Tommy, and Natasha. Gee drove the rental van away from the loading area. The small parking lot was jammed with bustling people, a pep band, and cars coming and going. TJ sat in the passenger seat, the kids in the back with the food, gleefully being flung from side to side.

"Look out!" yelled TJ.

Gee had miscalculated the closeness of a parked car and nearly sideswiped it.

"That's it, you're driving!" she said, pulling over to the curb.

"Women drivers," whispered Tommy.

"I heard that," Gee said.

The shift in drivers created a shift in roles, too. Now, she was the navigator, and he was the captain. She accepted the role reversal gracefully.

"Where do you want to go to first?" she asked.

"Well, I glanced at the one Knowles Avenue address. I know right where that is—let's go there!" TJ said. "You kids remember where Aunt Bessie lives?"

"Yes, sir," said Tommy.

"What color house, son?" he probed.

"White," Tommy said.

"Aunt Bessie is one of those people who will give you a job to do the moment you walk in the door. You know, 'Oh, good, the Lord has answered my prayers. The dishwasher has been broken for weeks.' She's too cheap to call a repairman. Right, kids?" he said.

"Yeah, one time she made me climb on a ladder and take leaves out of her gutters," Tommy said.

"Yeah, and one time she made me clean the bathrooms," added Natasha in a quiet voice.

"Well, I'm sure she means well," said Gee.

"We ain't going over there now, are we?" asked Tommy.

"*Aren't* going over there now," corrected TJ. "We will if you say *ain't* again."

"Are you kids warm enough?" asked Gee.

"Yes, Mom," Tommy said, smiling at his joke.

"Oh, so I'm not the only one who thinks you're not dressed warm enough?"

"No, Ms. Brooks, you're the second one."

"Maybe Moms are all alike!"

"Do you have kids?"

"No," said Gee.

There was silence. TJ frowned at Tommy in the rear view mirror.

They arrived at the first house and walked up to the front door, the food box in TJ's arms. A woman opened the door and Natasha said, "Trick or treat!"

Tommy whispered, "You idiot."

The elderly black lady of the house said, "Oh Lordy, treat, please."

Gee tried to explain who they were and what their purpose was. The lady seemed confused. A man in his thirties appeared over her shoulder.

"I know who you are. We got a call from the pastor's office. I'm her grandson. Come on in," said the man.

"What's happening, Dante?" said TJ.

"My, my, TJ! What you want to happen, Brother?" Dante said.

"Yeah, you know, I'm just doing this volunteer work.... Same ole, same ole," said TJ.

"Momma, these people be from the church. Remember, they're bringing you Thanksgiving food and such. Remember, Sissy is coming over to help you cook tomorrow? Remember?" said Dante.

"Well, praise Jesus Christ, our Lord and Savior. I knew he'd feed my family in his righteousness," she said.

The amateur crew turned on their heels, heading for the front door. "Well, have a blessed day, Miss Lady, and enjoy your family. Be sure to go to church, now!" Gee said, walking out the door. *What the heck*, she thought, *I might as well act like I'm from the church.*

As soon as they got in the van, the team burst into laughter and got out of there as quickly as possible.

"What was that all about?" TJ said.

"Yeah, trick or treat, Natasha?" Gee said.

"Go to church, Ms. Brooks? This ain't, uh, *isn't* no church mission," Tommy said.

They laughed hard and long.

"Who's that dude who said, 'What you want to happen?'" asked Tommy.

"Nobody. Just someone I know from—"

"Prison? Is he a prisoner, too, Daddy?" Natasha asked.

For a moment, Gee felt embarrassed, realizing how difficult it must be for TJ to put the past in the past with his kids.

"Fact is, he was. What he meant, Tommy, is did I want to do crime with him. Dante will be back in jail sooner or later. I never had nothing to do with him in prison, though. He and his guys would smuggle dope in the prison. I didn't want to get caught and have to spend more time inside those walls. I wanted to be home as soon as possible to be with you two. So, enough talk of prison. I'm not a prisoner anymore. What am I?" he asked.

"An IT expert, Daddy," Tommy said.

"My best Daddy," said Natasha.

"Well, IT man, can we get our stuff together a little better for the next visit from the Lord?" asked Gee.

They discussed options. TJ concluded that they better know their script because some of these folks might be confused about who they were and where they came from. As a group, they decided they didn't want to say 'church' or 'the probation office.' So they settled on 'community outreach,' although twice Natasha said 'community out-teach.' After the third visit, they decided, for efficiency, to pair up. While one pair carried the food, the other would do the talking. They'd take turns. TJ paired up with Tommy, and Natasha followed Gee, holding her hand wherever they went. They'd rate the "show," as they called it, after each event. Some were heartfelt, some were sad. The pair that did the carrying acted as evaluators of the presentation and found something funny about each stop. At the end of the mission, after a very late McDonald's lunch and thirty-seven deliveries, the tired team, with Natasha asleep in Gee's lap in the floor of the truck, pulled into the church parking lot, near Gee's car. A representative from Hertz was there to retrieve the van.

Gee carried Natasha to TJ's old, beat-up Toyota and placed her in the back seat. She kissed her on the forehead. "Bye, my sweet partner. Be good. You did great today. A lot of kids are going to get good food tomorrow because of you," Gee said.

"Bye, Ms. Brooks, thanks for being on my team. We're the best," she said, looking at her brother.

"No, you weren't," said Tommy, on cue.

She hugged Tommy. "You're a wonderful young man and I enjoyed being with you. I hope to see you again—after I get some rest," she laughed.

"Thank you, Ms. Brooks. You're funny and fun," Tommy said.

"You are too, Tommy," she said, brushing his hair with her hand and closing his door after he clicked his seatbelt.

She walked around the rear of the car to TJ's side, the sun setting early on this gray Wednesday before Thanksgiving.

"Thank you, TJ. I didn't expect to have such fun. What lovely kids. They're so smart, polite, *and* funny," she said.

"Junie raised them. I'm just trying to catch up. I enjoyed helping out. Thank you for inviting us. Can we help every year?" he asked.

"I'm counting on our team. Maybe Junie can join us, too. But you have to drive again, before you end up dying by my hands," she said.

"I don't want to die by anybody's hands," he said.

There was an awkward second. She felt like giving him a hug, a natural thing for her to do. Jesus, that's all I need, Gee thought to herself—Kingmaker hearing about me hugging a male offender.

He quickly held out his hand.

"Thank you, Ms. Brooks," he said.

18

BRICKHOUSE: SALVE FOR AN OLD WOUND

TJ Smith

The business of marital economics—who brings in what money and how it's going to be spent—is central to the equilibrium of couples. It was five days after Christmas, just over eleven weeks since TJ had started work with Art Coleman. The good news was that he had put in hundreds of hours. The bad news was that Art experienced delays in being paid himself for the work. But Art had sent a check for $3,000 and said that he expected to pay TJ the outstanding $8,000 within three days. TJ was elated.

Although TJ hadn't had a sip of alcohol since his release in September, he went to the corner beer and wine shop and bought a bottle of champagne. He planned to celebrate with Junie. The kids had already left to spend the night with friends.

It was six o'clock, and the champagne was chilled, as were two new champagne glasses, around which TJ had tied ribbons. When Junie arrived home from work, before she could take her coat off, he popped the cork in a sweeping gesture in the foyer. The joy in his heart, knowing $8,000 was nearly in his hands, also made him want to pop another cork, a little farther south.

"I don't approve of you drinking, TJ," she said, as she hung her coat and scarf in the hall closet. She took several steps toward the stairs—probably, he thought, to do homework in the spare bedroom, which the two of them shared as an office.

"What? Give me a break, Junie. I haven't had a drop of alcohol since I've been out! Junie, Junie, look at this: a check from Art for $3,000—three thousand! Another $8,000 is on the way! We already fixed your car, my mother's furnace, repaired this roof, bought the kids clothes, and paid some debts. This $3,000-check is fucking *free* for us—to spend on us!"

"Don't use that *street* language around me, or the kids!"

"Where is this coming from, Junie?"

"Yesterday, Tommy called his sister a pimp!" she said.

"Well, he's got it backwards, Ms. Nurse *Perfect*," he said. From the look on her face, he knew he'd made a mistake. He tried to give her a hug on the steps, but she turned stiff as a board.

"What's '*Nurse Perfect*' supposed to mean, TJ?" she asked.

"Nothing. Just give me a chance to celebrate being me, that's all. It can't always be about the wronged, the martyr left behind, can it?" he said.

"Oh, so you're the one who's suffered?" she said.

"Oh, come on, Junie," he said.

"Come on, what?"

"Have you conveniently forgotten that back when I couldn't find a job, except that 7-11 cashier shit, it embarrassed you? When I found better sources of income, you didn't mind spending that cash I laid on the table—no questions asked—not a word! You knew that money came from dope!" He gulped down a six ounce glass of champagne, chasing after her as she changed direction and headed away from the stairs toward the kitchen.

"I had no choice. You were one-third trying to find work, one-third pretending to be looking for work—probably laying up with Miss Suggar—and one-third trying to sell dope. So, what was I supposed to do? I had no skills 'cause I wanted to marry your sorry ass rather than go to school—where I should've been!" she said.

"I didn't keep you out of school, you liar. You know your father said he wasn't paying for your school."

"OK, Mr. I-been-home-three-months-and-haven't killed-anybody-yet, what're your big plans? I'm dying to hear them," she said.

"Either I'm going to use part of this money for a trip to the Bahamas with you and the rest on a down payment for a used BMW, or I'm going to use all of the money to lease a BMW! Pick your poison!" he said, thinking she would surely opt for a trip to the Bahamas, which would have made him a very happy man—and made him feel like a *somebody*!

"Have you lost it? We still have over $3,000 in bills for Tommy's braces from last year—you don't remember, do you? And we need money for Tommy and Natasha to go to summer camp. You don't think about that, do you? And, maybe your grandmomma will need help with her bills and such. But you don't think about that either, do you? That's right, *you* were *in prison* playing with Miss Suggar ... while I was out here trying to figure out all this stuff.... I forgot!" she said.

"So, I'm working to break even, huh?" he said. "To get back in your good graces.... To repay everybody on this *fucking* earth for being alive!" he said, grabbing the champagne bottle and pouring more into his glass.

"No, TJ.... This is our life ... our mess. There ain't *no* returning heroes on white horses!" she said.

"*Mess*? Fucking *mess*? Is that what you just said? Is that what you see us as? Or is it me? *I'm* the '*fucking mess*,'" he said. "Mess" hit him hard—the word sumed up what he projected his mother and father always thought of Dee and him, irrelevant *messes* to be left alone. He finished the bottle of champagne with one big gulp and banged it down hard on the kitchen table.

Before she could respond, he had grabbed his coat off the banister and walked out the door.

"TJ!" she screamed. "Oh, *shit*," she said to an empty foyer. *Oh, shit,* she thought.

~

TJ drove his car back to the wine and beer shop and this time bought a six-pack of Heineken in cans. Back in his car, he cracked open a can and finished it in thirty seconds. Less than an hour and four more beers later, he pulled up to Stardust Go-Go in Southeast Washington. Once inside, the music, the young, tough-looking crowd, and the flashing lights made him want to leave. It took him less than a minute to find her.

"Well, well, well," Taunja Suggar said, elbowing her cousin. "Look what just fell out of Hagerstown!"

"Hello, baby," he said and tried to give her a kiss, but she turned her cheek. She had on a skintight, black top that showed off her large breasts. Her straight, soft black hair was swept back in a ponytail. Her red lipstick glowed. Someone shouted out "Brickhouse!" her nickname at the club.

"I ain't heard from you in months! Ever since that woman went postal," she said.

"I missed you. The least you could do is dance with me," he said.

"Skip the blah-blah-dance shit, lover—let's get out of here. I know you got som'em stored up for me, all that time thinking and shit," she laughed to her cousin.

She put her coat on. Once in his car, he kissed her hotly.

"This is your lucky day. My momma's got my kids in Disney World, so we'll be all alone at my place," she said.

"You got—"

"Baby, Taunja always got what you need, *including* dope and cognac. Relax, Prison Boy."

Making love with Taunja was easy. TJ knew she liked to entertain. She also liked to please and was a student of what men really wanted. When Taunja teased it was not for long—she delivered and never tired. And she delivered in ways that would make a contortionist envious.

She told TJ that she had added pleasure hooking up with him tonight. "My baby's father just knocked up my best girl friend," she said.

Hours later, exhausted from the nonstop pleasures of the flesh, which were enhanced by pot and cognac, he headed home, arriving around 3:00 am. The night was a blur—a pleasant one.

~

Junie saw him on the couch as she was making her way out the door for work at 6:30 AM. She felt relieved. *Thank God he came home, instead of doing something stupid*, she thought. She peeked into his car, saw the empty cans, and figured he drove around, drank beer, and played pool somewhere. Drinking and driving would be a topic for another day.

Several hours later, he awoke on the couch and wondered if Tommy and Natasha had seen him there. They must have, he thought to himself. Then he remembered they weren't there the previous night. He had a splitting headache and went into the kitchen to make some coffee.

A wave of guilt came over him. Guilt was a feeling that he had very little experience with. He knew pain, regret, and feeling like a victim—but not guilt. *What am I going to do if Junie finds out? Or if*

Taunja spreads the word and Dee picks up on it? Shit, Dee and Taunja go to the same beauty shop! He looked at a picture of Junie and the kids on the wall. He forgave himself for the marijuana use—he had no plans to use any drugs again. He felt no compulsion to use alcohol. He didn't even want to hang out.

But computers ... the kids ... Junie ... a safe, happy home—it all seemed tied together. Never did he see himself out on his own with Taunja, or with anyone else, for that matter. *Taunja,* he thought this morning, *is a thing of the past.* But my, my, Brickhouse was hot. *Taunja,* he thought, *was a young man's pleasure—but not a family man's.* What was it in the fight, what words, what look from Junie hurt so bad? *What sent me running?* he asked himself over and over. *What?*

The memory of being dragged to church by his newly sober mother came to him. He recalled watching her as she cried at hymns.... She seemed so phony. Then, in a blink, he remembered his mother putting her arm around him as they approached Pastor Winston in the receiving line while leaving church. Her hugging him was something that he hadn't experienced before—and wouldn't again. Her hug made his skin crawl, unlike an embrace from Junie and certainly unlike the pleasures of being engulfed by the red-hot Taunja. He flashed back to Junie getting stiff when he tried to hug her last night. Somehow, on some level, that feeling of rejection devastated him. He shuddered.

Guilt and sorrow rolled over him. He felt guilty that if he failed with Junie and his IT road to success, he'd never get another chance. He realized that if Junie ever found out, they'd be through.

Later that morning, after two cups of coffee, he regained hope that Taunja would keep her mouth shut. *Fuck it,* he thought, *maybe things will work out after all.*

Hardroc was right, he said to himself with a laugh, *I do tend to get all wiggly before the band shows up.*

19

ZERO TOLERANCE

Gee Brooks

On a cold and blustery early January morning, just four months after TJ's release from MCIH, Gee looked forward to seeing him in her office and hearing his take on the IT work with Art Coleman. She had heard firsthand from Art two weeks ago that new business quickly pushed the hours well beyond full-time just three weeks after TJ started. Art told Gee that he couldn't be more pleased with TJ.

But Gee was sorry TJ had scheduled his meeting with her for today, because she had to attend a manager's meeting to update Kingmaker on the status of her assignments for the upcoming Baltimore conference. The mandatory meeting was a typical Kingmaker all-about-me micro-management exercise. Kingmaker's meeting was due to start in less than thirty minutes.

TJ was late. While she waited, Gee read a "Reminder" e-mail from Kingmaker. It announced that the deputy wanted all parolees to be drug tested at their next appearance in the office. The reminder e-mail was the first Gee had heard of the order—and reminder her that she had not caught up with her 158 unread e-mails. She noticed that "ALL PAROLEES" was underlined and bolded. She had no qualms with testing for drug use, but, *why now?* she asked herself.

The second TJ walked into her office, Gee's antennae began to flap due to the incongruence between Art's glowing report and TJ's sullen look.

"What's up?" she asked.

"Not much."

Just then, Chip knocked on the door.

"The deputy wants to see you *before* the meeting, Ms. Brooks," Chip said, calling her Ms. Brooks instead of Gee because a parolee was present.

Gee saw Huggie in the hallway. "Huggie," she called, "can you take a UA from TJ? I've got to go to the deputy chief's meeting." Before she ran out the door, Gee turned to TJ and said, "Are you all right? Is something wrong?" She wished he would tell her what was upsetting him—and quickly.

"No, I just feel disconnected," TJ said, looking at the floor.

"Give me a call tomorrow, and we'll talk." she said.

Again, Chip's head popped into the door, and he raised his eyebrows.

"I'm coming," shot back Gee, mumbling "wuss" under her breath.

Walking to the deputy chief's office, she thought to herself, *Why did I ask TJ to call me? I'm the one that wants the information.*

~

That night, Huggie left a message on Gee's cell phone, which was off. He asked her to call him as soon as possible.

Gee first listened to the message early the next morning, on her way to work. She called Huggie, who wanted to talk to her about his interaction with TJ the day before.

"TJ said, 'This guy in the hall asked about if a dude used some dope a week ago, would he be OK on a urine test. I told him probably, right?'

"'Wrong,' I said.

"'What about guys that aren't into the drug scene anymore—maybe just one little hit at a party. That ain't going to be a big thing, right?'

"I said, 'Probably wrong again. The new rules call for mandatory prison time of one year or more for marijuana—even one use.

"Then he said, 'Man, I fucked up. My wife and I had an argument over what to do with this big paycheck I got. I wanted a BMW—she wanted to put the money to bills. You know, like no more money was coming in, and I'd screw up again and go back to prison, and she'd need the money. Like ... like ... I'm some insurance policy. I stormed out and, you know, ran into this ole thing and maybe smoked....'" Huggie said. "'I can't do *no* more time,' he whispered.

"'Look, be strong, man. Be strong. Don't be stupid. Be strong!' I said.

"'And ... being strong, my brother.,... How's that going to help me?' TJ said.

"'I didn't know what to say, so I said nothing. TJ placed the half-full plastic urine bottle with his case number on the sink. He washed his hands, stopped, looked directly at me, and said, 'Thanks for keeping it real, man.' He turned and walked out."

"Oh God, Huggie. Sounds like he's going to have a positive for dope, doesn't it?" Gee said and hung up without saying good-bye.

Hours later, Junie called Gee on her cell phone. The timing of the call gave Gee goose bumps.

"Do you know where TJ is, Gee?"

"Junie, I'll get back to you. Let me check around," Gee said, trying not to use a panicky tone.

Gee called Huggie, who rounded up Pepe and Hattie, and Gee gave them the names of friends and local community advocates who might have information on TJ's whereabouts and state of mind. That afternoon Gee headed to TJ and Junie's house in Germantown.

"Gee, I haven't seen or heard from him—not a word—since yesterday. That's not like TJ. He doesn't answer his cell phone, or it's not working. I called Dee, and she hasn't heard from him either. She's calling around," Junie said, obviously upset.

"A colleague of mine and I noticed TJ looked upset yesterday. Do you know why, Junie?" Gee asked.

"Well, not really," said Junie. "But, after he went to your office, I know he came back home, because I found Tommy's glove on the pillow of his bed, and Natasha found her favorite doll on her pillow. They didn't leave them there. His keys are here, and so is my car," Junie said.

A chill shot through Gee. Were the keys a message?

As Gee was walking out of Junie's front door, Dee drove up with Tommy and Natasha in her car. She stepped out of her car and shook her head to indicate … nothing, no word.

Gee hugged the kids, said good-bye to Junie and Dee, and left hurriedly to continue her search. By night, Gee and her friends had combed the community, found no useful information, and, finally, agreed to call off the search. Gee had checked her messages at the office ten times. Nothing.

20

THE EYE OF THE TIGER

TJ Smith

When TJ left the courthouse, his head was spinning. *What will I say to Junie? Nothing. Should I call Ms. Brooks and try to explain? No. Could the urinalysis test come back negative, with no trace of marijuana? No. Will the court understand that the one-time marijuana use won't happen again? No. What can I do? Nothing…. There's nothing that will help you get out of this one.*

He could deny the drug use, but his trial had taught him that the prosecutors had their own agenda, and being understanding to defendants was not one of them. On this chilly January day, TJ headed for his car in the public parking lot. He looked down at the street, making no eye contact with anyone. He felt like he was a fugitive and had fleeting fantasies that at any moment a sheriff's deputy or Montgomery County cop was going to run him down and handcuff him. He thought of Dr. Richard Kimble hiding, looking over his shoulder in *The Fugitive. Who can I talk to? No one.*

Instinctively, he drove home—to Junie's home, which is how he still thought of the townhouse—though he had no plan. His mind raced. He felt like crying, as he did when he was a kid on the nights when his mother was out and about. Back then, he'd snuggle next to Dee on his grandmother's old couch, the one with the springs sticking out. If he moved too close to the center, a spring would poke into his back. They'd watch TV to take their minds off their fear of the dark. Maybe I'll call Dee. He called her cell number but got no answer. He left no message. Hearing her recorded message he felt anguished, further cut off, but also relieved she didn't answer her phone.

Once inside Junie's home, he walked through the living room and past the array of pictures. The thought of separating from his kids was wrenching. He shuddered and walked into the kitchen. It was 11:05 AM. Even the diva Taunja couldn't help him feel better now.

TJ sat on a kitchen chair and tried to imagine how to launch into a conversation with Junie that would explain why he was soon to be arrested for a violation of probation based on a positive urinalysis for marijuana. She simply wouldn't buy that officials made a mistake. She didn't think like that. If he tried to cover up the night when he used marijuana, she'd figure it out. She knew TJ only used marijuana as a way to boost his sexual pleasure. That would lead to Taunja. That would end their marriage.

Going back to prison for a year would end the marriage, too. He'd been allowed by Junie's grace to reenter her life, which was now far different than when he first went to prison nearly five years ago. She was not a dope user's wife. Thanks to the natural bonds between father and son and father and daughter, he had reentered his children's life. They were wonderful, sweet kids. Could they ever understand a second prison tour? *No*, came the voice in his head. Would they keep him at arm's-length? *Yes*, he thought. Could he negatively affect Tommy's self-esteem and vision of his own future? *Yes*, he said to himself. He'd be an embarrassment to his own children. The brief thought of the loss of a future with them bore into his soul.

He'd never be able to talk to Junie again.... *Never*, he said out loud to no one. He noticed the envelope on the kitchen table. Inside would be today's "Love Notes," a ritual Junie had started about six weeks ago. Because TJ often worked late into the night on surveys and slept late, sometimes the kids left for school with only a hug from a sleepy dad. So, every night the kids each put a "Love Note" in an envelope on the table. He read them as he drank his morning coffee. He hadn't read this morning's notes, because he had rushed off to the probation office early. He opened the unsealed envelope and pulled out two notes written on paper torn from the little notepads Junie had bought them. The kids were excited to have their own notepads.

> *Dear Daddy,*
> *Can we play catch tonight? I know it will be cold, so we*
> *can be faster.*
> *Love, Tommy*

> *Dear Daddy*
> *I love you and want to read the story about the bashful*
> *kittens to you tonight. OK?*
> *Love, Me*

TJ picked up the notes and put them in his pocket. He went over to a drawer beside the sink and found a $10 Metro farecard and put it in his wallet, which also contained $106. He also took a $20 bill, which he folded and put in his left sock. He headed upstairs.

TJ walked to his closet, put on a heavy black sweater, and put his Orioles baseball hat into a red backpack that he seldom used. He walked over to Junie's closet and searched around until he found a Nike shoe box on the floor, way in the back. Inside the box, inside an old sock, was a .32-caliber revolver and a small box of bullets. He had given the gun to her during the trial, out of the fear that some of his homeboys might believe he would testify for the state to save himself. He worried they might panic and come after the kids to silence him. Junie told him on a prison visit once that she had been so scared of the possibility that she couldn't sleep through the night until well after the trial was over.

The box looked like it hadn't been touched. TJ loaded six bullets in the revolver's chamber and returned the box to the back of the closet floor. He put the gun in his backpack.

TJ looked up and saw an orange and green silk scarf of Junie's. He touched it, rubbed it on his face, and put it around his neck. God, he wanted to hold her one more time.

He went into his office, grabbed two computer magazines he hadn't read, and put them in the backpack. He walked into Natasha's room and saw her doll, the one he had given her upon his release from MCIH. He smiled, noticing that she now had three barrettes in her hair. He put the doll on her pillow. He turned to leave but stopped, seeing a small bear on a broken clip, one that days ago had dangled from her school backpack. She had asked him if he could repair it. He put the bear in his backpack and walked down the short hall to Tommy's room. There on the floor was his baseball glove with a ball in it—the glove that was ready for today's catch. He kissed the glove and put it on Tommy's pillow.

He headed downstairs and sat at the kitchen table. He wondered where he'd go. Maybe California. Maybe New York…. Surely he could hide out there. What about Georgetown? *I want to see Georgetown.* He decided he wouldn't take the car. He headed for the pantry and grabbed a sixteen–ounce, red, plastic cup and put it in his backpack. Once more, almost out of duty, like at a wake where one feels compelled to look at an open casket, he returned to the living room. He sat in a large, stuffed chair, staring at the pictures. "Computer experts don't do prison," he said softly to Junie's picture. "I'm sorry, baby. I love you."

He walked toward the foyer, dropping his keys on an end table. In the foyer, he grabbed his heavy, black leather coat and put it on over the sweater and Junie's scarf, with the backpack over his shoulder. He couldn't bear to turn around again for one more look at Junie's home, which, he was realizing too late, was becoming his home, too.

He closed the door behind him and walked the mile toward Route 355, heading for a Ride On bus stop that would take him to the Metro station in Rockville. Two blocks from the bus stop, he walked into a county liquor store and bought three separate pints of Grey Goose Vodka and two sixteen-ounce orange sodas.

"Nothing but the best, sir! Must be celebrating again, huh? How was the champagne?" asked the clerk.

TJ nodded, but said nothing.

Outside the store, he knelt and poured half a pint of vodka into the red cup and topped it off with half an orange soda. He drank the mix as he walked to the bus stop. When the bus arrived, he gulped the drink to finish, then returned the cup to his backpack. The quiet ride to the Rockville station took eighteen minutes. Only two other riders were on the bus—two Hispanic women who spoke quietly to each other in Spanish and appeared to know each other. Both looked tired. TJ, too, felt tired in mid-afternoon on this partially overcast day. *God, I miss Hardroc. He'd disown me. He'd make sure I ended up in a maximum security prison—in a cell with some gang-banger, or a child killer.*

The bus pulled up to the front of the Rockville Metro station. In a short tunnel just outside the station, TJ spun his backpack around, crouched down near a trash can, and poured a second drink, identical to the first. One pint down, two to go. He walked into the station and up the escalator to the tracks. Within moments, he was on a train headed for D.C. He sipped his drink from the last seat in the back of a car. Georgetown.... *I'll get off at Dupont Circle.*

He was oblivious to the Metro cop in full regalia—gun, two-way radio, handcuffs, baton, badge, and pepper spray—who entered the train at the Grosvenor station. One glance at TJ sipping his drink and he was at him in a nano-second.

"You realize there's no eating and drinking on my cars?" the cop said, reporting the violation through a numbered code to someone by way of the two-way radio on his left shoulder, "You realize that?"

"Yes, sir. I'm headed to the doctor's office. I have the flu and a high fever. I'm trying to stay hydrated," TJ said.

"I don't care if you're dying. Get off this train—now—and if I catch you eating or drinking on my train again, I'm going to arrest you."

"Yes, sir," TJ said, walking toward the door.

When the train stopped at the NIH station. TJ exited the train. As he did, he heard the policeman shout for the benefit of the passengers, now his captive audience, "Rules apply to everyone!"

On the platform, TJ finished his drink in leisure, while glancing around for more Metro cops. He placed the red cup in his backpack and boarded the train that arrived seven minutes later. *Damn, I missed my one out*, he thought, laughing, feeling the effects of the vodka, *going to prison for drinking on the Metro. Everyone would feel sorry for me.*

He exited the subway at Dupont Circle and headed west on P Street, toward Georgetown. When he realized he was hungry, he stopped at the Oasis Delicatessen. The attractive, thirty-something, white clerk was snappy and friendly, treating him as if he was a valued customer. He ate the turkey sandwich at a small circular table in the corner, and he felt like a computer expert again as he paged through one of his magazines, which he held high so the clerk could see the cover. She kept glancing at him. He smiled at the casual flirting. When he left the store, he turned to her for one more smile, but she was occupied with a customer. *Maybe she was just being friendly*, he thought. *Nothing lasts forever.*

He walked out, staggering slightly, and headed toward the sun, west down P Street, crossing a small bridge. He saw a wooded area just over the bridge, jumped a small fence, and decided this was a safe enough place to drink and to urinate privately behind a tree. He sat down among the trees on the edge of Rock Creek Parkway and slowly worked his way through the second pint bottle, then started the third. Round and round his thoughts went. *Who can I call? Junie? No. Ms. Brooks? No. Dee? Not again. Hardroc? He'd never take the call, even if I could get through the prison maze and rules about incoming calls. What am I going to do? Prison? No fucking way. California? Maybe. New York? Maybe.*

He became distracted by passers-by, buses, and cars. He put his spinning head down on his knees. He was cold, even though the sun was shining. It was just around four o'clock.

He woke up to a brisk jab on his head with a firm object. Then came a smooth voice, for a second disguising the jolting words.

"Motherfucker, this is a Glock with a silencer on the back of your ugly-assed head. Hold still and you be living. Get jiggy and you be capped," said the voice. "Get his wallet, Q."

A second body pushed him forward just far enough to remove his wallet from his jeans. That voice reported, "Sixty-nine dollars."

"Cards?" said the first voice.

"One," said the second voice.

"Mr. Drunk-assed 1980 got a back-fucking pack," said a third voice. "Lemme see…. A fucking teddy bear! Some … what … fucking notes…." The pause suggested to TJ that the third person was reading the notes, but for some reason chose not to read Natasha or Tommy's love notes aloud.

"College boy here got commuter magazines…."

"*Computer* magazines, Slick, not commuter," said the first voice, still pressing the gun to TJ's head.

"What the fuck …? Prissy pants here got a .32 caliber revolver," said Slick, leading a chorus of whooping laughter.

"A fucking *starter* gun. Shit, I had a revolver when I was ten. Bang, bang, yo' dead. Shit, I be embarrassed to give this to some punk-assed homeboy…. Shit," said the first voice. "Now, listen up, shooter. We be leaving. You try to follow us and we'll cap yo' punk ass. You ain't doing no good, no way. Who'd give a shit if yo' dead, drunk man?"

Someone shoved TJ to the ground, and the three were gone.

TJ checked his backpack. The robbers apparently didn't see or want the last pint and orange soda. He poured all of the vodka into his cup and chased it with the remaining soda. His wallet was gone. He couldn't find the tiny bear, but retrieved his two love notes from several yards away and put them in his pocket. He tossed the backpack in the woods. He was very drunk, but he managed to get to his feet, staggering and unsure, walking west again on P Street. He asked a teenage girl how to get to the Kennedy Center, and she pointed left, down 29th Street. He concentrated on not staggering. At Dumbarton and 29th Streets, he noticed a black, teenage boy on a bike outside of Scheele's Market. Catty-corner was the boy's lookout. TJ recognized the setup, even in his drunken state. The kid on the bike crossed the street and approached him.

"Weed?" he said, softly.

TJ remembered the $20 bill in his sock.

"Two joints, rolled, matches. Twenty dollars," TJ said.

"No, no, no."

"Fuck off," TJ, the former street-master, said.

"Laced or not?"

"PCP?"

"Sumpin, sumpin," said the boy.

"Laced," said TJ. "Put the two joints and matches down on the sidewalk, over there," TJ said pointing. "Walk over here, and I'll hand you the $20."

The boy followed instructions.

TJ handed him the $20 bill.

"Shit be wicked, brother," said the boy and rode away quickly, his buddy at his side.

TJ walked south toward the canal. He wanted to get a good look at the Kennedy Center, where he'd promised himself he'd take Junie. Hardroc had told him he'd know he was really a professional when he saw a show at the Kennedy Center. TJ had Googled an image of the Kennedy Center, and many nights thereafter he went to sleep imagining he and Junie were attending a concert in formal clothes. Thoughts now were incomplete and short in duration. *Who can I call?* No one. *California?* Too far.

He found a wooded area on the south side of K Street, under the Whitehurst Freeway, blocks from Key Bridge. *Now* he could see the

Kennedy Center. He was sorry he saw it. It moved in and out of focus to him. *You're a prison computer expert,* he thought…. *That's all.*

He pulled the first joint out of his pocket and lit it. After a couple of heavy drags, he knew this was the real deal. And the boy was right…. It was laced with something. TJ felt paralyzed. Wild visions and images floated into his consciousness. Colors and patterns leapt out. He continued to suck on the joint, begging it to transform him. A wild tiger's mask appeared—orange and black, but with only one eye. TJ stared at it. It began to talk to him at a slow speed, as if it were coming from an echo chamber. The joint burned his fingers…. It was gone. He tried to find the second joint, but he couldn't get control of his fingers.

The mask spoke in waves, interrupted by Natasha's voice and then Tommy's.

"WHAT ARE YOU DOING, MR. COMPUTER?"

"Daddy, I need you, please don't leave me."

"Daddy, I be a junkie. See me, Daddy?"

"YOU BE A PRISON BITCH—THAT'S ALL. MISS JUNIE GOT A NEW MAN."

"Daddy, Mommy's crying. Help me, please."

"Daddy, Daddy, please come back … when you through prison."

"HARDROC SAID YOU DEAD TO HIM…. HA, HA, HA."

When TJ could focus again, he shut his eyes. Sometime later, he opened them and noticed lights around him. It was dark, and he felt cold. He managed to get to his feet and headed down K Street. He kept walking until he saw a sign for the Crescent Trail. The bike path looked scary to him, so he decided to sit by the trees again, overlooking the Potomac River. He feared the jump-out boys would return. He found the second joint and lit it. He sucked it hard. The lights all ran together in one wavy pattern.

Some time later he headed up nearby wooden steps. At the top, he could see the Key Bridge. He staggered toward it. A Rollerblader whizzed by him on the bridge sidewalk, heading toward Rosslyn, screaming something at him. TJ couldn't understand him.

On the windy bridge, he felt cold again. He saw the blue, warm waters of the Caribbean Ocean below, where he had hoped to take

Junie. A car rode by. He heard someone yelling at him from the speeding car—a car that looked like it was sixty feet long.

He looked down at the inviting blue waters. Again, he felt the coldness of the night. He found Junie's scarf tied to his neck and rubbed it gently.

"Daddy will find you, Natasha. Hold on, Tommy. I love you, babies," TJ said. Blue, black, yellow colors flashed, as sounds of speeding cars and an overhead plane roared in a deafening mixture. A gray prison cell clicked shut, encasing him. He screamed. The wind swirled around him, smacking his face.

He heard someone screaming, "Noooooooooooooooooo…!"

~

Junie stood at the front desk of the probation office, intentionally tapping her foot as the receptionist continued her phone conversation about Saturday's upcoming party.

"Excuse me, Miss, can you just tell me how to reach Ms. Brooks … please?"

The receptionist was annoyed with the interruption, and it showed on her face. Passing by in the hall on the way to his office, Huggie picked up on Junie's anxious tone and approached her. "I'm Huggie Winston, a colleague of Ms. Brooks. Can I help you?"

"I'm Junie Edwards, TJ Smith's wife, and—"

"Come on back to my office," he said.

Down the hall, less than fifty steps away, they entered his office, two doors from Gee's empty office. He closed the door behind her.

"I understand why you're here. Gee's my friend. Please have a seat. I have information for you, but none of it may be good. I'm breaking a confidence with TJ, but I'll talk in generalities.… That's the best I do," he said.

"So you know something, you've talked to TJ, but you're reluctant to speak directly. Am I correct? Who do you people work for, and who are you working *against*—me and my children? Look, I'm worried about his safety. We had a big fight the other night. He really hasn't been the same since. Now I can't find him. I'm scared. Can you help me, please?" she asked.

"I don't know where he is. I don't know. He came in here yesterday and was very depressed. He said he felt disconnected. He mentioned the argument with you, how he felt you didn't trust he'd make it. He appeared worried about the results of a UA test I gave him. He wanted to know what would happen if it was positive. I said a year in jail was likely. He said he couldn't do no more prison time. He thanked me for the information and left," Huggie said.

"TJ wouldn't do drugs … unless it was marijuana, and he'd only do that if…. Oh, my God … that bitch," she said.

Junie stood and looked at Huggie squarely. "Thank you. For what it's worth, you said nothing that broke his confidence. I'd figure it out sooner or later. I know TJ better than he knows himself. This isn't good. Did I really hear you right—one year for a stupid mistake? I'm not justifying it, but a year?" she asked.

"That's what I believe," Huggie said.

"My, my," Junie said, shaking her head, turning, opening the door, and leaving quietly.

On Thursday morning at 6:45, after a three-mile run, Gee was having her first sip of coffee when a short story in the Metro section of the *Washington Post* caught her eye. A man's body was found floating in the Potomac River one mile from the Key Bridge. Police speculated that it was suicide, particularly since a cab driver had reported seeing a man jump off the bridge. Death was instantaneous. Identification of the man was being withheld until notification of the family was complete.

She called a D.C. probation officer, an old friend who had worked as a liaison to her office. Gee asked her if she could find out the identity of the man who jumped off the Key Bridge. Within thirty minutes, she had her answer.

"Gee, a cop friend of mine said the man was Thomas Smith, Jr.," the officer said. "Why, do you know him?"

21

THE ABYSS

Gee Brooks

"Oh, God.... Oh, God, why?" She couldn't get beyond repeating that question to Dr. Weinman. TJ's suicide reignited the powerful business of grief, still lodged deep within her.

"Who do you feel you let down: TJ? Yourself? Who?" he asked.

"Both," she said.

"Start with the person you can do something about: yourself. What can you do now? Frankly, self-flagellation doesn't sell well," he asked.

"I'll never keep my mouth shut again when I feel I'm being given bullshit—from the system, Ed, anyone," she said.

"There are no do-overs in life, Gee. If there were, I wouldn't be such a mediocre golfer. No do-overs. What we've done, we've done. But, more to the point, there are also no chains on us—only those we place on ourselves," he said.

"You're damned right!"

"However …" he leaned forward, very near her legs, which stretched forward from the green leather chair, "Miss Congeniality will have to relinquish her crown."

She nodded. "I didn't like the stupid crown, anyway."

"Word of caution: There are consequences for everything we do. Be prepared to live with them."

"I understand. Maybe I'll take on the system," she said half-kidding, but, in a blink, realized she was quite serious.

"Well, the British have the loyal opposition. They're loyal, but they oppose mainstream politics. You might consider a blog. There's a blog out there for everything now. Who knows—you might have more supporters than you realize," he said.

She tried to image what that might be like.

"You know what my grandmother used to say?" he asked.

"No, what?"

"Expect the best, be prepared for the worst, and take whatever comes. What's the difference between grieving your mother's death and grieving TJ's suicide?" he asked.

She thought for a moment.

"I'm an adult now. I understand pain better now. Still, it really hurts," she said.

"I'm sure it does. A life wasted," he said.

On the way to her car, Gee picked up the phone and called in sick at the office. She thought, *maybe I should have warned him that one slip-up would set the system out to get him and I wouldn't be able to help him. God, why did I assume everything would just work out without a problem for TJ?* She just wanted to go home and go to bed. Maybe her awful headache would stop. As she headed up the elevator from the underground parking garage, she decided to stop by the lobby and pick up her mail. She was startled to see Ed sitting on a lobby sofa, apparently waiting for her.

He waved.

She walked over to the couch and sat at the opposite end.

"What brings—"

"Huggie told me about the suicide. I'm so sorry. Is there anything I can do?" he asked.

"I don't know what to say. No, I can't think of anything. I really don't want to talk about it anymore right now. I've got a splitting headache. You know, I'm sorting things out," she said. She considered saying "like you need to sort things out," and she considered inviting him up for a cup of coffee, but she did neither.

"I understand. Well, I hope you consider me a friend, one you can call on in a time of need," he said.

"*Je-sus*, Ed. That's a leap, isn't it? Mostly, I think of you as my ex and Ruppert's father," she said.

"I didn't come here to piss you off, Gee. I'm sorry if that's what I've done. Forgive me. Still, if I can help in any way, let me know. Take care of yourself," he said, rising from the couch and heading for the door.

"Thanks for the gesture," she said.

He waved without turning around.

22

OPERATION ØMAN

Gee Brooks

On the drive to Baltimore, Gee thought, *who in her right mind wants to be around yapping people?* On that Friday morning, January 9, her thoughts could best be described as scrambled. Strong emotions—anger, sadness, guilt, loss—overpowered her. She tried to deny to herself that TJ had guessed right—he would have been sent back to prison for the one marijuana use. But that denial, that sense of self-protection struck her now as empty. Of course The Kingmaker would have managed to send him back to prison. Sitting at the registration table for the T-Z attendees of the National Probation Officers Association's conference, at the Civic Center, she hardly spoke, and, when she did, it was without the typical humor and pizzazz that attracted people to her. To the casual observer, she looked dull and short on sleep.

At the moment, she felt enraged. Confusion was running in second place; loss third. She felt betrayed, but by whom: TJ, the system, Taunja Suggar? The next thought to roll in was the notion that *she* had done the betraying. It was she who misled TJ into thinking the system actually wanted him to succeed. Or that she could be trusted enough to help him solve problems and conflicts.

On and on somewhere between her brain and her heart went the struggle for a clear, unifying thought. Tommy and Natasha's images were burning in her stomach. She'd only seen Junie in person once but had spoken to her on the phone several times. Junie's a decent person, a good person, she thought. She grieved for Junie's lost hopes, too.

She flashed back to the Thanksgiving delivery team and had to get up from her seat and walk around to compose herself. Mostly, she felt the missed opportunity for TJ to be the involved and loving father she knew he wanted to be—the father he never had. She wanted TJ to feel useful and appreciated for his talents and gifts. She felt he deserved that. Junie wanted TJ to find balance and peace but not, Gee thought, in a grave. She knew that if she dwelled on the loss from the viewpoint of the two children, she'd lose it, quite publicly. She was terribly and profoundly sad, and very confused. She was in near-shock, feeling like a cork floating at sea. If she could've gotten away with wearing sunglasses, she would have. There was nothing she could do now to help anyone do anything, she said to herself.

Less than thirty minutes before The Honorable J. Trenton Axelrod, chairman of the Maryland Parole Commission, would deliver the keynote speech, he practiced that speech in the chauffeured state car. Always nattily attired and well-groomed, the tall, tanned Axelrod was a former Maryland state senator and, most recently, had run an unsuccessful bid for the United States Senate. As a consolation prize, after he turned over most of his sizeable political campaign war chest to the party, incoming Governor Ward appointed him chairman of the Maryland Parole Commission, at the encouragement of the political party. Axelrod knew little of—and cared even less about—the daily workings of the Commission. He had made millions in real estate before he turned to politics for amusement. Governor Ward and Axelrod had one brief discussion about the Governor's criminal justice views and wishes:

"Trenton, we have too many convicts running around the streets selling drugs and scaring citizens. Do your best to make us look good— whatever it takes!" the then-governor-elect said.

Two months before today's keynote address, a parolee on supervision in Baltimore had murdered his estranged wife and their three daughters before being killed in a police shootout trying to leave the city in his estranged wife's car. The girls were two, three, and five years old. All of the victims had their necks slashed by a hunting knife; all three girls were in their pajamas. The entire state was sickened. The Baltimore City Police Commissioner described the crime scene as the most disgusting, repulsive one he had ever seen.

As might be expected, the *Baltimore Sun* and local TV coverage of the crime was continuous and the event had even received national attention, especially on CNN. The media was focused on the gruesome details, labeling the killer the "Wanton Slasher," picking up on a label from a *Baltimore Sun* article. The incoming Parole Commissioner took the opportunity to try to pin the blame on the Baltimore-based parole officer, who actually had done a fairly good job of supervising a psychotic who had come apart after going off his medication. The central question posed by the media was, "Is any community in Maryland ever safe when parolees are released to the community?" Instantly, Axelrod had fodder, theme, and ample cover to do anything.

Gee and many probation officers had heard through the grapevine that since his appointment, and particularly after being cornered and blistered by a victim's rights group, Axelrod tended to give the same *go get 'em* speech no matter what the occasion—always centered on the victims of crime. It was hard not to agree with the general thesis of his pitch—we must protect society—unless you actually heard it live. In his first presentation as chairman, which Chief Probation Officer Kasten attended, Axelrod took twenty minutes to make this point: while those in attendance could enjoy life, many victims would never again enjoy the pleasures that others take for granted. He implied that no one was safe. Relief from the anguish caused by criminals under supervision will never be the companion of victims, Axelrod exhorted. Speech after speech, rumor had it, repeated the same message. Police loved it and stood proudly at attention behind him. Kasten warned Kingmaker that the guy was an idiot.

"They will never know peace again!" Axelrod would say, acting sad for emphasis. It was so over-the-top it became known in the law enforcement community statewide as "*the* speech." It was hard to imagine that one man, operating alone, could get people so turned off to talking about victims' needs. But Chairman J. Trenton Axelrod *almost* accomplished that awful feat. By targeting parolees as the enemy, he put a bull's-eye on his own office because of his obvious bias.

⁓

The Cuatro Amigos met in a small corner of the gigantic Civic Center foyer, coffees in hand, exchanging hugs and expressions of sorrow with Gee. Obviously, TJ's suicide hurt her deeply, as it did Huggie.

The Cuatro Amigos' sadness was in stark contrast to the mood of nametagged conference attendees and the speakers and presenters, who represented a favored, elitist group. For the latter, it was a time to boast among themselves about who had landed what grant from the

Department of Justice and how to seize other financial opportunities through connections. This was an art form for long-standing insiders: milking the government cash cow.

For some attendees, spread out in clusters in the long foyer, it was a chance to hear the latest ideas, touted programs, and trendy catchphrases—like "juvenile predators," Operation Nightlight, boot camps, and other catchy terms.

Conferences were also social gatherings for officers, particularly for those still young enough to burn the candle at both ends. Gee felt miserable, fighting every muscle in her body, all of which begged her to run out the Civic Center doors to God knows where.

She walked by officers swapping stories, hoping to be distracted from her pain. She heard about the "stupid" managers in their office, about how this person or that person had been unfairly promoted or not promoted or demoted. Stories abounded about hapless offenders who had made idiotic miscalculations during crimes. The stories started with "Did you hear the one about …?" Invariably, there were macho debates between officers as to whose district was the toughest on criminals. She retreated to a corner and held the wall up.

Had she continued to listen in, as Chip Faulknour and his managers did by moving from cluster to cluster, this is a sample of what she would have heard:

"We have this muscle-bound supervisor who lifts weights seven days a week. His name is Boyd Sutter. All of us in his unit call him 'Soup.' He thinks it means we have great respect—as in, Mr. 'Sup'ervisor. It's really code for 'he is so stupid his intellectual power goes from soup to nuts in a second.' When we call out 'Soup' he actually flexes his muscles like Popeye," laughed a young male probation officer.

In an "if-you-think-that's-something" mode, another male officer came back with, "We have this thing when some dumb new make-work policy is introduced at a meeting, two free beers for anyone who can get out 'bullshit' through a feigned cough within five minutes of the announced policy."

"Our huffy supervisor has been spotted inappropriately using his state car on the weekends. He's also been spotted taking the car to church—while giving us daily lectures on the strict state car usage policy. Unfortunately for him, his wife placed a bumper sticker on his car that said, 'Get Involved in Community Service.' The sticker was intended to promote her nonprofit community service business. That it did, until some *unnamed* officer," his eyes searching the ceiling, "pasted a cutout of a woman's handsome rack out of a *Playboy* magazine right over the 'Ser,' leaving 'Get involved in community (.)(.)vice," said a young officer, making circles for breast with his hands. Even female officers laughed at this story.

In a small group, an officer said, "We have a weekly bet on the most hard core officer of the month—the winner is the one with the most revocation requests to the court."

And in another cluster, a muscle-bound officer said, "Harris, our supervisor, has a tattoo on each arm; one says, 'Try me,' and the other says, 'Try this,' with a picture of cell bars.

And the story-topper from that group came from another muscular officer, "One of our supervisors has a tattoo that says 'Collars & Coffee.'"

"I don't get it," whispered a bookish young female officer to the person standing next to her.

"Collars are handcuffs," she said.

Followed by the next story-topper: "You think that's something, this scumbag—as we like to say—asked me, "What should I call you?" I said, "Mister."

From a smaller, somewhat more restrained group, came this story, "My caseload is so big, all I do is try to explain to my supervisor what I'd do *if* I had time to get organized," said an attractive blond officer. "The idiot always says, 'good job' about the job I'm *not actually doing!*"

"Yeah, well, 40 percent—I swear we figured it out—40 percent of my time goes to administrative stuff, like filling out data collection forms about what I'd do if I wasn't filling out data collection forms!" countered her buddy.

Chimes sounded, causing the convention goers to meander into the main meeting room. Officers rushed to fill the back rows first, where they could wiggle, giggle, and crack jokes freely. On the conference room walls were pictures of military victory themes from various wars.

The raised stage had one podium and chairs for speakers and honored guests.

After Baltimore City's Dunbar High School color guard's salute to the American flag and the Baltimore mayor's welcome, a Baltimore Circuit Court judge gave a brief discourse on the need for greater detail in presentence reports by officers, so that justice could be meted out in sentencing more uniformly.

Focus on this particular esoteric point struck a few academic experts as odd. In the third row, a University of Maryland criminal justice professor and recipient of numerous grants from the governor's office leaned over to his favorite graduate student and whispered to her, "Given the reality that statewide sentencing guidelines adroitly mirror federal sentencing guidelines, which, by Congressional intent, leave oh-so-little judicial discretion, what good are greater details? All prosecutors and judges care about are the severity of the offense and the offender's record. Who's he kidding?"

Making a late entrance, the Cuatro Amigos were motioned to the front rows by the self-designated assistant host, the seemingly agitated Chip Faulknour.

Chief Probation Officer Kasten, in his brief speaking assignment, welcomed everyone and then introduced Kingmaker, "who will serve as our official host."

To Gee, Dora Kingmaker looked very in-charge and pleased to be up front. She welcomed the national association attendees to Baltimore and then proceeded to introduce The Honorable J. Trenton Axelrod, chairman of the Maryland Parole Commission. Rising from a chair on the raised stage, although the applause was only politely cordial, Chairman Axelrod had the posture of a man who had just won an election as he walked toward the podium and microphone. Seven hundred faces stared at him. Chairman Axelrod spoke with such volume and excitement that even if he were talking in a foreign language, one could guess that something very important was about to happen.

"As I look out at you, you the defenders of truth and justice, I salute your long tradition of independent judgment and devotion to public safety."

A young female officer in the back row elbowed her friend and said, "Independent judgment? I need a hall pass from my supervisor to pee!" Her buddy giggled into her hands.

"Yours is a difficult task. You must look into victims' eyes day in and day out," the chairman said.

The graduate student leaned over to the professor and whispered, "Professor, what's he talking about? I bet 95 percent of the officers in this room never see or talk to a victim of crime after the sentencing hearing."

The chairman continued. "You must work with dangerous men and women—all of whom are so very talented at skirting our laws, so very proud to bring anarchy to our innocent children in the form of drugs, violence, and disrespect! With your help, we can do more!"

Since he was seeking it, the audience gave him applause, albeit mildly.

"Today, I'll ask for more! I'll ask you to work *extra* hours on nights and weekends.…"

"What does he mean—overtime? Are we fucking volunteers?" an officer in the back row asked his buddy beside him.

"I'll ask you to give more … more under the spirit that this great country was founded upon. Safety … safety is our first commitment to the public, and *more* safety is better!"

"Oh, shit, another more-is-better theme," mumbled a supervisor to her peer.

Only about six people were clapping, all on the raised stage.

"Today it is with *great* pride that we look to the future of parole and turn our eyes *away from* the leniency and enabling policies of the past. Today, the governor and I are announcing the most *forward-thinking* advance in community corrections—a data-driven system of accountability to reduce the number of victims in our community!"

Now, half the room was clapping, appreciating that the term data-driven was in vogue and certainly sounded advanced—and, since the word 'victims' always elicited sympathy, clearly something big was coming.

"It was with great pride that I promised the governor this: *today* will mark the beginning of a clear path for community corrections in Maryland and, I hope, back in your states, too; one that is a refined logical extension of all we know—but bolder than any past policy.

Today, the Maryland Parole Commission proudly announces ... *OPERATION ØMAN!*"

Axelrod was now shouting.

"*OPERATION ØMAN* stands for zero tolerance and mandatory revocation ..."

He paused for dramatic effect.

"... with a minimum one-year *mandatory* prison term with *no credit* for street time for the following—if all of you worked in Maryland, you'd be happy to come to work—with a minimum one-year *mandatory* prison term for one positive urinalysis for alcohol used outside a religious ceremony, one positive urinalysis for any illicit drug, one unauthorized missed appointment with a parole officer for anyone in a "high-risk" category, or one unauthorized presence outside the district of jurisdiction. The proud members of the Parole Commission expect the Maryland courts—and hopefully all parole authorities and courts around the country—to follow our lead!"

Chairman Axelrod swiveled around like Burt Parks announcing the new Miss America, pointing grandly now to a rolled-up banner hanging behind him.

"Ladies and gentlemen, I give you, OPERATION ØMAN!"

Down dropped a long banner that read:

As the banner unrolled, a hook broke off, and the banner swung violently to the left, directly behind the seated authorities, barely missing the Baltimore judge's head. There was a loud gasp and awkward laughter. Chairman Axelrod rushed over to the judge, then quickly back toward the podium to try to regain momentum. But from the second row came a voice that cut into the audience's stirring.

"This is outrageous! You should be ashamed!" shouted Gee, standing up to her full height and pointing directly at Axelrod, while glaring at the entire cast on the stage, which, of course, included Kasten and Kingmaker.

There was a buzz from the audience as folks in the middle rows repeated Gee's words to the folks in the rear.

Gee swiveled around, faced the roughly seven hundred stunned attendees, and shouted, "Stop this insane tail 'em, nail 'em, and jail 'em punishment crap toward offenders! Real people are being hurt!"

As Gee left the room with Huggie, Hattie, and Pepe in tow, Chairman Axelrod tried to corral the room's energy toward his new project. "True Americans don't run!" he called out. "We don't tread on victims! We're Americans first and foremost! I say to each of you, reach down into your patriotic heart and join me. No more crime victims. No more victims! *No more victims!*"

With each repetition of the chanted phrase, Chairman Axelrod picked up new voices—until the groundswell included nearly a third of auditorium. Still, just minutes into his prepared keynote address, Axelrod knew that the defining moment of his new anti-parolee, pro-victim advocate career had taken a detour south.

After the final "no more victims" shout-out, Kingmaker rushed up to whisper something into Chairman Axelrod's ear. Then, smiling, she seized the lectern's microphone, publicly thanked him for his thought-provoking project, and announced a brief break. The break turned into a forty-minute, very pregnant pause in the conference's scheduled agenda.

While Chairman Axelrod had planned to reintroduce Richard Nixon's overhead, two-handed, departure wave upon completion of his remarks, something told him *not* use the gesture on this particular day. Besides, as a practical matter, Kingmaker was effectively blocking the podium.

Bedlam broke out in the foyer.

In the chaos and throughout the day and into the next day, there was debate over *exactly* what happened—debate over what people *actually heard*. Some had heard something entirely different than their colleagues beside them had heard.

The initial comments in the hastily formed clusters of officers were wholly predictable. Mandatory revocations meant supervisors would be all over officers, checking every detail for potential revocations. Officers were angered about the idea of "voluntary" work on nights and weekends. They foresaw added paperwork, which they hated. They expressed anger at the idea of one more project ordered from above, without their input on the design. And, particularly at this moment, officers were convinced their leaders were operating, as one officer put it, at an "intellectual low tide."

It didn't seem like officers connected *empathetically* with the potential miscarriage of justice to "offenders" and their families. The plan was impractical. It was make-work. Officers who worked outside the state of Maryland feared their courts and parole authorities would pick up on Axelrod's idea. This policy shift could alter the role of probation and parole officers so adversely—by forcing mandatory revocations—that it played into officers' worse fears about their safety. Every offender would see them as the enemy. Any pretense of "helping" offenders would be over.

There were a few officers, on the margins, who wanted to be law enforcement officers anyway; they liked this mandatory revocation idea.

Many reported having heard booing, probably, they guessed, directed toward Gee's comment.

Others said they heard cursing, and it was directed to Axelrod.

Some remembered laughter or, at least, a nervous reaction to calamity.

There were gasps.

There were "Oh, my Gods."

And, although it made no sense, several reported hearing something like "Soup, soup."

There was equal debate about what folks actually *saw*.

Some said they saw a person in the audience flexing, actually flexing with his arms raised.

Others recalled seeing high-fives.

Still others reported seeing a look of shock on faces in the audience.

One person swore she saw the Baltimore judge pointing directly at Chairman Axelrod and cursing at Chief Kasten.

An officer from Montgomery County saw Chip Faulknour run up to the stage, motioning to Deputy Kingmaker—sort of like, "What should I do?"

When the participants returned to the conference room, an enlightened conference host might have made an astute, extemporaneous observation about the events. Instead, Dora and other officials handled the chaos like it was a minor interference and no big deal. No one bought this message.

The criminal justice professor told his student on the way back to the university, "I have an eerie feeling that the probation and parole system is shifting from incompetence to chaos and anarchy. Indeed, anarchy is close at hand: yesterday the *offenders* felt the brunt of punishment policies; today, it was the *officers* turn to be used for the governor's political motives. As Lyndon B. Johnson once said, 'It's better to have your enemies inside the tent pissing out, than outside the tent pissing in.' Right now, there were a lot of officers outside the tent."

"We ought to get a grant to study their morale," the student said.

"Great idea," the professor responded.

~

Meanwhile, the Cuatro Amigos had made a hasty exit from the building. They stood on Pratt Street looking toward Camden Yards. Gee was crying, then laughing. She was spaced out. Hattie, Huggie, and Pepe joined in one awkward laugh that Gee translated to mean, "What in the hell are we going to do now?"

The four friends knew well that Gee worked at the pleasure of the courts, without a union behind her, and could be fired or demoted for publicly disrespecting the chairman of the Maryland Parole Commission. The ever-composed Hattie Rogers barked orders.

"Listen up. I'm heading back to Rockville to talk personally with Judges Johnson and Clarke. Then, I'm going to call Maye Lee Williams at the Parole Commission. Pepe, you go see Judge Clarke."

Pepe balked. "But, Hattie, I don't like talking to judges."

"Do it anyway, Pepe."

"Huggie, get your father talking to the community activists about TJ's death. Here's how we pitch it: the Governor and Axelrod are trying to usurp the authority of the courts by publicly shaming judges and administrators into making 'zero tolerance' policies that the courts *in their infinite wisdom* and, God forbid, probation officers, should be making. Get the community activists to understand that the targeted group includes their sons and daughters!" Hattie said.

Gee just rolled her eyes.

"Oh, Gee, reach out to Jon Rhodes or Carrie Springer as soon as possible. Maybe they can get the story *on* Axelrod and *off* of you!" ordered Hattie.

"OK," Gee said.

Pepe said, "It's too risky to hide or appear to be cowering."

So, they agreed to meet at the scheduled happy hour where hundreds of probation and parole officers from all over the country, for better or worse, would be gathering at a closed-door event.

"We're out there now without a net. But, after all, haven't we *really* had enough?" Huggie asked.

~

Hattie's view that the Cuatro Amigos could somehow slow down an attack by Dora Kingmaker and her management jester, Chip Faulknour, by quickly talking to select judges and community leaders was a good one—but not exactly accurate. No more than thirty seconds after the conclusion of the Axelrod debacle, Kingmaker was pulled aside by the deputy director for State Probation and Parole, accompanied by the state regional administrator, who had oversight of Montgomery County.

"Listen, Dora, we can't bring charges against your officers, but please know we'll do anything possible to help you get them fired. We can testify at hearings, whatever. Maybe Internal Affairs is the route to go. Think about it and call me," said the deputy director.

"Oh, believe me, I'll handle this one personally," Dora said, as the state officials scurried off to report the incident to their absent director.

Dora motioned for Faulknour to come to her side. "Come to the faculty room," she whispered.

"Why?" asked Chip.

"Well, Chip, had I wanted to explain it here, in public, I wouldn't whisper to meet me in the faculty room, would I?" she added.

"Shit, I'm not going to get the blame for my officers' behavior, am I? They're going to fall before I do. I warned Brooks to keep her mouth shut. Officers can't talk to the chairman of the Parole Commission like that," he said.

Kingmaker didn't answer, just frowned and turned on her heels.

Chip waited a few minutes, then followed Dora to the faculty room. He knocked on the door.

"Come in," she said.

"What do you think, Dora?" he asked, closing the door behind him.

"Let me say it real clear: I suspect somebody's head is going to get chopped off for this mess. We now have an over-reaching, idiotic parole chairman suggesting—telling, really—how Chief Judge Brayer and the other judges of Montgomery County should manage revocations!" she whispered in a stern posture.

"But, Dora, he's only talking about parolees—not probationers under court jurisdiction, right?"

"Chip, Axelrod expects the courts' handling of probation revocations to follow his lead for parolees. If the press jumped on this like the new, best thing, the courts will have insurmountable public pressure to follow suit. He's pitting the governor against the courts, the executive branch against the judiciary branch. Long-lasting bad blood usually follows moves like that. And our Ms. Brooks has stepped right in the middle. We should thank her. Now, how do we come out of this without blame, and turn this to my—I mean, *our*—advantage?"

"Why don't you call your friend?" Chip asked, raising his eyebrows.

"Who?" she asked, thinking to herself, *does he mean the governor?*

"*You* know—your *special* friend," he added, raising his eyebrows again on the word "special."

"What the fuck are you saying? Do you mean the governor?"

"Well, *yeah*. Wouldn't he want to help you?"

"You idiot. The governor is not my—screw it, never mind. The Governor wouldn't jump into this fray to benefit me. He'll have his hands full staying clear of this mess. My guess is he'll deny he knows anything about Axelrod's policy, and, in fact, he may not know anything. On second thought, I doubt he knew *nothing* before today's grand announcement," Dora said, thinking out loud.

"Is this going to land on us? Do you think we're going to be demoted?"

"Not if I can help it. Let's weigh our options. I've already cornered Kasten and suggested a meeting Monday morning with Ms. Brooks. I'll make sure Kasten thinks we had no knowledge of the details of Axelrod's Operation Øman." she said.

"But, Dora, we did! We had an advance copy! You sent out e-mails, reminder e-mails, and had mandatory drug testing for all of the parolees!" he said.

"Deny it, Chip. Or, better, say you thought the new policy was cleared through channels. Mention the time required to put this conference together. Got it?" she said, glaring at Chip.

"Got it. But you, not Axelrod, ordered mandatory UAs for all parolees," he said.

"I'll say I assumed Axelrod's policy called for mandatory urinalysis. Who can we go to? Not Chief Brayer. He's too removed."

"What will Kasten do? I don't want this landing on me! I've done nothing wrong. Damned Brooks," he said.

"Kasten will fall on his sword. He's counting the days until he retires. He gets irritated by pressure and criticism, but usually not really shaken."

"Well, good. Then we're home free!"

"Chip, I don't want to just avoid blame. How do we turn this to our advantage? There's one way. Separate ourselves from Kasten. The governor is pals with Senior Judge Cox. They play poker together, I've heard," she said.

"How'd you know that?"

Her glare cut off follow-up questions.

"I have my sources. I can go see Cox and talk about the embarrassing event—how Kasten was asleep at the helm and how upset the officers are. But, to make that work, we've got to speak to the inappropriate behavior of Brooks, Winston, Gonzalez, and Rogers. I'll describe them to Judge Cox as appearing to start a rebellion," she stated, liking the sound of her own plan as it was coming out of her mouth.

"But Cox is so old. He only works part-time. Who'd take him seriously?"

"Chip, it's possible to have little leverage within the courthouse, but a great deal of leverage in statewide politics. Judges don't get to be judges by judicial talent, you idiot!" she said.

She took a long drink of water.

"I want to paint a picture of Brooks's rudeness and Gomez, Winston, and Rogers marching out—like a 1960s demonstration, like they're leading a rebellion. But we'll need more. We'll need samples of poor performance on their parts, the troublemakers' parts. I think we can get Brooks fired, and I know we can get Gomez fired! Winston and Rogers are too well-connected politically. They'll just end up with black eyes," she added

Upon seeing his you-made-a-politically-incorrect-statement look, she added, "Excuse my poor choice of words. Stay with me, Chip—this is our chance to get Kasten out of the way, one way or another, and you and me promoted to chief and deputy."

Chip didn't move a muscle.

"We've got to get evidence from their case files showing that they're not doing their jobs—that this *rebellion* is just the tip of the iceberg," she said.

"How?"

"Tomorrow, we'll review their files. We have keys to their offices. You're their supervisor. Make up a reason why you're looking at their files. It's not that hard, Chip, just make the shit up. If we can find enough errors or oversights, we'll prepare a confidential summary report for Judge Cox, which I'll allude to, but won't give him unless he asks for it. I'll say the following: We have problems with the parole chairman, but there are bigger morale problems brought on by Kasten's poor leadership and the four rebels. The rebels —I like that … 'rebels'— should be fired or demoted. 'But,' I'll say, 'I fear Kasten will do nothing about it.' Last, I'll say that all of this reflects badly on the judges."

She took another sip of water, then added, "I'm guessing this is the kind of thing folks talk about at poker games. My hunch is that the governor and Judge Cox will get the ball rolling for us."

"What will we look for in the case files?"

"Anything and everything," Dora said. "Anything and everything."

"Oh, Dora, one last question. Why do you hate her so much?"

"Hate? OK, I'll bite. I *hate* everything she stands for—her bubblegummed, ponytailed idealism. I had to hear about her father being a federal probation officer even before she was hired."

"But, Dora, I'm around her every day. I've never heard her mention her father."

"She doesn't have to mention it, Chip—it's her trump card … like she knows better than us. You can take her and every whiny public defender and all of those bogus community mouthpieces and stick their make-a-difference, mushy crap with the supposedly *helpless* thugs and put it where the sun doesn't shine. I hate her cutesy smugness. I hate her phony utilitarian Princess Sunshine routine. The world is made up of decent people and thugs. Now, it's our jobs—and we get paid to do this—to protect the public from thugs. If Princess Sunshine wants to hold hands and sing 'Kumbaya,' that's cool, but not on my watch. The streets of Hell are paved with her good intentions. How's that for a biblical reference? I didn't get a hand up. I picked myself up. Not on my watch—there's too much at stake."

"You're not ... ah ... jealous ...?"

"Chip the Chipster, I beg you to shut the fuck up before I send you back to your last job."

After five hours of snooping, Kingmaker and Faulknour had the goods. Nothing terribly serious—just enough information from the files to raise questions about "failure to perform duties pursuant to policy." Each of the four had submitted late reports to the court and turned in untimely statistical reports. Gee Brooks's defense of Viv Watson would be brought up. Gomez's inability to write acceptable pre-sentence reports would be used against him. Twelve times Hattie Rogers had refused to take more supervision cases. That would be the focus for her. Huggie Winston had been criticized by Faulknour for spending too much time in the community and refusing to be an office duty officer twice, saying he had more important things to do. There was also the "shady" car sale reprimand letter in his file.

Their legal representatives, if they chose to retain lawyers, would try and rebut, she said to Faulknour, by arguing that with high caseloads, every officer is guilty of not touching every base in every case, every time. But the damage would be done. Kingmaker knew the burden to defend themselves would be on the Cuatro Amigos and on Kasten—as in, how did he let this happen? Isn't the public unsafe? Besides, Kingmaker had never been turned down by the court in her personnel requests, including firings and demotions. Now, she figured, was the time to yank the lever.

~

"Put a summary of the specifics into talking points for each of the four, and make up a potential witness list, including the deputy director of Parole and Probation and the state regional administrator. If Judge Cox weighs in, we'll follow his lead. Otherwise the two of us will present our inquiry and recommendations to Kasten. When the court takes action against the four of them, that can't be good for Kasten," she said.

"Sure, sure. You started to say something about your conversation with the Internal Affairs Unit. What did they say?" Chip asked.

"Oh, have I got great news! Even Kasten has no idea that Internal Affairs has agreed to use surveillance to track Brooks's and Gomez's movements for five days! The deputy director and regional administrator bought our argument that her disrespectful outburst and Gomez's defiant physical gesture toward the Commissioner when he walked out of the room were sufficient grounds for action. For good measure, I threw in tracking Gomez with all that Hispanic community stuff. We got 'em!" Kingmaker said.

Gee felt her outburst had, at the very least, put an abrupt end to the Cuatro Amigos operating below the radar. Everyone knew, she said to Pepe, that they didn't agree with the mainstream viewpoints of the deputy and the managers. They had overtly opposed the punishing practices—railed against them, some said. Now, they'd be targets for the deputy chief and perhaps others who were desperately in need of scapegoats.

"I'm sorry, Pepe," she said on a cell phone call.

"What is ... is," he said.

The night of Gee's outburst, the Cuatro Amigos entered the happy hour celebration at the Colts4Evr Bar and Grille, off North Street. The sign outside said, "Closed for Private Party!" On the walls were countless pictures of old Baltimore Colts football players. The waiters and waitresses wore Colts jerseys. One long oak bar wrapped against the wall in a semicircle, and around the facility were circular tables for eight. Walking into the bar, Gee felt the noise level suddenly drop 1,000 decibels—or so it seemed. The foursome marched straight to the bar, led by Huggie. Gee felt every eye on her. Then it came: a sudden hoot, a follow-up yelp, a loud scream—until it seemed like the entire bar broke into roaring approval directed at the Cuatro Amigos. But it turned out *not* to be the entire bar. A counter-wave of jeers started with shouts of "yellow bellies," "Al Qaeda lovers," and "gang-bangers" and ended with a chorus of "boos."

Huggie's hand lightly touched Gee's arm, and Hattie backed toward Gee, as if they were circling the wagons. Pepe glared at three large Texans. A small group of officers approached the Cuatro Amigos. A short, nasal-pitched spokesman said to Gee, "We just want you to know we hate everything you stand for!"

"And what does she stand for?" Huggie asked.

"You know—*them*. We don't protect *them*. We protect the good guys!"

Pepe shot back, "What do you mean '*we*,' gringo? You got a turd in your pocket?"

The small group snarled curse words and pretended to physically restrain some of their crew, like baseball players do in fake fights. Then they turned and walked back to their table.

The room, filled with about 250 probation and parole officers, erupted with laughter and a buzz, repeating Pepe's punch line for those who couldn't hear it.

"It's OK—it's *OK!*" shouted Gee over the din of noise. Now, like Axelrod earlier, she was shouting. "But *we've* had enough of targeting *them!*"

The crowd of young officers cheered.

"Enough punishment! Enough inventing ways to 'catch' people making mistakes! What good is sending folks back to prison for stuff that half the population does—like smoking a joint, like 75 percent of you have?" she said.

One guy shouted out, "*Busted!*" to a roar of laughter.

She went on, "We've got work to do. We've got to learn how to be good—no, excellent—probation *and* parole officers. I'm not very good. I had a young man kill himself...." She started to choke up and had to stop.

"Take your time, sister. Tell the truth," said Huggie.

"Go on, sister!" Hattie said.

Gee pulled herself together, now in touch with her rage.

"I'm not a very good probation officer. When I needed to listen, really hear a young man, a man with a wife and two small children that love him just as much as *your* children love and need you—I wasn't there. I was too busy with busywork to hear his cry for help. I swear to God: this is the last day on this job I will ever, *ever* drown out my own values!"

Pausing, Gee looked first at Pepe ... then Hattie ... then Huggie ... and then into the gathered crowd....

She was welling up, but she managed to eke out, "Together, we can make a difference—join us!"

The next sound was the kind you hear when the home team scores the winning points in the last seconds of a basketball game.

Like the losing team's fans, a group of snarling, cussing officers left the bar in obvious protest, led by the contingent from Texas.

"How?" said a woman's voice rather softly, as the noise subsided.

"Yeah, how?" came another voice from the pack.

Seeing the cluster of antagonists leave the bar gave Gee a sense of safety. She had seen the opposition. Her internal voice said *Bring it on.* She had a white-hot, steely look of certainty.

"I want us to start asking ourselves one question: how do we learn the essential ingredients for excellence in our profession?"

"Isn't that kind of fancy?" asked one muscular female officer.

"Sorry, let me say it another way—suppose there were four or five skills we could learn that would change everything. Would you be interested in learning them?" Gee asked.

"Hell, yeah," said Pepe.

"But you better teach them in five hours, 'cause that's all the training we get a year!" said another officer, to laughter.

"Isn't that what the national association is supposed to do?" asked a woman.

"Not really. The association is about trends and news. There's a serious question we have to ask ourselves: if probation and parole is to become an elite profession, what do we need to know? I guarantee you this—the answers will come from *us*, from those that do the work, not from governors, asinine politicians, judges, *parole commissioners*, prosecutors, managers acting without input from us, or supervisors acting like editors. *We* must define *our own* profession."

There was loud applause.

"What will the name of this *thing* be, and how will you get the ball rolling?"

"The Nuevos Principios Society—With Support, People Can Change," said Gee, glancing at her friends, who only shook their heads.

"For us *gringos*, what do the words mean?" asked a young woman, smiling coyly at Pepe.

"Nuevos Principios means to find a *new way* of looking at things. We'll define our own vision," said Gee.

"How will we communicate?" asked a techie-looking fellow.

Gee pointed to her three friends, who stood with mouths noticeably agape, "My three friends here have already committed to setting up a Web site and blog where we can communicate. It will be up in ten days. Look for www.nuevosprincipios.com." She told no one that she had obtained the use of the domain name two hours earlier from her laptop.

"Tell everyone about it, please. I know this—no one can stop the truth," said Gee.

Then Gee invoked the words of former president Ronald Reagan, "If not us, who? If not now, when? Thank you for caring."

~

The conference ended the next day at noon. The Cuatro Amigos were simply in attendance, listening to the concerns of others and thanking them for expressing their views. Most folks appeared to be pleased just to be taken seriously. Gee also felt she received a few "God bless you" looks, looks she felt meant, "There's no way you're going to pull this off." She also felt that any minute someone was going to give the Cuatro Amigos the old "the boss would like to see you" gesture. The message would probably be delivered by Chip Faulknour.

Before they left, Hattie approached Gee and said, "Did you get ahold of Carrie Springer?"

"Not yet, Commander, but I will today."

"Good. My mother said she is one sharp cookie. She doesn't say that about too many people. Who knows what could come of it?" Hattie said.

~

Gee was able to get Jon Rhodes on the phone at home early Sunday morning. Jon said he was getting ready to leave town, but he gave her Carrie's home phone number and encouraged Gee to call her.

"Ms. Springer, this is Gee Brooks. I'm a probation—"

"Sweetie, call me Carrie. I know who you are. Olivia Lopez spoke highly of you," Carrie said.

"Oh. Well, I've got a story to share with you. Actually, several stories that have erupted—"

"When you say *erupted*, does this involve the court?"

"Absolutely," Gee said.

"Honey, we need to meet. Are you comfortable talking to me off the record?" Carrie said.

"Comfortable? I'm very anxious," Gee said.

"Comfortable" was a stretch, Gee thought. She corrected her thought to say to herself that she was relatively *un*comfortable talking to Carrie—or anybody else for that matter. Like cops, probation officers were drilled to be insular and trust few outsiders, particularly those with the power of the pen. If something embarrassing about her bosses or the organization leaked to the press without Kingmaker's prior approval, Gee would be fired on the spot. Gee worried about what Carrie might do with the information she shared. *But what choice do I have?* she asked herself.

Twenty minutes later, she rang Carrie's doorbell.

"Listen, I've already lied to you," Gee said, as Carrie ushered her inside.

"Oh—"

"Yes. Actually, I'm very uncomfortable talking to anybody about recent events."

"Look, I understand more of the politics of the environment you work in than you might think. Consider me an investigative reporter. I like to shed light on areas that are simply unjust. I'll keep everything you say off the record and protect you as my source. I think you've called me because you think that WWTS is interested in the ends of justice being served. Am I right?"

"Yes, that's true. Also, I don't want an attorney yet, and I have no one else to turn to *inside* the system."

"OK. Let's start there and see where things go. I think you'll be pleasantly surprised by how common our interests are."

Gee exhaled and took in the ambiance of Carrie's kitchen, where she'd entered the house. It was exquisitely decorated—professionally designed, she guessed, in modern furnishings. The kitchen had a huge island with gas burners, an overhead brass hood, and hanging copper pots and pans. Gee noticed that bold black cabinets offset the nearby black and tan, oak dining room chairs and a rectangular table in a nearby dining room. The kitchen also had a dark maroon marble countertop that seemed to encircle the room. Black leather stools stood near the countertop. They chose two.

"I've always dreamed of having a house like this. It's so beautiful," Gee said.

"Thank you. Aren't you sweet! My former husband and I raised our two boys here. The house has so many memories. Since we divorced, I just haven't had the heart to sell it. Maybe I have some unfinished business before I move on...." Carrie didn't finish her sentence.

Gee noticed the soft tone and tried to blend into Carrie's admission of vulnerability without making Carrie feel awkward. "It takes a lot of time. I'm separated from my husband and have a new condo. Everything feels so new. My dad still lives alone in the house we lived in when my mother died. I'm not sure he'll ever move from that old house. I know he doesn't need all the space."

"Now tell me, what happened?"

"I don't know how much you know about our office. It's a top-down environment where the agenda is being as tough on crime and offenders as possible," Gee said.

"So I've heard," Carrie said.

"Last Wednesday one of my favorite parolees, TJ ... committed suicide."

Gee stopped, her eyes watering.

Carrie said, "Oh, sweetie, I'm so sorry."

As Gee cried, Carrie retrieved a tissue box. After a minute, now better composed, Gee told of TJ and his likely marijuana use, of Junie, TJ's kids, and his computer aspirations. Gee then shifted to the Baltimore conference and Axelrod's Operation Øman.

"It stands for zero tolerance and mandatory violations," Gee concluded.

Carrie looked confused. "I'm sorry," she said. "Does this new policy affect the courts, and does it differ from current practices?"

"The court—well, really, our office and the state's attorney's office and the Parole Commission, have been cracking down harder and harder for the slightest infractions. I don't mean—"

"You don't mean new arrests and convictions," interrupted Carrie.

"How'd you know that?" Gee asked. Outside the Cuatro Amigos, she had thought no one knew or cared.

"We'll get back to that," Carrie said, waving her hand.

"So, current practices aren't too different than what the parole chairman's stupid new idea calls for, but it adds something: he institutes a *mandatory* revocation policy for parolees with only *one* event—say a positive UA for marijuana or one missed appointment—and a *mandatory* prison setback of one year or more. That's insane!" Gee added.

"What happened at the conference when what's-his-name announced this?"

"Well, Houston, we have a problem.... I, uh, stood up and said something like, 'This is stupid and you should be ashamed!' I think I even pointed to Axelrod on the stage. And my boss. And our deputy, who hates me. Oh, and a Baltimore judge...."

"Holy smoke, girl. Too bad the governor wasn't there, too. Did they hear you?"

"Oh, they all heard me. Then I screamed something like, 'Stop this tail 'em, nail 'em, jail 'em punishment crap!'"

"Actually, I like that: tail 'em, nail 'em, jail 'em. What was the reaction of the Baltimore judge? I want to know where the political heat will come from. Do you remember?"

"No."

"Have you heard from Kasten, or the deputy?" Carrie grilled.

"No."

"*No* is a good thing. Now, let's go back a minute. Does this new policy affect the courts?"

"No, not directly."

"Honey, Congress itself loves to trim judicial discretion by putting mandatory minimums into sentencing law. But tell me if I have this right: this Øman thing could *indirectly* affect the courts if the idea gets a favorable response from the press and if noise from the press affects public opinion. Then, I suppose, even the judges in the Circuit Court in Montgomery County would feel pressure to follow suit, either formally or informally. Right?"

"Yes, and all of these tough-on-crime schemes add up to severe punishment, mostly for blacks and Hispanics," Gee added.

"What's the connection between the parole chairman's announcement of the new harebrained idea and TJ's suicide?"

"About ten days ago, every officer had direct orders from our deputy—I guess in anticipation of the new policy announcements at the conference in Baltimore—to take mandatory UAs from all parolees the next time they saw them. Carrie, you know how police always start some 'Operation Clean Sweep,' or whatever, with busting folks for outstanding warrants to make a big splash? The mandatory UAs were the same thing. Anyway, one of my colleagues told TJ last Monday about the mandatory one-year sentence for a positive UA. We believe he had recently smoked pot. He said something about how he wasn't doing anymore prison time. Anyway, we know he went home—and then disappeared. He jumped off of the Key Bridge, rather than go back to prison," Gee said. "He left behind a wife and two small children."

"That's terrible."

"Three other friends and I are pissed off and decided we're going to come out swinging. We have some ideas I'd like to share with you," Gee said.

"Just pissed off?"

"No. I feel like I've embarrassed ... others. Maybe my mother. I know that sounds silly. She died when I was twelve...." Gee stopped in mid-sentence and began crying.

"How?" Carrie asked, passing the tissue box again.

"From cancer," Gee managed to get out.

"I'm so sorry. Do you remember ...?"

"Oh, God, I remember how brave she was. She never let us know how bad she hurt. My dad told me that nurses said Mom was a horse—in fact, he called her 'The Horse,'" Gee smiled through the tears.

"I bet there are other stories you have about her character—her strong will—apart from cancer?" Carrie asked, taking Gee's hand.

Gee nodded, hard, but was unable to say anything.

Shaking her head from side to side, Carrie said, "I can only imagine your mother standing in your corner. Mothers love their babies. That's what they do."

Gee cried harder.

"We'll talk more about this another day. Deal?" Carrie said, her hand lifting Gee's chin. "Deal?"

"Deal," Gee said.

"Right now, we need to see if we can keep you employed for a few more days! There—that thought ought to brighten up your weekend!" Carrie laughed.

"What're you going to do?"

"Something before Monday morning—you can be sure of that!" Carrie laughed again.

Gee started to say something, but Carrie overlapped her.

"You go enjoy the rest of the day. Be around friends. I'll get back to you tonight," Carrie stood and ushered Gee toward the door. "I mean it. Go have some fun. Give it some thought, Gee—your mother was a fighter, and fighters admire other fighters. She'd be proud of you!"

"How can I—"

"You already thanked me by coming here today. The WWTS might turn out to be a great resource for you, if you'd like."

"Yes, my friends and I need your help."

"Good! We'll figure it out together," Carrie said and opened the door. "Oh! Before you go, let's exchange cell numbers. Would you be a dear and program mine? My son does that for me."

The numbers exchanged, Gee squeezed Carrie's hand and was off.

~

It was just before noon. Bill Brayer was reading the Outlook section of the Sunday *Washington Post*, enjoying his second cup of coffee, when the phone rang. His wife, Mildred, who would typically answer the phone, hadn't returned from church.

"Hi, Bill, it's Carrie.… How are you?"

"Fine, Carrie. Good to hear your voice on this gray January day. I was just considering starting a fire. To what do I owe this privilege?"

"I need your help."

"Anything, dear—within the laws of this great country."

"Have you heard about the events at the probation officers' conference in Baltimore on Friday?"

"Well, yes. I got a call yesterday from Kasten who said that one of his officers—maybe more than one—shouted at that idiot Trent Axelrod.... He's the governor's new parole chairman."

"I know, Bill."

"I'm sorry—you probably know more than I. Anyway, what I heard was that the female officer shouted at Axelrod as he announced some new mandatory revocation policy for parolees. I asked Kasten who was on the dais, and he mentioned his deputy, Commissioner Williams, and Judge Leonard Thompson from the Baltimore Circuit Court. I know Len, so I called him to find out if he was offended and if my court needs to express a formal apology. His exact words were, 'Hell, no. Screw the nitwit,' meaning Axelrod. Len said he got a kick out of the officer's guts and he joked about the way her buddies stuck by her side. He's a former Marine colonel. Len and I agreed to hold a conference call with the statewide Judicial Council next Wednesday to frame a response to Axelrod's policy—which, by the way, I had not heard of. I'm sure my colleagues on the bench will be up in arms, Democrats and Republicans alike. We don't like being surprised or cornered. How'd you find out, Scoop?" he asked.

"I just met with one of the officers in this made-for-TV drama. This, of course, is something WWTS is very interested in," she added.

"Good, I'm glad to hear it. Officially, I say nothing on the record. Harry Johnson and I will serve as deep background, if that's your pleasure. Whether you need my information or not, it's nice of you to have thought of me. The short, off-the-record version is that I'm furious. I'll have a talk with Bob Kasten about how he got blindsided. Clearly, he needs to grab hold of the reins, rather than have one foot in retirement! That, of course, is *also* off-the-record," he added.

"Are the officers going to be the scapegoats?"

"Carrie, I understand your interest in protecting her. I plan to let Kasten know the issue is Axelrod, not the spontaneous—albeit overly aggressive—outburst from one of his officers. But realize that pressure to punish officers usually comes one step down the hierarchy—from Deputy Kingmaker, not Kasten."

"Thank you, Bill. May I make an appointment with you for next week to talk about an issue for WWTS?"

"Dear, I don't keep my calendar. Call Gabby White. She just points me in certain diretions."

~

When she got off the phone with Judge Brayer, Carrie called Gee.

"This is what I know. Powerful forces in the court are not going to let you guys take the fall for reacting to Axelrod's stupid new idea. Trust that judges will be talking about Axelrod—not you—behind closed doors. Still, be on guard for Deputy Kingmaker. Keep her in front of you," warned Carrie.

"I can't thank you enough!" said Gee. "Listen, Carrie, there's more we need to talk about."

"What's up?"

"Can you meet my friends Huggie, Hattie, and Pepe this Saturday morning at Starbucks in Bethesda?"

"Gee, why not meet here? Was the coffee that bad?" Carrie asked. "I think we can talk more privately here."

"I do too! You'll love the Cuatro Amigos."

"Lord help us, you even have a secret club name!"

"Thank you so much."

"Balls to the wall, girl—balls to the wall!"

"What?"

"It's a saying my pilot ex-husband taught me. It references a short runway where a pilot has to yank the throttles—the sticks with balls at the top—back hard and quick before the plane runs into a mountain or a bank of trees. Honey, it means to give an all-out effort!" Carrie said, laughing.

"Well, balls to your walls, too, Carrie," Gee laughed.

23

POWER INTERRUPTED

Carrie Springer

When judges are embarrassed or angry, somebody pays for it. On Monday morning, when Carrie called Gabby White to schedule the appointment, Gabby whispered that a meeting was in progress in Chief Judge Brayer's chambers with Chief Probation Officer Robert Kasten. Gabby loved to be the source of gossip in the courthouse. Carrie, of course, didn't mention that she already had insider information.

"I asked Judge Brayer what he wanted me to record as the purpose of the meeting in his office log. He barked, 'Just put down a Come to Jesus meeting,'" Gabby said, with a giggle.

What Carrie really wanted was to get Judge Brayer's view on some staggering statistics she had collected regarding the escalating number of revocation hearings in the court during the past two fiscal years. She planned to report to the judge that her estimates were just that—estimates. She expected to complain that hard data was difficult to come by from state probation officials and from the probation office's meager Web site statistics. She also planned to discuss the suicide of TJ Smith and more about the conference in Baltimore. Carrie didn't want to print any information that would harm the goodwill between WWTS and the court or her friendship with Bill Brayer.

As she waited outside an empty courtroom in a cove in front of heavy wooden doors, Carrie heard a man and a woman conversing nearby. The tone of their discussion caught her attention. She peeked around the corner and recognized Faulknour. She didn't know the woman. Just outside Judge Cox's chambers, next door to Judge Brayer's chambers, the pair stopped.

Before buzzing the intercom outside the chamber doors, the woman said, "Chip, we're going to nail Kasten, Brooks, and the other three with this information. I know Cox will take this to the governor. Brayer will have to do something to save face. He doesn't like to dabble in office politics, but he will. Judge Brayer will be cornered into taking action against all of them. Think of it—insulting a state official in front of 700 people, a mandatory revocation policy inserted right under Kasten's nose without the court's knowledge, pressure on the courts to respond, poor performance by four officers—we got 'em!"

"Right, right, Dora," Chip said.

Oh, that's Dora Kingmaker, Carrie thought.

Kingmaker entered Judge Cox's chambers, and Chip turned and walked away.

~

After chatting with Gabby White, Carrie was waved in by Judge Brayer, who was on the phone. She stared at the countless family and professional pictures behind him on the paneled walls.

"Good afternoon, Judge, and thank you for seeing me," she said, smiling, after he hung up.

"What's up, Carrie?"

Carrie raised her concern about the poor quality of data she was able to access regarding technical violations.

"Hold on, let's see what I can do," he said. "Gabby, get the State Director of Information Technology in Baltimore on the line."

Seconds later, he asked—well, ordered—that Ms. Springer be provided a clearly worded report as soon as possible with the number of revocation hearings over the past five years, statewide and in Montgomery County, and the results of those hearings.

"Furthermore, I want her to receive a breakdown showing, within those persons revoked, how many didn't have new criminal offenses—technical violators, I believe you classify them as. Send me a copy, too," he added.

"Yes, sir, Judge, I will see to it myself," responded the official.

"Thank you, Bill. I was going to ask you about the chairman of the Parole Commission's Operation Øman speech, but I changed my mind. I'm meeting with Gee Brooks and some other probation officers this Saturday to see how I can help them with their concerns about mandatory minimums and technical violations. Apparently, they're interested in doing something," Carrie said.

She waited anxiously for his response.

"Good for them! This *is* America. If you're fishing for a public reaction regarding Axelrod, here's my say: the court is always interested in new ideas to reduce crime and its terrible impact on citizen-victims," he said.

"Thank you for the quote. One more thing: I'm sort of like the media, right? And, well, the media does pass along information, right?"

"Go on."

She told him, verbatim, what she had overheard Kingmaker say to Faulknour in the hallway.

"I don't want you blindsided, Bill," she added.

"Interesting. Thank you, Carrie," he said, and he stood, concluding the meeting.

"Interesting," Judge Brayer repeated out loud to himself, as Carrie closed the door behind her with a smile on her face.

Meanwhile, Dora Kingmaker was ushered into Senior Judge Cox's chambers. She sat before him, crossing and uncrossing her legs slowly, as he held his hands under his chin at a ninety-degree angle, as if he were focused on riveting testimony in a trial. She was familiar with nearly all of the pictures of politicians over his shoulder, having seen them on TV and in the paper. It was as if the pictures were a look back at power in Maryland—their terms had all ended decades ago.

"How can I help you today, Ms. Kingmaker? Have you up and gotten married on me and changed your name since we last spoke?" said Judge Cox, peering over his desk at her legs.

"Now, Judge Cox, I wouldn't get married until you absolutely told me there was no chance you'd marry me and take me out of my lonely misery!" Dora Kingmaker said.

"Oh, you little devil! How long has it been since we've talked?"

"Well, we did have that case last year—the Hawkins murder—and, oh, I guess at the governor's speech on the cleanup of the Chesapeake Bay last summer," she said, intentionally reminding him of her connection to the governor.

"What brings you to my chambers today?"

"Judge, I'm concerned about, well, the direction of the probation office. We've got four ring leaders who demonstrated at our national professional association conference in Baltimore—"

"I'd demonstrate, too, if that fool, Axelrod…. I'm sorry. I've diverted from your point. Please continue."

Well, he knows the issue, she thought. "Well, of course, Chairman Axelrod overstepped his authority. I couldn't be more outraged! Who is he to tell *us*—or the judges—what we should do? But I'm worried, Your Honor. Chief Kasten should have *never* let that happen. Now we've got four poorly performing probation officers leading a damned—excuse my French—a *darned* revolution."

"When did you learn of their poor performance, Ms. Kingmaker?"

"Well, after the demonstration. I understand they're starting some sort of society to question the court's authority!" she said.

"Hell, I question the court's authority every day. But go on, please," he prodded.

Suddenly, she felt as if she were on a slippery slope, unable to get traction with him. "Well, we have a structure in the probation office. The inmates can't run the asylum," she added, having no idea what to say next. *Damn it. He's drifting,* she thought.

"So, what would you have the judges do, Ms. Kingmaker? Reprimand the four officers? Fire the chief? Demote the chief? And, if we did demote him—you know, or put him out to pasture until he retires—who would take his place?"

She wanted to crawl out of her skin. "Well, Your Honor, that, that certainly isn't my domain. I just wanted you to know—"

"Ms. Kingmaker, trust me. I get your message. Here are the facts: I like the governor. I've never asked him why he appointed Axelrod. I never will. The governor didn't appoint Kasten chief of the probation office—that was this court's call. The chief judge really has the say about the chief's appointment and tenure. I don't know if His Majesty Judge Brayer, will fire Kasten. But, again, that's *his* call. Now, if Judge Brayer brings it up in a judge's meeting and asks for our views, I'll weigh in. But otherwise it's Brayer's call. Do you understand what I'm saying to you?"

"Yes, sir."

"Well, thank you for sharing your concerns. It was good to see you again," he concluded, standing up.

"Thank you for seeing me, and best wishes to your family and particularly to that lucky wife of yours!" she said. As soon as the words "lucky wife" came out of her mouth she regretted them, since the earlier flirtation had failed.

"Good day, Ms. *Kingmaker*."

As she closed the door behind her, she wondered if he added special emphasis to her name and was, thereby, sending a message. *God, he's such an asshole*, she thought to herself as she left his chambers.

~

"Dora, what happened?"

"I think it's too soon to tell. Maybe the old bastard was just messing with me."

"Well, have I got information for you—Ms. Brooks is seeing a psychiatrist!"

"Are you sure, Chip?"

"Yes. I overheard her making a personal call to someone and mentioning she had an appointment to see her psychiatrist today."

"Great! Let's see if we can't pressure her to take a leave of absence. If she bites, when she comes back, I'll give her assignments so awful no one could take it."

~

Collectively, the Cuatro Amigos were beyond edgy. The stress level was so high they decided they couldn't wait until Saturday; they met at Starbucks on Thursday morning, huddled at their favorite indoor table because they were gun-shy about being seen outdoors.

"Did you read that shit?" Gee asked the three.

"OK, I'll bite. What shit?" Pepe said.

"The Kingmaker's new policy. From here on out, it's not sufficient to write 'doctor's appointment' on a leave slip request—now you have to put the *name* of the doctor or the name of the facility."

"So?" said Huggie.

"You don't get it? What business is it of hers the name of the doctor we see? It can only be used for her to get more stuff on us," Hattie said.

"How?" Huggie said.

"I've been seeing a psychiatrist since—" Gee started to say 'Birdshit,' but, in deference to Huggie, who was still friends with Ed, she shifted in mid-sentence to his name, "—Ed and I broke up. I don't want that information to be public or to be used against me."

"My hunch is that, somehow, she already knows," Hattie said.

~

The first leave slip Gee submitted with the name Dr. Steven Weinman resulted in an immediate reaction, just five minutes after she put it in Chip Faulknour's inbox. After asking her permission, he closed her door and sat down very politely before her.

"I, uh, noticed that you have an appointment with Dr. Steven Weinman. Isn't he a psychiatrist?"

"What business is that of yours?"

"Dora and I have been concerned about you for some time. You seem to be so over-stressed."

"I'm fine."

"Well, if you need to take a leave of absence to get yourself together, we're quite sympathetic. All of us go through difficult times, Gee. Sometimes we just need space. You don't need the stress of this place, too."

"Well, thanks, Chip, but working with you and Dora is just the medicine I need."

~

Two weeks later, in a briefly worded policy announcement, Chief Kasten cancelled the medical identification policy, calling it unnecessary. Through back channels Carrie learned that Kasten thought Kingmaker was abusing her power. She shared that information with Gee. But the horse—the information about her psychiatric requirement—was out of the barn.

24

THE NEW ALLIANCE

Gee Brooks

Ready, fire, aim! That's it—ready, fire, aim, Gee thought to herself over a cup of coffee at her kitchen table, now distracted from the Sunday *Washington Post* before her. That's what she'd done. She had committed her three friends to an unknown, risky path—one that could affect their livelihood.

She called Hattie and set up a meeting to talk about the new Web site and blog before they met with Carrie and Jon on Saturday. Both ladies liked structure and certainty—there was little of either now. About 300 officers around the country were waiting for an action-oriented blog site. Finding common ground with her friends was easy, but finding common ground with officers in different districts, counties, states, and systems, that part was the great unknown.

Gee wanted a big-tent approach, one that included those who disagreed with the direction she hoped to go. The effort to make probation and parole systems less punishing was moving forward, and those who couldn't join that movement could keep their place in the mainstream. Already they had a label. The *Baltimore Sun* had sent a female reporter to cover the conference, and she had slipped into the happy hour at Colts4Evr Bar and Grille, unnoticed. On the Sunday right after the conference, the reporter's article referred to the Nuevos Principios Society's movement as a "humanistic revolution." The writer quoted the president of the Police Chiefs' Association of Maryland, who viewed the "humanistic revolution" as a "miserably out-of-touch, soft-on-crime, revival effort. But what can you expect of social workers?"

Gee remembered reading that early in any change process nothing is aligned. It's like being in the desert, alone. Old values are disrupted beyond repair. There's a sense of betrayal and of loss. It was like the day she moved into her new condo and nothing felt comfortable. She remembered that she was neither *there* in the old house or *here* in the new condo. She only knew then that she couldn't go back. So it was with this effort. *The genie can't go back in the bottle*, she thought.

On Thursday, January 15, Carrie Springer wrote a two-hundred-word article about Operation Øman in WWTS, referring delicately, without names, to the *scene* in the Baltimore Civic Center. Carrie had made the use of prisons for technical violations a public matter. Now the issue was a conversation piece throughout the state.

On Friday, January 16, Chief Kasten announced by e-mail that, by agreement with the courts, the Maryland Parole Commission had decided to delay implementation of Operation Øman until additional research was available. Tragically, Gee thought, the formal policy reversal could not bring TJ back to life. Quite the spin, officers gossiped. Still, there was a sense that mandatory revocations were around the corner. The practice of setting sentencing policy had become the newest trend for lawmakers. The belief that the powerful supported every tough-on-crime initiative, real or imagined, tended to shift managers to reinforce officers' behavior toward catching offenders' possible missteps with more zeal, not less.

That same Friday, the Cuatro Amigos held court at a corner table in Houston's over lunch. There were many questions fired at Gee. How do we get a blog started? Who, exactly, was going to pay for the Web site? What were the movement's essential ingredients?

"I don't like the term 'essential ingredients.' It sounds so … fancy," said Huggie.

"Be patient, Huggie. What I'm after is a new image for probation and parole," Gee said.

Hattie added, "God knows we have an image problem. If you asked average folks to give you *one word* that describes nurses, coaches, and bankers, they could answer. And my guess is that the word would be 'positive.' If you said probation or parole, who knows what you'd get back."

"OK, so what are you trying to get at—the basics, common sense?" Huggie asked.

"If it was common sense, it would be common. It's not basic. I think reaching difficult people with real challenges is an art, backed up by skills. That's what I'm after. What are those skills? Right now I don't know, but I see them in you three. I know we can identify those skills and learn them. Hang with me, we'll figure it out," Gee said,

"This, folks, is why people buy mystery books," Gee said, with an exaggerated smile.

"Bite me!" said Huggie.

No one else was smiling. So much for humor, she thought. She shared that her grandfather often used the expression, "Master the essential ingredients and the rest will follow." She had used this saying in many diverse situations in her life. She added that the probation and parole systems no longer operated with any real knowledge or skills, and, as a result, newer officers had mastered no skills. It was like the profession had meaning in other cultures but not here in the United States. She stated that, in her view, the place to start was to gather the pulse of other probation and parole officers through the blog. What were they thinking about? What turned them on? What turned them off? From that baseline of information, the Cuatro Amigos would seek leaders from the responders—hopefully motivated leaders who would emerge and share the workload. They'd make a decision about whom to seek out to help them formulate the "essential ingredients" of the profession. Then there would be the hard part: influencing the field officers.

"I know that Carrie Springer is eager to help us set up the Web site and link our articles to their Web site. Think about it—that link means that the Nuevos Principios Web site will be linked to countless other Web sites associated with WWTS. We'll become very public, very fast," Gee said.

"The easier to nail us, too, with our own words," Huggie said.

"Who are they linked with? Give me an example," Hattie said, ignoring Huggie's comment.

"Here are a few she mentioned today: the National Trial Lawyers Association, the Montgomery County Bar Association, the National Association of Women Judges, the National Sheriffs' League, the NAACP.... Need I go on?" Gee asked.

"Whoa! You're right. Huggie, our butts will be out there!" Pepe said.

With that, Huggie stood up and started to sing at the top of his voice about having no place to run or hide.

Hattie joined the chorus, followed by Gee and finally Pepe, to the amusement and applause of most of Houston's customers. In unison, the four danced and sang their way out the door.

When they stopped dancing, Pepe said, "I ask one thing and only one thing, my brother and sisters."

"What's that?" Gee asked.

"When I'm working at that car wash on Georgia Avenue near 495, you guys promise—paper-only tips!"

"We'll try, Pepe. We'll try, my brother," Huggie said.

After the laughter, they divided the tasks and started on their separate ways.

"We're going to do this!" they heard Gee shout from about thirty yards away, probably using the same tone Orville Wright used to assure a critic that he was sure "this thing will fly," long before he knew whether he and Wilbur were nuts and if the damn thing would ever get off the ground.

Jon Rhodes arrived at Carrie's house first, followed quickly by Gee, and then Hattie and Huggie, who drove together. Only Pepe lagged behind. The women chose white wine, while Jon and Huggie each grabbed a cold Heineken. When there was a knock on the door, Carrie rushed to greet Pepe, who had on his favorite Yankees baseball hat.

"You must be Pepe!" Carrie said, unable to take her eyes off of *his* eyes. "Oh, no, another Yankees fan!" she teased. She went over to the closet, pulled out a Red Sox hat, and propped it on her head.

"How quickly we move from hospitality to war!" Hattie said.

"Now, now, I can leave my hat on the table—if you would kindly remove yours! Truce?" Pepe asked.

"Pepe hasn't taken his hat off since July when he went to New York—claims he had it on and it helped get him into Nobu without a reservation!" chirped Gee.

"Did you meet Nobu in July?" Carrie asked.

"Yes, he did! How'd you guess that, Carrie?"

"I didn't.... You know.... Sometimes those chefs meet and greet...." Carrie said, her words tailing off.

The look on Pepe's face is strange, thought Gee. *What was that about?*

"Well, why don't we sit down and see how WWTS and the Nuevos Principios Society might work together," Carrie said.

Gee spoke for her group. "First, the *good* news. We have our Web site and blog up and running. My father's friend Art Coleman helped us create a very simple survey for the Web. That survey asks officers to anonymously rate what they think is the most important skill in the profession.

"Secondly, they were asked on a scale of one to six, with six being excellent, how well they rated themselves on this important skill. Then they were asked to write briefly how they might improve that score.

"Exactly 767 officers responded within six days. We think word is spreading quickly about the Web site. Of the 767 respondents, their response to the most important skill question was roughly—help me with the numbers, Hattie."

"Well, let's see," Hattie said, pulling papers out of her leather folder. "Thirty percent said being engaged in the local community is most important, another 22 percent mentioned communication skills, about 20 percent addressed listening skills, 10 percent said learning to work with difficult people, and the balance was all over the place.

"As for Question Two, their own personal ratings, most respondents generally provided no rating. Art suggested that this might have something to do with trust over how the information would be used. It was the third question, how they could be better, that was the real eye-opener. Looking back, it was an existential moment for us: you know, when the truth is quite miserable, is that really bad news?"

Everyone laughed.

"Hattie, if I may, the information from Question Three was a pinprick into the balloon of a notion I had that 'we' will lead this group, hungry for knowledge, to the promised land. Read a few responses," Gee said.

"OK," said Hattie, "here goes: 'We have only have eight hours of annual training.' 'My only job is to monitor the four to eight special conditions of the court.' 'Nobody cares what skills I have—I get rated for timeliness of field notes and reports.'"

"The responses seemed very passive-aggressive, hopeless, and without an ounce of personal responsibility or accountability," Huggie said.

"We did find three officers, each from different areas of the country, who volunteered to work on the blog and a bi-weekly newsletter. One was a supervisor. We agreed to take turns writing the lead articles," Pepe said. "Every lead article raises a specific point and asks readers to weigh in and, if they choose, to add general information on their local practices, but without a requirement for hard data. Some officers do gather statistics."

"Instead of hard data, respondents are sharing information and stories through the blog—a picture of the world from the ground up," Gee said.

"OK, we have a sense of what you're trying to do. Right, Jon?" Carrie asked.

"Two questions. What do you want to stop? What do you want to start?" Jon asked.

"We want to stop the punishing culture where it's 'us against offenders,'" said Gee, "where the goal is to send them back to prison by any means possible. We want to teach the essential ingredients of excellence and help create an atmosphere where offenders are seen as humans worthy of help and support."

"Not bad, girl!" said Pepe, giving her a high-five.

"OK, then our train is on the same tracks as yours. Let me propose we work together. I recently joined WWTS.... Let me back up. Jon started WWTS after his wife was murdered. He wanted to make sure justice was administered fairly. Since then, Jon and I have realigned that mission. Justice in the Montgomery County courts remains a primary goal. But WWTS is becoming aware of how revocation hearings have increased significantly over a long period of time, and no one seems to be examining why this is. It appears that prisons are used for mere rules violations, whereas rules or special conditions are used as trip wires. We find this to be a mindless attack on the powerless and an outrageous waste of financial and human resources. How can we work together to stop this madness?" Carrie asked.

The Cuatro Amigos heads wiggled like bobble-headed dolls in the back of a pick-up truck.

"Whoa! That's the first offer of community support we've gotten.

We want to start by collecting the story and then working to improve the knowledge and skills of officers, so they don't rely on punishment techniques," Gee said.

"How are you funded?" Carrie asked.

"By the seat of our pants," said Pepe.

"I'll pay all of your expenses for a year," Carrie said.

"No, Carrie, we'll split that bill," Jon said.

"How can we—"

"Thank us, Gee? Work with us. Why don't we do a summary of every article you write for your newsletter and run it in *our* newsletter? Also, we'll link you to other organizations through our Web site. We'll take the lead on the special conditions fight. We have more political cover than you. You guys focus on the skills and how folks get trained on them, OK?"

"Pepe and I have some exciting things going on in the black and Hispanic communities. We could use your help, I'm sure," Huggie said.

"Why don't we sit down separately and see how Jon and some friends of mine can help in that area?" Carrie asked.

"Good deal!" Huggie said.

There was excitement and a sense of common purpose in the room as everyone exchanged phone numbers. The meeting drew to a close. Gee went to the bathroom before leaving.

When she returned to the living room, Carrie asked her, "Do you have dinner plans?"

"No, not really."

"Let's order Chinese and eat here. Come on, I'm lonely. How's that sound?"

"It sounds great."

"So, you're a single girl again!" Carrie teased.

"*Nominally* single. I don't feel single. I haven't dated since Ed and I separated."

"Are you angry at Ed, numb, in pain—or all three?" Carrie asked as they ate Chinese food and drank white wine in the comfort of the living room. Carrie had oak logs burning in the large fireplace on this chilly February day. The smell reminded Gee of being in that rustic cabin in West Virginia with Ed.

"Mostly hurt, I guess," she said.

"Hurt is what I felt entitled to feel, until I allowed myself to let the rage out. I was a good mother, faithful wife, and, I thought, pretty caring. What does your father say about the separation?" Carrie asked.

"I think he hopes we'll get back together. But he doesn't say much."

"But you don't know, right?"

"Right."

"Well, go ask him. Maybe he'll surprise you. And what do you imagine your mother would say about the divorce? Do you think she— what was her name?" Carrie asked.

"Anne."

"Would Anne be angry? Is that your fantasy?"

"Why angry?"

"Maybe angry at Ed. Somebody's got to feel angry!"

"What do you mean?"

"Well, I think sometimes it's hard for women to express their anger. Maybe like it's not allowed, like—"

"Everyone else needs them to be strong," Gee finished her sentence.

"Exactly. I needed to be strong for my two boys. It took me a year of turning inward and blaming myself before I realized … I'm not perfect, but I tried. And then I said to myself that now I'm going to stop trying with Carl. Men will do one of two things when you stop beating yourself up—realize what they're missing and try again, or move on. Either way, there's not much you can do about it. But if you try to leave out your anger and settle for being hurt, darling, you're just wasting your own precious time," Carrie concluded.

Gee noticed on the fireplace mantel a picture of Carrie and her two boys when they were in their early teens and said, "They're adorable."

"We build ourselves around men and then wonder why it doesn't work," Carrie said.

"I'd love to be able to talk to my mother like you and I are talking now."

"Honey, I would've loved to have had a daughter like you to care for and watch over," Carrie said. "How 'bout if we settle for friends?"

"Now that's something I would cherish."

"Go through the pain, Gee, not around it. Go through it. Be open to your dad. I'm always here to talk, too," Carrie said.

~

The Cuatro Amigos began the work of writing articles that appeared on their Web site and through WWTS. Hattie wrote the first lead article in the newsletter: "The Use of Multiple Special Conditions: Are They Really Trip Wires for Failure?"

Hattie raised the view that the use of not only general conditions of supervision, but, more specifically, multiple special conditions of supervision, had been added on to virtually *every* new case. Turns out, Hattie argued, that the special conditions had become a "Judicial Honey-Do List" and, in practice, were trip wires for failure. On and on the list of "special rules" went until they became impossible for probation officers to reinforce because of their sheer volume. She pointed out that over 90 percent of those in her district who were sent back to prison for technical violations of the conditions of their supervision had multiple special conditions. Hattie also used the term "punishment überalles mentality," which she described as the love of punishment above all else. She compared this culture to judges seeking re-election in Texas displaying large posters of criminals they had been responsible for executing. The blog responses rippled with stories and anecdotes, mostly supportive of her view.

Next, Pepe wrote a piece with Gee's editorial assistance: "Hispanic Males on Supervision: Does One Size Fit All?"

Pepe cautioned officers not to assume the quiet nature of a person with limited English skills meant that the individual was stupid, hostile, a member of a gang, disinterested in learning, or uneducable. He suggested that the appropriate place for members of the MS-13, Crips, Bloods, and other similarly violent gangs was prison, or deportation. He also stressed the importance of prevention of gang membership for younger kids and suggested officers become involved in community events. He added that learning the pro-social values of the individual Hispanic offenders in their families and communities was far more valuable than an office interview. Pepe borrowed a visual image from a colleague and created this picture:

Solve Problems Early...Before They Grow Large

The blog responses to Pepe's article were almost uniformly focused on the fear of the separation of the Hispanic community and their gangs from mainstream society.

Then, Carrie Springer wrote a piece: "Technical Violations and the Use of Prisons as a Sanction: At What Costs and Impact on the Community?"

Carrie wrote that states were spending more money on corrections than education, and, as a taxpayer, she wondered if the public really knew this fact. She argued that the use of jails and prisons for noncompliance to the conditions of probation and parole was the most egregious failure of community corrections, because most could have been dealt with more effectively with community-based resources. Her research, supported by the work of several graduate students, led her to conclude that somewhere between 20 and 40 percent of persons in Maryland's prisons, at any given time, could be there for technical violations—rules violations—and that at a rate of about $30,000 per person, per year.

"Imagine," she wrote, "what we could do with that money to solve problems in the local community without reliance on prisons. If we rely instead on local resources, we could have already laid the last brick toward construction of new prisons. Imagine that."

The number of blog responders to Carrie's article was over 2,500. Many readers expressed feeling blindsided by the information.

It was clear the blog respondents were not just officers within the district, or even just the state. Respondents were multiplying like rabbits. By September, blog responses to each article averaged 3,500. A new culture emerged: readers felt it was their responsibility to respond to the articles, surveys, and comments made by other bloggers and to send a link to the blog site on to colleagues and friends. By December, the number of responses rose to 21,000 separate e-mail addresses. They included probation and parole officers from countless state and local systems, some even from the federal system. Surprisingly, they also included judges, researchers, academics, students, supervisors, managers, and bureaucrats from Washington.

Huggie next wrote a lead story: "The Children of Persons on Supervision: *Laissez-faire*, or Should We Care?"

In this article, Huggie suggested that probation and parole officers were not, in reality, merely working with the person on supervision, but that every time an offender went to prison, it was likely they left behind a family and kids whose plight was made exponentially harder for economic, social, and spiritual reasons. Although the blog responses often stated interest in the well-being of the next generation; they differed strongly about who was responsible for the current state of affairs.

Still, Gee Brooks was miserable.

She recognized that there was valuable information and soft data coming back from bloggers. But what could be done with the hopeless tone, the "but what can we do?" tone, that left her feeling angry and very unsure of what she had gotten herself into? Better to have promised nothing than to have raised hopes falsely, she thought to herself.

Returning to her office on a Friday afternoon, Hattie saw Gee getting into her car in the parking lot.

"Guess what," Hattie said.

"OK, what?" Gee said.

"My mother's going to see her old friend Barbara Washington next week, and she's going to ask for her help!"

"Who?"

"Barbara Washington, as in Maryland Senator Barbara Washington, idiot. Mom's going to position this thing—punishing offenders with unnecessary prison time—as a civil rights issue. Hold on to your hat!"

"Now I know we'll be fired."

"We'll work at Pepe's car wash. You know, cute little shorts, tank tops—"

"Funny. Good-bye, trouble," Gee said.

~

"I've found our niche! I've got the answer!" Gee said to Huggie, Hattie, and Pepe over lunch in the courthouse cafeteria.

Hattie interrupted, which was unusual for her. "One time this guy came up to me at the beach and said, 'Have you found Jesus?' I said, 'I didn't even know he was lost.' Honey, what's the question?"

They had to wait for Huggie to stop howling.

"In addition to the Web site, blog, and newsletter, what tangible product can we offer?" Gee asked.

"Balloons, T-shirts, pens?" asked Pepe.

Gee punched him in the arm. "Stop it. A reader asked last week where she could get training to be more effective. Nobody offers what we want to get at: the business of listening to and communicating with difficult people—changing behavior. That's it. We're going to develop it with someone and sell it. There's the door to the future."

This time there were no cute remarks.

Walking back to her office, Gee decided it was time to call her father.

25

HAPPY ANNIVERSARY

Gee Brooks

Funny, Gee thought, driving to Starbucks, *today is the one year anniversary date of the big crash,* or the "Big Crawl," as she referred to it with Dr. Weinman—the day she crawled out from under her desk and had to choose between dialing 9-1-1 and an unknown psychiatrist.

"I must admit, the rescue squad guys are pretty cute," she had said to Dr. Weinman two days ago.

"And I'm not? Listen, wisdom and sagacity win every time," he said.

She was early, twenty minutes actually. Today she drove, which was unusual. The Cuatro Amigos usually arrived at 10:00 AM on Saturdays, although Huggie and Hattie were typically late.

Ten minutes before the hour, Pepe arrived on his mountain bike.

"Save me a seat," he said to Gee. There were five empty outdoor tables, although business was booming inside.

Pepe joined her, armed with his Caramel Macchiato.

He kissed her on the cheek, as was his custom with the ladies. "You look like a million bucks, after taxes," he said.

In fact, she looked like she had just run five miles, although ten was the exact distance, and then driven directly to Starbucks.

She wondered whether she would mention the anniversary. A more confident and open Gee said, "You know, Pepe, a year ago today, you scraped me off the bottom. I don't know what would've happened if you hadn't picked me up outside the courthouse and taken me to the psychiatrist—I should say, my psychiatrist."

"I thought you were nuts, trying to catch a cab in Rockville at six o'clock," he said.

"Seriously, thank you. It didn't hurt that you stalked me for two weeks either. I think Ed thought you were some lover."

"He did. You're welcome. I've been there. I learned…. Well, the thing I try to focus on is not a bunch of magical words or outrageous deeds. It's just to be there," he said, looking down, his tattered Yankees cap dangling threads here and there.

Gee reached over and pulled off two threads with one sharp downward snapping action, a motion a veteran seamstress would appreciate.

"You look great…. Let me say that another way. You look more open … free," he said.

"I'm trying."

They sat in silence for a few minutes.

"My father committed suicide when I was teenager," he said.

"Oh, my God—" Gee said.

"Oh my God, what? You pregnant, girl?" asked Huggie, arriving from behind Pepe, coffee in hand, sliding his muscular body into a smallish chair at the table. "It ain't my baby, I swear."

"Whose baby?" said Hattie, partially hidden behind Huggie. She too, was holding a cup of coffee. They had driven together, as usual.

The silence felt awkward for Gee.

"Oh, shit. Is something wrong?" Huggie asked.

"Naw, my man. I was just telling Gee my father committed suicide when I was a teenager. This is twice as many times as I've ever said those words to someone who isn't in my family," Pepe said.

Gee noticed he didn't look down this time as he uttered the word "suicide." He was hiding nothing.

"I miss him at times. I'd just like to talk to him. I try to get that fucking scene out of my mind—of a rope around his neck. But I guess some things are so terrible they shouldn't be forgotten," Pepe said.

"I'm sorry, man. I feel like a jerk," Huggie said.

"I'm sorry, too, for you and your family," Hattie said. "It does explain something about you."

Pepe jerked his head back and frowned, which Gee picked up on.

"What the heck does that mean?" Gee asked.

"I've never seen a man—make that a person—who is so alert to other people's pain and suffering. That kind of sensitivity, with antennae locked in an 'up' position," she made a grand sweeping motion, like she was locking a submarine's periscope in an 'up' position, "constantly scanning the environment, can't be taught. It comes out of pain. I've always admired that quality in you. I try to be like you. I'm sorry, my honey, that your skill came from such an awful experience," Hattie said, getting up, going around the table, and hugging Pepe from behind.

"I'm sorry, baby," Hattie said.

Pepe held his right hand over his eyes.

Silence followed.

"There have been times when I wished my father would die—right there, when he was preaching. When he preached about the 'sinners,' 'the wrong doers,' 'the backstabbers,' I always felt that he was really talking about me. I hated that feeling. I wanted him to die. I feared him," Huggie said. "Funny, you'd like your father back—I've wanted mine gone."

After a pause, he continued.

"When TJ killed himself, I thought about how he used to get his butt dragged into my father's church. He didn't do nothing wrong. Poor guy. There's my father yelling down at me, TJ nearby, about sin and sneaking around. TJ didn't do nothing. Just tried to be loved, that's all, by that liquored-up sponge of a mother. I didn't do nothing. Fuck him. The community is *my* church. I been out there with Pepe ten times as much as my father ever was. He stayed in his office, writing his sermons. I could hear him practicing. If it's such divine intervention, how come you gotta practice it?" Huggie said.

There was a pause, but no one laughed. Gee had never heard Huggie speak so openly.

"A phony, really. I remember this little four-year-old girl from our church got run over by a bus. Turns out, the bus driver was drunk. The kid had a nice, respectable family—friendly and all. She had this tiny little coffin, closed because she was flattened, I heard some kids say. The family asked me to be a pall bearer.... I don't know why. I didn't want to. I was thirteen. I begged my daddy not to make me. He said some shit about doing the Lord's work, the Lord's call to duty. Fuck that shit. All I could see in my mind's eye was that poor girl all mangled, and he gave some fire and brimstone speech about the Lord calling her to duty in heaven. 'Weep not for the righteous.... Weep not for Sandy.... God needs her in heaven.' Her mother fainted at my feet. I cried so hard. I looked over at my father and felt his steely, piercing stare—like I was messing up his delivery. I hate my father."

"When did you stop fearing him?" asked Pepe.

"When I started this story," said Huggie with a straight face.

Gee tried hard not to laugh, but she spit out a mouthful of coffee, just missing Pepe's shoulder. Hattie and Pepe joined in, unable to hold back any longer.

"Hey, it's a start!" Huggie said, laughing that big, bold laugh of his. "Hey, it's a start."

Hattie said, "My mother ran my house. In many ways, I'm like her. But it's odd. With all of her civil rights work, with all of her causes. I don't know. It's my father I admire and try to be like. If you want to get some big, sweeping, complex task done—world peace, for God's sake—you'd get my mother. But my father," she had to slow down to get the words out, "my father was there in the painful times, the lonely times. He's like Pepe. You never had to say a word about your pain—he knew it. Odd. It's odd that I'd learn nurturing from my father when thousands of people know my mother as a voice for the underprivileged. My father ... God, I hope my fiancé, Breighton, turns out like him."

After a long pause, Gee said, "My mother died from cancer when I was twelve. My father and I lived together at that same house in Rockville. After I went away to college I never moved back. I've tried to be like her and him, I guess. But I can't stand going over to his house anymore. Ed was always a great buffer. He'd help my dad with projects while I'd clean up, mop, iron, scrub, bake—"

"Really? I need someone on Saturdays," Hattie said.

"Bite me. I'd do anything not to look at them...."

"Look at ...?" Huggie said.

"The monuments. The Burns Memorial Monuments. Pictures.... There must be fifty pictures of her, her and my father, her and me. It's like time stopped. There's no me—no Gee—in the present. I'm five, six, seven years old when I go over there. I'm *her* daughter, not me. I hate it," she said.

"Why don't you tell him?" Pepe asked.

"I don't know."

"Jesus, you don't know? We're tied to you, the leader of a revolution,

Ché, and you can't talk to your father? By the way, same for you, Huggie," Hattie said.

"Same for you and your mother, Hattie," Huggie said, smiling.

"Point taken," Hattie said. "Gee, you can't be afraid to talk to another probation officer, your father?"

"It's the monsters that are closest to us that are the hardest to slay," Gee said.

"Here, here. To slaying the monsters—inside, nearby, and those in pinstriped suits, if necessary," said Pepe, holding up his coffee cup.

"You mean the Yankees?" asked Huggie.

"I mean Kingmaker and all of the jerks like her that don't care about our people."

And the Cuatro Amigos banged coffee cups, gently.

~

Walking toward her car, Gee took one look back at the table and thought to herself, *what an amazing conversation.* Then she noticed that Huggie had left his cell phone on the table. Lost and found was a familiar activity for the forgetful Huggie. Usually, he misplaced his keys. As she headed back for the phone, it began to vibrate.

"Hello, Huggie's phone service," she said, answering it and expecting to hear Huggie calling from Hattie's cell phone.

"Gee? Is that you?" said Ed.

"Ed, I'm sorry, I was just grabbing Huggie's phone that he left on the table at Starbucks. You might try Hattie's cell. Do you need the number?"

"Well, yes. I'm in the emergency room at Suburban Hospital. Can I give you a number here and have him call me?"

"Are you OK?"

"I fell on my bike on Bradley Boulevard. I'm OK. I have a bruised shoulder and a bunch of stitches in my hip. I need a ride home. Can you reach him?"

"I'll try. Someone will call you back. I'm sorry you're hurt," she said, hanging up.

Gee called Hattie, but her phone was off. She decided to head to Suburban Hospital; it was less than two miles away. She found herself racing to the hospital, out of instinct. *Whoa!* she said to herself, dropping her speed from 48 to 30 mph. *He said he had stitches.... That's all.*

She parked her car and headed into the emergency room entrance. Outside the entrance, next to some bushes, she saw Ed's bike with a twisted front tire. She identified herself as his wife to the receptionist, and she was guided, without delay, to his bed, in a holding area. The beds were separated by white cotton curtains. She pulled the curtain back and saw Ed with a bandaged hip—and naked from the waist down.

"Whoa! Well, it could have been worse," she said.

He glanced up, startled. "Oh, I thought—"

"I couldn't reach Huggie. I'll give you a ride home."

Seeing Gee enter, a nurse followed and said, "He's ready to go, if you're ready for him, Mrs. Brooks."

When the nurse said Mrs. Brooks, Gee noticed the look on his face was as if he had received a low-voltage shock.

"Thank you, Nurse. Men!" said Gee.

"First, I suggest you have him take his pain pills. He's going to feel that hip when the Novocaine wears off. Mrs. Brooks, I'll get you the prescription. Don't leave without it. Your husband is going to be grumpy," said the nurse.

"Oh, he's always grumpy. I just give him space."

"Remember, dear, make him use ice for the swelling, but keep the stitches clean. They'll come out in eight days. Remind him to have his primary care physician take them out." The nurse gave him two pills and a cup of water, which he swallowed. She added, "I'll get the wheelchair. Get dressed, and don't forget, get those stitches out a week from Monday."

"Well, I can't take him to the doctor," Gee said, stopping the nurse in her tracks. "Didn't he tell you we've got three kids to care for, and I have a full-time job?"

The nurse frowned.

"It's OK, Nurse, we'll get a babysitter," Ed said.

"Listen, we've left them alone too long already, dear," she said.

The nurse frowned again and left the room.

"It's easier to get in if you're a wife," she said.

"Kids?" he said, looking uncomfortable.

It was an aha moment for Gee. *Why have I ever believed Ed really wanted kids? I'm not waiting another five years for him to change his mind.* The prefix "ex" sprang to mind; ex-husband seemed to fit now. It was the first time that she saw and accepted, truly accepted, the end of them as a couple.

They made their way to the exit, and Ed lowered himself carefully into her front seat. Gee took the front wheel off the bike and stuffed the bike into her trunk.

"What happened?" Gee said, realizing she had forgotten to ask.

"Some truck came around the corner, halfway in my lane, heading for me, going around 50 to 60 mph. He swerved back on his side, but a car came from out of nowhere behind me. I saw in a glance it was swerving and braking. I felt it was going to clip me, so I bailed out, to the right. I think my hip caught part of the pavement on the side of the road; I know my shoulder hit a tree. I'm lucky," he said.

Gee noticed his shirt was torn on the side. He had scratches on his neck. His scraped and badly bruised right arm was in a tan sling. They had given him blue paper shorts with an elastic waist to wear home. He had blue paper slippers on, too. The rest of his torn riding gear was either thrown away or in a paper bag in his hand.

"Does the arm hurt?" she asked.

"It could be worse."

Silence followed until he said, "Why'd you say kids?"

"I have no intention of being Aunt Gee. It just came out. You know, a role play around 'Mrs. Brooks,'" she said. "Actually, kids like it when their mother is *at them*!"

"Oh, God," he said.

She pulled in front of the house and headed for Ed's bike. He got out of the car gingerly and limped to the house.

"Well, hello! Oh, my, what happened?" asked Ed's neighbor, whom Gee knew only as Flo. Gee disliked her long-windedness and her penchant for gossip.

"Hello, Flo! Got an injured rider, but he'll be OK," Gee said.

Flo stopped, waiting for Gee to chitchat. She did not stop, but headed inside.

"She's not my burden anymore," Gee said, peeking out the front window. Flo stood on the sidewalk with her hands on her hips. Gee let Ruppert in from the small, fenced backyard.

"Hi, baby," Gee said to Ruppert, who wagged his tail like an oscillating fan on high speed.

"Why don't you sleep downstairs on the couch? I wouldn't climb the stairs," she said to Ed.

"Like old times, huh?"

"Well, it was one of the last places you could take refuge."

"I guess this is poetic justice."

"Actually, 'poetic justice' sounds cavalier when you say it."

"I'm sorry. I was making a joke at myself. I was a jerk to ever say you were—whatever I said. The truth is—"

"Excuse me, why do I need a new version of the truth from you now? I stop my car and pick up turtles so they don't get crushed in the road. Funny thing: when you pick them up, they pee, sometimes on you. I thought I'd help you get settled. Now that you're settled, you can be alone or have a special friend come over. It's your chance for solitude, reflection, or one-legged potato races. I don't care. Come on, Ruppert. One night in the condo shouldn't throw the planet off its axis. I'll bring him back tomorrow afternoon."

"That'd be great. Thank you."

She opened the car door for Ruppert, who sprang into the back and took his window seat. She started the car and took off, lowering Ruppert's window. "Oh, shit," she said aloud, "I left the prescription in the kitchen." She made a U-turn at the corner, intending to pick up the prescription and have it filled at a nearby CVS. She slowed down and then, seeing Flo, gunned it right past the house.

Flo put her hands back on her hips.

Gee felt bad for Ed, but not that bad. *Pissing turtles must have friends for the bad times*, she laughed to herself.

26

THE INVASION

Gee Brooks

Banter went back and forth about the recent blog responses. On a bright, crisp Saturday morning in January, at the Bethesda Starbucks, the Cuatro Amigos sat at their favorite inside table near the window, facing Woodmont Avenue. Gee spoke of the recent help she had received from Carrie Springer, now a trusted ally and friend. They spoke of the blog's momentum in finding a common platform with fellow officers around the country.

Huggie changed the conversation's tone.

"Is it me, or is somebody messing with our files?" Huggie asked.

"Oh, here we go.... 'They're out to get us!'" said Pepe.

"Hold on, Pepe. What do you mean?" asked Hattie.

"This past Monday, things in five of my files were out of place. Maybe I'm just paranoid," Huggie said.

"You're not going to believe this, but I've had the sense that things in my office have been moved around. I can't tell you exactly why I think that," said Hattie.

"Hell, my files are so disorganized, I'd never know!" laughed Pepe.

No one else laughed.

"And you, Oh Fearless One?" asked Huggie.

Gee sighed.

"I wish you'd...." Gee paused, looking at Huggie directly. She took an exaggerated deep breath and exhaled. "I don't know, but something about my office felt *weird* Monday. It's just a feeling. I can't explain it."

There was a pall over the table.

"Who gives a shit? Who cares, really?" Pepe asked. "They already run the place. What more do they need?"

"Power, Pepe, power. Power for power's sake. What're we going to do?" asked Huggie.

"They're coming after us, gang. Brace yourselves. My dad always says, 'When you don't know what to do, do nothing,'" Gee said.

"What the fuck. Here's to *nothing*," said Hattie, hoisting her fist into the air for a group smash of knuckles.

Huggie stood and leaned over the table, pulling Gee, Hattie, and Pepe closer, and whispered, "Yo, sniff this out of my files!" Then he farted. It was most out-of-character for the preacher's son.

Gee adroitly avoided looking directly in the eyes of any patrons as the Cuatro Amigos rolled out of Starbucks, overcome by laughter.

"Oh, my God," Gee repeated over and over again, shaking her head.

"Huggie, I wish your long-suffering wife had seen this middle school, boy's locker room behavior," Hattie said.

"Tell the wolves there ain't nobody here but us chickens. Come get us! We're ready for you," Huggie screamed.

"Huggie, that's a deal breaker," said Hattie.

Pepe tried to talk, but couldn't stand up straight, he was laughing so hard. Finally, he eked out, "At least you're not long-winded."

Gee punched Pepe in the arm.

Hattie punched Huggie in the arm, and off they went in different directions, one united team toward four different homes.

Gee's fears about impending doom were almost dashed by the disgusting Huggie moment. Almost dashed, but not really. Gee suspected her friends were as scared as she was, whether they chose to talk about it or not. She worried about getting fired or demoted. It would require legal representation and be expensive, time-consuming, and emotionally draining. The "adversarial action," as the firing or demotion would be called, would be bad for future employment; it would be something that would always have to be explained—and it would be embarrassing. Every quirk and vulnerability would be exposed. It would be ugly.

The Cuatro Amigos were on edge but moving full steam ahead. Gee accepted that they no longer had control of events or even their futures. She felt vulnerable and angry, but not intimidated.

Back at Starbucks, aka the Bethesda Refuge Center, as Hattie now

279

called it, on a sunny day, Gee said, "On three different days this week, while I was driving in the field to see offenders, I was being followed by this small, white Chevrolet driven by this white guy with messy hair. Some kind of stalker or sicko. When I looked at him in my rearview mirror, he sorta covered up his face. I'm thinking about reporting this to the cops. I even wrote down the license number: SG 1254."

"Cesspool. You're being followed by Cesspool," Huggie said.

"What on earth are you talking about?" Pepe said.

"Well, the cars we use out of the motor pool all say 'LG'—they're local government cars from Montgomery County. Some of the staff of the State Division of Parole and Probation have state cars assigned to them—their tags start with 'SG.' One year after I came here, the division started an Internal Affairs Unit. Get it now? They do shit like investigate wrongdoing, including officers who are believed to be doing second jobs during the day. I got recruited, probably because they needed some minorities to bust minorities—the real estate gig thing is popular in Baltimore with officers. So I spent the day with Cecil Poole—Cesspool—messy hair and all. That is one sick dude. I was supposed to be there all week. On the second day, instead of going back to Baltimore to join Cesspool, I walked into Kingmaker's office and said I thought being in the IAU's office put me in the wrong minority: those without integrity. She gave me that sick smile of hers. Cesspool's on your trail," he said.

"Damn," said Hattie.

"Damn," said Pepe.

"*Je-sus*.... Now that's creepy," Gee said.

"Very creepy," said Hattie.

~

The next day, bursting with angst, Gee decided on a lengthy mountain bike ride that would end at Starbucks, where she'd have coffee and head the short distance home. She leaned her bike against Starbucks's window and knelt down to feel the firmness of the rear tire, which looked low on air.

Crouching, she felt a gentle, small touch on the left side of her back, so soft it didn't startle her. She turned and saw a blond-haired, adorable girl in a blue dress, five or maybe six years old. But the gentle touch on her back had come from a little towheaded boy, maybe three or four—the girl's brother, she guessed.

"Is that a girl's bike or a boy's bike?" asked the little girl.

"Well, honey, it's either. Your mother or your father could ride it," Gee said.

"Mommy's in hever," mumbled the little boy, looking at her squarely.

"What, dear?"

"He said, Mommy's *in heaven*," said the sister, as Gee noticed an adult man's sneakered feet now appearing next to the little girl.

She looked up at him and said, "Oh, I am so sorry—"

"It's OK. He's proud he knows the word 'heaven,'" said the father. "Car accident, last year. In California, I used to have a mountain bike, but I could never get used to riding in traffic here, so I gave it away."

Noticing that the little boy's hand was still on her back, Gee said, "I hate traffic, too. I prefer riding on the Crescent Trail."

"I haven't ridden in—sorry, my name's Brad. This is Sarah, and that's Bradley, who's apparently attached to you."

"Well, hello, Bradley and Sarah … and Brad. How old are you two?"

"I'm this many," Bradley said, holding up four fingers.

"I'm six-and-a-half," said Sarah.

"My name is Gee, and I'm very happy to meet all three of you," Gee said.

"Do you have a wife?" Sarah asked.

"Sarah!" Brad said.

"It's OK," said Gee, laughing. "No, dear, I don't have a wife. I don't have a husband either. I used to, though."

"Bradley's fish died," Sarah said.

"Sorry. Well, we won't hold you up," said Brad.

"Well, bye for now, and how nice to meet you three," Gee said, shaking each one's hand. Both children shook her right hand with their left hands.

"Bye, Miss Gee," Sarah said.

27

THE GALLERY

Gee Brooks

It was an unusual Sunday morning. Gee's back was tight. She chose to stay in bed instead of biking or running. She tried to process the reason for the stiff back. Around ten o'clock, the phone rang.

"Gee, it's the man in your life. Join me for church."

"No, not today, Dad. But can I see you after church at your house?" Gee asked, then wished she could cram those words right back into her mouth.

"Sure. Is something wrong?"

"No, I'd just like to talk. See you at noon," she said. Bam! She was as anxious as a novice actor on opening night. Oh, God, is this the day?

She arrived sharply at noon and greeted her father at the door of the four-bedroom Cape Cod she had lived in from the time she was two until she went away to college.

"How's my long-lost daughter?" he asked.

"Found. Can we talk?"

"Sure. Coffee, water, Coke?".

"A Coke would be great. Thanks, Dad. I'll get it."

Gee poured two drinks in familiar glasses, probably twenty years old, and joined her father on the old, brown couch in the living room. Gee looked at the exact spot where he had held her and told her that her mother had died. She hated that spot.

She looked around, as if she needed one last reminder. The pictures of Anne Burns were everywhere—on every wall, on end tables, on the coffee table … everywhere. There were pictures of Gee as an infant, at her christening, at birthdays, on her first solo bike ride with Mom's outstretched hand barely removed from the seat, camping, and at the beach. There were countless mother-and-daughter pictures: hugging, cheek-to-cheek, smiling, making faces, doing rabbit ears to each other, and holding hands. And, of course, there were pictures of Thomas and Anne together, some actually taken by a young Gee. Nearly every picture included Anne.

Gee prolonged the silence by sipping her Coke.

"I hate coming over here—"

"Why would you hate—"

"Dad, this is hard enough. Let me talk," she said.

He folded his arms, crossed his legs, and sat back in silence. Although he appeared closed, he actually listened best in this posture.

"Excuse me. Linda often says I treat you like a child. Please go on," he said.

"I hate coming over here because of all these damned pictures—"

"But, Gee—"

"These pictures stopped time for you. And for me—"

"But, Gee—"

His unusual interruptions—he was always a great listener—signaled that the topic made him anxious, and that, in turn, was making her anxious. She had a decision to make: retreat or plow ahead.

"They're a monument. I'm back then when I come over here," she said, pointing to a picture of her at six with Mom beside her. "She's everywhere, smiling, laughing, looking warm, loving. Dad.... She's dead. She's not coming back. Dad ... you ... I ... *we* ... must move on."

Silence followed.

"I can't believe that you'd—"

"Goddamn it, believe it. I'm a human being. My mother is dead. Your wife is dead. Can't we accept that?"

"Gee, I don't like this—"

"Why is it every time I'm here, magically, Linda is not? Are you keeping us separated for some reason?"

"Well ...."

"Are you in a relationship with Linda?"

"Jesus, what kind of question is that?"

"Why, do you think I'd disapprove? Am I a child who'd think you're disloyal to Mom?"

She noticed he turned red.

"Yes. Linda and I have been having an affair for years, after your mother and her husband died."

"An affair? You're a single man!"

"I didn't know how to bring it up. I felt guilty for so long, like I was cheating you out of a memory."

"Maybe I would have reacted that way. I'm not acting like that now, and that's what counts. I don't know. Who knows? Can I be around you two, go to dinner, something? No more secrets."

"OK. Is this connected to the pictures?"

"In a way, yes. You put all these pictures up when Aunt Susie gave Mom's clothes and personal effects to Goodwill. Why?" Gee asked, looking straight at him.

"This is awkward...."

"My feelings are awkward, too, but they're my feelings."

"Your mom and I had this thing, a playful titillation. God, she was sexy to me. She'd hang the clothes she was going to wear on her closet door the night before. I'd walk by her things and just touch them. She'd get dressed in the morning and pretend I wasn't staring at her. She was very coy. The act, of course, always got my attention. When I came home that day and all of those reminders...."

He paused, crying.

"... all of her clothes were gone.... I felt violated."

"I used to wear Ed's T-shirts when he was out of town, when we were together. When we separated, I made sure I took two of them before I moved. I slept in them for months. It was as if he was with me, his smell. I threw them away, though," Gee said.

"When all of those reminders were stolen from me ... before I decided it was time to let go...."

"You built this photo gallery."

"Linda calls it the Arlington Cemetery North Memorial Gallery. I built this nutty gallery."

Silence followed.

"And ...?" she said.

"I don't know how to take it down. Some time—not today—will you help me take it down?" he cried, softly.

"We don't have to throw anything away. One day, you'll have

grandchildren who you'll want to share them with," she said. "They'll be in my house and in the kids' bedrooms," she said.

~

Two Saturdays later, he invited her over again. She arrived after lunch. He greeted her and headed to the basement. He brought back four large cardboard boxes and a hammer.

He said only, "Would you help me?"

"Sure," she said.

Slowly at first and then faster, they went from one picture to the next. Thomas took down about two-thirds of the pictures, handing them to Gee, who wrapped them in newspaper, taped the paper, and put them neatly, carefully, in the boxes. Almost every displaced picture merited a short story. They went from room to room.

"I'll have to fill in the holes later," he said.

"In the walls, or in you?" she asked.

He smiled at her.

In one of the boxes, she noticed a picture of her mother with her arms around Gee, at age six. Gee remembered exactly where they were, right outside Kings Dominion, just before first grade started.

"May I have this picture?" she asked, pulling it out of the box.

"Of course. You can have any of them. Why don't you take this—"

"No, thanks, Dad, just this one."

"Well, I'll clean this mess up later."

"There's one more thing," she said, turning to sit on the couch.

He took a deep breath, exhaled, and followed her to the couch.

"Why did you write down every word Mom said when she was dying?"

"Let me explain."

"Do you remember the words?"

"No, but listen—"

"No, you listen first. I've been haunted by those words. I've tried to win her approval in everything I've done. I read those two pages you wrote countless times, looking for instructions on how to live my life. In part, the words helped; but, mostly, I've allowed them to put a muzzle on me."

"Oh, Gee—"

She held up her hand to cut him off, "You make me happy, Sunshine. From the moment I saw your fuzzy blond hair and held you in my arms for the first time, I've been happy and always, always very proud of you. Proud you were *my* daughter. My little darling, my time is up. I know you'll be OK, won't you? I'm going to be waiting for you and Dad on the other side. I'll be there for you again. I'll see my little darling again—but not just anymore now."

"That's enough, Gee."

"The hell it is. You need to hear the final order: 'I want you to promise to use your life to take care of yourself, your father, and other people. Promise me that, my little darling.'"

She started crying. Her dad appeared to be in agony, but she soldiered on. "Why did I need my dying mother's words etched in my soul? Why?"

"Why didn't you tell me before?"

"I thought I was being a good little girl."

"I'm *so* sorry. No wonder you're angry. I'm not going to try to justify what I did. I'm so sorry. It was just stupid. But please, please hear me out. God, that was stupid. In her last few weeks, when it was clear that your mother was near death, she and I talked endlessly it seemed, day and night in the hospice, about her emotional pain—the pain of leaving you. She and I had reached our ... separation. We had faced the end of her life, but she couldn't come to grips with her desire to die to be out of pain, because it meant separating from you."

He paused a very long time.

"'Apart from Gee,' she kept saying, 'apart from my little girl.' Morphine shot after morphine shot barely dulled the pain, and then only for a short time. I'd ask her if it was time. 'No,' was all she'd say. And then, around two o'clock one morning, she woke up and asked me if I'd be in the room when she said good-bye to you. It was a different conversation."

He paused to cry hard.

"I said I would. She asked me to remind you later that she loved you and how proud she was of you. 'God help me,' she said, 'I'm not equipped to say good-bye to my angel.'

"I was an emotional mess. So, I came up with this stupid idea to write down what she said. I didn't tell her I was going to write things down, and, in her state, she didn't know I did. The truth is, it was my way of holding on to to her, too. I made a copy for myself and read it for a couple of months. Then I threw it away.... It was too painful to read. I guess I was so self-centered that I didn't consider your needs. I'm so sorry," he said.

"Thank you for that. I'm going to keep the picture you gave me today and throw the letter away. I loved Mom, but I just don't want to cling to her death anymore."

After a few moments of silence, as he cried, she stood and took the picture that was leaning against the couch, indicating she was leaving.

At the front door, he said, "Thank you, Gee. I'm so—"

She put her finger over his lips, like an adult woman would do to a child, and shook her head side-to-side.

"In time, I'll forgive you. Give me some time, Dad. Let me sort things out. Oh, and I'll be invited to meet Linda?"

"Yes, yes, you will."

"Bye, Dad, I love you," she said, turning to leave.

"I love you, too," he said to her back, as she waved without turning around.

28

FREEDOM FROM

Gee Brooks

Just a couple of months after the "gallery session," Gee's relationship with her father felt renewed ... and open. In his car on the way to Outback Steakhouse, she actually looked forward to meeting Linda, and her father expressed the same sentiment.

"I need your help," Said Gee, as she drove.

"Of course."

"But first, I'm curious. What do you think about Ed and me being separated? You haven't said much."

"Well, you didn't ask. Frankly, I'm pissed off at him. I'd like to tell him.... Well, let me say it this way: I like Ed, but if he can't see what he's got right in front of him, I have no sympathy for him."

"Thank you," she said. *Well, Carrie was right*, she thought.

Gee described the events of late, including the blog and Web site she and her friends had set up.

"Honey, I can review the articles and read the blog comments. Just cut to the chase. What's bothering you?"

"Officers sound discouraged, without hope that anything could ever change, probably because of the "tail 'em, nail 'em, jail 'em" mentality. You know, like the beliefs supporting Operation Øman. How do we get officers off helplessness?" Gee asked.

"I'm not sure what your expectations are. Taking responsibility and being accountable are adult roles. You can't expect officers who are left out of the decision-making process and treated condescendingly, like mushrooms, to suddenly take risks that could get them in hot water."

"Good point."

"Probation and parole officers don't work for the money—what little there is. It's in their genes to help others. Most of them, anyway. It's who they are. I know your values and trust that what you're doing is helping others. You can't possibly fail at that—or let anyone down."

There was silence for a moment, as his words seem to bore into her: "or let anyone down."

The words lingered in mid-air and then in her throat. Images flashed in front of her: Ed's frowning face, TJ's slight smile in the MCIH administration building, Tommy's shyness, Natasha asleep in her lap, her dying mother, and her Cuatro Amigos. Had she unintentionally harmed all of them?

"Thank you. I've been avoiding me," she said.

"You're missing a question."

"What, Dad?"

"Well, are you interested in the question?"

She nodded, trying to focus.

"Why do you do this work?" he asked.

"I like to help people."

"Do you need others' approval—your bosses, your peers, your friends, or mine?"

"I've already talked to you about how I've been haunted by trying to get Mom's approval. Maybe others', too. But that's in the past. Today, the answer—I hope—is no. I'd love others' approval—and yours too. But I can live without it."

"Do you think I was an OK probation officer—at least through the stories I told you? Or am I too 'old school' to be relevant?" he asked.

"Oh, Dad, I'm sorry if I haven't made it clear to you how much you've shaped my life, my values, my hope to be useful. I love your stories. I'm *so* proud of you. I want to have stories like yours that I can share with you."

"Then why have you never asked me *how* I got the skills to reach folks—or do you think that I was just *lucky*?"

He told a story of a time early in his career when he felt like the system wasn't reaching folks. A metaphor came to him rather simply one day: junk stacked is still junk. People who have junk in their basement decide it's time to fix the mess. They go down and stack the junk in clever piles. They weigh it, count it, color-coordinate the various sectors, and even give the categories special names. It's still junk. "That was what my probation office was doing, creating trendy new junk piles," he said.

"I saw how rude or, at least, insensitive the staff was to folks on supervision. I knew that the system shouldn't treat folks on supervision rudely. Offenders would never respond favorably. Would I? I figured out that officers took on simplistic, condescending roles with folks on supervision, because they didn't have the skills to communicate effectively; they were just stacking junk. Then, as a monument to failure of human understanding, we build more prisons and jails to warehouse the people we can't communicate with. I told myself, 'Let it stop with me,'" he said.

He went on to say that he had decided to learn ways to be more effective with difficult people in difficult circumstances. He made a decision not to acquiesce to the stupid practices that didn't work. He became curious: Why do people drop out? To what degree does mainstream society screen certain people out? Do those who take on anti-social attitudes experience isolation and pain, and, if yes, can that pain be useful to learning? Can others actually help someone help themselves, or is it just a matter of will? Is there a group of people for whom prison is the only answer?

"I read everything I could: journals of other professions, child-rearing books, principles of mediation and negotiation, coaching strategies, mentoring, and therapeutic interventions. Your peers don't read enough! I devised a plan to get as much training outside of the profession as I could afford. It probably cost you a nice used car at age sixteen," he said.

"Just when I was liking your ideas—"

"Sorry! I had one rule: the training had to have a likelihood of carrying over to my work, though, at first, I felt I had to stretch that rule. Nobody at work was talking about negotiating with offenders. After a few years, I wanted to find the 'key elements' of this profession."

"Gramps called them 'essential ingredients.'"

"I stand corrected. Will you remember my words with such sharpness?"

"Always."

"I took a communication course from Dr. Larry Howe. I was enamored by his insights. I found it ironic that I was the only person in the class from the criminal justice field. And then it hit me like a bolt of lightning: The criminal justice system doesn't act like a business. Probation and parole are not in the business of business. Before the field can produce a great product, it will first need a better understanding of the concept of satisfied customers—for *all* of the customers. I took fifteen seminars from Larry Howe and his colleagues. They changed my life. The training changed my entire focus. Two weeks ago, Larry asked me to join his staff as a senior consultant for the Chesapeake Group."

"Dad, I'm so proud of you!"

He smiled.

"It's your search … your journey. And, of course, I mean that of your friends, too. Do it right, girl. So much depends on it."

Gee asked for Larry Howe's phone number.

"Larry is going to be at the Chesapeake meeting in Crofton next month. Would you like me to see if he would adjust his schedule and meet with you before the meeting?" he asked.

"Would you do that?"

"Write up a one or two page summary of what you'd like to get out of the meeting and e-mail it to Larry, with a copy to me. I'll send you his e-mail address. In the meantime, I'll let him know it's coming. He has plenty of experience adapting his work to community settings."

"Will you be part of the meeting?"

"I'll introduce you and play it by ear."

"Cool! I'm anxious."

"What?"

"Anxious!"

"Gee, what have I taught you? You're not anxious—you're excited!"

"Right again, Dad. Oh, look. Is that Linda in front of the restaurant?"

"Yes it is."

"Oh Dad, she's so pretty," said Gee.

~

Gee dropped her father off at home after a wonderful dinner with Linda, who felt like a new friend. As she was pulling out of his driveway, she heard him holler, "Oh!"

She stopped and rolled down her window.

"She would be very proud of you," he said, looking at the ground. And, with that, Thomas Burns went inside the house without making eye contact.

Mom, she thought, and smiled.

29

CLARITY OF ROLES

Gee Brooks

The next day, on a conference call, Gee worked out a newly defined role for herself in Nuevos Principios, and, in so doing, helped Hattie, Huggie, and Pepe redefine their roles.

Gee's plan was to dedicate her time to defining the "essential ingredients" of excellent probation and parole work and to develop a strategy to get those elements into the profession through training. She agreed to plow new ground, but to gain a consensus first. This approach was consistent with their practice of inclusion. They had agreed to test every idea through an article or blog dialogue for resonance with field officers.

Hattie was particularly interested in the views of female judges and other minority judges. She said she sensed that the persistent punishment theme must be out of alignment with these judges' notions of individualized justice. She thought that women have a broader sense of nurturing than men, and, surely, some offenders must trigger a feeling in female judges that the young men before them could be their sons. She knew Judges Clarke and Johnson would be helpful. She also wanted to expand the inclusion of family and child advocates into their efforts; all of them, she guessed, would know the effects of so many minority men going to prison. So, she engaged in a comprehensive outreach effort with the assistance of her willing and energetic mother.

Hattie expressed her excitement about her mother's upcoming meeting with her friend Senator Washington.

Huggie and Pepe wanted to focus on continuing the development of community support using an asset mapping strategy. Huggie was impressed with Pepe's argument that many minorities needed a chance to show what strengths they had—not just what labels could be stuck on them.

The foursome realized that that left exactly no one to administer the Web site and keep the blog dialogue going. They turned to three volunteers who had been with them since the Baltimore Civic Center debacle, Rick Volzano, Maria Sanchez, and Abba White Cloud.

They talked about greater coordination of efforts and communication with Volzano, Sanchez, and White Cloud, and how this communication would have to occur primarily through e-mails and conference calls. They agreed that all phone calls and e-mails would be returned on the same day, and if an e-mail had criticisms, and the response was edgy, the parties would pick up the phone and iron things out. The Nuevos Principios Society graduated from the work of four friends to a real organization.

30

THE CHESAPEAKE CONSULTING GROUP

Gee Brooks

Gee bought four hours of time from the Chesapeake Consulting Group, paid for by Carrie and Jon. The escalating blog responses were uplifting, but they were opinions—not a call to action. Gee had an anxious feeling she was running out of time. She had to develop a strategy that would lead to a training product before she was drawn into an adverse action by Kingmaker. When and if that happened, everything would have to go on hold. Perhaps her career and income would abruptly end as well.

She knew, too, that if the quality of the training was a joke, she and her colleagues wouldn't get a second chance. The training product had to reach a lofty threshold. It had to inspire officers and staff to do two things without management support: to help change the culture of the system and to teach new knowledge, skills, and attitudes to help officers work more effectively with offenders. It was a vexing problem. Many people do just enough to get by at work, she thought. What would motivate officers to want to do more?

Gee had no doubt that Kingmaker had targeted Pepe, Hattie, Huggie, and her for adverse action. It was the subject in the office. No one knew what was real and what was idle gossip, but she could feel the stares from her colleagues, who also kept her at arm's length at the courthouse. Time was not on their side. The gap between their grandiose idea of a "human revolution" and the development of an actual training seminar felt like peering across the Grand Canyon.

~

Gee felt wiggly in Dr. Weinman's waiting room. She knew what she wanted to talk about.

She wanted to share a disturbing dream, one in which she woke up sweating, trying to scream.

"Your unconscious at work…. Good. Go on," Dr. Weinman said.

She described that at first she saw a horse, a palomino, galloping along a narrow trail. Then she was riding it. Empty leather saddlebags flapped up and down. The horse morphed into an Appaloosa with two heads. She was terrified and wanted to go back, but lost her sense of direction.

"And the author thinks …?" he said.

"It's like the first horse was me. I think the empty bags remind me of my mother and me somehow. The Appaloosa seems to be a blend of my three friends. The two heads and the terror, who knows?"

"Might two heads be about who's in charge? Or, what direction?"

"Wow! That's it. The meeting tomorrow is about direction. God, we're becoming entrepreneurs. Actually, I'm terrified."

She began to talk about her "essential ingredients" concept. He interrupted.

"Be careful not to use too many sophisticated concepts. Then you're getting into theory. They're metaphors, right? I believe you're onto some very important concepts, like problem solving, conflict management—good stuff," he said. "Your saddlebags are empty of any old baggage. Remember, you didn't ask your friends to follow you…. They chose to."

"I wish I knew how things would turn out tomorrow."

"Don't we all! Listen, you're bright—a pathfinder, really. What could go wrong, Mrs. Edsel? They've named the car after you!" he said, laughing. "One last thought: whatever you try to get started, it's important to demonstrate it locally. You need a proving ground."

~

In the conference room of the Chesapeake Group offices in Crofton, Maryland, Thomas Burns introduced Gee to Dr. Larry Howe and excused himself.

With that, Gee said, "I sent you an overview statement."

"I read it, thank you. Very interesting challenge," Larry said.

"Let me state my goal: Before I leave here today, I want to determine if your group will work with us, under an acceptable financial arrangement, to create training that will produce the knowledge skills and attitudes that will help our Nuevos Principios Society change the culture of the criminal justice system … one person at a time."

"That's a pretty tall order, but we've had success in other organizations," Larry said.

"Officers from all over the country are talking about wanting more effective listening and communication skills and better ways of working with difficult people. They want to change the punishing tone of the officers. Trust me, the time is right. Our focus is to lift up the 'essential ingredients' of being an excellent probation or parole officer and drive those skills down into daily practices," she said.

"You're in luck: enhanced listening and communication skills have great applicability to our personal lives and our best futures. You can market them with the message that the Society has something for you that will change your life! So the motivation—why should I invest my time and money?—is self-improvement in one's personal life and on this, or any, job. I appreciate that you're using a rather unique strategy to get there—change the officers, change the managers. That said, the culture of an organization is usually 'the way we get things done around here.' It's also a tone. You can feel it. And, over time, it bends and is shaped by key leaders and staff, whether they are kindhearted or quite nasty. A cold receptionist may be seen as relaying the attitude of the whole staff. Changing that tone, as you described it—punishing, cold, condescending, mean-spirited—is a critical first step.

"But the culture, or tone, is tied up with beliefs about the people you work with. If they are the enemy and you just want to catch them making mistakes, it doesn't matter what you say to them. So, the current tone would be appropriate. If, however, you believe those on probation can change their behavior toward pro-social values and that building a relationship with a probation officer will help an offender change and will support his or her successes, then the tone must change, and it does matter what you say and how you say it. And it has to be clear to everyone—as in everyone—what the tone should be and why. We'll cover this thoroughly in training," Larry said.

"For God's sake, Gee, slow down. What happened?" Hattie said from her cell phone.

"I just left the Chesapeake Consulting Group's office. I faxed a draft agreement to Carrie and Jon. Please set up a meeting with Pepe and Huggie. We've tentatively agreed to their designing generic training on the listening and communication skills for officers and a wide audience, like court personnel and community agencies, and training for officers on mastering the essential ingredients of probation and parole work, including listening and communication skills. The Nuevos Principios Society would sponsor both training initiatives!" Gee said, almost screaming.

"Well, who does what?" Hattie asked.

"They will not market or 'host' workshops; that would be our job. The proceeds from the workshops would be divided. Larry would teach the listening and communication skills in a two-day workshop. The essential ingredients training, once we nail them down, would be two, three-day workshops spaced several weeks apart. The training would feature in-district exercises between the training events to enhance the participants' skills. They agreed to hold developmental costs to a bare minimum."

"Wow. Great job, girl! Now let's see if our own folks will support us," Hattie said.

31

GROCERY CART COLLISION

Gee Brooks

Gee stopped by the grocery store to get some household supplies for her father—he never seemed to think about the little things, like tissues or trash bags. There, rounding a corner on aisle seven, Gee literally ran her basket into Junie's cart. They laughed and then paused in a brief, awkward silence. At Gee's initiative, they hugged. Finding words was more difficult. She knew Junie in the context of TJ. The last time she saw Junie was the brief meeting at her house, the day Gee searched for TJ, while his body was, in fact, floating in the Potomac River with Junie's scarf still tied around his neck and the kids' love notes in his pocket.

"How are you, Junie?"

"Fine, Gee. Well, getting stronger. You know: two steps forward, one back. There's so much to process," she said, looking down at the floor. "I guess maybe I'm learning to forgive TJ. One day I'll learn to forgive myself. I keep asking myself, what was the big deal about a working man buying a car for himself, one he's proud of? Nothing, really. I've even forgiven Taunja. I know he must've smoked dope with her the night we fought. A couple of weeks ago, Dee told me Taunja's baby's father beat her to within an inch of her life. She's all messed up. No woman deserves that."

"No, they don't. I'm trying to take something out of TJ's death that will help others. He would've liked that, I think," Gee said. "How are the kids?"

"Natasha is running the house. Oh, Tommy is playing in his first game on a Little League baseball team on Saturday."

Gee remembered the glove TJ bought Tommy.

"This baseball thing came out of nowhere," Junie said. "Last Saturday this baseball coach shows up at my door with two kids beside him in baseball shirts and hats and tells me he's 'heard' about Tommy's skills from other kids in the neighborhood and he wanted him on his team. That struck me as odd—what kids would be talking about Tommy's skills? I told him it wouldn't work for two reasons. I knew, because I looked into it, that kids had to be nine years old, and he's barely eight. And I work and go to school. I can't drive him to practices. I told him Tommy and I have already talked about this a thousand times. That didn't slow this coach up one bit. He said that'd be no problem. He said he had a 'special waiver' on the 'age thing' from the Commissioner and that volunteers from local churches would handle all the transportation to and from practices and games, as they would the drinks and the snacks. Plus, local merchants covered all equipment costs. I knew Mr. Nosey heard every word from his room, because he yelled out, 'Please, Mom?' Can you believe it, thirty seconds later he was out the door on his way to his first practice? He's got great new friends and that wonderful coach. He even sleeps in his uniform with his glove by his bed. I'm so happy for him. I only wish…." Junie's voice trailed off.

"I know."

They closed their conversation, hugged, and started toward different aisles, when Gee turned and said, "Who's the coach?"

"Oh, Coach Pepe. Isn't he a—"

Gee nodded and said, "Yes, a probation officer," and turned away, a millisecond before her eyes welled up.

"Yes, a probation officer," Gee said quietly to herself. Then she smiled. For God's sake, he could have come up with something better than "a waiver from the Commissioner." She started to laugh out loud, right past the quick-sale bent cans cart.

~

The Cuatro Amigos, sitting at an outdoor Starbucks table, complained about the growing support among probation and parole officers throughout the country for a movement to carry firearms. Probably one-third of the separate systems—state, county, and federal—authorized the use of weapons, and the number was increasing daily. These four unanimously opposed the trend toward carrying guns.

"If you wear a gun, then, in everyone's eyes, you become a law enforcement officer—as in, cop," said Hattie.

It looked to Gee that Pepe was prepared to say something, but he stopped before he started, and no words came out. She felt a small tapping on her back. Pepe was staring at the little tapper.

"I have a boo-boo," said Bradley, holding his Spiderman Band-Aid-affixed finger up for her to inspect.

"Oh puh-*lease*," said Sarah, just behind him.

"Well, it's my two buddies! I'm *so* sorry, Bradley—let me kiss it," Gee said. She made an exaggerated kissing sound and squeezed his little hand gently. His broad smile made his ears seem farther apart. Gee barely restrained a laugh.

"Kids!" said their father, hustling to the table from several steps away.

"Well, hi, Brad! Everybody, these are my little buddies Bradley and Sarah and their dad, Brad. Brad, Sarah, Bradley, these are my best friends, Pepe, Huggie, and Hattie," Gee said.

Hattie made a fuss over Sarah, as did Pepe with Bradley. Huggie stood close to Brad and welcomed the entourage to join the four friends.

"Well, another day, but thank you. Oh, Gee, I've ordered a new mountain bike!" Brad said.

"Cancel it! I have a better deal. I'll trade you my bike for those two," she said, pointing at Sarah and Bradley.

"Some days I'd take you up on it," Brad said.

"Join us!" Gee said with a sweeping arm motion. She caught a glimpse of Pepe rolling his eyes in a gesture she took to mean "how obvious."

"I can't today, Gee. Maybe next time, though," he said.

"Well, we're up here every Saturday morning at ten o'clock. Join us," she said. *I hope he heard the ten o'clock*, she thought.

"Thank you, Gee. I will," Brad said, gathering the kids, saying good-bye, and entering Starbucks.

Gee waited for comments. She was prepared to downplay the feelings Brad, Sarah, and Bradley evoked in her.

With Brad and the children inside Starbucks, neither Hattie, Huggie, nor Pepe said a word.

"What?" said Gee, scanning the troublemakers.

No response.

"What?" she repeated louder, annoyed.

Pepe started snickering.

Huggie started a slow, groaning, whining giggle.

"The idiots are trying to say that they liked that scene," Hattie said.

"No, I wasn't—" Pepe started to say, until laughter interrupted his words.

"What?" Gee said.

"Gee's got a boyfriend, Gee's got a boyfriend," Pepe teased in singsong.

She punched him hard in the arm.

"We're fucking with you, Princess. Those children adore you. Brad's not exactly ugly, you know," Huggie said.

"Hattie, why do we bother to try to help them?" Gee said.

"Actually," Hattie said, bursting out laughing, "they're right for once."

32

COMMUNITY ALL-STARS

Pepe Gomez

Pepe heard them—the rumors—which were all over the office and the subject du jour. *When*, not *if*, would Kingmaker lower the boom on Gee, Huggie, maybe Hattie, and certainly himself? In numerous conversations with Olivia, Pepe came to accept the reality that he was swimming in the wrong pond. Rules, procedures, and fitting in had never been a priority. In fact, fitting in scared him. He didn't fit in at the public schools in San Antonio. He really didn't fit in at the University of Texas at Austin. But he used those experiences, looking in from the outside, to find his passion—to help the disadvantaged make it. That vantage point gave him a sense of peace with his father. He stood for the little people, who, at times, couldn't stand up for themselves, he told Olivia, without boasting.

Pepe's vision was focused on mobilizing communities. Yet, outside that passion, he was well aware of The Kingmaker factor, the constant stress on Gee, Huggie, and even the strong-willed Hattie. Under times of high stress, Pepe had learned to dig in deeper. Aside from humor, digging in was the primary skill he used to cope with his anger.

Pepe also felt Huggie was asking for more of his time, which was a good thing. They knew different communities. Huggie knew the African-American neighborhoods; Pepe, the Hispanic. Each had limited experience crossing over into the other's communities.

Over beers at Tommy Joe's, Huggie asked Pepe, "How're we going to get officers comfortable working out in these neighborhoods?"

"You mean to join two guys who are about to be fired?" Pepe said.

"I ain't talking about that shit."

"Your face is."

"I do have three kids to feed."

"OK, you can be the shift boss at the car wash."

Huggie didn't laugh. "Comfortable where?"

"Well, how'd you get comfortable in lower-class black neighborhoods? You're not lower–class."

"I don't know."

"Well, you do it every day."

"What?"

"You seem to find out quickly what you have in common with offenders. You leave yourself open to them. I've watched you and tried to do the same," Pepe said.

"Really? I guess it's second nature. I have this spooky way of tapping into what people need," said Huggie.

"Spooky? The only thing spooky around here is the fact you never pay for beer."

"Seriously, though, how do we build a network of community allies that are motivated to help our folks, Pepe?"

"You appeal to their self-interest. Give them a title!"

"Now that's just great, Pepe, really. Ladies and gentlemen, I present the Duke of South Algonquin Street!"

"You couldn't hotwire a car, could you?" asked Pepe. He didn't wait for an answer. "We need connectors—people who like to hook people up with other people—businessmen, the retired, the gifted, the kindhearted. They have to demonstrate one common attitude: to understand what it feels like to be hurt, to be alone, to be without. We want people who like the underdog. That's what we are looking for," Pepe said, sipping his beer, as a thirtyish blond walked by and smiled at him.

Seeing Pepe return the flirtatious smile, Huggie said, "Chumster, could you stop that for just for one second? Where do we start?"

"You're half asleep, aren't you? You and I started this process two or three years ago!"

"What?"

"Were you and Rosa up late last night, you know, playing hide the harpoon? Focus, man. Now, we just add a twist. We give 'em a title. We recognize them publicly in front of their peers. All of this helps them be what they want to be: connectors and givers. Then, we lead them to tell us how they'll be helpful to us—and how we can be helpful to them. Now, the 'we' also means people on supervision. All of them have grandmothers, someone who loves them. And offenders care about little children not being hurt—it's just matching strengths.

Then all of these 'they' out there help us find more of *them*. It's a new twist on the 'us' and 'them' game. The connectors become 'us,'" Pepe said.

"I get it. Community All-Stars. We'll call them Community All-Stars." Huggie suggested.

"Man, you're good."

"How do we get them together?"

"Everyone eats. We'll have a special dinner—no, a community breakfast event. We'll get folks from a variety of communities to come to a probation/parole-sponsored unity breakfast."

"We can't raise money. We're public servants, remember? You're handing Kingmaker the last peg for our coffins. Who's going to pay for it?"

"Oh, Hugster, you worry about little things. Do you arrange your SpaghettiOs letters before you eat them?"

"I'll visit you in jail," said Huggie.

"Can we have the breakfast in your father's church?" asked Pepe, ignoring Huggie's fundraising legality issue.

"I'm sure. He has a very large social hall and kitchen."

"So, if I get the food donated, we can cook it there, right?"

"I bet we could get the women in my father's church to volunteer to help cook and serve. I just hate to get my father involved."

"Do you have an alternative?"

"No."

"OK, then. I'll get people to help, too."

"Now, we need Hattie and her sources and Gee and Carrie to tell us who to invite and who should speak—oh, and how to get the manager's approval."

"So, you're leaving the impossible to Hattie?"

"Girl's good. You watch."

Hattie agreed to the impossible task with joy, but under one condition: some women on her caseload and the cleaning staff could attend with their children. The men acquiesced quickly. She had, after all, the art of knowing exactly what buttons to push. Whatever Hattie said or did, Pepe never questioned. She managed to convince Judge Glenny Clarke to gain Chief Kasten's approval. Judge Clarke never shared with anyone what she said to gain Kasten's approval for the

Community Unity Breakfast—only that the events had the court's approval and that she and Kasten would manage the public speaking.

At Hattie's insistence, Gee brought Carrie Springer into the planning. Carrie knew many key staff members of social service agencies on a first name basis. One phone call from her was enough to assure the attendance of organizations' movers and shakers.

Twenty days later, the probation and parole district sponsored its first Community Unity Breakfast. Seventy-eight people attended, about half of whom were community leaders, advocates, and neighborhood advisors. Judge Clarke and Chief Kasten publicly recognized ten community people. Some were quite ordinary people—ordinary, that is, until they received their Community All-Star patch and framed certificate, signed by Chief Judge Brayer. Now, they were part of Pepe and Huggie's connectors group. The All-Stars and community agencies were invited back to the second Community Unity Breakfast the following month.

The second breakfast had a topic: "Reaching Our Children in Need." That breakfast had 138 participants, including six community police officers. More All-Stars and two community police officers were awarded patches and certificates.

The third event hosted 147 folks. It was becoming hip to be at the events. Again, more All-Stars were added. The fourth event was moved from Huggie's father's church to a large synagogue's meeting room. Other organizations vied for the prize of holding it. A local printer produced 400 posters for community agencies and businesses that said:

We want you to make it!

Come in for a hand up!
www.nuevosprincipios.com

The breakfasts ended quietly. The production had gotten so time-consuming it was beyond the ability of Pepe to continue to come up with his magical solutions. However, the Community All-Stars recognition process and the connections between the community, the people on supervision, and their budding new advocates—probation and parole officers—had begun in earnest.

33

FOUR LIVE WIRES

Carrie Springer

Following the meeting at Carrie's, when Pepe and Huggie asked for support for their community initiatives, Carrie got to work looking for that support.

"Our group usually receives presentations at the Chevy Chase Club, in their Lincoln Room. Jon Rhodes may join us, too. We've found that if we control one variable—the setting—it's fairer to the applicants. Let's have the Cuatro Amigos pitch their ideas on their program," Carrie said.

"Presentation, application ... ah, well, Carrie.... Damn.... I better get ahold of the boys and Hattie and get them prepared," Gee said.

"That would be a wise thing to do."

For the next three weeks, the four friends prepared as thoroughly for this presentation as they did for their final exams in college.

On a Saturday afternoon in March, Carrie gave last-minute instructions to employees of the catering staff regarding the placement of the sandwiches, salad, snacks, and drinks. The meeting was held in the privacy of the Lincoln Room, a room that could hold seventy-five people. Today, a room divider made the room small and cozy. Spring was in the air, and the large, pillared, three-story, white club complex, covering nearly a block on Connecticut Avenue, was made even more attractive by freshly cut flowers in the large marbled foyer. A technician was busy setting up a LCD projector and screen, as Carrie placed notepads and pens on linen-covered tables. *Surely*, Carrie thought, *countless CCC members had begun or sealed thousands of deals on these very tables.*

At 12:45 PM, Carrie was joined by her very close friends of over twenty years, Laurie Woolworth, Myrtle Block, and Eleanor Spaulding. Together, at each other's sides, the four friends had been through weddings, funerals, illnesses, divorces, and most of life's joys, heartaches, and pains. They liked to call themselves the "Four Live Wires." They had reached the age where they complemented each other; they didn't compete for attention.

The Four Live Wires shared numerous things in common. With regard to their financial matters, they were all very conservative. All were raised as true blue bloods. Each lived a privileged life, without financial worries, but none was shallow or haughty. Each was quite passionate about serving the underprivileged and demonstrated this interest with their time on various nonprofit boards and with their money. In this regard, they were more like classic liberals. And none was a fool or an easy mark for anyone. They didn't particularly care what others thought of them, and they had no time or patience for phonies. They were socially accepted at the Chevy Chase Club, but, still, they made some women at "the club" uncomfortable with their directness.

Eleanor, the oldest at sixty-seven, was a widow who spoke the least. She looked much like Eleanor Roosevelt and could size up a person's character within ten seconds. She was elegant in her articulate, poised manner, with gray hair and a slight bend in her posture, the result of early osteoarthritis. A colleague once said that Eleanor was grace and dignity, splattered with Tabasco sauce.

Laurie was the outward spirit of the four friends. Like Carrie, Laurie was attractive and an extrovert. The youngest, in her early fifties, Laurie looked like a cheerleader, which she had been in college, but now with mileage. She was a charmer who invigorated others with her enthusiasm and trademark laugh, which was contagious.

Myrtle was distinguished in her physical appearance, but not especially attractive. She appeared to be a descendant of the Queen of England. Myrtle was the relative introvert of the group, a plodder. She wore distinct black Ralph Lauren glasses, which gave her an international flair. For Myrtle, every point had to make logical sense, or she would stop the conversation until it did. The other three ladies called Myrtle's tortured pace "The Myrtle Mile."

Together, their collective net worth was in the neighborhood of one hundred million dollars.

Long ago, they had made a pact that if they decided to enter into a "project," as they liked to call them, they would do so with equal energy and financial commitment, but only with unanimous agreement. Still, behind each other's backs, "anonymous" donations appeared, even *after* they had met their agreed-upon share. This backdoor practice was understood, but never discussed openly.

Carrie told Gee absolutely nothing about her three friends, other than that this was an opportunity for the Cuatro Amigos to give a presentation to folks who might be interested in funding their community ideas for the underprivileged, particularly in the crime prevention area.

The Cuatro Amigos arrived together in Pepe's car. Moments before they entered the front door of the CCC together, Pepe said to Hattie, "At the worst, we get a free lunch!"

Hattie pinched him on the arm. "Freeloading irritates me. Oh, by the way, my mother said we have no idea of the social influence we are about to encounter. Be on your toes!"

Gee, Hattie, Huggie and Pepe entered the Lincoln Room right on time. Each was nattily attired, although Pepe had received last-second needling from Hattie because he had his NY Yankees hat on.

Carrie, seeing Pepe, made a big fuss over him.

In a flash, Myrtle was talking to Hattie about community work she had done with Hattie's mother, Dr. Emilee Rogers.

The bouncy Laurie spoke to Huggie about her past civil rights activities with his father. "Give Dr. Winston my best, please. He's such a hoot, you know!" Laurie said.

"Have you got the right Dr. Winston?" Huggie deadpanned.

"Kidder. He's an inspiration, isn't he?" Laurie added. "And an apple doesn't fall far from the tree."

Carrie noticed that Eleanor was reserved, as usual, but she appeared to be at ease talking to Gee.

"Well, why don't we all find a seat? Huggie, you said you have a PowerPoint presentation, so while you connect your PC to the projector, let me introduce everyone and frame why we're all here today," Carrie said. She waited for everyone to be seated.

"Let me begin by saying that I'm sorry Jon Rhodes couldn't be with us today. He's traveling to California to visit his sister, who's ill. Let me make clear, I take no responsibility for my three friends—"

Hattie jumped in, "Nor, Carrie, do Gee and I take responsibility for Huggie and Pepe!"

They all laughed.

"Well, now, we've already agreed on something! Cuatro Amigos, we have a pet name, too! We're the Four Live Wires!" Carrie said.

The room broke up in laughter.

Pepe turned to Laurie, touched her shoulder with his index finger, and made a sizzling sound, like he received a shock.

"We like to get involved with worthy projects addressed to the needs of the underprivileged. We've worked on civil rights projects, the creation of a secondhand clothes distribution center, food drives, child care issues, supporting mothers with children who want to enter the workforce, educational issues.... You get the picture. We decline proposed projects by about ten to one, particularly if they don't pass a 'Myrtle Mile' threshold," Carrie joked.

"The cross I'm caused to bear!" Myrtle said, dramatically crossing her arms over her heart.

"Laurie, Myrtle, and Eleanor know of my work with WWTS. They know of the governor's interest in being popular, which has led to the continuation of punishing 'tough-on-crime' policies that hammer the African-American and Hispanic offenders and their communities disproportionately. We've been around the block—"

"Darling, can you find another metaphor?" Eleanor asked, while looking straight at her notepad.

Pepe kept snickering, so Laurie said, "Watch it, buster—you can't stay young and dashing forever!"

My God, thought Carrie, *Laurie's flirting with him!*

"We have plenty of experience with governments that turn their backs on the needs of people. I've spoken briefly to these ladies about your Nuevos Principios activities—we love that name—the Web site, newsletter, and blog and your efforts to change the culture of your probation organization and maybe even the culture of the court and parole authorities. We're your allies. We'll help you get connected to others of influence, but—how shall I say this?—we're stealthy. We do our best work in the dark!" Carrie said.

Laughter shook the room.

"Why have we invited you here today? The reason for this

meeting is to determine how, if at all, we can help you bring about better, sustainable community associations and organizations. While we care about helping individuals in need, like your offenders, we're more process-oriented. Like you, we want to bring about systemic, permanent—if anything is permanent—change. We can be the system's worst nightmare. So, how might our paths cross? That's the purpose of this meeting," Carrie said, gesturing to Gee to start.

"OK. Thank you for inviting us. We like your clubhouse," she said.

Everyone laughed.

"Here's where we are today. We try to be good probation officers and work within our own individual value systems. At the heart of our shared beliefs is the view that with sufficient support, people—offenders, the powerless—can change their behavior toward pro-social values. But we, those who work within systems, must want offenders to make it. Our system is neither civil nor respectful to the people on supervision. We can't pretend any longer that those aren't the facts. Recently, because of his apparent one-time use of marijuana, and faced with the certainty of another year in prison, TJ, one of my promising parolees, committed suicide, leaving behind a wonderful wife and two small children. For us, that was the point of no return," Gee concluded.

The tears welling in Gee's eyes did not escape Carrie and, she guessed, the other ladies.

Hattie stepped in quickly, "We've decided to try to reach our colleagues all over the country. We want to start, as the *Baltimore Sun* put it sarcastically, a 'humanistic revolution.' We want to change the culture in our business."

"How long has your profession had this—what is it—mean-spiritedness?" Myrtle asked.

"Probably about thirty-plus years," Gee said.

"How can you change a culture without the support of management?" Laurie asked.

"Folks, let's not slide into conventional wisdom—'only managers can create a vision'—when, in fact, nothing—*nothing*—we have *ever* done has pleased the management of one organization. Screw management," Carrie said.

"Oh, there goes our rebel, shifting into gear!" Laurie said.

"Ironically, officers are wonderful people, but, within the organization, they follow the lead of their managers, which is to rely on stereotypical thinking. So, without taking on management, we think we must tap into officers' existing values. But, to change our system, we need new skills. Creating training opportunities to teach those skills is our primary target. Now, here's our dilemma. We're focused on changing the organizational culture, one officer at a time. We're optimistic. But we'll need folks from outside to put pressure on the system to abandon the punishment—what we call the 'tail 'em, nail 'em, jail 'em' mentality," Gee added.

"If it weren't so tragic, that slogan would be cute," Myrtle said.

"We're optimistic that help from folks like Carrie at WWTS will make a huge difference. But that still leaves the enormous problems in the community. No matter how good officers get, if communities won't offer a hand up to offenders, well, we're just howling at the moon. That, I think, is where we could use help from you. How exactly, we don't know. We can visualize a fuzzy image of what the future could look like. We want to see probation officers in the community working with advocates at the neighborhood level. Before I turn things over to Huggie, then Pepe, are there any questions?" Gee asked.

"I thought probation officers were, sorry, bleeding-heart social workers. Where does this punishment stuff fit in?" Laurie asked.

"Crack cocaine and gangs have led to the political conclusion that prisons are the only answer. Tough-on-crime is how you get elected. Punishing people on probation and parole supervision, *catching them* doing something wrong, is the trendy new sport. It's like the steps you would take to stop violent gang members are being applied to penny-ante behavior. The net is too wide. And the net is getting wider. There's no end in sight."

"Why don't managers do something more humanistic, to use your term?" Eleanor asked.

"I'll answer that," said Hattie. "They want to be promoted. If one offender harms someone in the community, the press conducts a witch hunt to determine who to blame. How could this happen? Why didn't the officer prevent it? On and on. So, one case—remember the 'slasher' in Baltimore?—or even the fear of one case failing and doing harm, sends a shockwave of overreaction. The system's response is to nail 'em. The consequence of a notorious case—a Willie Horton—is a career killer."

Next, Huggie carried the four ladies through a brief deficit-based depiction of three Hispanic high-crime communities, sometimes called Hotspots, and two large black communities. He beat the typical drums: lack of community organizations, gangs, drugs on the corners, and fear of crime that kept citizens inside their houses after dark. Within a few minutes, the gloom in the room could be cut with a butter knife.

"Hopeless, isn't it? Depressing ... it seems. We don't think from deficits, however. We think from strengths that are already out there. So, let's flip this negative image upside down and look at what Pepe and I have turned up in about two years of community work. Pepe...."

"First, let me say it's a great honor to speak to women of passion. I've always heard that if you want to get a tough job done, give it to small group of concerned women. My grandmother and mother are such women. They've made me rich beyond my wildest dreams with the value of caring for the less fortunate. Huggie and I realized that he was comfortable in the African-American communities and I was comfortable in the Hispanic communities. What's wrong with that picture? If we couldn't get out of our own comfort zones, how did we expect others to? So, we decided to join forces and see what would come from our collaboration.

What I'm about to show you is a sample, just a small sample, of Community All-Stars, as we call them. Think of them as community assets. I guarantee you that you don't know them. But, like you, they're very special, caring people. They're the unseen glue that cares for the small and the meek—whether they are young or old. We learn every day that there are gobs of them doing marvelous things without fanfare. We're just scratching the surface. We believe the offenders we work with should both *receive* community support and *offer* it to others. We've seen that when young offenders—whom you might think of as taking *from* the community—become needed by those who have nothing, particularly children who remind them of themselves, or the elderly, who remind them of their mothers or grandmothers—bam!—a powerful switch gets flipped on. They *want* to help. Here, then, are just some of the stories of these Community All-Stars," Pepe said.

One after another, up came a still photo of a Community All-Star. Most photos were action shots, rather than photos in posed positions. The Cuatro Amigos had overlaid brief interviews on a camcorder with either the Community All-Stars directly or with community members telling stories about the acts of the All-Stars.

For every individual pictured, stories about them were full of their caring and "being there" for others. Strikingly, each All-Star interviewed directly seemed uncomfortable being praised for acts that apparently came to them as easily as breathing. Pepe stacked the presentation so that the deeper he got into the slides and interviews, the more touching the stories became.

"Janelle is a fifteen-year-old black girl in Rockville who's organized a homework club for poor young kids in her neighborhood.

"Juan is a gardener from Argentina who plays soccer with twenty to thirty boys and girls every day, weather permitting.

"Raymon is a black barber who, by blunt negotiation skills, makes sure drug dealers stay away from middle school and younger kids.

"Shauntelle is a black hairdresser who takes care of young girl's hair for free in her home on Mondays, her day off.

"Clinton and Bruester are two retirees who, on their own initiative, work helping offenders to set up their own businesses. To date, three offenders have succeeded in small businesses.

"The Catholic priest at St. Mary's, Father Rice, has helped start a center for abused children from the local neighborhood.

"Anna Rivera has just started an afterschool sewing club for latchkey girls.

"Willie Brown, a Montgomery County Police Officer, is in his fourth year coaching black kids in football and baseball.

"The Rockville AME Church, headed by Lynore Thoms, has started an afterschool computer program for young kids," Pepe said.

The final All-Star presented was a black woman identified only as Ms. Lilly. On a sepia photograph, which was a side view of her holding a young child, Ms. Lilly appeared to be in her seventies, maybe eighties.

Pepe told this story:

"Huggie discovered from young offenders in the black Lincoln Park neighborhood that sometimes the local kids would get hungry and have nothing to eat because their mothers were strung out on crack or on a bender. Sometimes they waited for their mothers to come home for days. Then, apparently, they would give up and meander down to Ms. Lilly's, day or night. Ms. Lilly's son, DeWayne, had paid cash for the six-bedroom, four-bathroom, two-story, wooden-framed house across from Montgomery College. Rumor has it that DeWayne hit it big on a drug deal, just months before he was murdered by drug dealers. Community police officers told Huggie that DeWayne tried to get to the next tier of crack distribution by double-crossing his suppliers. Folks say that Ms. Lilly has never slept well after that incident, some twelve years ago.

"Today, she's very heavy, probably over 250 pounds, and has high blood pressure, diabetes, and walks with a cane. She mumbles to herself, almost Tourette's-like, partly, folks say, to remind her of what she's thinking and partly, they say, in anger, most probably because she can't take a shoe to the neighborhood kids' irresponsible parents.

"These kids arrive at her house, we're told, sometimes sheepishly, sometimes crying, sometimes clutching dolls. Ms. Lilly told Huggie that they ball up in the fetal position, racked with fear, in order to fall asleep. Ms. Lilly says she holds them and hums gospel songs for hours, if that's what it takes. She always says to them when they're not in a crisis, 'Ms. Lilly is slow coming down those steps. So, you just be patient. You keep ringing that bell. Someone always wake Ms. Lilly. You remember—you always remember—Ms. Lilly is *so* happy to see you!'" Pepe said.

Pepe went on to say that, during the week, she usually wore one of two housedresses. But, on Sundays, she wore broad-brimmed hats and a fancy dress to church. At home on Sundays she hummed hymns and never scowled.

Hattie interrupted, "Huggie and Pepe know this firsthand because they drop food by there all the time—they think Gee and I don't know that."

Pepe frowned but continued his story by saying that on Sunday afternoons her house was always open for neighborhood children, young and old, to enjoy fried chicken, mashed potatoes, gravy and biscuits, spinach, and seasonal pies. Numerous adults, after giving Ms. Lilly a mandatory kiss on the cheek, would help with the preparation.

When Ms. Lilly received a kiss, it meant she accepted someone in her house. As Ms. Lilly has gotten older, she's tended to give "instructions" for others to carry out specific duties in the kitchen. Teenaged kids in the neighborhood keep watch over Ms. Lilly, like going to the store for her, taking out her trash, cutting her grass, and giving her a heads-up on the neighborhood *crisis du jour*. There isn't a thief that could stay alive if he stole from Ms. Lilly.

Huggie added, "She has what she calls a 'Jesus Bowl.' Older kids are 'allowed' to put money in the Jesus Bowl to help take care of the small children, but she will throw large bills from teenagers, like twenty-dollar bills, out on the front porch, if she believes the money comes from drugs. Of course, it's OK if they put in one hundred $1 bills. They just have to be wrinkled and not in a neat pile. The little ones are asked to put a penny in the Jesus Bowl every time they spend the night to pay for their meals, 'so you don't be owing *nothing* to nobody.' Ms. Lilly repeats these words every day, we're told."

"Of course, the little kids could get pennies off the kitchen counter to put in the Jesus Bowl in the dining room, if they had none," added Gee.

The next segment showed an attempted interview with a skinny little black girl of about four or five years old. The video caught the voice of Pepe, obviously shooting the scene and giving instructions to Huggie, while the huge Huggie tried to make himself small by kneeling at the child's side. Huggie asked her, "What does Ms. Lilly do for you, sugar?"

After twenty seconds of the little girl looking at her shoes, Pepe took the camera off of her.

"I assumed she wasn't going to talk," Pepe said.

Then the camera's microphone picked up this tiny voice. Huggie asked her to repeat what she said, as Pepe quickly brought the little girl back into focus.

"Well ... Ms. Lilly says ... she always gladest to see me. Ms. Lilly say I'm special," said the girl.

"This little warrior is a child who's seen, up close, more ugly brutal scenes and experienced more abject neglect than most adults will experience in a lifetime—all the while, clutching that worn-out little doll," Pepe said.

There was a very long pause.

Three of the four ladies, veterans of life's ups and downs, looked quite touched.

Last, on the screen came a collage of the Community All-Stars. Huggie left that image in place.

Carrie was the first to speak. "What fool said the four of us are tough? Well, thank you. Do I take it, then, that somehow supporting this Community All-Star notion, this natural wealth of assets in the five locations you mentioned, would be of help?" Carrie asked.

"Yes," said Pepe and Huggie in unison.

"Yes," added Gee and Hattie.

"Well then, thank you. We have much to talk about. I'll get back to you with a formal response, probably in the next few weeks. Your work is very important. Thank you. Why don't we all enjoy lunch," Carrie said.

~

In an unusually swift follow-up meeting, only one week later, the Four Live Wires met at Carrie's house for lunch. They ate in her formal living room, eating sandwiches from plates on their laps.

As was their custom, independently, they checked out the Cuatro Amigos from multiple perspectives. Collectively, they had talked to twenty-two people about Huggie, Hattie, Gee, and Pepe.

Because Carrie had a personal relationship with the Nuevos Principios Society, the hostess yielded to Eleanor to start the discussion.

Eleanor asked, "Well, is this something we might be interested in?"

No one knew exactly what to say, so there was a pause.

"Since I sponsored them, so to speak, I'll speak last," Carrie said.

"Well, there're all sorts of 'Myrtle Mile' issues, which, on their face, make this a very difficult project to support. For example, all sorts of government agencies already have responsibilities to provide the kind of care we heard about from them," Myrtle said.

"I agree. So many churches, nonprofits, as we even heard from them, are already doing the things we hope for in the community," said Laurie.

Realizing that the others were waiting to hear her response, Eleanor stood and leaned toward the three friends on her cane, shortening the already close distance. "What is it? What *is it* I'm experiencing? Someone help an old lady out. There are more reasons *not* to support this loosely strewn idea than there are to give it a boost. That part's easy. But what do we have on our hands? What is it that so disturbs my equilibrium with regard to these four? I mean this quite seriously. Help me out, *please*. Why do these puppies move me so?" she asked, and sat back down in her chair, staring into space.

"Well, they have guts, brains, and their reward system is inward. Gee reminds me of myself when I was young. I'm so proud of her courageous acts—it's like she's a daughter I always wish I had. I know that's not on-point to our mission, but she's a young woman we should want to mentor," Carrie said.

Laurie started to say "Pepe is—"

"Oh, for God's sake, Laurie. I thought menopause had killed all that lust!" Myrtle said.

"Hell, Myrtle, maybe a good, old-fashioned toss in the hay is just what you need!" said Laurie.

"Could the she-wolves pipe down, please? Go on, Laurie, I assume you had a point," said Carrie.

Tears rushed to Laurie's eyes. A hush followed. "There are so few people, my father was one, whose sincerity and kindness touches you and comforts you in ways that defy words. These people can touch your very soul. This young man, Pepe, is capable of great things. Heck, we hear from good people wanting to do good things all the time. I sleep at night when we say no. But this man understands the moment. He knows how to reach people's hearts. He knows what's inside of you and how to link with you. I'm telling you, community people will follow him. He's clearly, *clearly*, in the wrong profession. We can manage his transition out of the system he's in. He's the real deal."

The usual bantering was absent.

"Well, Hattie's brilliant and clearly devoted to children's rights. Rest assured, one day we'll read about her on the front pages of the *Washington Post*. She's tough, but not belligerent," Myrtle said.

"And Huggie?" asked Eleanor.

"Huggie Winston is authentic. The black community will follow him," said Laurie.

Eleanor continued, "Then, as I understand it, we have four courageous young people who stand a good chance of getting turned into mincemeat by the vicious aspirations of those who have dominion over the criminal justice system. That's an old script. Their sin is caring about the powerless, which, I suppose, was once the bedrock of our American experience. They bear all of the risks. 'Corporate punishment' waits for them—for wanting to help offenders make it. Their hope of turning around the stereotypical thinking will fall on its can when offenders can't get support in their own communities. This asset building thing is critical. God knows, I'm sorry to say, they will probably have to weave things through sports—maybe they need to. But they should realize that efforts must be rooted in advancing education. Be clear, these folks are talking about changing how people care about the outcast. My God, ladies, did you pick that up? Changing the whole culture! Now, that alone ought to dismiss them from our consideration! I call for a vote."

It was standard practice that when one person called for a vote, a vote followed without further debate

Eleanor said, "Do we support this project?"

"Yes."

"Yes, indeed."

"Absolutely."

"Done," said Eleanor.

The Community All-Stars were about to get a big boost.

"At what individual level?" asked Eleanor.

No one spoke.

"Well, then, I establish the sum at $100,000 each," declared Eleanor.

"Wouldn't that be a record high?" said Myrtle.

"Well, yes, indeed it would!" said Eleanor.

~

Carrie set up a meeting with the Cuatro Amigos at brunch in her home on Saturday morning. She called Olivia and asked her to attend the meeting, too.

"I'd be delighted to attend," Olivia said.

At 9:45 AM, Olivia and Pepe arrived, hand-in-hand in Carrie's foyer.

"Well, hello—" Carrie started to say, then, noticing the locked hands, added spontaneously, "I see you two—"

"Let me explain, since I don't make a practice of sharing my personal life with my work world. More importantly, I don't make a practice of being deceitful to friends," Olivia said.

They settled at the kitchen island as they poured coffee.

"When you and I were in New York, Hector—sorry, Pepe, as you know him—Hector and I were on our second date. I expected nothing to come of the relationship. Frankly—"

"I expected true love," tossed in Pepe.

Olivia smacked him on the arm, as Carrie burst into laughter.

"Anyway, I learned quickly how truly lost he was without proper guidance and structure. So, I guess you could say, I adopted him—you know, as a project," Olivia said.

"Of course, dear, I understand fully," Carrie said.

"Oh, you two—" Pepe protested.

"But I soon found out my distant approach wasn't providing enough guidance. It became necessary for him to move in with me for 24/7 care. I consider Hector ... my social burden," Olivia said.

"God bless those who suffer in silence," said Carrie. "I understand, Olivia. Of course, you appreciate that we wouldn't bring you here for bad news. I thought that there may be some legal issues that might emerge for which we'll need advice, or any other role you may find appropriate, including a board position. But, really, I rule nothing in or rule nothing out. I just wanted you in on the ground action. We'd welcome your creative ideas."

"I'm flattered. That gives me a chance to watch lover boy in action," Olivia said, touching Pepe's cheek warmly.

"Good deal," Carrie said, as the doorbell rang. Within minutes, everyone had arrived. It was as if they had taken the same cab together. In came Eleanor, Myrtle, Laurie, Gee, Jon Rhodes, Hattie, and Huggie. A surprise attendee was Rosa, Huggie's wife.

"I couldn't help but bring Rosa along—" Huggie started to say.

Before he could get his sentence out, Laurie, Eleanor, Hattie, and Gee were all around Rosa, making her feel welcome.

"I just felt, perhaps, there's something an educator might address, if you had any questions—" Rosa said, cutting off her sentence.

"It only takes a few good women...." Laurie said, smiling at Pepe.

"Do you women want Jon, Huggie, and me to wait outside?" Pepe said.

"That won't be necessary," said Carrie.

"Rosa, I'm delighted you came. Also, let me introduce Pepe's *special friend*, Olivia Lopez. Olivia is an Assistant Public Defender," Carrie added, looking at Olivia, who stood shoulder-to-shoulder with Pepe.

"Why, Pepe, you little rascal," Gee whispered.

The social conversation, mixed with guests loading their plates with bagels, fresh fruits, lox, and assorted breakfast treats, could have had a life of its own, that is, until Carrie marshaled everyone into the living room.

"By the way," Pepe said, "these ladies are known as the Four Live Wires.

Everyone laughed.

"True, true. We still have some spark left in us. Right, ladies?" said Carrie.

"We can only hope," said Eleanor.

"Well, Eleanor, our spokesperson in most matters, will you make our little announcement?" Carrie asked.

"Of course, and thank you, Carrie, for bringing these folks to us and for hosting this brunch," Eleanor said. Then she rose, again leaning on her cane.

"Unfortunately ..."

Carrie noticed Gee's face turn ashen.

"Unfortunately, we can't give you Ft. Knox, because that's what you folks deserve, with this project. But we gladly and proudly choose to support you financially and in any other way we can think of, within our time and resources," Eleanor said.

There was a burst of shouting and hugging. Gee and Hattie cried. Jon, Huggie, and Pepe high-fived. There was absolute joy in the room. Olivia and Rosa smiled at each other.

"What can we say?" asked Gee, tears rolling down her face.

For five minutes there was no attempt to thwart the joy. Then, Myrtle handed out a one-page talking point document.

"This is how we propose to tackle this mission," said Eleanor. One could have heard a pin drop, though it would have landed on a lush, two-inch-thick carpet.

The document had bullets that Eleanor proceeded to walk everyone through.

"Here's where we propose to start: the Four Live Wires and Jon, our spark plug, will make an initial donation totaling $500,000. Our fundraising abilities will make that figure look small. The five of us will be in charge of fundraising. Immediately, upon your approval today, a 501(c)(3) educational organization application will be filed with the IRS, so the entity can receive tax-deductible funds. Perhaps Olivia would ..." Eleanor paused for Olivia to respond.

"I'd be pleased to handle that aspect," Olivia said.

"Good and thank you, dear. Unless someone has a better idea, the organization would be known as the Community All-Stars in Perpetuity, or CASI, for short," Eleanor said.

"Cool," said Huggie.

"Good, it was your name, really. We just added the in perpetuity to suggest the organization intends to be around for some time. Like us old ladies," Eleanor said.

"We'll form a nonpaying Board of Directors. Today, I ask Olivia Lopez, Carrie, Jon, and, on my own authority, Rosa Winston, to serve on that board. Is that something you would appreciate, Olivia, Carrie, Jon, Rosa?" Eleanor said, looking at each one, waiting for a response.

Olivia and Jon responded affirmative by short, quick answers, Carrie with a nod.

"I don't want you to think that you should feel obligated to—" Rosa started to say.

"Honey, after my wedding night, I haven't felt obligated to do anything in my life!" Eleanor said.

It was the first off-color remark that Carrie, Laurie, and Myrtle had ever heard Eleanor make, and it brought down the house.

"Well, then," said Rosa, trying to catch her breath from laughing, "I'd be honored. I'll be most interested in the educational component."

"You raise a good point. We'll talk a little more about our vision for oversight of education and other functions. We plan to find a center in each of the five locations you've identified and staff the centers with a small, paid staff and volunteers. And let me speak to one very personal goal we have: we'd like to buy Ms. Lilly's home for a considerable fee and lease it back to her for $1 annually. We'd set up a trust fund for her to live on. With her approval and meeting zoning requirements, we'll fix the house up, at no expense to her, and use several rooms for offices and help her expand her efforts. Her house, then, would be the first center in operation," Eleanor said.

Pepe and Huggie's faces displayed unbridled pride.

"We have considerable experience in organizational design, but we'll rely on the board and president to make the staff selections. We've put our heads together to select a president and recommend the appointment of Admiral Theodore Pendleton, who is, of course, an African-American, and the former deputy chief of staff of the Navy. He will bring with him countless retired Navy and military folks as volunteers. We have spoken with him, and he will accept the position under one condition—he will serve for one year and one year only. Then, he will hand off the job to one of you, if you'll have the job. That's his condition. Do you join me in supporting his nomination, and do we accept this plan?" Eleanor asked.

"That's not quite far-reaching enough," said Huggie.

"Huggie?" Gee said.

"Hear him out," Hattie said.

"I'm listening," said Eleanor.

"This gracious offer—and your design—is thoughtful. It's smart, really, to have a veteran organizational man with lengthy, proven credentials. But I don't associate organizational skills with passion, particularly in this environment, which requires special character traits—someone who can go freely over the humongous bridges that divide the court from the community, the rich from the poor, blacks from whites, whites from Hispanics, and minorities from the mainstream. In my culture, people often talk about the long awaited someone—the *one*—to carry us out … to show the way. The older folks tend to talk about a new savior, one who could split the Red Sea again. The younger generation looks for more pragmatic goals, like economic justice," Huggie said, pausing for a long, deliberate drink of water.

All eyes were on him.

"Over the past few years, I've learned our spiritual leader is among us," Huggie said, pointing at Pepe with his enormous hand. "He's *the one*. He's us in the community," Huggie concluded.

Gee stood, walked over to Pepe, put her left arm over his shoulder and said, "Yes, he is."

Hattie stood, took a few steps, and stood beside Pepe. "Yes, he's our man."

Pepe's head was down, his face hidden underneath his NYY hat. Gee had an arm around him, and Olivia was nestled against him.

"Unless Pepe objects, by the powers vested in me, which I just made up, this oral contract is herewith amended. Pepe is our second president, whenever he's comfortable with the organizational structure and has sufficient administrative support," Eleanor said.

Pepe started to speak, but got only a far as, "I'm touched...."

"Well, good. Soon you'll have two jobs," Gee said.

"Not exactly. Hector and I have made two decisions. He's asked me to marry him ... and he's decided to leave the probation office when he finds a suitable position in the community," Olivia said.

There was a gasp of joy and excitement.

"Well, then, Pepe, we offer you a suitable position in the community. Would you like to join CACI as the Vice President and help us get established and then work out a transitional process with Admiral Pendleton?" Eleanor asked.

"I'd be pleased to learn the organizational side as the vice president first," Pepe said.

"Done," said Eleanor.

The joy was unrestrained and bled into numerous sidebars, until Eleanor got the group back on task.

"Now, we've always sought for our projects, rightly *your* project in this case, to become self-sustaining, with donations, contributions, and grants secondary, after the startup. In other words, we'll look to business models to support CASI. Jon, please," Eleanor said, sitting down and yielding the floor to Jon, who stood up. His appearance was anything but dour.

"When I headed a real estate firm, one of the most difficult tasks was finding outfits to make repairs quickly, and at a fair price for the houses that went on the market. You know, putting up a new roof or repairing one, making plumbing repairs or replacing fixtures, painting, exterior landscape improvements, on and on. Right now, it would be hard to ever meet the demand. Let me ask this two-part question of our Cuatro Amigos: Do you think we could generate an interest on the part of inmates or persons on probation, men and women, to be trained to do these jobs? Secondly, could they do them honestly and behave in a trustworthy manner?" he asked.

"Absolutely to the security issues; we'd screen out those that aren't ready. As to the other part—their interest—as long as the wages are fair, they'd be hungry for jobs where they work independently," said Pepe.

"I wholeheartedly agree," said Huggie.

"Count on women with children being very interested," added Hattie.

"Yes. And I'm sure the prisons can be counted on, too, to provide elementary skills for painting, roof repairs, and carpentry work. To some degree, they're already teaching those skills. Parolees just usually have no opportunity to apply the skills when they're released," said Gee.

"Here's one proposed model, just to get us started: every offender goes through our internal training for thirty days. We hope probation/parole officers will take an active role in participating with us—you know, be on the team, type of thing. Offenders will be under the direct supervision of a coach. They'll be paid, of course. If they demonstrate skills and have sufficient discipline, they'll be promoted after the thirty-day training period to then serve on a team. After twelve months, or thereabout, they'll enter positions as team leaders for six months. During this time, they'll be coached, mentored, and supported to break off and start their own business. They may choose *not* to start their own business, but the option is there. By then, by eighteen months, surely, the label 'offender' will have disappeared in the eyes of real estate agencies. They'll just be people who can be trusted. What do you think?" he asked.

"Nothing short of boss," said Pepe.

"Good, because right now, I have commitments from six real estate businesses that are prepared to give all of their work to CASI—that is, if the teams perform well. I have fifteen to twenty mentors lined up ready to train, ready to go," Jon said.

"Wow!" was all Huggie could get out of his mouth.

"Carrie," Eleanor said.

"Oh, yes. CASI will seek separate funds to establish a memorial fund, an annual TJ Smith Award of around $5,000 to a community person, or offender, who best demonstrates the spirit of—how shall I put it—integrity and pro-social behavior. We'll figure out the exact language," Carrie said.

Rosa put her arm around Gee.

"Honey, TJ helped get this started, didn't he?" Carrie said to Gee, softly.

"I'm sorry to say, yes, Carrie, he did," Gee said.

"We join you in your sorrow. But, understand, everyone in this room believes that you did the best you could. It's also true that Lucy Rhodes had a hand in forging what we're doing today. May God comfort both of their souls," said Carrie.

The group collectively paused for Gee and Jon to compose themselves, which they did quickly.

"Olivia, you've seen Pepe and Huggie's presentation on the Community All-Stars?" asked Eleanor.

"Yes, I have," Olivia responded. It dawned on Carrie then that Olivia's hand had been all over Pepe's work.

"Will you work with Jon to manage the early public relations effort, including producing a more elaborate DVD from their work—expanding it, as necessary? I'll pay for that myself," Eleanor said.

"We can do that, right, Jon?" asked Olivia.

"With pleasure," said Jon.

"Now onto an area that we are, like Rosa, most drawn to: education for young adults and children in these five communities. We don't have to reinvent the wheel. There are plenty of folks who have their oars in this educational water. But we *do* want to support them, collaborate with them. Organizations like religious institutions, or the Boys & Girls Clubs. We want every center to have computers and life skills opportunities. I know Rosa and others will be instructive as to what's needed and how to be effective in this area. And Rosa, we know plenty of retired teachers who would work with us," Eleanor said.

"I'd be pleased to help in whatever capacity you'd like. Huggie, it's now up to you to cook dinners and clean the house—I've got CASI work to do!" Rosa said, elbowing him.

"Finally, you have to reach children where they are. So, we'll rely on Huggie and Pepe to spearhead the sports aspect. We wouldn't know a softball from a soccer ball. Perhaps Gee, Hattie, and Olivia can focus on the social and cultural aspects, with our active support. But again, the job is to do as much personally as you like, but also to organize the work of others," Eleanor added.

"It'll be a ball," said Olivia.

"This is just marvelous," said Hattie.

"Wow!" was all Pepe could say.

"Wow!" tossed in Huggie.

"So that's all we have. I take it then, we move forward today as a team. Am I correct in that assumption?" asked Eleanor.

The room erupted in applause.

34

THE CONGRESSWOMAN PLAYS HARDBALL

Senator Barbara Washington

Hattie's mother, Dr. Emilee K. Rogers, was the college roommate at Harvard and the best friend of U.S. Senator Barbara Washington. Washington was the first black and the second female senator in Maryland's history. Barbara Washington was a bootstraps civil rights attorney who the other side of the aisle tried to paint as soft-on-crime. The labeling effort went both ways. At a recent fundraiser, the now-divorced Senator Washington shared a brief update with her friend Emilee about her daughter, Amora, who had been having "maturation issues." In their brief conversation, Emilee suggested a lunch meeting, saying she had a problem she needed help with. Barbara summoned her nearby administrative aide to calendar the lunch.

Several days later, after Senator Washington's typical "meet and greet" public display of grandeur to restaurant well-wishers, whom she always thought of as voters, and a quick scan of the room for the lurking press, she was seated with Emilee. The two friends spoke quietly and to the point. Emilee shared the story of Hattie's most recent work "adventures."

"Sounds like us, raising hell back in the day, doesn't it, girl?" said the senator. "How can I help?"

"Barbara, I leave the strategy in your capable hands," replied Emilee, with a smile.

Since Emilee, who was quite capable of extemporaneously creating a seventeen-point, multi-tiered plan, offered *no* specifics, Senator Washington understood the message. The senator was being called upon to find the political, or budgetary, vulnerability of those administrators at the highest levels who were responsible for the current state of unwarranted punishment in criminal justice. Washington's ability to inflict fear was unsurpassed—the fear of unending oversight and threats of "downward budget adjustments." She knew, without any doubt, that the morons managing the probation and parole systems in Maryland, the ones causing folks, particularly minorities, to be sent to prison under the false color of public safety, couldn't hide from her. Emilee Rogers knew this, too.

Senator Washington agreed to the task—it was, after all, an opportunity to display her core belief that equal justice belonged to every citizen. Her staff quickly arranged a private meeting in her Senate office with seven of her key press *pets*. In the off-the-record meeting, the senator described her view of the state of the probation and parole system. Preliminary data, provided to the senator through Emilee Rogers, by way of Hattie and Carrie, and carefully screened by her staff, suggested that, nationwide, nearly 25 percent of those inmates in prisons, at any given time, were incarcerated for technical violations of the conditions of release—*not* for new criminal offenses. The senator referred to this practice as a *faux* public safety practice from Hell. In fact, she added for emphasis, it was nothing more than a "tail 'em, nail 'em, jail 'em" policy, one that disproportionately targeted minorities. She tipped her pets off to a press conference and shared a copy of a letter she had just sent to the General Accounting Office (GAO), Congress's investigative sleuths. The request sought an examination of technical violation practices in federal, state, and county court systems and in parole systems.

Before her press conference, four articles were generated by her press pets, mostly focusing on the growing use of prisons for very minor "human" problems and on the costs of this endeavor. One story pointed out it was cheaper to send one student to Harvard for a year than to incarcerate a technical violator for a year for smoking a joint.

The senator opened her press conference with outrage about the misuse of prison cells for technical violators, while at the same time urging more white-collar fraud perpetrators to have "reservations" set aside in prison. This "reservations" expression deftly avoided her being criticized as soft-on-crime by her adversaries.

She remarked, "In my view, probation and parole officers are some of the finest, most dedicated public servants I've ever met. I promise to do everything in my power to use the money saved from the misuse of prisons for penny-ante rules violations to advance job training for every inmate who wants to walk the straight and narrow path. If offenders, on the other hand, want to tear up *our* communities, we'll keep the light on them. And, instead of more prisons, I vow to earmark additional money saved from unnecessary use of costly prison space for training for probation/parole officers. Theirs is a difficult and dangerous profession. The balance of savings should go into the educational needs of public school systems," she added.

And so, the war was on.

News of the press conference spread quickly and shook the criminal justice world. She was already a hero to civil rights enthusiasts and a monster to government administrators. Academics wondered if she was acting alone or just the advance guard.

Two days later, the senator added an amendment on the floor of the Senate to a reauthorization bill for the Department of Justice (DOJ) that would, in effect, curtail federal prison expansion until further review of existing prison cell usage. No one objected. The amendment was quite nettlesome, if for no other reason than its timing: eight new prisons were in some stage of development. This amendment would create chaos.

The amendment almost slipped into law before a young, eager congressional aide from the political opposition discovered it while reviewing a congressional mark up at 1:30 AM, over pizza. The aide called the Bureau of Prison's Congressional Liaison Office the first thing the next morning. That office referred the matter immediately to top-level officials at Justice. The prison-industrial complex was furious, and their lobbyists went into code red damage control mode.

The next morning, at 8:00, Senator Washington graciously agreed to a hastily called breakfast conference with the deputy attorney general and his aide.

Behind closed doors, and off-the-record, the deputy attorney general and senator banged heads. Still, they managed to find common ground. The DOJ agreed to conduct an extensive review of contemporary prison and jail cell use for technical "rule" violations. If, and only if, the senator's assertions were supported—they quibbled over what constituted supported—the DOJ would initiate a comprehensive dialogue with the federal and state courts, federal and state prisons, and local jail representatives. There were no promises made as to what the various agencies would do as a consequence of this "dialogue." The

DOJ promised, in effect, to ask this question: "Are current revocation policies and practices resulting in unjust outcomes?"

The deputy attorney general also promised to commit sufficient grant money to study the issue after the initial dialogue. In exchange, Senator Washington agreed to drop the amendment with the following caveat: the DOJ would agree *not* to oppose future efforts to add mandatory certification of all federal probation officers. She reasoned that state probation and parole systems would quickly follow suit with the certification effort. Two days later, her amendment to review the existing use of federal prisons disappeared … quietly.

The request for the GAO investigation did not disappear. It just hung there. Whether acted upon or not, the threat of an expansive GAO review and report to Congress on the use of prisons as a sanction for technical violators remained useful to her cause—and good theatre. Suddenly, Senator Washington's request of the GAO became the subject of interest in criminal justice circles and started a series of politically oriented discussions with federal and state administrators. A good portion of the dialogue was focused on whom to blame and who should take the fall for the over-reliance on prisons.

Senator Washington's next move was to introduce legislation requiring mandatory use of local resources for federal technical violators, unless there was a clear and present danger to citizens or family members. She announced hearings for the fall session. She stated in the Congressional Record that she intended to hear from the Nuevos Principios Society. She believed their testimony would secure funds for the training required for mandatory certification of federal officers.

With news of forthcoming Congressional oversight hearings on the use of prisons for minor behavioral issues, came reinvigorated debate from academia regarding whether people really could change their behavior.

35

CARRIE'S BET

Carrie Springer

To suggest that Carrie's reactivation of her membership at the Chevy Chase Club was received with pleasure by every member was inaccurate, but that didn't surprise her. In fact, the cold shoulder was one of the reasons she avoided being at the club after her separation and divorce. She never cottoned to the notion of being a spouse *of*. There was still a small group of male members, particularly golfers, "Friends of Carl," as it were, who'd rather she not return. She knew well that some men at CCC despised her. She hated the feeling of being despised. Del Topping, particularly, was one of Carl's best friends and golfing buddies who went out of his way to deliberately ignore her at the golf complex.

Carrie sensed coldness from Carl's friends through passive acts: turned backs or, at times, apparently, she just became invisible. Carrie had heard the standing joke at CCC—that she had picked a divorce attorney that ate small children for breakfast.

On a bright September day, Carrie and Jon were joined at the club by Judges Brayer and Johnson for golf. They were at the first tee box when Del Topping accidentally backed into her while chatting with his waiting foursome.

"Well, Carrie, how are you?" Del said.

"Fine.... Busy, and you, Del?" she asked.

"Well, thank you. I spend a lot more of my time now with my favorite charity, the MS Society."

"Really.... I'm spending more time with a new foundation called CASI."

"Never heard of it. What's that?"

"Well, in short, Del, we work to strengthen the community by crime prevention and helping offenders make it in the community."

"Make it? As best I can tell, they all belong in prison! That way, we're all safe from them."

"Del, that's such a provincial notion."

"Nobody buys into that liberal crap."

"Don't bet on it, Del. Just keep an eye on us."

"Do you typically play with these guys, Carrie?" Del asked, pointing to Bill Brayer, Harry Johnson, and Jon Rhodes.

"Yes, I do."

Looking at Jon Rhodes, he said, "I'm glad he's back into circulation—you know, after one of your offenders murdered his lovely wife. Well, Carrie, I'm a betting man, and I also do fundraising for MS. I play with George Evans and Bill and Tommy Wright. You know all of them, right?"

"I know who they are."

"Well, how about a little bet? My foursome against yours? The winner contributes to the other's charity."

"Well, I don't know—"

"Now, Carrie dearest, I know you—how shall I say this—came out OK with the Carl divorce thing. Certainly...."

"You're on. Let's talk about the details after the round. Marcus needs to sit in, too."

"Deal," he said, smiling.

"What was *that* all about?" Jon asked, approaching Carrie in the wake left by Del's departure.

"Oh, nothing," she said.

On the eighteenth green, Carrie decided to break the news to her playing partners that she intended to bet Del's foursome that they could beat them.

"Do you think that we could beat Del's group?" she asked.

"I've watched them all day. I'm sure of it," said Jon Rhodes.

"I think so," said Judge Brayer.

"Probably," said Judge Johnson.

"Good, because I've agreed to make a bet with them. The winner makes a contribution to the other's charity," she said.

"Well, Carrie, understand clearly that Harry and I can't officially be part of a bet. Not even the appearance of a bet. We'll find some way to pay you in cash if we lose, of course, but remember, we're not on the bet," said Bill Brayer.

~

Inside the clubhouse bar, it appeared to Carrie that Del's buddies wanted no part of the disagreement. Marcus, in his assistant pro capacity, was the official guru in charge of protocols in handicap squabbles for member's bets. He was seated in a chair near Del. Carrie thought that Marcus's body language suggested that he was trying to display neutrality. Carrie noticed Jon and Judges Brayer and Johnson leaving for the men's locker room.

Del said, "As Marcus will attest, we have handicaps of four, seven, nine, and twelve. Yours are three, ten, twelve, and you, Carrie, play to a fifteen. Sounds like a fair bet is even-up."

"Even-up, *my ass*. Better, you give us twelve strokes. You have four men!" said Carrie.

"Out of the question," Del said.

After twenty minutes of haggling, with Marcus serving as a non-invasive referee, they reached this decision: the match would be medal play, based on electronically stored handicaps. Del's foursome was the better golfers. To win, Carrie's team would need to stay within seven strokes of Del's foursome—a score of eight strokes or higher, and Del's team would win the match.

Marcus stated that Del and a fellow named George would be paired with Judge Harry Johnson and Carrie.

"Oh good, it'll be Harry-Carrie for you two—and *we* get to watch!" howled Del.

Harry Johnson, reappearing from the locker room, heard the remark as he walked by the table and looked at Carrie with raised eyebrows, as if to suggest—*that is* pretty funny. In return, Judge Johnson received a scowl from Carrie.

"Marcus, will you set the event up for next Friday at one o'clock? I have two conditions: Marcus supervises the match by physically being on the course with us," Carrie said.

"Marcus?" asked Del.

"Fine," said Marcus.

"The men play from the black tees and I play from the reds," Carrie said.

"Try to keep up, dear," said Del.

"Oh, I will, Del, I will."

"And the wager?" asked Del.

Del's playing partners turned their backs at the bar. Marcus excused himself.

"For reasons I care not to go into, the bet is between me and your team," Carrie said. "What'd you have in mind?"

Del grabbed a napkin and wrote the following: "Total team: $4,000." He handed it to Carrie.

Reading his offer, Carrie grabbed another napkin and wrote: "Team total: $20,000." She shoved the napkin toward Del, abruptly.

A seasoned poker player, Del didn't blink. He went over to his playing partners and had a brief conversation. He returned in thirty seconds.

Del grabbed another napkin and wrote the following: "Team total: $60,000." He pushed the napkin toward Carrie with a velocity that caused it to take flight. Carrie caught the napkin an inch above the table.

Carrie grabbed yet another napkin and slid it toward Del: "Team total: $100,000."

Del went back to his partners and whispered to them in a huddle, like a football team calling a play. Carrie saw them smile, collectively. He returned to the table.

"Deal. Let's both sign two napkins with the $100,000 amount and each keep a copy," Del said.

Carrie tried to stop her hand from shaking as she signed the napkins.

~

She found Bill, Harry, and Jon in the parking lot waiting for her with arms crossed, leaning against Bill's black Cadillac STS.

Carrie said, "The bet for each of you is $2,000."

"What do you mean, 'each of you'?" Bill Brayer said.

She started to lie but knew her astute colleagues would see right through it. She felt embarrassed.

"Well, it's $94,000 for me," she said.

"Jesus Christ, Carrie," said Harry Johnson.

"Carrie, are you completely nuts?" Jon said.

"Carrie, I'd love to back you, but I'd be looking for a new wife if I bet $25,000," Bill Brayer said.

"You men don't get it, do you? Why would I expect men to get it?"

Fire came into her eyes. The men uncrossed their arms and stood erect.

"It's your world, your club, isn't it? Women belong on the tennis courts or in the card room or playing mah-jongg. Men can decide to trash a woman's reputation, throw adultery in her face, make her feel lost and crazy, and then insinuate she's a gold digger while playing by the legal rules. I know how they talk behind my back around here. I was somebody *before* I married Carl, *before* I joined this club, and I'm somebody *after* the divorce. I want to see that bastard Del squirm. Screw him," she said.

"I appreciate your sentiment. Still, Carrie, I can't bet that kind of money," Bill said.

"What the hell. Carrie and I will split the exposure on the $96,000," Jon said.

"Jon—" Carrie started to say.

"You hush ... for once. I owe you. For more than I care to share right now, right here in this parking lot. Forty-eight thousand is nothing compared to what I owe you. I'll make that in interest on my investments in a few months. I believe the worm will collapse under pressure, too. Bill and Harry, just stay within your games."

"OK. In Carrie We Trust," Harry said. "Jesus, a $100,000 bet that I know nothing about! The largest bet I've ever made was $2,000."

"Me, too. But I think Carrie and Jon are right. Del will fold under pressure," Bill Brayer said.

Captain Bill Brayer's team met for dinner on Wednesday night at McCormick & Schmick's in Bethesda. The team expected Bill and Jon to play even-up with their two adversaries in the first foursome. It was essential, therefore, for Harry and Carrie to stay within seven strokes of George and Del. The collective view was that George would play solidly; Harry would have to stay with him. But Del would collapse under the pressure. That was the thinking and everyone bought into the group mindset.

Bill Brayer and Del were team captains.

After eighteen holes, in spite of their optimism over drinks at McCormick & Schmick's, Bill Brayer and Jon Rhodes lost by three strokes—not the even score they had imagined. Playing slower, the second foursome was about to hit their drives on the seventeenth tee. Harry and Carrie had seven strokes higher than George and Del. So, Carrie and Judge Brayer's foursome, collectively, was ten strokes over Del's foursome and running out of holes to get within seven strokes to win.

With stellar play by Carrie and obvious choking by Del, at the end of seventeen holes, Brayer's team trimmed the deficit to six strokes to take the lead. If they held on, they would win by a stroke.

Carrie's mind raced as she walked toward the eighteenth tee. She thought of Carl. She wondered if Carl ever mentioned his dalliances to Del. Stop it, she said to herself. As she had been taught by Marcus and reinforced by Jon, she tried to visualize her winning shots.

But the eighteenth hole favored long hitters: advantage, Del's crew. On the eighteenth tee box, the two pairs huddled away from each other. Whatever George said to Del, Carrie noticed, Del seemed to be comforted—the cockiness returned to his posture.

On this long par five, 512-yard hole, Harry and George were on the green in three shots and both easily pared.

Carrie and Del, however, were both in greenside sand traps in three shots. Del loved sand shots. She hated them. They scared her to death. She had been known to choke badly in the sand. Carrie waited beside the trap for Del to hit. Her heart pounded. Her knees shook. She looked up to see Bill and Jon smiling at her. Jon made a hand motion, one he had used hundreds of times at sand traps to remind her to hit *under* the ball, as if a tee were propping the ball up under the sand. *Hit the tee*, the hand gesture meant. She got his message and smiled as if to say, "Sure, now I just have to do it."

Del hit out of the left trap. It was a lovely swing, and the ball hit six feet from the pin. Unfortunately, it didn't stop, and ended up twenty-two feet from the flag. His putt would require a crafted, severe right-to-left break *back* to the flag to make a par five.

As she stood over her ball, Carrie became iron-like. The stance made Jon twitch. She blasted at the ball. It moved exactly three feet, still in the sand. Now, she too, had taken four strokes. The crowd around the green, about thirty members, made an awful moan. All of them had heard about the bet. They clustered together in separate groups of men and women, as if this were the Billy Jean King Battle of the Sexes, Part II. She trudged to the ball and thought to herself: *You* weren't *listening to Jon. You were* pretending *to be listening to Jon. Jon is your friend. Jon isn't Carl. Now hit under the goddamned ball, hit the goddamned pretend tee under the sand, and try and keep it somewhere in goddamned Montgomery County. You can do this, Carrie.*

Her stroke was more relaxed, and the ball floated out of the sand, landing fourteen feet from the pin. She had taken five shots.

Three ladies actually clapped.

Del hit his twenty-two foot putt, his fifth shot. The ball rolled toward the hole. It broke left, dead-on the hole, as planned. Victory was in sight, and he started to jump in the air, until he saw his ball hit a pebble, which threw it off line, further left, by about half an inch from the left lip of the hole, ending some seven feet from the hole. He was, everyone agreed, simply robbed. He had taken five strokes, too.

Carrie then putted to within two inches of the hole. George conceded the tap in, which appeared to piss Del off. Her score was a double bogey seven.

Del missed his seven-foot putt, his sixth shot and one that would have tied the match. He angrily picked up his ball, conceding the match.

Only six strokes more than the score of Del's team, the match belonged to Judge Brayer's team.

Bill whispered to his teammates, "Act like you've been there before. Don't let that bastard know we sweated!"

Then everyone shook hands.

Bill, Harry, Jon, and Carrie, surrounded by friends and well-wishers, had several drinks in the clubhouse.

Del walked up to her and whispered out of earshot from the others, "Congratulations. Good luck with your project."

~

They drove together in Judge Brayer's car to McCormick & Schmick's that night. Captain Bill's foursome drank and told stories of the day with robust laughter. Each was getting snockered. Brayer's law clerk agreed to drive the foursome home.

"What are we doing with the money?" asked Bill Brayer.

"I'm donating my share to a 501(c)(3) foundation we're just starting in the community. Jon, this is our TJ award money!" Carrie said, hugging him.

"So will I…. I like that. Mildred will hear about today's events, I'm sure. I can deny the bet and say no money ever touched my hands," Bill Brayer said.

"Carrie, you can have my share, too," said Harry Johnson.

"Dinner's on you three. Never doubt a determined woman…. Oh, and it helps to be surrounded by such clutch players!" she said.

Captain Bill's team drank and closed the restaurant, recalling key moments in their conquest.

36

THE LOVE BIRDS DO LUNCH

Judge Harry Johnson

He was, as usual, on time. She was, as usual, late—by about ten minutes this time. In his courtroom, he would have grilled an attorney for tardiness. But he'd never grill her. Judge Harry T. Johnson, the distinguished, articulate, black judge and Carrie's golfing buddy, waited at the couple's usual corner table, away from the hubbub at the restaurant Citronelle. With her familiar flare, Senator Barbara Washington joined him, with a kiss on each cheek. Just seeing her sent a rush through his veins—and one vein in particular. To him, she was the sexiest woman alive. The physical aspects of their affair, by agreement, had ended long ago; the excitement that each caused in the other had not. Theirs, he believed, was an endless teenage-like version of puppy love. He hung on her every word; she, he thought, paid close attention to everything he said. He always listened to a favorite romantic CD on the way to meet her. Their time together barely, just barely, made up for the emptiness he felt when he was apart from her. He had sufficient reason to believe the same was true for her. Unsaid was his belief that some day, somehow, they'd be together. Harry and Barbara were in love.

They first met at a fundraiser for her nearly ten years ago. She had consoled him when his wife walked out on him and their children. Soon after, at his initiative, they had lunch. They dined together five or six times before she invited him back to her condo, where she lived alone. The physical component of their heated love affair lasted nine months. It ended months before she was elected to her first term as senator; the same time Harry's wife decided she would return to being the Judge's wife and mother to her three children. Something had died in Harry Johnson's relationship with his wife, though. It could best be described as spontaneity.

When Senator Washington called him to arrange this lunch, she said she needed help with an issue. For him, helping Barbara would be a thrill.

"There's an issue in your court, Harry, and with the Maryland Parole Commission. You know I'd never presume to tell you how to manage your court, but I want to share my concerns directly," she said.

"Go on, Barbara," he said.

She told him of Hattie Rogers and gang. She reminded him, as he painfully knew, that the Congress had gone too far in the creation of mandatory tough-on-crime sentencing guidelines, herself included, but she was very concerned with the number of persons going back to prison for technical violations of the conditions of release, not for new crimes. She handed him a two-page report on the violation rates for Montgomery County, supplied by a Hattie-Carrie collaborative effort. The paper showed that over several years, 57 percent of all cases closed on parole and probation were revoked, or a total of 7,057 persons. Of that group, 2,117 had committed new crimes—felonies or misdemeanors. The balance, 70 percent, were closed by violation, were technical violators—*without* new arrests or new crimes. A few, she said, as best her staff could tell from the records, were for absconding. Catching them and sending them back to prison made sense, she reasoned.

"But the rest? My staff estimates that somewhere between 10 and 45 percent of persons in prisons in Maryland, at any given time, could be there for technical violations—rules violations—at a cost of $30,000 per year.

"Are you sure this data is accurate?" he asked.

"As best as we can tell, darling," she said.

"'Darling' always means something's coming … so to speak," he said.

"Stop playing."

She told him of her recent actions with the Department of Justice and how she cornered the deputy attorney general into examining the use of prisons and jails for technical violators.

He had already heard of "the request." He smiled at her tactical skills. She talked about Hattie and her friends' interest in the essential ingredients of the profession. She reminded Harry that the Cuatro

Amigos, like both of them, believed people could change their behavior.

"I'm fully aware of the J. Trenton Axelrod debacle. So, Barbara, could you get to the point? There are no votes here for you.... I can't vote twice," he said.

She started to tell him the story of TJ.

"I know the circumstances through Hattie Rogers," he said.

"It's so easy to pigeonhole people, Harry, until we see the very *real* people our policies effect," she said.

"Interesting concept coming from the legislative branch," he said. But, as a black man, he understood her point quite well. "And ...?"

Barbara plowed forward. "Will you do something for me? Will you arrange for Officer Brooks to present TJ's case in a case study format to the judges—with a twist: bring in TJ's widow to hear her version?"

"That would be highly unusual!"

She didn't blink. "Lots of things are highly unusual—my love for you is highly unusual! I understand TJ's widow, Junie Edwards-Smith, speaks well on her feet. It wouldn't be a bloodletting. Harry, we owe this to all the young black men, women, and children who are left behind. We owe them, Harry. They need us, Harry, to tell their story." She said, appearing to be finished, but only taking a breath.

"We—you and I—owe *our* people, Harry. They've given us so much. There are very few things that I love that I've let slip out of my hands, Harry," she said, pausing for emphasis, while staring into his eyes as only she could do with him, "I don't want this one—help me not let this one, this *opportunity*—get away."

"Barbara, Barbara, Barbara.... What am I going to do with you?" he said, as his hands slid across the table and squeezed her arms. His words would have seemed appropriate in a transcript of the conversation; however, the look on his face and the warmth in his touch gave the comment an obvious double meaning.

"Now that's a penalty, Harry. Illegal use of the hands!"

"My hands would be just a start!"

They laughed, as only lovers do when enjoying an inside joke.

37

TRAINING: THE RUBBER MEETS THE ROAD

Gee Brooks

It was time to put up or shut up in a conference call. Gee led Rick Volzano, Abba White Cloud, and Maria Sanchez, surrounded by Hattie, Pepe, and Huggie, and she gained their support for the idea that listening and communication skills were the gateway to their humanistic revolution. The newsletter had assiduously stressed that their interest was *not* the development of projects, programs, or initiatives.

"Now I'm prepared to bet the farm that the training is on target. This is the point of no return," Gee said.

Volzano agreed to announce in the newsletter and on the Web site that the Nuevos Principios Society was pleased to offer two-day Listening and Communication Skills workshops. This announcement would also be carried by the WWTS newsletter. The announcement would include sites, provide the dates, and establish cut-off dates for registration.

They agreed that if the registration for a workshop did not reach twenty-five attendees by the end of the registration period, the event would be cancelled.

Gee announced, too, that, by agreement, participants would receive a certificate of completion from the Chesapeake Consulting Group. Gee emphasized that the workshops were for everyone, not just probation and parole officers.

Rick and Abba reported that twenty-three workshops were scheduled in the first six months.

Six months later, again by conference call, Gee reported what everyone already knew: nineteen Listening and Communication workshops were actually presented, four were cancelled. The attendees' evaluations—

conducted by an independent Ph.D. candidate—of the workship, blog responses, and follow-up e-mail interviews on the lasting applications of the training, found that evaluations were exceedingly high, but, more importantly, that the skills taught, respondents said, were believed to be useful and relatively easy to implement, both on the job and in their personal lives. A total of 546 persons completed the training. Strikingly, beyond the expected probation/parole professionals, attendees included eighteen clerks, Olivia Lopez, six community police officers, seven lay leaders from two churches, two community outreach specialist, twelve domestic violence workers, thirty-six teachers, six clergy or youth pastors, 135 community organization representatives including Jon Rhodes and Carrie Springer, representatives from the YMCA, Boys & Girls Clubs, a Teen Pregnancy Prevention Task Force, twelve retirees, thirty volunteers with attendance paid by their agencies, twenty-seven nurses; two bus drivers, and one judge—Judge Glenny B. Clarke, representing the Association of Women Judges and a referral of Hattie Rogers.

Gee walked the team through the second featured strategy: to advance the essential ingredients training for officers. There was both a mystical and practical quality to the formation of the essential ingredients.

Gee explained, "We couldn't create them—who'd care? They couldn't be retread old stuff—who'd pay attention? If they were derived from common sense alone, they probably wouldn't make much of an impact. They come from what people are saying is *missing*. Now, that's art at work! The question remains, will they resonate?"

One by one, Rick, Abba, and even Huggie began to express long withheld doubts about this essential ingredients business. All along, they said, this aspect felt dicey. Hattie stepped in quickly.

"Hey guys, guys, hold on! We've operated on trust that Gee would bring back something good from her consultations," Hattie said. "Our job was to get the pulse of what the officers felt was really important in their work. We all felt that it was critical to incorporate the consensus from bloggers. We've done that. Take a deep breath. Here's what Gee's said all along: everything has essential ingredients and if you don't get them right, you'll never succeed. That's all. It's not rocket science. It's a foundation for working with people. Let's give her some room."

There was a long pause.

"OK, fair enough. This is what I propose—" Gee started.

In spite of Hattie's brushback pitch, Rick interrupted, "OK, I give up. What are the five essential ingredients?"

"I'm getting there, darling. First, the process: We announce in the newsletter that the next five newsletters will address the Five Essential Ingredients—let's just start calling them the 5-EI—that probation and parole officers need to reach excellence. Each newsletter will address one essential ingredient. We'll stress that, without feedback and consensus, the essential ingredients would be of no more value than the useless mission statements in their manuals."

"OK," said Pepe.

"OK, here's one: don't chew bubble gun while making out with a girl with braces," said Rick.

"My, aren't we anxious? Stay with me, I'm getting there," Gee laughed. "Pull up the attachment I just e-mailed you guys, while I hand the 5-EI to my local knuckleheads. Here goes:

1.   LISTENING & COMMUNICATION SKILLS
       Learn listening skills that help us understand what offenders are saying to us and techniques to build rapport.

2.   FIRM-FACTUAL-FRIENDLY TONE (FFF)
       The culture of our organizations is what we decide to make it. It should have three qualities:
       Firm: Firm means individuals in the organization say what they mean and mean what they say. Firm is not to be confused with punishing or being rude.
       Factual: Being factual increases an understanding of the requirements and boundaries.
       Friendly: Be friendly means be respectful. Friendly doesn't mean 'being friends.'

3.   BE THERE
       Be in the moment.

4.   FIND COMMUNITY SUPPORT
      Find the sources of help that are already in the communities
      and neighborhoods.

5.   MINING FOR GOLD
      Every person has special gifts, talents, abilities and motivation.
      It's the job of officers to seek them out in those on their case-
      load and find points of resilience that can be expanded upon.
      State clearly, 'We want you to make it.'"

~

Weeks later, again in a phone conference, the same team members discussed the blog comments on the 5-EI.

Gee said, "Pepe and I read every comment. We guessed that 90 percent of the responses were positive. It doesn't get any better than that. What do you think, Houston, do we have a go?"

"The responses were better than I thought they'd be. I just don't like the name 'essential ingredients.' Then again, I didn't like Nuevos Principios Society, either," Rick said.

After considerable discussion, the Nuevos Principios team endorsed the 5-EI. Later, they laughed as they quizzed each other to repeat them in thirty seconds. Out went thousands of 5-EI cards, the size of a credit card, to bloggers, paid for by *WWTS*. It read simply:

The Nuevos Principios Society
With Support ... People Can Change
The 5-EI

"Back to the Chesapeake Group to finalize the training they've already started developing. Most of the training will focus on a solutions-focused approach, asset mapping, boundary setting, mediation, negotiation, conflict resolution, role clarity, and, most importantly, creative problem solving techniques," Gee said.

~

A modest retreat location was found with a meeting room that could hold up to sixty participants. Financial challenges aside, the Cuatro Amigos realized that if the number of participants making the commitment of time and money numbered only four—namely, the Cuatro Amigos—they would certainly lose momentum. Attendance at the training was the new point of no return. The next newsletter announced the first training. It read:

The Five Essential Ingredients Toward Excellence in Probation and Parole

Sponsored by the Nuevos Principios Society
November 1-3, 2004
Hallowood Retreat Center, Comus, Maryland

For more information contact the Nuevos Principios Society at www.nuevosprincipios.com

---

Participants were given until August 1 to sign up.

The Cuatro Amigos, Rick Volzano, Abba White Cloud, and Maria Sanchez waited.

Within ten days, the number of attendees who had placed a $100 deposit for the training reached fifty-seven, of whom thirty-three were from Montgomery County. This news signaled to the Nuevos Principios team that there was both national and local interest.

However, the old theatre adage applied to the post-training evaluations and responses: if you show a gun in Act One, you'd better fire it by Act Three. If the training flopped, Gee knew the Cuatro Amigos would be remembered as overachieving dreamers. They'd be dead in their tracks. Then what?

There was concern on everyone's part about the training. Most participants worried, among themselves, that the two three-day training sessions wouldn't be applicable. They were willing to give the process the benefit of the doubt but with a small margin for error. Several questions, in particular, were circulating: Would the training be boring? Would participants get lost in squabbles about "in my district?" Would they leave thinking that they'd heard good stuff but would never use it on the job? There was a lot of doubt as the training began. Even though Gee knew that her father said the trainers changed *his* life, days before the first three-day event, she was wigglier than a three-year-old child on a wooden pew in a long, hot church service.

Everyone would have had *more*, not *less*, doubt, had they been privy to the debate going on between the two Chesapeake Consulting Group trainers about how to condense eighty hours of materials into less than forty hours of classroom time. And the participants would have to have fun—it was their nickel.

The closing event of the last day was a feedback session. One participant described the power and influence of the opening exercise on Day One as, "You had me at hello." She was referencing what happened after an icebreaker. The two trainers pulled out Automated Responder System equipment to conduct a spontaneous survey designed by Art Coleman. Used on TV quiz shows, this radio frequency equipment had the audience using individual keypads to enter responses to PowerPoint questions. The participants' responses were displayed immediately, with percentages. Some key questions and the answers from the fifty-seven attendees in the opening exercise were:

1. MOST CITIZENS IN MY DISTRICT FEEL UNSAFE WITH REGARD TO CRIME.

Answer: 90 percent responded "strongly agree."

2. HOW MANY TIMES IN THE PAST YEAR DID YOU MEET WITH COMMUNITY GROUPS OR ASSOCIATIONS?

Most frequent answer: "less than two."

3. WHAT WOULD OTHERS SAY IS THE CHARACTERISTIC THAT YOU MOST OFTEN DISPLAY ON THE JOB?

Answer: 80 percent responded "tough-minded, but fair."

4. THE MAIN REASON THAT BROUGHT ME TO THE JOB OF PROBATION OFFICER WAS:

Answer: 95 percent responded "to make a difference in the lives of others."

5.IN MY CURRENT ACTIVITIES, WHAT PERCENTAGE OF TIME DO I FEEL THIS VALUE (ANSWER TO QUESTION 4) IS ALIVE AND KICKING?

Most frequent answer: "11-25 percent of the time."

6.I BELIEVE MOST PERSONS ON SUPERVISION HAVE *AT LEAST ONE* SIGNIFICANT PERSON IN THEIR LIVES WITH PRO-SOCIAL VALUES (FAMILY, CHURCH, AND COMMUNITY).

Answer: 100 percent agreement.

7.HOW MANY OF THESE SIGNIFICANT PERSONS (FROM QUESTION 6) DO YOU TYPICALLY KNOW, PER CASE?

Most frequent answer: On average zero or one per case.

It appeared to Gee that differences between participants faded away as their answers appeared in the aggregate. A saying was displayed: "We didn't come over on the same ship, but we are in the same boat together now!"

With similarities in beliefs and attitudes displayed using the spontaneous electronic survey equipment, participants talked frankly about what they referred to as the "dismal swamp" of their profession. There was a consensus in the room now, expressed by one participant's comment: "We can do better than that!"

Summing up his views at the end of the training, one participant said emotionally:

"I feel like I've been handed one of those foreign language translator headphones at the UN. After three days, I hear and understand things clearer. I never imagined I missed so much before. This is what I came into this field to do. There are also some family members at home who will benefit from my new skills. My wife will be startled."

At the end of the training, alone in her car on the way to meet Huggie and Rosa, Hattie, Pepe and Olivia, and Carrie and Jon at Carrie's house, Gee didn't know whether to scream with happiness or cry with joy ... so she did both ... all the way down Route 270.

Gee was in a state of euphoria. She felt brain-dead and tired, yet happy and relieved. She had underestimated the stress she was carrying over the success of the training. The entire group gravitated into a circle at Carrie's house and told or *re*told stories—fears of being fired, the Baltimore Civic Center ordeal, the Happy Hour at the Colts4Evr Bar and Grille, the misplaced files, Dora Kingmaker's threats, the Four Live wires, Ms. Lilly and CASI, and other stories. There were no periods, no pauses—just endless, connected joy.

After many beers, Gee said goodnight to hugs and kisses.

"You mean after waiting months to do five days of tailing Brooks and Gomez, they have nothing? Nothing? You mean we couldn't catch them arriving late, leaving early, meeting on government time for some BS activity? They couldn't even catch Gomez? Holy shit," Kingmaker said.

"Dora, Inspector Poole said it was almost like they knew they were being tailed," Chip said.

"Shit, Poole is an asshole," she said.

Kingmaker decided to express her concerns about the comments being made on the Nuevos Principios blog. In a memo she wrote, "I find many of the comments objectionable and clearly anti-management. I seek your permission to initiate adverse action against Brooks, Gomez, Winston, and Rogers."

"Maybe, Chip, we'll have our answer soon," she said to Faulknour the next morning over coffee.

38

CHIEF KASTEN'S REVIVAL

Robert Kasten

Chief Probation Officer Robert Kasten, one week into October, felt buoyed by the news of the two 5-EI training events. His officers were buzzing about applying what they'd learned. The two trainings, including the previous Listening and Communication workshops, were described as the best the officers had ever attended.

He also had three memos on his desk: one from Judge Clarke, another from Assistant Public Defender Olivia Lopez, and a third from Dora Kingmaker. Clarke's and Lopez's memos praised the Listening and Communication workshop; Kingmaker's complained about the blog.

Kasten had been slowly shaken out of his automatic pilot approach to leading the office. Chairman Axelrod's debacle, miraculously, hadn't landed squarely on him; he was able to claim that he hadn't been fully informed about Operation Øman, which was partially accurate and a little in the gray area, by way of a Clintonesque "what constitutes fully informed?" He told his wife that Judge Brayer bought his explanation with a caveat. Brayer said to him that "the Parole Commission had better not step in the court's domain again—and the court better not be behind the eight ball again on your watch again." Message received, Kasten told his wife. She told her sister that it was the first time Bob had talked about his work in over five years.

What followed after Judge Brayer's warning equally shook Kasten. He got a phone call from an old colleague in Oklahoma City, who wanted to know about this Nuevos Principios Society thing.

Kasten's response was, "What do you mean?"

The caller thought Kasten meant, "What do you mean, questioning me?" Kasten meant, "What do you mean?"

The caller ended with, "Robert Kasten, you're a gutsy guy. Keep up the good work. It's about time we kicked some butt."

Kasten was in the dark.

Two days later, an irate chief probation officer and colleague from another district called and said, "Why don't you fire the bastards? What do they want, to empty the prisons?"

Kasten allowed that he was on top of the situation.

That same day, a reporter from Oakland, California, called and asked if Kasten was in jeopardy of being fired for being soft-on-crime. Robert Kasten brushed the reporter off, but Judge Brayer's words were still ringing in his ear—"not on your watch again."

He dug into everything the Nuevos Principios Society wrote. He was pleased with what he read. He began to get up to speed on national criminal justice issues. He was appalled by the macho, law enforcement bent the field had taken. He realized his own officers and his court had followed suit blindly.

All of this paled in comparison with the jolt he got from another phone call, one he had waited for anxiously.

At 10:30 AM, his sister-in-law called from his wife's internist office.

"Robert, meet us at home," she said.

For a week, Margaret Kasten complained about double vision, weakness, and slurred speech. Today, his wife was told that she had progressive MS, which would eventually be terminal. What lay ahead was a long struggle for survival. Margaret and the chief both knew that. For reasons of potential health care costs, income, and the recent sparkle back in Robert's eyes, Margaret insisted that the last thing she wanted or needed was for him to retire.

"I don't want you moping around the house," she said.

He was grateful and relieved. He wanted something to do to balance the daily agony of watching her suffer.

After conferring with Judge Brayer, who was sympathetic to Margaret's illness, he received permission to continue working—at least for the four year tenure of Judge Brayer's administration.

~

Kasten received a second e-mail from Dora Kingmaker and Chip Faulknour requesting a meeting to discuss their plans for adverse action against Gee Brooks, Huggie Winston, Hattie Rogers, and Hector Gomez.

He summoned them into his office. As they sat in front of him, side-by-side in thick leather chairs, Dora stared at the multitude of framed photographs over his shoulder.

"It's past time to take action, Chief. I suggest that we take this all the way to the end game for the four of them," said Dora. "Strike while the iron's hot. We've got damning information from their case files: oversights, late entries, blog stuff, insulting the parole chairman, terrible recommendations for sentencing, poor writing skills, on and on—enough to fire them, or at least demote them, and run them off."

There was something particularly irritating to Kasten about Kingmaker's tone. It was as if he was hearing a tone in her that he had chosen to be deaf to before this moment. It struck an unpleasant nerve, like dental hygienists do when using picks to scrape gums and teeth clean. He realized that months ago, maybe even days ago, he would have acquiesced to Kingmaker's will. But it dawned on him that it was Gee and the others who were expressing the very same spirit that he had when he came into the system some thirty-two years ago, before he was burned out, before he stopped caring. It was then, when he stopped caring, that something died in him at work and at home. Now, he regretted that he had allowed that to happen. He felt particularly guilty for losing his spirit around Margaret. *I've become a dullard,* he thought. Now, time was precious.

He put an end to Kingmaker's recommendation with this statement, "I'm ordering you two to leave them alone. I'm not asking you—I'm *ordering* you. Do you two understand me?" he asked.

"Yes, sir," they said in unison.

"Make no mistake—if either of you does *one thing,*" he held up his index finger, "to bring harm to them, I'll have your jobs—and I don't care how high up or how powerful your friends are.... I have friends, too!"

Kasten had wanted to say that to Kingmaker for some time. He had just never had the passion, until now.

"Now, if you've gone through their files, go through everybody's to the same degree. And then, after you've done that, I want you two to plan how you're going to fix the problems you find, and then give me a report on your plans. I've let you two have your day. That day is over. Wake up and smell the coffee! Walk down the halls—listen, as I have, to how excited the officers are about the recent training their society held! I don't give a rat's ass if we diametrically oppose everything that's being held up as cool by every probation and parole office in the country. My money's on them and their vision. They got it right. And so will we get it right around here. Neither one of you will send out one more policy memo or e-mail that is not expressly cleared through me. Got it?"

"Yes, sir," they said.

Kasten swiveled his chair toward the windows and away from Kingmaker and Faulknour. They rose and departed without a word.

"Jesus, Dora—" said Faulknour, entering the hallway.

"I'll get his ass fired.... I will," she said.

Dora Kingmaker tried fourteen times in the next ten days to reach her friend, the governor. Her voice messages were not returned. Finally, she stopped trying.

Upon delivering the news in a manager's meeting that he had the court's nod to continue as chief, a tacit sign of support, Kasten sent an e-mail to all staff that contained word of his wife's illness and his plan to continue as chief for the foreseeable future. Kingmaker was furious. She knew this meant that Kasten had Judge Brayer's support, or else Brayer wouldn't have blessed an open-ended tenure. She surmised that her plan to have Judge Cox drop the word to the governor to influence Judge Brayer to fire Kasten didn't work—for whatever reason. *Assholes*, she thought.

She scheduled a trip to San Juan, Puerto Rico, for mid-December and left the dates and hotel information on the governor's cell phone. Maybe that would attract his attention—he was the one who had raised the possibility of getting away together. She knew if she got him alone outside the country for several days she would have a chance to reinvigorate her career, hopefully in Washington, D.C.

Following Senator Washington's manipulations in Congress, including the threat of a GAO investigation on contemporary revocation practices, rumors abounded throughout Maryland's criminal justice agencies that statewide policy changes were imminent. Robert Kasten liked the wave of action—it touched something in him. In Montgomery County, the collaborations fueled by the Community Unity Breakfasts inspired Kasten to experiment with a team-oriented idea he called the Weekly Meeting Format. He picked up elements of his plan from an article in a Harvard Business Review. Kasten first discussed his idea with Judge Brayer, who gave his approval, then with seven officers and their supervisor. Gee heard about Kasten's idea through other officers. The plan was for officers to form area-based community teams, plan what they'd do with every offender, seek ideas and feedback from teammates, and reach out to the local community.

It was brilliant in its simplicity. The supervisor and officers were encouraged to innovate, but to stay with the concept. Officers were floored. "Direct feedback" officers kept repeating to each other, incredulously. Kasten had stumbled into a new day. After just four weekly team meetings, the supervisor and officers in the experimental unit raved about the process.

Chip Faulknour volunteered to be the second unit to try out the process. Waiting for his officers to arrive for their first team meeting, in a small conference room, he said to Gee, the only officer present, "You know, it's funny—Kingmaker appears to be out of the loop on this team meeting thing."

"I noticed," Gee said.

She also noticed that Faulknour was slowly distancing himself from Kingmaker, too. Speaking as individuals, the Cuatro Amigos supported the team process to Faulknour. For once, Huggie didn't mumble in the unit meeting. Gee was surprised by Kasten's action—and from the head of the department, no less.

39

THE JUDGE'S EPIPHANY

Chief Judge Bill Brayer

Days after the sterling golf match victory at the CCC in September and back in the role of judge, Bill Brayer listened intently to testimony from a witness in a jury trial. The witness was guided by an able defense attorney. Out of the corner of his eye, he noticed Carrie entering his courtroom in a stunning, blue, patterned dress. He noticed, too, that she tried to be quiet, tiptoeing as women do, to avoid clicking her heels on the marble floors. He watched her find a seat in a middle row of the crowded courtroom. He glanced at her, trying to be inconspicuous. She made eye contact and gave him one of those silly little waves with her fingers only. He, in return, smiled ever-so-slightly.

Brayer knew well the line of reasoning the defense attorney's argument was taking, and, in fact, he agreed with her presentation. He drifted into thought, as he glanced at Carrie, about how differently we see our friends when they're *outside* of their professional roles—when they're out of their element. Like a minister with a glass of wine in her hand or cops helping little children learn something new or teachers in their roles as mothers. Like the TV coverage of a well-known conservative Christian pastor caught having sex with a hooker. The associated images change a person in our eyes, forever. *We never*, he thought, *see them in the same light again.*

Sometimes that's sad, even tragic, he thought. Other times, when we see a friend out of their element, such as at a christening, a wedding, or a funeral, it can shift the relationship toward greater intimacy. We feel we've seen a more human, vulnerable side.

He looked again at Carrie, who was listening intently to the defense attorney. Her presence had an eerie effect on him. He felt humbled. He took a long breath and exhaled. Immediately, it no longer felt necessary, or even appropriate, for him to use his typical, haughty judicial tone. In fact, it seemed overbearing and out of character. He could never act

356

that way in front of Carrie. *For God's sake*, he thought, *she would laugh out loud.*

It was the last moment Chief Judge William Brayer ever carried himself in a haughty manner or used an officious, overbearing tone in his courtroom. Instead, he adopted a factual, and, well, almost *friendly* demeanor in the courtroom, one more fitting his real character.

40

THE JUDGES GET A JOLT

Gee Brooks

Gee waited in the halls for Junie Edwards-Smith. She paced and thought, *please don't be late—they'll never give us a second chance.* Besides, Chief Kasten had been explicit, "Be prepared to tell about TJ's death, briefly, and then let Mrs. Smith tell her side—but tell her to be brief, too. Ms. Brooks, don't piss them off! You'll never get a second chance."

This meeting was risky. She was surprised by the invitation—well, order—to appear. She had no idea of its origin.

Judges give great deference to other judges, in part because they're from different political parties or generations and in part because they believe they're each independent captains of their own courtrooms—with the minor irritating factor of the appellate review process looking over their decisions.

When in a group, such as at this monthly judges' meeting, judges tend to get off track easily. Fueled by deference, they also tend to get lost in the magnificence of their own voices. So, judges' meetings can go in any direction, and they can go on forever. For this reason, Chief Judge Bill Brayer, responsible for the administration of the Montgomery County Circuit Court, ran a very tight monthly judges' meeting.

Judge Brayer opened the meeting with this statement, "As you know, Judge Johnson has asked us to take about fifteen minutes, removed from our busy calendars, to consider whether we are 'on target,' as Harry puts it, with the supervision of the persons on probation."

Judge Brayer ignored, by way of a slight smile, the rumbling comments about "*never* being removed from busy calendars." More than one judge sounded like Phineus T. Bluster of the old *Howdy Doody* television show: jabbering about God knows what. Judges like to talk about their long hours the same way construction workers brag about how much overtime they've worked in a busy summer week.

"More specifically, Judge Johnson would like to address what happens to offenders that don't make it, because we revoke their supervision. I thank Chief Probation Officer Kasten for joining us today. So, let me turn the balance of the meeting over to Judge Johnson," said Judge Brayer.

"Ladies and gentlemen, like you, I pride myself on interpreting the law. It is, I suppose, what we do best. Recently, I've been informed that in this district alone, over several years, 57 percent of persons on parole or probation supervision have had their cases revoked." He continued, giving the figures provided by Senator Washington's staff.

"Those violations were mostly, I believe, for failure to abide by the special conditions so near and dear to our hearts. A goodly number of those revocation hearings were heard by you. No wonder our calendars are stacked! The balance was handled by our friends at the Parole Commission. Now, I don't know the racial make-up of those returned to prison, but I'd guess they would look a great deal like Judge Clarke and me. Ladies and gentlemen, what monster have we created?" Judge Johnson asked.

All hell broke loose. The implication that judges, albeit unintentionally, may be part of a racist problem, broke judicial protocol.

The judges offered competing explanations for why so many offenders came back to their courts for violating the many special conditions of their supervision.

"They don't live by our rules!" said one.

"They can't hold jobs!" said another.

Judge Johnson reasserted command and control, as he did in his courtroom every day.

"Many are wondering what condition our special conditions are in. Have they become Judicial Honey-do Trip Wires?" he asked.

Now, there were fourteen conversations underway—that is, fourteen talkers and no listeners.

Judge Brayer came to the rescue to restore order.

"I have the utmost confidence you'll be open-minded as you examine your own practices. I also have confidence that you'll give thought to the use of multiple special conditions," Judge Brayer said, over the noise, trying to corral the breakaway conversations.

"But I thought that multiple special conditions *helped* the probation officer keep the difficult cases on the straight and narrow!" said Senior Judge Cox. "You mean someone is saying they don't help? Why didn't someone say something before now?"

"Maybe it's because the senior Democratic judge bit their heads off too frequently," said a junior Republican, with the effect of rolling a hand grenade into a craps game.

"Come now. They were never afraid to speak up to me when I was the chief judge, were you Mr. Kasten?" asked Judge Cox.

Chief Kasten smiled, but said nothing.

The younger Republicans snickered.

A moderate Republican judge said, "Sometimes, we forget that most of us gave much of our time and plenty of our money to be *appointed* to these judgeships—not *anointed* by the Almighty."

Snickers erupted around the large mahogany conference table.

Fourteen individual conversations erupted again.

Judge Johnson sought to control the flap. "I'm asking Judge Brayer to explore this issue with Chief Kasten and report back to us for next month's meeting. What can we learn from reviewing the data? Maybe we'll find a correlation between multiple special conditions and the high rate of revocations based solely on technical violations. And, if we do, we should consider adjusting our own practices before the governor, some goddamned DOJ official, or an academic researcher tells us what we need to do. Of course, I'm not suggesting anyone here has acted in any way other than to pursue justice at the highest degree of integrity. But I do ask for a few more minutes of your time to hear a brief, personal case study. Is that OK, ladies and gentlemen?"

"What? This is unprecedented!" said one judge, looking at other judges for support.

After a few more grumbles, Judge Johnson continued. "I've asked Officer Brooks to present the case study. This is a parole case handled by our friends over at the Commission."

He waited for the predictable chuckles to subside.

"The issue is: what can we learn from this case about our court practices? Ms. Brooks will be joined by a parolee's widow," he said, gesturing for Chief Kasten to summon Ms. Brooks and Junie Edwards-Smith, before the judges had a chance to pontificate further.

Admittedly, the mood was somewhat lighter now that the judges realized they would be considering a Parole Commission case, and not one of the brethren.

As Chief Kasten returned to the meeting room, he had an awkward look on his face. Behind him, as expected, was the easily recognizable Gee Brooks, followed by an attractive thirty-something black woman *and* two small children—a boy and a girl.

Judge Johnson started to stumble all over himself, as his colleagues sat up stiffly. Even he didn't expect the children!

"Ms. Brooks, it was my understanding ..." Judge Johnson started to say.

"I'm sorry, Your Honors. I think I know how this might appear. My name is Junie Edwards-Smith. These are my two children, Tommy and Natasha. I've told them what a wonderful job you judges do to keep all of us safe, and I just wanted them to meet you and for you to meet them, before I send them out of the room. They may want to be judges one day, too. Now, they have school work to do," said Junie, with one hand on each child's head.

The children said simultaneously, "Nice to meet you," indicating that slight pressure was being applied to the backs of their heads by their mother's hands and that they had rehearsed this humble greeting.

The judges acted charmed and reached out to these children with kind small talk. Then, their mother whisked them out of the room, as promised.

The judges appeared to sit back more fully in their heavily padded, black leather chairs.

Gee told the story of TJ, from meeting him in prison to learning of his suicide. She made it clear that, in her view, his probable one-time use of marijuana should have received a negative consequence—perhaps a weekend jail-based work detail—but not a year in prison, which TJ projected accurately for himself and refused to abide by—even though it meant death by his own self-inflicted method.

Then it was Junie's turn.

Although Gee knew her as a bright, intelligent woman, she wondered what she would say today.... They hadn't rehearsed.

"Thank you for inviting me here today. I'm here hoping that maybe this story will help others. I intend to tell you the truth, as I know it, without leaving anything out," she said.

Gee scanned the room quickly. Most judges seemed interested in what Junie Edwards-Smith was saying. A few simply looked down at their hands, as if she were another witness in a trial.

"TJ had his faults. He tended to panic, or overreact, usually when he feared the loss of something important to him. Days before he jumped off the Key Bridge—he hated water because he couldn't swim—we had an argument over whether to save a large paycheck he received for computer work that Ms. Brooks had gotten him or spend it on a car.

"I was so selfish and wrong. He had worked for the money. I was working. We could afford for him to buy a car. I acted like I didn't trust our future together, and he sensed it. I remember saying something like, 'Go ahead, spend the money—you don't care about us!'" she said.

She began to tear up, but she never lost pace.

"I think I pierced his dreams. He left and went straight to this ole thing," she said.

Some judges at first looked puzzled, until the lone female judge, Glenny Clarke, voiced a sympathetic "uh huh"—which meant she understood that Junie meant men can't help but be weak when it comes to sex. Only after Judge Clarke's sound did the male judges catch on, Gee saw.

"It's pretty clear now that they smoked some dope that night. Young black men do that to show off, you know. Later, I heard from Ms. Brooks that TJ learned about a new—what's the word?—*mandatory* policy that was going to send him back to prison for a year. I could have told you that TJ couldn't do no more time. You see, he didn't see himself anymore as a *convict*—he saw himself as a computer expert. All of his family was talking about him: 'TJ's going to get me a computer and teach me how to use it.' 'TJ's so smart.' He promised to take Tommy to a baseball game. Natasha was going to join Brownies, because he could take her to meetings while I worked and went to school. We were going to the Kennedy Center on a date. He had dreams, and he was on his way. Prison wasn't an option.

"I'm truly sorry for what I did—and what he did. But he didn't deserve to die, and he didn't need to be in prison. I'm sorry that he didn't become what he wanted to be most: a successful man and a good father. And, mostly, I'm sorry for my children," she pointed to the waiting room, "who were just getting to know their father again. All they wanted was his love and attention," Junie said, bowing her head.

With that, her tears flowed like a river.

Gee put her arm around Junie, and Judge Clarke quickly got out of her seat and came over to give Junie a hug.

"Thank you for sharing your story," said Judge Clarke.

Junie's head remained bowed.

"Look at me, dear. Look at me! I assure you—beyond your wildest dreams, the lessons learned today from you, from TJ, and from your little angels will not be forgotten by this court. God bless you, dear, and good luck to you," Judge Clarke said.

Encouragement and kind wishes to Junie came from most judges as Judge Johnson escorted Chief Kasten, Gee, and Junie out of the room.

Upon Judge Johnson's return and after the doors were closed, Judge Clarke thanked Judges Johnson and Brayer for the experience. She said softly, "If we let ourselves, every single case can look alike—if we let ourselves."

It was a powerful moment for several judges of the court.

Thereafter, without referencing this event, judges began to ask different questions, and this new line of questioning spread quickly throughout the bench. For instance, in receiving sentencing recommendations from probation officers, if judges thought that too many special conditions were being proposed, they simply denied them. Special conditions requests now had to pass a new test: are they doable, and are they reasonable? While Chief Judge Brayer never put this threshold test in writing, he guessed it emerged from informal conversations between judges.

Data collected by probation managers, at the insistence of Chief Kasten, uncovered an amazing fact. In the previous year, of the number of offenders returned to prison for technical violations of the conditions of supervision, without a new conviction—the vast majority had four *or more* special conditions. The evidence was clear beyond a reasonable doubt; the more special conditions placed on offenders, the more likely they'd end up in prison. Kasten reported this finding to Judge Brayer, who shared it with the judges. No judge wanted their special conditions to be the sole reason for another prison term.

Coincidentally, similar data showed up in the WWTS newsletter, as if they had conducted independent research. Carrie wrote that as a matter of public policy, it would be very hard for taxpayers to understand why a person in prison for murder was sharing a cell with a person who did not pay all of a fine.

~

Within months, another mindset emerged about special conditions. Upon officers' requests, many excessive special conditions were dropped from persons already on supervision. Memos about dropping special conditions between officers and judges became an everyday occurrence. Rather than piling on nice-sounding special conditions that could never be met, by district-wide judicial consensus, and now policy, judges officially ratcheted up their threshold questions into one simple test: an *if and only if* test. *If* the condition is necessary to the outcome, such as drug treatment, it was added—and *only if* it was necessary.

By the spring, just six months after the special conditions issue came to light, out of 312 new cases, the number with four or more special conditions was six, the number with three special conditions was twelve, cases with only two special conditions were twenty-seven, and the rest had one or no special conditions. No one complained, not even the prosecutors. Judges were relieved by the very small number of revocation hearings that landed on their calendars. Now, they could spend more time on weighty judicial matters.

Data showed that within six months the number of revocation hearings for technical violations had dropped by 76 percent.

State officials began to look at the district's data with disbelief. The number of technical violators in jail awaiting revocation hearings nearly disappeared from the Montgomery County Detention Center. And, more importantly, the number of probationers and parolees returning to prison for technical violations was, well, miniscule.

Carrie, Jon, Gee, Pepe, Huggie, Hattie, and Olivia were delighted beyond words.

Upon learning of this newly released preliminary data from Chief Kasten through Judge Brayer, instead of lunch, Judge Johnson and Senator Washington celebrated over dinner at the Inn at Little Washington, their scheme having played out better than even they could have hoped for.

41

ANNUAL AWARDS CEREMONY

Judge Bill Brayer

On the morning of the court's annual awards ceremony, Gee decided to go in late, since the affair often lasted until midnight. She got a cup of coffee at Starbucks and headed to her car.

Brad ran toward her, hollering from a distance for her to wait.

"Gee, I've been hoping I'd run into you! I bought a mountain bike and have ridden twice. Would you like to go riding with me tomorrow morning on the Crescent Trail?" he asked.

"I'd love that!" she said.

"I, uh, how can I say this?"

"Just say it," she said, smiling.

"I've wanted to call you hundreds of times…. I just never know whether having two kids, uh…."

"Brad, I love your adorable children, and I'd love to get to know you," she said. *I felt that way two seconds after I first saw you*, she thought to herself.

—

The Montgomery County Circuit Court's annual court awards ceremony, held in early December, was typically a good affair to miss, if you could come up with a sufficiently legitimate-sounding excuse. During Chief Judge Brayer's administration, the ceremony was held at the Chevy Chase Club, because CCC discounted the drinks and hors d'oeuvres for him, and it was a place where he felt comfortable. Chief Judge Brayer's past opening remarks about how pleased he was with the court personnel never really seemed authentic. But they had at least been brief.

Next in the ceremony came his announcement about the outstanding employee from each office—that is, the clerk's office, the public defender's office, the court security office, the maintenance office, the probation office, the pretrial services office, the court stenographer's office, and the court translator's office.

This year, the nominations from the probation office were controlled directly by Chief Kasten, forgoing his traditional use of a committee headed by Dora Kingmaker.

On this night, Judge Brayer was about to have a great deal of fun—needling, cajoling, leading, entertaining, and exposing some of his great, but well-hidden, compassion. On the way to the club he tried to articulate to his wife, why, after all these years of being staid and formal in his courtroom and in the courthouse, he had chosen this event to display his true character.

"I feel so different this year. Something has changed in me. It has been unfolding for a long time. It's hard to explain. At that judges' meeting when Mrs. Smith and her two children appeared, something changed in me. I began to ask myself over and over again, what can be greater than human understanding? What have I missed out on? What have I not seen that has been before me all along? And, after Carrie showed up in my courtroom, I've even changed my courtroom demeanor. I've decided to enjoy life. It's the oddest thing," he said.

"Well, I know the real Bill, so I'd have to see you in your courtroom to appreciate the difference," his wife said.

"I think you'll see me tonight," he said.

Except for the location, this year's awards ceremony was quite different. The courthouse buzz had one persistent question: why does it feel so different this year?

For one thing, Gabby White, Brayer's administrative assistant, could usually be counted on to leak the awards winners to Carrie and others. It was great sport to watch the winners trying to act unaware. This year, upon direct orders, Ms. White was anything but gabby, and she intentionally avoided talking to her usual sources, saying little more than that there was a "judicial code of silence." Bummer, said her cohorts.

A way-too-friendly tone was being set by Judge Brayer himself! For weeks preceding the ceremony, he said to everyone—inside and outside his courtroom— "Looking forward to seeing you at the awards ceremony." Besides the award winners, attendees had previously looked to the ceremony the same way they looked forward to a root canal.

Everyone agreed this year was different because each department received explicit orders from Judge Brayer to submit the exact number of attendees to Gabby White by the Wednesday before the Friday night event.

~

Beyond the courthouse buzz, Gee had her own questions about why it seemed so different this year. She learned through Carrie that Huggie and Pepe had been instructed by Judge Brayer to invite their Community All-Stars to the ceremony. Before tonight, no community folks had ever been invited to this court-centered event.

"What's going on, guys?" she asked Huggie and Pepe over coffee. The pair gave a palms-up gestures of ignorance. "Now, that's irritating. Stop it. What's going on?"

Pepe changed the subject.

Junie Edwards-Smith called Gee yesterday and asked her what she should wear to the affair. Gee didn't question her presence, but it felt odd. When they got off the phone, Gee surmised that maybe Judge Johnson or Clarke had something to do with Junie's attendance.

All of this annoyed Gee, who, like a reformed cigarette smoker intolerant to smoking around her, couldn't tolerate secrets.

Cocktails and hors d'oeuvres started at 6:30 PM, sharp. Gee arrived precisely on time. With a Heineken in hand, she saw Jon and Carrie arriving and gave them hugs. They chatted briefly before Carrie and Jon were pulled elsewhere by friends.

Stunning flower arrangements were centered on circular tables, each of which held roughly eight guests. Names and table assignments were on a sign-in table outside the main room, manned by Gabby White and a clerk. There was only one head table.

A modest podium was placed near the forty feet of windows on the west side, allowing a view of the golf course's eighteenth green. Gee noticed Carrie, Jon, Judge Brayer, and Judge Johnson pointing at the green and laughing, just before the staff pulled the curtains shut.

Soon, Huggie and Rosa arrived, looking dashing as always. Then, Pepe arrived with Olivia Lopez locked tightly on his arm. They looked very chummy, and the suspected intra-court "special friendship" was confirmed as a fact. One look at the two of them together led one probation officer to elbow his buddy and say, "Shit, no wonder the Chumster retired."

The stylish Hattie Rogers made an arm in arm entrance with her mother, followed by her father and her handsome fiancée, Dr. Breighton Taylor, III.

Gee rushed over to hug an arriving Laurie Woolworth, Myrtle Block, and Eleanor Spaulding. *Odd,* she thought. *Why are they here?*

Suddenly there was quite a buzz. People seemed to turn in unison to see an arriving guest. Gee thought she recognized the woman causing the stir—then realized it was Senator Barbara Washington. The senator was greeted first by Judge Harry Johnson, as if, Gee noted, they were old friends. Senator Washington quickly fell into a pool of judges, all anxious to speak with her. Gee also noticed a nosy reporter hanging around within earshot of the judges, talking to no one.

Huggie sidled up to Gee and said, "Check out The Kingmaker and Chip over in the corner. They look like two cats that live in the same house but don't like each other. They look rather grim, don't they?"

"I hear she's planning to leave," Gee said.

"Really…. No shit. Maybe there is a God."

"Poor Chip. What'll he do now?"

"Don't know. Don't care."

Gee noticed Junie and excused herself to greet her.

"Well, aren't you beautiful!" Gee said, hugging her.

"I know, I know, what am *I* doing here?" said Junie.

Before Junie could answer her own question, Hattie joined them, and the three ladies chatted like old friends.

Judge Johnson came over and almost pulled Junie from her lady friends to introduce her to Senator Barbara Washington, Judge Brayer, Hattie's mother, and Carrie and Jon. Gee noticed the conversation appeared to be quite warm and friendly.

Hattie drifted away to mother the workers of the courthouse, her "little people."

Carrie approached Gee, looking exquisite in a dark green dress, white wine in hand, gave Gee a big hug and kiss on the cheek, and said,

"I'm so proud of you!" Then Carrie seemed to *surge* away—like surfers do when they catch a big wave—toward the other Live Wires.

Gee's eyes followed Carrie to Laurie Woolworth, Myrtle Block, and Eleanor Spaulding. Carrie leaned over and began talking to a woman Gee didn't recognize. *My God*, she thought. *that's Ms. Lilly.* She rushed over, her second Heineken in hand, and chatted with Ms. Lilly.

Judge Brayer walked by and approached Gee. "You look lovely, dear. I'm quite proud of you and the Cuatro Amigos bandits," Judge Brayer said, winking.

"Thank you, Judge," she said.

Judge Brayer disappeared.

Cuatro Amigos? How did he learn about that name? she wondered. *Bandits? What did he mean by that?* Gee's head was spinning. This was enough action for a month: the buzz before the ceremony, Huggie and Pepe's mysterious behavior, Hattie's parents being here, Senator Washington's attendance, Junie's presence, Carrie's remark, and Ms. Lilly.

Gee waved to Pepe, but, before they could reach each other, Judge Brayer stood over the lectern, tapped the microphone, and asked everyone to be seated.

⁓

Gee was seated at the table with Pepe and Olivia and a group of public defenders.

"I'm especially excited about this year's awards ceremony. I think you'll understand why in short order. First, I'd like to recognize our honored guest, Senator Barbara Washington, who'll speak to you shortly. Senator Washington," he said, nodding in her direction, where she sat at a table with Judge Johnson next to her. She rose, waved, and received a warm standing ovation.

"And, of course, my esteemed colleagues of the bench," he added, waving widely, as they were seated throughout the room. They chose not to stand.

The applause was somewhat friendly, slightly beyond obligatory.

"At this time, I'd like to honor thirty-eight Community All-Stars who have joined us tonight. As you know, their contributions to the lives of the people we work with, their families, and the neighborhoods and communities they live in, is truly a blessing—every day. I call on Pastor Alonzo Richardson to tell a story about one of our All-Stars in attendance tonight, Ms. Lilly, perhaps our most veteran All-Star," Judge Brayer said.

Pastor Alonzo Richardson rose and stood next to Ms. Lilly, who remained seated with her head bowed, looking at the floor, obviously very uncomfortable with the attention. Pastor Richardson told the story of Ms. Lilly's community efforts, as Pepe had to the Four Live Wires in this very same facility.

"Now, as you watch a videotape of many of our All-Stars here tonight, please carefully observe a little one's heartfelt appreciation—someone whose life Ms. Lilly has influenced *forever*—and, ask yourself this question: what do Ms. Lilly's acts call me to do in the community?"

On a screen behind him came the stories of the Community All-Stars, and, finally, Huggie's interview with the little warrior regarding Ms. Lilly, except this updated version, orchestrated by Jon and Olivia through a professional studio, with music and titles, looked like it was ready to be aired on *60 Minutes*.

Based on the expressions on the faces of the audience, the videotape sent the message Judge Brayer sought to deliver.

"Would Ms. Lilly please stand to accept our heartfelt appreciation?" Judge Brayer said. TJ's sister Dee and Eleanor Spaulding, pushing her cane away, as if she herself was twenty-something, sprang up to hold Ms. Lilly's arms and help her rise to receive a long, standing ovation.

"And would the rest of our Community All-Stars, whose actions play out every single day in our communities, please stand and be recognized?" he commanded. Thirty-eight community leaders, advocates, and ordinary-looking citizens stood and received public recognition.

After a deliberate pause to shift gears, Judge Brayer continued.

"I want to make sure that tonight, tonight of all nights, I don't speak *only* in my public language tone—or, as my grandchildren would say, all my 'blah, blah, blah' stuff. Tonight, I want to share with you some of my heartfelt feelings."

"I hope this night will not be remembered as just an awards ceremony. I think of it more as a celebration. Recently, I've been contacted by members of the media wanting to know how this district has become such an interesting place to work. In my humble view, I told them, this year we've achieved an unspoken goal—one that I didn't set, one that Robert Kasten didn't plan, but one that was a fallout from—do I have this right?—a *humanistic revolution.* And I do hope my critics in the press don't try to spin this with a soft-on-crime slant," he paused for effect, "because they'll look like fools!" He smiled thinly at the lead crime reporter at Table Two.

"The difference to which I am referring is that we're becoming a true court *family* and a true community of concerned, involved citizens."

The attendees applauded.

"As their leader, I'm trying to figure out, which way did they go?" he laughed.

The audience laughed, too.

"I'm trying to figure out all of the pieces of the puzzle. I'm still not sure I have them. I know this: there's been a lot of *noise* coming from the probation office this year!" Brayer said, glancing at Chief Kasten.

Laughter and guffaws followed, which made him smile.

"And, I understand, our friends at the Parole Commission may have heard some of that noise, too," he added.

The crowd roared.

Gee thought to herself that it seemed like Judge Brayer was having fun.… He was at play.

Judge Brayer's tone shifted. "I understand a tragic event may have been the springboard for great actions. A young parolee named Thomas Smith, or TJ, as he was called, committed suicide rather than be sent back to prison—probably for a year, maybe longer—for smoking a marijuana joint while on parole. Other than that one act, for which he should have received a consequence, he was doing quite well. He was married to a wonderful woman and had two well-mannered children, whom the court has met.… Lovely children, really. TJ was an IT expert, and he had a very good job."

One could hear a pin drop.

"This tragic death led one probation officer, Virginia Brooks, to say, '*No mas,*'" he said, looking squarely at Gee.

She smiled and looked down.

"Virginia was joined by Hattie Rogers, Woodrow Winston, and Hector Gomez," Judge Brayer said, pausing to smile at each of the three.

With the judge's announcement of Hector Gomez's name, spontaneous hoots and hollers erupted. The astute Judge Brayer recognized the subtle point being made by the audience's reaction.

He paused for quite a while, again for effect.

"In response, they started a Nuevos Principios Society.... Did I get that right?"

Gee nodded at him and smiled.

He paused again.

"A thought-provoking newsletter and a blog—" He pronounced the word blog, "bloog," intentionally or unintentionally, and the Internet-savvy audience broke into laughter. After three unsuccessful tries and a corrective shout-out from the audience, he frowned and said, "*Whatever*," mocking the relatively youthful audience. "Whatever you call that thing. Well, I understand that blog thing has captured the attention of probation officers, parole officers, politicians," he smiled at Senator Washington, "academics, community activists, and even judges—well, some Internet-savvy judges, anyway. Thankfully, folks that read and responded to the newsletters slightly outnumber the appellate review judges that reverse my decisions!" he said, looking at his fellow judges.

The laughing audience was in lockstep with him.

Judge Brayer pointed at Gee, Hattie, Huggie, and Pepe as he said, "Now these Cuatro Amigos, as they called themselves, Brooks, Rogers, Winston, and Gomez, went on a journey to find the elements—the essential ingredients, or 5-EI—of success in their profession. Did I get that right, Chief Kasten?"

Kasten nodded.

"I'm told they went outside the system and gathered knowledge from management consultants that work with successful businesses to find what makes those businesses thrive. They arrived at listening and communication skills and the essential ingredients—the knowledge, skills, and attitudes officers must have to excel in their profession. Officers went off and got trained—at their *own* expense. The society's simple notion was that until officers excelled at these skills, there was no chance they could be effective with people on supervision. Do I have this right, folks?" he asked. He looked at the Cuatro Amigos slowly and individually.

Each nodded.

"I understand that underneath this essential ingredients notion, the philosophical underpinning, as it were, is the belief that everyone, *everyone*, can change their beliefs and behavior. Do I have that right?" he said, using another rhetorical question for effect.

He again looked squarely at the Cuatro Amigos, one at a time. He got a smile from Gee, Huggie, and Hattie, but a "damned right" look from Pepe.

"Even judges can change their behavior?" he said, looking for his peers in the audience with his right hand shading his eyes—as if the *brightness* of the question bothered his vision.

There was yet another thunderous outburst of laughter. The judge noticed that even the newspaper crime reporter was smiling. *God forbid*, Brayer thought to himself.

"I'm told fifty-seven officers—thirty-three from this district—have been trained in the 5-EI," he said. "My first announcement tonight, then, is that I have authorized the Clerk of the Circuit Court to pay all of the expenses that officers from this district have incurred for that training, *nunc pro tunc*," Judge Brayer said, using the Latin term meaning "now for then."

His colleagues on the bench knew it was fiscally irregular, at best, to approve funding retroactively.

At least thirty-three officers cheered loudly, some punching each other in the arm.

"I am further advised that this simple understanding of the work of probation and parole officers is catching on around the country. Catching on so much that the district has been nominated by the national probation officers' association for its outstanding contribution to the advancement of justice, and somehow they're giving me some of the credit—fools!," he said.

Warm applause followed.

"I've already approved Chief Kasten's request for all remaining officers on his staff to receive this same training in the next fiscal year— even the managers."

Judge Brayer received Chief Kasten's smile, while also noticing Deputy Chief Kingmaker staring into her lap. Two days before, Chief Kasten had advised the judge that Ms. Kingmaker was leaving on vacation for Puerto Rico in four days—and that she had informed him in writing that she felt it was time for her to move on in order to further her career goals. She asked Kasten for his patience in her job search.

"Ah, but don't think they're having all the fun! Every court family member in the next fiscal year will receive two days of listening and communication skills training from the society!" said Judge Brayer.

Gabby White turned to the clerk beside her and said, "I can't wait to spread the word."

The startled clerk responded, "But, Gabby, everyone's here."

"Oh, yeah, that's right," Gabby said, as her shoulders slumped.

"Well, then, I suppose *congratulations* are in order, Mr. Kasten." Chief Judge Brayer said.

Chief Kasten stood and received the applause, but redirected it by gesturing with his hands to the Cuatro Amigos.

"Now, I'd like to ask the Cuatro Amigos to come up to the podium and join me. It's getting lonely up here!" said Judge Brayer.

"Oh, *Je-sus*," Gee mumbled out loud to herself.

Once beside Huggie, she whispered, "I guess we're out in the open now!"

"Easier to shoot," he whispered back.

As they gathered awkwardly beside the judge, like clustered penguins, the emcee continued, and Gabby White, dressed in a stunningly simple black dress, rushed over to retrieve a cart from the corner. Despite her very high heels, she deftly pushed the cart to the podium and awaited the judge's cues.

"Let there be no doubt in anyone's mind that their sheer display of tough-minded determination in the face of massive criticism, disbelief, and ridicule bordering on harassment, was a continuing act of courage, compassion, and care. Therefore, first, I want to recognize the outstanding contribution of Ms. Hattie Rogers to this effort with this plaque identifying her as a co-winner of the Probation Officer of the Year Award. Congratulations, Ms. Rogers," he said, shaking her hand and hugging her gently, as Gabby handed him her plague, which he, in turn, handed Hattie.

Gee was thrilled for Hattie, whose loyal courthouse entourage yelped.

"I now present Mr. Woodrow Winston with this plaque recognizing him as a co-winner of the Probation Officer of the Year Award," he said, offering a strong handshake and pat on the back. A warm response from his peers erupted with calls of "I ... I!" Judge Brayer asked him, in a whisper, if he had been in the Navy. Huggie whispered back it was an old office joke.

"Next, Mr. Hector Gomez is the recipient of two awards. First, he is a co-winner of the Probation Officer of the Year Award. Congratulations, Mr. Gomez," he said, with a smile and a small bow.

Huge applause erupted for the legend.

"Secondly, Mr. Gomez, I hear endless stories about all the lives you have touched, year after year, day after day, with your community outreach efforts. I wish my humble legacy as chief judge would include the qualities you exemplify. Therefore, it is a great personal honor to appoint you an Ambassador of Goodwill for this court. Your portrait will soon take its rightful place in the Clerk's Office as a permanent part of the history of the court," Judge Brayer said. And with that, he handed Pepe two plaques: the Probation Officer of the Year Award and a second one—one of those plaques that started with "Whereas." But it was what Judge Brayer did next that appeared to touch Pepe most deeply. Judge Brayer, away from the microphone, stood close to Pepe. While the applause thundered, Gee alone could hear the judge apologize for his courtroom tirade two years ago. Bill Brayer sought a very personal reconciliation with Pepe. Placing his hand on Pepe's shoulder, he said very quietly, "Mr. Gomez, I am only sorry your parents aren't with us tonight."

At that very public moment, Pepe cried. His fiancée cried, too. Pepe tried to smile, but his contorted, tearful face betrayed him. Judge Brayer and Pepe hugged briefly, defying heretofore conventional wisdom and permanently altering the court's folklore.

The audience rose to its feet with great respect and appreciation for what they had just witnessed. Save for a few judges and a handful of officers—and Dora Kingmaker—there wasn't a dry eye in the house.

Judge Brayer composed himself and returned to the lectern. The judge saw Ms. Lilly waving broadly to Pepe.

"I now call upon a special guest to present the 2005 Court Employee of the Year Award," Judge Brayer announced. "Mr. Thomas Burns."

Hattie grabbed Gee's arm, while Gee's father walked across the stage.

"Be cool, General," Pepe whispered.

Judge Brayer shook Mr. Burns's hand, then deftly stepped out of his way. The young lady that ran twice as far as the boys and, perhaps, could run even farther than Chip Faulknour, didn't appear to be capable of running a half a block now.

Thomas Burns kissed his daughter on the cheek.

"Well.... *Well*. Your Honor and distinguished guests, it's a great honor for me to accept Judge Brayer's invitation to present this award. More precisely, Chief Kasten asked me if I, rather than he, would do the honor. Thank you, Robert, for that kind gesture. Second only to accepting her mother's proposal for marriage, it's the greatest honor of my life," he said, smiling at Gee.

"I'm pleased, Gee, that you and your allies and a growing number of officers throughout the country have focused on how to *re-root* your honorable profession. You've accomplished—*are* accomplishing, I should say—something I dreamed about but was unable to do. As you well know, it's not just the people on your caseload—it's their families, their children, their children's children, and the entire community—that you affect when you help people change their behavior for the better. I'm proud of you, Virginia Brooks, and ... I know your mother is, too. Congratulations, honey," he said.

She fell into his arms, as Gabby handed her the Court Employee of the Year plaque. It was a touching father-daughter moment. She handed the award to her father. There was little doubt in Judge Brayer's mind that most people in the room were touched by Thomas Burns's remarks.

Gee took time to try to compose herself. False start. Stop. False start. Stop. Another deep breath, all the while looking out at a roomful of colleagues happily engaged in a standing ovation. Quietly, from behind her, Huggie whispered in his baritone voice, "You can do it, girl."

Huggie's words comforted her. Finally, Gee began, and the audience was seated and hushed.

"Thank you, Dad. Thank you, Judge Brayer. Thank you, Chief Kasten. I'm deeply touched." With that, she paused again.

"My friends, Hattie, Huggie and Pepe, I'm so proud of them. My friends and I started our ... adventure ... in anguish over the loss of TJ. I felt very ineffective at my job. I had always admired the skills of Huggie, Hattie, and Pepe and what they were able to accomplish, but it was almost as if they had to work upstream—frankly, against a tone of meanness. 'How could this be?' we asked ourselves. When we looked around—at you—we saw nothing but good people, caring people with good values. But somewhere, somehow, the profession got lost. That's the simplest way I know to explain a complex problem. We didn't know how to fix it; so, we did what my father taught me to do: we asked for help. And help we got. Plenty of it—some from surprising sources, most of which are here in this room. Thank you to all of the people who reached out to us, and thank you for this award. But ... I don't deserve the credit..."

She struggled mightily now.

Through a burst of tears came, "Thank you, TJ, for showing us the way, and thank you, Mom and Dad, for showing me the way."

She hugged her father. He continued to hold his arm around her shoulder until they arrived back at her table. The standing ovation continued. Huggie, Hattie, and Pepe returned to their tables and hugs.

Judge Brayer continued at the podium. "My colleagues and I on the bench, with the concurrence of the heads of the various offices, wish to finish an incomplete piece of justice. I call on Senator Washington to announce this next award. Ladies and Gentleman, the distinguished United States senator from our proud state, Senator Barbara Washington."

Moving rapidly, as was her custom, Senator Washington, in a beautiful black suit with a white blouse, seized the podium, and the room fell silent.

"I am so pleased at what I have observed tonight, and I know my dear friends on the bench and the loved ones and parents of these officers are pleased and proud as well. This court family is on the path toward true justice and community reconciliation. Nothing more, nothing less," she said. She paused. She made eye contact with every single person in the room, or so it seemed to Judge Brayer.

"TJ's death was a wake-up call, wasn't it? Wasn't it?"

Many heads were nodding.

"A wake-up for you *and* a wake-up call for me. Out of darkness and misguided notions has come the light of reason. Out of frustration has come a new idea—a new way. The old is giving way to the new. The new way will shine until it, too, becomes old and gives way to yet another newer and better form.

"This is the way of a humanistic revolution. So it has always been, and so it will be in the future.

"No one who has died needlessly because of injustice has died in vain. No one. But never, *never* forget that this bold humanistic revolution was born of *many* discarded lives, broken dreams and promises, and unnecessary deaths.

"Heretofore, *before* TJ's death, the toll was mostly unseen. Not anymore. Make no mistake; the toll has been great. But this is *not* the time for blame. It *is* the time for you and me to stare directly into the darkness and ask, 'Which path do I take?'

"Which path do *I* take? Do I want to merely punish people *or* reach them? Do I want prison bars or rising stars? Which path do *I* take? What do I want to give to the next generation? What do I find necessary to take from a person, on bended knee? Which path do *I* take? If not to reach a hand out to those on bended knee, what will I offer?

"Which path do *I* take? If not the milk of human kindness that saved *me*, what did?

"If not us, you, me, who will save us from our desire to punish the punished? Who will save us from ourselves?

"Let the madness stop with us. Let it stop *now*.

"Let us witness tonight ... the end of the end. In its stead, the beginning of a new day is here, and the new beginning has begun!

"Which path do *I* take?

"Come, join hands. Let us go into the light ... together!" she concluded.

The audience jumped to their feet in salute of Senator Washington.

Unlike most politicians on most occasions, Senator Washington wanted little lasting attention now; so, after about thirty seconds, she interrupted the ovation with a hand gesture.

"It is with great privilege—it is with *great* privilege—that I ask a young widow, Mrs. Thomas J. Smith, Jr., to please come up here, dear," she said.

Barbara Washington and Junie hugged like sisters.

Gee's heart was full of joy. Tears rolled freely down her face as she watched this festival of a circle closing.

"Mrs. Smith—Junie—through the generosity of the CASI Foundation, I am pleased to announce the creation of a permanent trust that shall be named the TJ Smith Award. The annual award is to be given to a Montgomery County citizen who has demonstrated the greatest pro-social change in the past year. TJ fought as hard as he knew how to fight to reach his full potential, his dreams. May his memory, though this annual award and its financial reward, help others achieve their dreams," she said.

Gabby handed the senator a framed letter.

"The first annual award goes posthumously to Thomas J. Smith, Jr. The money is to be used for the benefit of his children. The court also appoints you, Mrs. Smith, as a permanent member of the selection committee for this award," Senator Washington said, handing Junie the plaque and kissing her on the cheek.

The audience was again on its feet but hushed quickly out of respect. Junie handed the plaque back to Gabby to hold, as she moved toward the podium to address them.

Gee noticed that when the kitchen door opened with scurrying servers carrying dessert trays, she could see standing just inside the kitchen a man in orange prison garb, with handcuffs secured behind his back and in leg irons, with a skinny prison guard standing nearby. That explained the presence of a second, beefy prison guard right outside the kitchen doors, to the right. *My God*, she thought, *it must be Hardroc*. She guessed this was the work of Judge Clarke, who now stood beside the guard outside the kitchen doors. Gee had no idea how long the guards, or Hardroc, had been there. She reasoned that only a temporary furlough at the request of the court could have made this possible—the prison authorities wouldn't do this on their own initiative. Gee concluded, too, that Hattie must have had a hand in this. Gee could see Hardroc watching with rapt attention. This was his protégé, his little brother's final victory lap.

"Thank you, Senator Washington. On behalf of TJ and our

children, Tommy and Natasha, I'm honored. His death has created much darkness for us and his extended family. That darkness is not over. But I realize that others—the judges of this court, the Cuatro Amigos—many have felt my family's pain and expressed empathy. Thank you for reaching out to us," Junie said.

Gee watched as the audience, including the judges, gave Junie their rapt attention. As Junie told her story, the power of justice's unseen impact on ordinary people was unfolding.

"TJ made me laugh. He made his kids laugh. He didn't fool me though. I know he laughed so he wouldn't feel all of that pain inside him in places ... in places I couldn't reach and he couldn't make go away. The pain was too deep. The damage was done," Junie said.

Junie talked of TJ's pride at being an IT expert and how that vision of himself no doubt made it impossible to square with the notion of returning to prison. She spoke of the loss to the children. But it was the last thing she said that seared itself into Gee's heart, and she guessed, into the hearts of the audience, too.

"TJ ... the man ... who was no longer a criminal ... died a criminal's death. My God, that was wrong," Junie said, with conviction, but without blame. "I thank you, and one day my children and their children will thank you, for seeing to it..."

Junie cried now, openly.

"... for seeing to it ... that this never happens again. On behalf of TJ ... thank you for caring."

Gee moved quickly to meet Junie at her table. She sat and squeezed her hand as Judge Brayer continued with other awards.

"I'm pretty sure Hardroc's here, in the kitchen. Sit tight," Gee said. She hurriedly approached Judge Clarke.

Out of the corner of her eye, Junie caught a glimpse of the beefy guard talking to Judge Clarke outside the kitchen.

"That's Hardroc, isn't it?" Gee asked Judge Clarke.

"Yes, it is. I got a temporary furlough under the conditions he could watch the process from a secure area away from the guests and that he be returned by 10:00 PM, which means he's got to leave in five minutes. These guards want to take him out of here now, but I want

Junie to meet him first. I'm out of judicial clout. Any ideas?" Judge Clarke said.

"Give me a minute," Gee said.

"Hurry," said Judge Clarke.

Gee walked over to TJ's sister Dee and whispered in her ear. Dee picked up an uneaten piece of carrot cake and a fork. With her index finger Gee gestured for Junie to join them about thirty feet from the prison guard. Judge Clarke joined the sidebar.

"Junie and I are going to talk to Hardroc," Gee said.

"He's here?" Dee asked.

"Yes. Now, Dee, I want you to go over and flirt with that guard," she said.

"Judge Clarke, give Dee time to stall, then you tell the guard that Junie and I are saying good-bye to Hardroc," Gee said.

The skinny guard opened the kitchen door, craned his head, caught the eye of the beefy guard, pointed to his watch, and returned to the kitchen.

"Got it, but please hurry, girls," the judge said.

Dee executed the plan to perfection. The guard was torn between gobbling the cake and visually trying to undress Dee.

Judge Clarke breezed by him with her ducklings in tow, and, before he could respond, she said, "We'll be in the kitchen for one minute," as Dee rubbed his arm provocatively and babbled about the wonderful cake and questions about where the guard liked to go to dance.

Once Gee and Junie were through the swinging doors, Judge Clarke stood outside the doors as if she, too, was a sentinel.

Hardroc was leaning against a kitchen counter. His body looked like TJ's—thin, but more muscular. The skinny guard, now frowning, was standing at the kitchen door next to the parking lot exit sign, nearly forty feet away from Hardroc.

"You have one minute. Make it snappy," he growled at Junie and Gee.

Gee stopped near the door and said nothing, but smiled and nodded to Hardroc. He burst into a smile and nodded back at her.

Junie walked up to Hardroc and stood before him at arm's-length.

"Thank you for coming, Mr. Hardroc," she said. "TJ knew how

much you cared for him. You, above anyone on this earth—counting me—believed in him. I thank you. My children thank you," she said.

"TJ was a wiz ... a real IT expert. I'm never wrong about people. He was a good man," Hardroc said, staring at the floor, seemingly, Gee thought, finding the intensity of Junie's eye contact difficult to maintain.

"May I write to you, Mr. Hardroc, to keep you informed about the kids?" she asked.

"I would consider it an honor to receive information about your family ... TJ's family," he said.

Junie noticed the guard pointing to his watch.

"I'm sorry we lost him," he added.

Junie approached him and kissed him gently, respectfully, on his cheek.

Walking toward the swinging kitchen doors, she stopped, turned around, and said, "May a merciful God watch over you and keep you safe. You're a kindhearted man." She turned again and approached Gee as the beefy guard burst through the doors and, with the aid of the skinny guard, grabbed Hardroc's arms and turned him toward the exit door.

The guards allowed Hardroc to turn around one last time.

"Mrs. Smith ..." Hardroc called out, stopping her in her tracks before she reached the swinging doors. She turned around slowly and faced him.

"I know because I talked to him every day—can't hide the truth from a cellmate—that *other* woman—she was about his fears, his inadequacies. You were his hopes. He loved you deeply, and the kids. You were his life," he said.

Junie smiled, slightly, looked at the floor, and nodded once. Then she turned to Gee's open arms and cried.

"I know, baby ... I know.... I'm here," Gee said, as the guards whisked Hardroc out the door.

THE END

Printed in the United States
138924LV00004B/1/P

9 780595 498734